MONTALBANO'S FIRST CASE
AND OTHER STORIES

Also by Andrea Camilleri

Inspector Montalbano mysteries

THE SHAPE OF WATER

THE TERRACOTTA DOG

THE SNACK THIEF

THE VOICE OF THE VIOLIN

EXCURSION TO TINDARI

THE SCENT OF THE NIGHT

ROUNDING THE MARK

THE PATIENCE OF THE SPIDER

THE PAPER MOON

AUGUST HEAT

THE WINGS OF THE SPHINX

THE TRACK OF SAND

THE POTTER'S FIELD

THE AGE OF DOUBT

THE DANCE OF THE SEAGULL

THE TREASURE HUNT

ANGELICA'S SMILE

GAME OF MIRRORS

BLADE OF LIGHT

Other novels

HUNTING SEASON

THE BREWER OF PRESTON

ANDREA CAMILLERI

MONTALBANO'S FIRST CASE AND OTHER STORIES

Translated by Stephen Sartarelli

MANTLE

First published 2016 by Penguin Books,
an imprint of Penguin Random House LLC

First published in the UK 2016 by Mantle
an imprint of Pan Macmillan
20 New Wharf Road, London N1 9RR
Associated companies throughout the world
www.panmacmillan.com

ISBN 978-1-4472-9838-0

Copyright © Sellerio Editore 2008
Translation copyright © Stephen Sartarelli 2016

Originally published in Italian 2008 as *Racconti di Montalbano* by Sellerio Editore, Palermo

The right of Andrea Camilleri to be identified as the
author of this work has been asserted by him in accordance
with the Copyright, Designs and Patents Act 1988.

1 3 5 7 9 8 6 4 2

A CIP catalogue record for this book is available from the British Library.

Typeset by Ellipsis Digital Limited, Glasgow
Printed and bound by CPI Group (UK) Ltd, Croydon, CR0 4YY

Visit **www.panmacmillan.com** to read more about all our books
and to buy them. You will also find features, author interviews and
news of any author events, and you can sign up for e-newsletters
so that you're always first to hear about our new releases.

Contents

Author's Preface

The task of creating a sort of personal anthology from all of the short stories I have written was almost enough to drive me to despair. I did once edit a volume of selected writings of a great author, but working in another's skin is always easier.

The problem that immediately arose was that my first book of short stories, *Un mese con Montalbano* (*A Month with Montalbano*), was published by Mondadori in May 1998, when four novels with Montalbano as their protagonist had already come out, and the character had therefore already had the time and opportunity to attain a certain completeness.

In other words, in these stories, Montalbano appears as an already developed, well defined character, and thus I do not have the option of discarding any stories still weak or uncertain in design. They are all, from this point of view, written on the same terms.

I should also add that twenty-seven of the thirty-nine stories that appeared in that first volume had been written for the occasion, and that there was a precise but unstated intention guiding their creation.

This intention was to compose a series of 'portraits' of Sicilian characters, and therefore the stories didn't necessarily have to revolve around murders but could also concern investigations into memory, false robberies, conjugal infidelities, petty vendettas, and so on. I used the 'police procedural', in short, only as a pretext.

I followed the same guidelines with the twenty stories in the second short-fiction collection, *Gli arancini di Montalbano* (*Montalbano's Rice Balls*), published in September 1999. Here, too, the more or less 'procedural' circumstances served as a springboard to explore characters, settings, and situations.

Things, in part, changed substantially, and I would say even visibly, with the third volume, *La paura di Montalbano* (*Montalbano Afraid*), published in May 2002. Here, while the three shorter stories followed the guidelines of the first two collections, the three longer stories were no longer a pretext, but revolved around bona fide police investigations, however *sui generis* at times (but this is in the nature of Inspector Montalbano himself).

The fourth and final volume, *La prima indagine di Montalbano* (*Montalbano's First Case*), published in April 2004, brought together three long investigations, none of which stemmed, however, from murders.

These guidelines made the process of selection even more difficult, owing to a curious — at least to my eyes — interchangeability between one story and another.

I must, moreover, confess that none, not a single one, of the stories of Montalbano was written without a specific prompting — or even necessity, I am tempted to say. Writing just for the sake of writing is not my sort of thing. I would even say I'm incapable of it. And this, at the moment of selection, created an additional problem.

There was no problem whatsoever, on the other hand, from an affective point of view, so to speak. Many writers claim they consider their works as their 'children'. This is not the case with me. I make a clear distinction between children and books, in favour of the former. Anyway, with the fifty-nine stories that make up the four Mondadori volumes as well as twenty-one Montalbano novels, I would be in a position to beat a biblical patriarch!

Well, after having beaten around the bush, I've run out of subjects and now have no choice but to enter the quicksand of reasons for accepting some stories and rejecting others.

Three preliminary statements.

I want to emphasize further – since it seems rather clear to me in the prior paragraphs – that the stories included are not intended to be an 'elite' or 'best of', because it's quite possible they're not. Second, I am also keen to point out that the order in which the stories are presented in this anthology does not respect the chronology of the publication dates. For, example, I open the collection with a story that is in fact the one written most recently of all. Third, this is a book necessarily consisting of a certain number of pages, since if there were any more, it would become unwieldy. My ideal personal anthology would have included a few more stories.

So, to be brief: there are twenty-one stories here.

The first one features Montalbano's first case and opens when he is still a deputy inspector, not yet with Livia, and dreams of being transferred to a seaside town like Vigàta. The first time that Montalbano ever appeared in print was in the novel *La forma dell'Acqua* (*The Shape of Water*), published in 1994, and in that book he's forty-four years old, has already been Chief Inspector of the Vigàta police for some time, and is very much with Livia.

Well before the readers started wondering, I had begun to ask myself: what did Montalbano do before coming to Vigàta? I answered myself in those pages.

And, in fact, almost all of the stories collected here try to answer questions I had, or to settle bets I had made with myself, or treat narrative problems I had set for myself.

I hardly intend to specify, story by story, the reasons for my choices, but, as the reader will already have gathered, there are two main threads: one that favours situations not specifically procedural, and one that, while treating material of a clearly procedural stamp, very often arrives at conclusions that underscore the inspector's humanity more than his rigour in seeing that the law is respected.

One such story, for example, is 'Fellow Traveller', about which I'd like to say a few words. In 1997, I think, I was invited by the organizers of 'Noir in festival', at Courmayeur in north-west Italy, to write a short story that would be read during an encounter with a French mystery writer who, in turn, would read a story of his own, written for the occasion. Well, my story was read first. And I didn't understand why, during the reading, the French writer kept looking at me with increasing astonishment. Then it was his story's turn. And it was I who was profoundly astonished. Because the stories were essentially the same: both unfolded inside a railway sleeper cabin with two beds, one occupied by a police inspector, the other by a killer. Those present at the conference didn't want to believe that it was a coincidence; they were convinced that the French writer and I had worked it out together. But in fact we had never met or spoken before then. At a certain point, Ed McBain stood up and explained the mystery in his own way, by claiming that since we were both European writers particularly attentive to the psychology of the characters, as opposed to their actions, it was inevitable that we should both end up having the policeman and the killer meet face-to-face in an ideal space such as a stifling sleeping compartment.

Finally, a few words about another story, 'Montalbano Says No', which ends with the inspector making a late-night phone call to me, his author, in which he tells me in no uncertain terms that he refuses to continue the investigation into which I've thrust him. This was the time of the so-called 'cannibals' of contemporary Italian fiction, who scorned my writing for what, they accused, was 'feel-goodism', and I decided to respond. But for me that story

is still very relevant, and is, in fact, a sort of manifesto. A refusal, that is, to delight, narratively, in violence.
    And that's all. Happy reading.

Andrea Camilleri

MONTALBANO'S FIRST CASE

1

It was by rather circuitous channels, through a sort of prediction, that Montalbano learned of his forthcoming promotion to the rank of inspector exactly two months before the official, stamp-covered announcement.

Indeed, in every self-respecting government office, predicting (or forecasting, if you prefer) the more or less imminent future of every element of said office – and all neighbouring offices – is a common, daily practice. There is no need, say, to examine the entrails of a quartered animal or to study the flights of starlings, as the ancients used to do. Nor is there any need to read the patterns of coffee grounds at the bottom of a cup, as we have been known to do in more modern times. And to think that in those offices, whole oceans of coffee are drunk each day . . . No, for a prediction (or forecast, if you prefer) to be made, a mere word, casually dropped, a hint of a glance, a subdued whisper, or the first, upward movement of an eyebrow about to be raised, is quite enough. And these predictions (or forecasts, etc.) concern not only the career trajectories of bureaucrats – transfers, promotions, reprimands, citations of merit or demerit – but often involve their private lives as well.

'In three weeks, at the very most, Falcuccio's wife is going to cheat on him with Stracuzzi, the consultant,'

Piscopo the accountant says to Dalli Cardillo the surveyor while watching their colleague Falcuccio head for the toilet.

'Really?' the surveyor queries in puzzlement.

'I'd bet my house on it.'

'What makes you so sure?'

'Just take my word for it,' Piscopo the accountant says with a grin, tilting his head to one side and putting his hand over his heart.

'But have you ever seen Mrs Falcuccio?'

'No, I haven't. Why do you ask?'

'Because I know her.'

'So?'

'She's fat, Piscopo: fat, hairy, and practically a dwarf.'

'So what? You think fat, hairy women who are practically dwarves don't have the same thing between their legs as all the rest?'

The beauty of it all is that, without fail, seven days after this exchange, Mrs Falcuccio ends up in the spacious, wifeless bed of Stracuzzi the consultant, moaning with pleasure.

And if this is what happens in every normal sort of office, imagine the high percentage of accuracy the predictions (or forecasts, etc.) made in police stations and commissioners' offices must have, since there, all personnel, without hierarchical distinction, are expressly trained and instructed to notice the tiniest clues, the slightest shifts in the wind, and draw the inevitable conclusions.

The news of Montalbano's promotion did not take him by surprise. It was all in due course, as they liked to say in those offices. It had already been a good while since he'd finished his period of apprenticeship as deputy inspector in Mascalippa, a godforsaken backwater in the Erean Mountains, under the command of Chief Inspector Libero Sanfilippo. But what had Montalbano worried was where they would now decide to send him — what, indeed, would be his next destination. For that word, *destination*, was very close to another: *destiny*. And a promotion most certainly meant a transfer. Which meant changing home, habits, friends: a destiny yet to be discovered. In all honesty, he was fed up with Mascalippa and the surrounding area – not with the inhabitants, who were no worse or better than anywhere else, having more or less the same proportion of hoodlums to honest folk, cretins to smart people as any other town in Sicily. No, quite frankly, he just couldn't stand the landscape any longer. Mind you, if there was a Sicily he liked to look at, it was this same Sicily of arid, scorched earth, yellow and brown, where little clumps of stubborn green stuck out as if shot from a cannon, where little white dicelike houses clinging to the hillsides looked as if they might slide down below at the next strong gust of wind, where even the lizards and snakes on summer afternoons seemed to lack the will to take cover inside a clump of sorghum or under a rock, inertly resigned to their destiny such as it was. And above all he loved to look at the beds of what had once been rivers and streams – at least that was what the road maps insisted on calling them: the Ipsas, Salsetto, Kokalos – whereas they were now nothing more than a string of sun-bleached stones and dusty shards of terracotta. So, yes, he liked to look at the landscape, but to live in it, day after day, was enough to drive a man crazy. Because he was a man of the sea. On certain mornings in Mascalippa, when he opened the window at dawn and took a deep breath, instead of his lungs filling with air, he felt them emptying out, and he would gasp for breath the way he did after a long dive underwater. No doubt the early morning air in Mascalippa was good, even special. It smelled of straw and grass, of the open country. But this was not enough for him; indeed it practically smothered him. He needed the air of the sea. He needed to savour the smell of seaweed and the faint taste of salt on his lips when he licked them. He needed to take long walks along the beach early in the morning, with the gentle waves of the surf caressing his feet. Being assigned to a mountain town like Mascalippa was worse than serving ten years in gaol.

On the same morning that a man who had nothing at all to do with police stations and commissioners' offices had predicted his transfer – he was a government employee of a different sort; that is, the director of the local post office – Montalbano was summoned by his boss, Chief Inspector Libero Sanfilippo. Who was a true policeman, one of those who can tell at a glance whether the person in front of him is telling the truth or spouting lies. And even then, that is, in 1985, he already belonged to an endangered species. Like doctors who used to have what was once called a 'clinical eye' and could diagnose a patient's malady at a glance – whereas nowadays if they don't have dozens of pages of test results obtained by high-tech machines in their hands they can't tell a thing, not even a good old-fashioned flu. Years later, whenever Montalbano happened to review the early years of his career in his head, he always put Libero Sanfilippo at the top of the list. Without appearing to want to teach him anything, the man had actually taught him a great deal. First and foremost, how to maintain one's inner equilibrium when something terrible and shocking happens in front of you.

'If you let yourself get carried away by any reaction whatsoever – dismay, horror, indignation, pity – you're done for,' Sanfilippo would repeat every time. But Montalbano had managed to follow this advice only in part, because at times, despite his great efforts, he was overwhelmed by his feelings and emotions.

Secondly, Sanfilippo had shown him how to cultivate the 'clinical eye' that he so envied in his boss. But, here too, Montalbano could only absorb so much of his example. Apparently that sort of Superman X-ray vision was for the most part a natural gift.

The negative side of Chief Inspector Sanfilippo – at least in the eyes of former sixties radical Montalbano – was his utter, blind devotion to every sort of instituted Order with a capital O. The established Order, the public Order, the social Order. In his early days in Mascalippa, Montalbano wondered in bewilderment how a rather cultured gentleman like his superior could have such an iron-clad faith in an abstract concept which, the moment you translated it into reality, took the form of a cosh and a pair of handcuffs. The inspector got his answer the day when, by chance, his boss's identity card ended up in his hands. The man's full name was Libero Pensiero Sanfilippo. That is, 'Free Thinking' Sanfilippo. *Madonna santa!* Names like Libero Pensiero, Volontà ('Will'), Libertà, Palingenesi ('Rebirth'), and Vindice ('Avenger') were what anarchists used to like to give to their sons and daughters! The chief inspector's father must certainly have been an anarchist, and his son, just to be contrary, not only had become a policeman, but had also acquired a fixation for Order, in an ultimate attempt to annul his paternal genetic inheritance.

'Good morning, sir.'

'Good morning. Please close the door and sit down. You can smoke, but don't forget the ashtray.'

Right. Because, aside from Order with a capital O, Sanfilippo also loved order with a small o. If even a little ash fell outside the ashtray, the chief would start squirming in his chair and grimacing. It made him suffer.

'How's the Amoruso–Lonardo case coming along? Any progress?' Sanfilippo began.

Montalbano hesitated. What case? Filippo Amoruso, a seventy-year-old pensioner, while reworking the edge of his vegetable garden, had shifted it slightly, eating up barely three inches of the bordering vegetable garden of one Pasquale Lonardo, an eighty-year-old pensioner. Who, when apprised of the fact, had claimed, in the presence of others, to have engaged several times in sexual congress with the deceased mother of Amoruso, known far and wide to have been a big slut. At which point Amoruso, without so much as a peep, had stuck a three-inch stiletto blade into Lonardo's stomach, without, however, taking into account the fact that at that same moment Lonardo was holding a mattock, with which he dealt him a vicious blow to the head before collapsing to the ground. Both men were now in hospital, charged with disorderly conduct and attempted murder. Inspector Sanfilippo's question, in all its uselessness, could therefore mean only one thing: that the chief was taking a roundabout approach to the subject he wanted to discuss with Montalbano, who assumed a defensive position.

'It's coming along,' he said.

'Good, good.'

Silence descended. Montalbano shifted his left buttock about an inch forward and crossed his legs. He did not feel at ease. There was something in the air that made him nervous. Meanwhile, Sanfilippo had pulled his handkerchief out of his trouser pocket and was buffing the surface of the desk with it, making it shinier.

'As you know, yesterday afternoon I went to Enna – the commissioner wanted to speak to me,' he said all in one breath.

Montalbano uncrossed his legs and said nothing.

'He told me I'd been promoted to deputy commissioner and would be transferred to Palermo.'

Montalbano felt his mouth go dry.

'Congratulations,' he managed to say.

Had he called him in only to tell him something that everybody and his dog had already known for at least a month? Sanfilippo took off his glasses, looked at the lenses against the light, then put them back on.

'Thank you. He also told me that within two months, at the most, you too will be promoted. Had you heard any mention of this?'

'Yeth,' Montalbano exhaled.

He couldn't form the letter s, his tongue having sort of

solidified, and was as tense as a bowstring, ready to spring forward.

'The honourable commissioner asked me if it might not be a good idea for you to take my place.'

'Here?!'

'Of course, here in Mascalippa. Where else?'

'Bu . . . bu . . . bu . . .' said Montalbano.

It wasn't clear whether he was babbling incoherently or simply stuck on the word *but*. This was what he'd been fearing! The moment he entered Chief Inspector Sanfilippo's office he'd expected this very bit of bad news! And his boss had not failed to deliver it. In a flash he saw the landscape of Mascalippa and environs pass before his eyes. Magnificent, yes, but for him it just wasn't the thing. For good measure, he also saw four cows grazing on parched, wilted grass. He shivered, as if sick with malaria.

'But I told him I didn't agree,' said Sanfilippo, smiling at him.

But did his bastard of a boss want to give him a heart attack? To see him writhing and gasping for air in his chair? In spite of the fact that he was one step away from a nervous breakdown, Montalbano's polemical instincts got the better of him.

'Would you please explain why you think it's a bad idea for me to work as inspector in Mascalippa?'

'Because you're utterly incompatible with the environment here.'

Sanfilippo paused, smiled faintly, then added: 'Or, more precisely, the environment is incompatible with you.'

What a great policeman Sanfilippo was!

'When did you realize it? I've never done anything to show—'

'Oh, you certainly have! Certainly! You've never talked about it, never said anything, I'll grant you that. But you certainly showed it! Barely two weeks after you were first assigned here, I understood everything.'

'But how did I show it, for Chrissake?'

'I'll give you one example. Do you remember the time we went to question some peasants in Montestellario and we accepted an invitation to eat with a family of shepherds?'

'Yes,' said Montalbano, teeth clenched.

'They laid the table outside. It was a beautiful day, and the mountaintops were still covered with snow. Remember?'

'Yes.'

'You sat there with your head down. You didn't want to look at the landscape. They gave you some fresh ricotta, but you muttered that you weren't hungry. And then the father of the family said that one could see the lake that day, and he pointed to a distant spot far below, a little jewel sparkling in the sunlight. I asked you to come and have a look. You obeyed, but immediately closed your eyes and turned pale. You didn't eat a thing. Then there was that other time when—'

'Please, that's enough.'

Sanfilippo was having fun playing cat and mouse with him. To the point that he hadn't even told him what the commissioner had finally said. Still shaken by the memory of that nightmarish day spent at Montestellario, he began to suspect that his boss still hadn't mustered up the courage to tell him the truth. Which was that the commissioner had stuck to his original idea that Montalbano should be the inspector at Mascalippa.

'So, in the end, the commissioner . . . ?' he ventured.

'In the end the commissioner what?'

'What did he say in response to your observation?'

'He said he would think it over. But if you want to know my opinion . . .'

'Of course I want to know your opinion!'

'In my opinion, I persuaded him. He'll let the higher-ups decide where to send you.'

✼

What would be the irrevocable decision of the Higher-Ups, those Supreme Gods and Deities who, like all self-respecting deities, were headquartered in Rome? This troubling question was preventing Montalbano from properly savouring the suckling pig that Santino, the restaurateur, had proudly prepared for him the day before.

'You're disappointing me today,' said Santino, slightly offended, having watched him eat listlessly.

Montalbano threw up his hands in a gesture of resignation.

'Forgive me, Santì, I just don't feel right.'

Walking out of the trattoria, he immediately found himself fumbling about in the void. When he'd gone inside to eat, the sun was out, and in little more than an hour, a dense, gloomy fog had descended. That's what Mascalippa was like.

He started walking home with a heavy heart, dodging head-on collisions with other human shadows by sidestepping at the very last instant. Darkness in the daytime, darkness inside him. While walking he made a decision he knew was final and irrevocable: if by any chance they assigned him to another town like Mascalippa, he would resign. And he would become a lawyer, or a legal aide, or the office manager of a law firm, so long as it was by the sea.

He lived in a small two-room rented flat, with kitchen and bathroom, right in the middle of town so that he wouldn't have to see any trace of mountains or hills when looking out of the window. There was no central heating, and despite the four electric space heaters that he never turned off, on some winter evenings all he could do was get into bed and cover himself entirely but for one arm, which he kept outside the blankets to hold a book. He'd always liked to read and then reflect on what he had read, and for this reason the two rooms were overflowing with books. He was capable of starting a book in the evening and then reading till dawn, without interruption, in order to finish it.

Luckily there was no danger that he would be summoned in
the middle of the night for any violent crimes. For some
inexplicable reason, killings, shootings, and violent brawls
always seemed to happen during the day. And there was
hardly any need for investigations; the crimes were all without mystery: Luigi shot Giuseppe over a matter of money
and confessed; Giovanni knifed Martino over a question of
adultery and confessed. And so on. If he wanted to use his
brain, Montalbano was forced to solve the rebuses in the
Settimana Enigmistica, which had a whole week's worth of
puzzles. At any rate, at least his years in Mascalippa, spent
beside a man like Sanfilippo, were not time wasted. On the
contrary.

That day, however, the idea of spending the evening
lying in bed reading, or watching some idiocy on TV,
seemed unbearable. At that time Mery was home from the
school where she taught Latin. He'd met her at university,
during the years of protest. They were the same age, or
almost: she was four months younger. They'd liked each
other at once, at first sight, and quickly they'd gone from a
sort of amiable affection to an absolutely open, amorous
friendship. Whenever they desired each other they would
call one another and meet. Then they drifted apart and fell
out of touch. In the mid-seventies Montalbano learned that
Mery had got married and that her marriage had lasted less
than a year. He ran into her by chance one day in Catania,
on Via Etnea, during his first week on the job in Mascalippa. In a moment of despair he had jumped into his car
and driven for an hour to Catania with the intention of
seeing a first-run film, since the ones that made it to Mascalippa were all at least three years old. And there, inside the
cinema, as he waited in the queue to buy his ticket, he'd
heard someone call his name. It was Mery, who was just
coming out. And if she'd been a beautiful girl in full flower
before, maturity and experience had now made her beauty
more composed, almost secret. In the end Montalbano

didn't get to see his film. He'd gone to Mery's place, where she lived alone with the intention of never marrying again. Her one experience of marriage had more than sufficed. Montalbano spent the night with her and headed back to Mascalippa at six o'clock the following morning. Thereafter it had become a sort of habit of his to go to Catania at least twice a week.

'Hi, Mery. It's Salvo.'

'Hi. You know what?'

'What?'

'I was just about to call you myself.'

Montalbano became disheartened. Want to bet Mery was going to tell him they couldn't get together because she was busy that evening?

'Why?'

'I wanted to ask if you could come a little earlier than usual, so we could go out to dinner. Yesterday a friend of mine from work took me to a restaurant that—'

'I'll be at your place by seven-thirty, OK?' Montalbano cut her off, so happy he was practically singing.

*

The restaurant was called, rather unimaginatively, Il Delfino. But the imagination lacking in their sign was abundant in their cooking. There were some ten antipasti, all strictly seafood, and each more heavenly than the last. The *polipetti alla strascinasale* melted even before touching the palate. And what to say about the grouper cooked in an angelic sauce whose various ingredients Montalbano was unable to identify in full? And then there was Mery, who when it came to eating was just as much of a bon vivant as he was. For if, when you are eating with gusto, you don't have a person eating with the same gusto beside you, the pleasure of eating is as though obscured, diminished.

They ate in silence. Every so often they looked each other in the eyes and smiled. At the end of the meal, after the fruit, the lights in the place went dim and then off. One of the customers protested. Then through the kitchen door came a waiter pushing a cart carrying a cake with a single lighted candle on it and a bucket with a bottle of champagne in it. Bewildered, Montalbano noticed that the waiter was coming to their table. The lights came back on, and all of the customers applauded as a few of them cried out:

'Happy birthday!'

Surely it must be Mery's birthday. And he'd completely forgotten. What a heel he was! What an airhead! But he could do nothing about it. He was simply incapable of remembering dates.

'I . . . I'm so sorry. I forgot today was . . . your . . .' he said, embarrassed, taking her hand.

'My what?' Mery asked, amused, eyes glistening.

'It's not your birthday?'

'*My* birthday? It's *your* birthday!' said Mery, unable to hold back her laughter.

Montalbano, flummoxed, could only look at her. It was true.

When they got back to her place, Mery opened a wardrobe and pulled out a package all prettied up in what shop owners like to call 'gift-wrapping', an orgy of coloured ribbons, bows, and bad taste.

'Happy birthday.'

Montalbano unwrapped it. Mery's present was a heavy sweater, for the mountains. Quite elegant.

'It's for your winters in Mascalippa.'

As soon as she'd said it she noticed that Salvo was making a strange face.

'What's wrong?'

Montalbano told her about his promotion and conversation with Inspector Sanfilippo.

'. . . So I don't know where they're going to send me.'

Mery remained silent. Then she looked at her watch. It was ten-thirty. She shot out of the armchair to her feet.

'Excuse me, I have to make a phone call.'

She went into the bedroom and closed the door so she wouldn't be heard. Montalbano felt a slight pang of jealousy. On the other hand he could hardly object to Mery having a relationship with another man. A few minutes later, she called to him. When he entered the bedroom, she was already in bed, waiting for him.

Later, as they lay there in each other's arms, Mery whispered into his ear.

'I called my Uncle Giovanni.'

Montalbano hesitated. 'And who's he?'

'My mother's younger brother. He adores me. And he's a big cheese at the Ministry of Justice. I asked him to find out where you're going to be assigned. Was I wrong to do it . . . ?'

'No,' said Montalbano, kissing her.

*

The next day, Mery called him at the office around 6 p.m.

She said only one word.

'Vigàta.'

Then she hung up.

2

Thus it was not some common soothsayer in the lofty reaches of the Roman Olympus, the Empyrean Palazzi of Power, who had uttered those three syllables – *Vi-gà-ta* – but a supreme Deity, a God of the Religion of Bureaucracy, one whose word marked immutable destinies. And who, when duly implored, had given a clear, precise response quite unlike the oracular utterances of the Cumaean Sibyl or the Pythia or the god Apollo at Delphi, which always needed to be interpreted by high priests who were never in agreement about the actual meaning. '*Ibis redibis non morieris in bello*,' the

Sibyl would say to the soldier about to go off to war. Sincerely yours. But one had to put a comma either before or after that *non* for the soldier to know whether he would leave his hide on the battlefield or come away safe and sound. And deciding where that comma should go was the job of the priests, whose interpretation usually depended on the amount of the offering made. Here, on the other hand, there was nothing to interpret. Vigàta, the Deity had said, and Vigàta it would be.

After receiving Mery's phone call, Montalbano was unable to remain seated at his desk. Muttering something incomprehensible to the guard on duty, he went out and started walking around the streets. He had to make a great effort, while walking, to restrain himself from breaking into a boogie-woogie, which was the rhythm to which his blood was circulating at that moment. Jesus, how nice! Vigàta! He tried to remember the place, and the first thing that came to mind was a sort of picture-postcard image showing the harbour with the three jetties and, to the right, the squat silhouette of a massive tower. Then he remembered the *corso*, the main street, about halfway down which was a large cafe that even had a billiards room with two tables. He used to go there with his father, who liked to play a round from time to time. And while his father played he would regale himself with an enormous triangular chunk of ice cream, usually what they called a *pezzo duro*, or 'hard piece', usually of chocolate and cream. Or cassata. The ice cream they made there had no equal. He could still taste it. Then the name of the cafe came back to him: the Castiglione. Who knew whether it still existed and still made the same incomparable ice cream. Two blinding colours then flashed before his eyes, yellow and blue. The yellow of the very fine sand and the blue of the sea. Without realizing, he had come to a sort of lookout point from where he could admire a broad valley and the mountaintops in the distance. They were hardly the Dolomites, of course, but they were still mountaintops. Normally they were enough to plunge him into the gloomiest sort of melancholy, a sense of unbearable exile. This time, however, he was able to look at the landscape and even enjoy it a little, comforted as he was by the knowledge that soon he would never see it again.

That evening he phoned Mery to thank her.

'I did it in my own interest,' said Mery.

'And what interest is that? I don't understand.'

'If you were transferred to Abbiategrasso or Casalpusterlengo, we wouldn't be able see each other anymore. But Vigàta's only about two hours from Catania. I looked at a map.'

Montalbano didn't know what to say. He felt touched.

'Did you think I was going to let you go so easily?' Mery continued.

They laughed.

'One of these days I want to dash down to Vigàta, to see if it's still the way I remember it. Of course I won't tell anyone that I . . .' He trailed off. An icy serpent slithered fast up his spine, paralysing him.

'Salvo. What's wrong? Are you still there?'

'Yes. It's just that something occurred to me.'

'What?'

Montalbano hesitated. He didn't want to offend Mery, but his sudden doubt was stronger than any sense of etiquette.

'Mery, can we trust this Uncle Giovanni of yours? Are we absolutely certain he—'

Her laughter rang out on the other end.

'I knew it!'

'You knew what?'

'That sooner or later you would ask me that. My uncle told me your place of assignment has already been determined, already been written down. You needn't worry. Actually, tell you what. When you decide to go to Vigàta, let me know a few days in advance. That way I can request a leave of absence and we can go together. Will I see you tomorrow?'

'Of course.'

'Of course what? Of course we're going to Vigàta together, or of course I'll see you tomorrow?'

'Both.'

But he knew at once that he had told a lie. Or at least a half-lie. The following day he would of course be going down to Catania to spend the evening with Mery, but he had already made up his mind to go to Vigàta alone. Her presence would definitely have distracted him. Actually the verb that had first come to mind was not 'distract' but 'disturb'. He had felt a little ashamed of this.

*

Vigàta was more or less the way he remembered it. There was, however, some new construction on the Piano Lanterna, horrendous sorts of mini-high-rises of some fifteen or twenty storeys, while the little houses once built into the marlstone hillside, stacked one on top of the other and forming a tangle of little streets throbbing with life, were all gone. They were all hovels, more or less, single-room dwellings that during the day got air only through the front door, which was necessarily kept open. As one walked through those little streets, one might get a glimpse of a child being born, a family quarrel, a priest giving last rites, or a group of people getting ready for a wedding or a funeral. Right before one's eyes. And the whole thing immersed in a babel of voices, cries, laughter, prayers, curses, insults.

He asked a passer-by how the small houses had all disappeared, and the man replied that terrible flooding and landslides had washed them all the way down to the sea a few years before.

He'd forgotten the smell of the harbour. A combination of stagnant sea water, rotten seaweed, sodden cordage, sunbaked tar, diesel, and sardines. Each single element making up that smell might not be so pleasant to the senses when taken alone, but together they formed a highly agreeable aroma, mysterious and unmistakable.

He sat down on a bollard, but didn't light a cigarette. He didn't want the newly rediscovered scent to be polluted by the smell of tobacco. And he stayed there a long time, watching the seagulls, until a rumble in his stomach reminded him that it was time for lunch. The sea air had whetted his appetite.

Returning to the *corso*, which was actually called Via Roma, he immediately spotted a sign that said 'Trattoria San Calogero'. Putting his trust in the Good Lord above, he went inside. There wasn't a single customer. Apparently it wasn't time yet.

'Can one eat?' he asked a waiter with white hair who, hearing him enter, had come out from the kitchen.

'No need to ask permission,' the waiter replied drily.

Montalbano sat down, angry at himself for asking such a stupid question.

'We've got *antipasto di mare*, spaghetti in squid ink or with clam sauce or with sea urchin.'

'Spaghetti with sea urchin's not so easy to make,' Montalbano said, doubtful.

'I've got a degree in sea urchin,' the waiter said.

Montalbano wanted to bite his tongue into little pieces. Two to nothing.

Two idiotic statements and two intelligent replies.

'And what've you got for the second course?'

'Fish.'

'What kind of fish?'

'Whatever kind you like.'

'And how is it cooked?'

'It depends on what fish you choose.'

He'd better sew his lips shut.

'Just bring me what you think best.'

He realized he'd made the right decision. By the time he

left the restaurant, he'd eaten three antipasti, a dish of spaghetti with sea urchin sauce big enough to feed four, and six red mullet fried barely one millimetre deep. And yet he felt light as a feather, and so infused with a sense of well-being that he had a doltish smile on his face. He was convinced that once he moved to Vigàta, he would make this his restaurant of choice.

It was already three o'clock. He spent another hour dawdling about town, then decided to take a long walk along the eastern jetty. And he took it one slow step at a time. The silence was broken only by the surf between the breakwaters, the cries of the seagulls and, every so often, the rumble of a trawler testing its diesel engine. At the end of the jetty, directly below the lighthouse, was a flat rock. He sat down on it. The day was so bright it almost hurt, and the wind gusted every so often. After a spell he got up. It was time to get back in his car and return to Mascalippa. Halfway up the jetty he stopped abruptly. An image had appeared before his eyes: a sort of white hill, blindingly bright, descending in terraces all the way down to the water. What was it? Where was it? La Scala dei Turchi, that's what it was! The Turks' Ladder. And it couldn't be too far away.

In a flash he got to the Castiglione Cafe, which was where it had always been. He'd checked beforehand.

'Could you tell me how to get to the Turks' Staircase?'

'Of course.'

The waiter explained the route to him.

'And I'd like a *pezzo duro*, please, in the billiards room.'

'What flavour?'

'Cassata.'

He went into the back room. Two men were playing a round, with a couple of friends looking on. Montalbano sat down at a table and began to eat his cassata slowly, savouring each spoonful. All of a sudden an argument broke out between the two players. Their friends intervened.

'Let's ask this gentleman to settle the matter,' said one of them.

Another turned to Montalbano and asked:

'Do you know how to play billiards?'

'No,' said Montalbano, embarrassed.

They looked at him disdainfully and resumed their argument. Montalbano finished his ice cream, paid at the cash register, went out, got in his car, which he'd parked nearby, and headed off to the Turks' Ladder.

Following the waiter's directions, he turned left at a certain point, went a short distance downhill along a paved road, and then stopped. The road ended there. One had to walk on sand the rest of the way. He removed his shoes and socks, put them in the car, locked the car, rolled up the bottoms of his trousers, and walked to the beach. The water was cool but not cold. Just past the promontory, the Turks' Ladder suddenly appeared.

In his memory it had seemed much more imposing. When you're small everything seems larger than life. But even cut down to size, it retained its astonishing beauty. The silhouette of the marlstone hill's crest stood jagged against the crisp blue of the cloudless sky, crowned by hedges, intensely green. Towards the bottom, the point formed by the last few steps of land descending into the turquoise sea sparkled in the sunlight and took on nuances of colour tending to bright pink. The part of the hill that stood further back lay instead entirely on yellow sand. Montalbano felt so dazzled by the bright colours, which practically screamed at him, that he had to close his eyes and cover his ears with his hands for a moment. He was still about a hundred yards from the base of the hill, but he chose to admire it from a distance. He was afraid he might end up inside the unreality of a painting, a picture, afraid he might himself become a spot — surely jarring — of colour.

He sat down on the dry sand, spellbound. And he remained there, smoking one cigarette after another, mesmerized by the chromatic variations in the glow of the sun on the lower steps of the Turks' Ladder as it slowly set. Once it had set, he got up and decided to drive back to Mascalippa after dark. He decided it was worth his while to have another meal at the Trattoria San Calogero. Walking slowly back to his car, he turned around every so often to look. He really didn't want to leave.

He drove back to Vigàta at ten kilometres an hour, bombarded with insults and obscenities by other drivers who had to pass him on the rather narrow road. But he didn't react. He was in the sort of state of mind where, even if someone were to cuff him on the head, he would turn the other cheek. At the gates of town he stopped at a tobacconist's and stocked up on cigarettes for the journey home. Then he went to a service station to fill up the tank and checked the tyres and oil. He glanced at his watch. He had another half hour to kill. Parking the car, he walked back to the harbour. Now there was a large ferry tied up at the quay.

A line of cars and trucks were waiting to go aboard.

'Where's it going?' he asked a passerby.

'It's the mail-boat for Lampedusa.'

At last it was late enough to go to the restaurant. And, indeed, when he entered, three tables were already taken. The waiter now had a younger man helping him. He approached Montalbano with a grin on his face.

'Shall I decide for you, like we did earlier?'

'Yes.'

The waiter bent down towards him.

'Did you like the Turks' Ladder?'

Montalbano looked at him in astonishment.

'Who told you I . . .'

'Word gets around quickly here.'

They probably already knew he was a policeman!

✣

A week later, as they were lying in bed, Mery came out with a question.

'Did you ever end up going to Vigàta?'

'No,' Montalbano lied.

'Why not?'

'I didn't have the time.'

'Aren't you curious to see what it's like? You said you'd been there when you were a kid, but it's not the same thing.'

Oh, what a pain! If he didn't make an immediate decision, the questions might go on for ever.

'We'll go next Sunday, all right?'

They agreed that Mery would set out in her car and wait for him at the bar at the junction for Caltanissetta. She would then park in the car park and they would go the rest of the way in Montalbano's car.

And thus he was forced to return to Vigàta pretending he hadn't just been there a few days before.

*

Montalbano took Mery first to the harbour and then to the Turks' Ladder.

She was enchanted. But, being a woman – that is, belonging to that species of creature who is able to combine the loftiest heights of poetry with the hardest of concrete facts – she turned to Montalbano, who couldn't take his eyes off all that natural beauty, and said, in Sicilian: 'I'm really hungry.'

Thus Montalbano found himself confronted with the most Shakespearean of dilemmas: should he go to the Trattoria San Calogero and risk being recognized by the waiter, or try a new restaurant and risk, with a high degree of probability, being served a bad meal?

The idea of having to drive all the way home with his stomach churning, at grips with food that even dogs would have refused, dispelled all doubt. Back in Vigàta, he

manoeuvred things so that he and Mery ended up as if by
chance under the sign of the familiar trattoria.

'Shall we try here?'

Once inside, he tried to catch the waiter's eye and
succeeded.

They needed exchange only the briefest of glances.

You have never seen me before, said Montalbano's eyes.

I have never seen you before, replied the waiter's eyes.

*

After feasting in heavenly fashion, Montalbano took Mery
to the Castiglione, advising her to order a *pezzo duro*.

When she'd finished her ice cream, Mery said she
needed to go the loo.

'I'll wait for you outside,' said Montalbano.

He went out onto the pavement. The main street was
practically deserted. Before him stood the town hall with its
little colonnade. Leaning against one column, a policeman
on his beat was talking to two stray dogs. A car approached
slowly from the left. Then all at once a sports car appeared
at high speed. Right before Montalbano's eyes, the sports
car skidded slightly and sideswiped the slow-moving car as
it passed it. Both drivers stopped and got out. The one
driving the slow car was an elderly gentleman with glasses.
The other was a young sort of ruffian, tall and mustachioed.
As the elderly gentleman bent down to assess the damage
done to his car, the young man put a hand on his shoulder
and, when the old man stood up to look at him, punched
him hard in the face. It all happened very fast. As the old
man fell to the ground, a fat man got out of the sports car
with a determined look on his face, grabbed the youth, and
forced him back into the car, which then set off again with
a screech of its tyres.

Montalbano went up to the old man, who was unable to
speak. His face was all bloodied. The blood poured out of
his nose and mouth. The policeman arrived at a leisurely

pace. Montalbano sat the victim down in the passenger seat, as he was clearly in no condition to drive.

'Take him to A&E at once,' he said to the policeman.

The policeman seemed to move in slow motion.

'Did you get licence number of the other car?' Montalbano asked him.

'Yes,' the policeman said, pulling a pad and pen out of his pocket. He wrote down the number. Montalbano, who had memorized the number himself, noticed that the man had written it incorrectly.

'Listen, the last two numbers are wrong. I got a good look at them. They're not five-eight, but six-three.'

The policeman corrected the two numbers with bad grace and put the car in gear.

'Wait. Don't you want my name, address and telephone number?' Montalbano asked.

'Why would I?'

'What do you mean, why would you? I'm a witness.'

'All right, all right, if you really care so much.'

He wrote down Montalbano's personal particulars as if they were somehow offensive to him. Then he closed his notepad, gave Montalbano a dirty look, and left without another word.

As he was driving off to take the old man to the hospital, Mery reappeared on the pavement.

'I decided to freshen up a little,' said Mery, who hadn't noticed anything. 'Shall we go?'

*

A month went by without so much as a leaf moving. No messages of promotion or transfer were forthcoming from the Higher Spheres. Montalbano began to be convinced that it was all a joke played on him by someone trying to get his goat. Which put him in a bad mood and had him dealing imaginary kicks left and right like a horse being assaulted by horseflies.

'Try to be reasonable,' Mery said, trying to calm him down, especially as she had become the principal target of his outbursts. 'Why would anyone want to play a joke like that on you?'

'How should I know? Maybe you and your Uncle Giovanni know!'

And it always ended in a squabble.

Then, one fine morning, Chief Inspector Sanfilippo called him into his office and, beaming a broad smile, at last gave him the response of the Council of Gods: Montalbano was to be Chief Inspector of the Vigàta police.

Montalbano's face turned pale at first, then red, then began to verge on green. Sanfilippo became worried he might be having some sort of attack.

'Montalbano, are you OK? Sit down, please!'

He filled a glass from the bottle of mineral water he always kept on his desk and handed it to him.

'Drink.'

Montalbano obeyed. Because of his reaction, Sanfilippo got the wrong idea.

'What's wrong? Don't you like Vigàta? I know it pretty well, you know. It's a delightful town. You'll love it there, you'll see.'

*

Montalbano returned to the 'delightful town' – as Sanfilippo called it – four days later. This time in an official capacity, to introduce himself to Inspector Locascio, whom he was to replace. Police headquarters was located in a decent sort of building, a three-storey construction situated right at the start of the main street for those entering from the Montereale road, and at the end of the main street for those coming in from the Montelusa road. Montelusa was the provincial capital, where the Prefecture, Commissioner of Police, and courts all were. Locascio, who lived with his wife on the third floor in an apartment belonging to the police department, immediately told Montalbano that he would have it cleaned up before leaving.

'Why?'

'What do you mean, why? Don't you intend to use the apartment?'

'No.'

Locascio misinterpreted this.

'Ah, I get it. You don't want people to see your comings and goings. Lucky you, who can have night-time guests!' he said, elbowing him in the ribs.

On the day Montalbano was to take command, Locascio introduced him to all the men on the force, one by one. There was one man, a little older than Montalbano, whom the inspector immediately took a liking to, Sergeant Fazio.

Montalbano wanted to take his time looking for the right place to live. In the meantime he rented a bungalow that was part of a hotel complex a little over a mile outside town. He'd put his books and other few belongings in a storage facility in Mascalippa, until he found a home.

3

The day after his arrival in Vigàta he got in his car and went to Montelusa to introduce himself to Commissioner Alabiso, whose fate was already sealed. The soothsayers predicted that at the first sign of movement at the ministry, he would be given his marching orders. He'd long been the chief of the political team (which still existed, though every so often they changed its name), and by now he knew too much. The last straw was his scarcely flexible character; indeed he'd never met a compromise he liked. In short, there are men of quality who, when appointed to certain positions, turn out, precisely because of their quality, to be unfit in the eyes of men who have no qualities whatsoever but who, to make up for it, engage in politics. And

Commissioner Alabiso was now considered unfit because he wasn't afraid of anybody.

The commissioner received Montalbano at once, shook his hand, and asked him to sit down. But he seemed distracted. Every so often, as he was talking to Montalbano and looking him straight in the eye, he would hesitate, as if confused. Then he suddenly said:

'But tell me something. Do we know each other?'

'Yes,' said Montalbano.

'Ah, so that's it! I was sure I had seen you before! Did we meet on duty?'

'In a way, yes.'

'And when was that?'

'About seventeen years ago.'

The commissioner looked puzzled.

'But you were just a child then!'

'Not quite. I was eighteen.'

The commissioner visibly put up his guard. He was beginning to understand.

'In '68?' he ventured.

'Yes.'

'In Palermo?'

'Yes.'

'I was an inspector at the time.'

'And I was a university student.'

They eyed each other in silence.

'What did I do to you?' the commissioner asked.

'You kicked me in the arse. So hard that it tore the seat of my trousers.'

'Ah, I see. And what did you do?'

'I managed to punch you.'

'Did I arrest you?'

'You weren't able to. We wrestled for a few seconds, but I managed to break free and escaped.'

Then the commissioner said something incredible, and so softly that Montalbano wasn't sure he'd heard right.

'Those were the days,' Alabiso sighed.

Montalbano started laughing, and the inspector joined in almost at once. They embraced in the middle of the room.

Then they got down to more serious matters. Mostly concerning the turf war between the two local Mafia families, the Cuffaros and the Sinagras, a struggle that yielded at least two killings a year on each side. According to the commissioner, each of the families had a saint in heaven.

'I'm sorry, sir, but what heaven are you talking about?'

'Parliament.'

'And do the two honourables belong to different parties?'

'No. They both belong to the majority party and the same bloc. You see, Montalbano, I've got this idea, but it's very hard to prove.'

And it's because of this idea of yours that they want to shaft you, Montalbano thought.

'Perhaps it's completely unfounded. Who knows,' the commissioner went on. 'But there are certain coincidences which . . . I think it's worth looking into.'

'But didn't you discuss this with my predecessor?'

'No.'

No explanation.

'And why are you discussing it with me?'

'Chief Inspector Sanfilippo is a dear friend of mine, like a brother. He told me all I needed to know about you.'

*

Every morning when he left the hotel to go to headquarters, after a series of bends he came to a straight stretch of road parallel to the long, broad beach. The area was called Marinella. There were three or four small houses built right on the beach and standing rather far apart from one another. They were quite unpretentious, all single-storey constructions that spread out horizontally, with rooms that probably lined up in a row, railway-style. And all inevitably with giant cisterns on the roof for collecting water. On two of them, however, the tanks were situated at the edge of a sort of terrace that served as a roof and solarium and had an external staircase in masonry for access. Each house also had, in front, a small terrace where one could eat in the evening with a view of the sea. Every time Montalbano drove past he felt his heart throb. If he could somehow manage to move into one of those houses, he would never leave! What a dream! To wake up in the morning and take a walk along the seashore. And perhaps, if the weather was right, go for a long swim.

*

Montalbano hated barbers' shops. Whenever he was forced to go to one because his hair was hanging down to his shoulders, it put him in a dark mood.

'Where can I get my hair cut?' he asked Fazio one morning in the tone of someone asking where the nearest funeral home was.

'The best place for you would be Totò Nicotra's salon.'

'What do you mean "the best for me"? Let's get this straight, Fazio. I refuse to set foot in one of those salons full of mirrors and gold trim, I'm looking for . . .'

'Something more discreet, sort of old-fashioned,' Fazio finished his sentence.

'Exactly,' Montalbano confirmed, looking at him with a touch of admiration.

'And that's why I mentioned Totò Nicotra.'

This Fazio was a true policeman: a few bits of information were enough for him to know a person inside and out.

When the inspector walked into Nicotra's shop, there were no customers. The barber was a taciturn old man well past sixty who looked a bit melancholy. He didn't even open his mouth until halfway through the haircut. Then he decided to ask:

'How do you like Vigàta, Inspector?'

By now everyone knew who Montalbano was. And so, as they got to talking, he learned that one of the little houses in Marinella was now vacant because Nicotra's son, Pippino, had gone to New York and married an American girl who'd even found him a job there.

'But they'll want to come back for their summer holiday, won't they?'

'No, sir. My son already told me he's going to go to Miami. Who knows when I'll see him again! So I had the house whitewashed and cleaned up inside for nothing!'

'Well, you could always go there yourself.'

'To Miami?!'

'No, I meant the house on the beach.'

'I don't really like the sea air. My wife's from Vicari. You know it?'

'Yes, it's up high.'

'Right, and my wife's got a little house there, where we like to go now and then.'

Montalbano could feel his heart throb with hope. He leapt into the breach:

'Do you think your son would be willing to rent it to me for the whole year?'

'What's my son got to do with it? He left me the keys and told me to do whatever I want with it.'

*

'Hi, Mery. Want to hear some good news? I found a house!'

'In town?'

'No, a bit outside. A small three-room house, with kitchen and bathroom. Right on the beach at Marinella, just a few yards from the water. It has a solarium and a veranda at the front where you can eat outside. A little jewel.'

'Have you already moved in?'

'No. Day after tomorrow. I've already arranged for my stuff to be brought down from Mascalippa.'

'I want to see you!'

'Me too.'

'Listen, I could come to Vigàta this Saturday afternoon and go back to Catania Sunday evening. What do you say? Would you put me up?'

✿

The following day was a Thursday. And a beautiful day it was, which put him in a good mood. Entering his office at the station, he noticed a sort of postcard on his desk, addressed to him from 'The Courthouse of Montelusa'. It had been postmarked fifteen days before. Which meant it had taken a good two weeks to travel the less than four miles separating Vigàta and Montelusa. They were convening him for the coming Monday at 9 a.m. His good mood faded. He didn't like having to deal with judges and lawyers. What the hell did they want from him? The card didn't say anything, other than the division where he was supposed to appear. The third division.

'Fazio!'

'At your service, Chief.'

He handed him the summons. Fazio read it and looked questioningly at the inspector.

'Could you have a look and see what this is about?'

'Sure.'

Fazio returned a couple of hours later.

'Chief, before coming to Vigàta to start your new job, you'd been through here a couple of times, hadn't you?'

'Yes,' Montalbano admitted.

'And you witnessed a scuffle between two motorists?'

Right! He'd forgotten all about it.

'Yes.'

'You're being called upon to testify.'

'What a pain in the arse.'

'Sir, apparently you're a good citizen. And good citizens

who testify are usually subjected to pains in the arse, at least around here.'

Was Fazio making fun of him?

'Are you saying it's better not to testify?'

'Chief, what kind of question is that? If you want me to answer as a policeman, I'll tell you it's your duty to testify. But if you want me to answer as a civilian, I'll tell you it's always a big pain in the arse.'

He paused.

'And sometimes one pain in the arse leads to another, like mushrooms.'

'Look, this involves a routine incident. Following an ordinary traffic accident, some bully broke an old man's—'

Fazio raised a hand to cut him off.

'I know the whole story. The beat officer filled me in.'

'The one who took down the licence-plate number?'

'Yes, sir. He said he'd written down the wrong number and you made him correct it.'

'Yeah, and so?'

'Well, if not for you, who were in Vigàta for the second time and whom everyone knew was an inspector, that wrong number would have been written down correctly.'

Montalbano looked bewildered.

'What the hell are you saying?'

'Chief, the beat officer says he was right to write the number down wrong.'

Montalbano could feel his nerves beginning to fray.

'Fazio, you're talking in circles. Could you be a little clearer, please?'

Fazio answered with a question.

'Can I close the door?'

'Go ahead,' Montalbano consented, increasingly flummoxed.

Fazio closed the door and sat down in one of the two chairs in front of the desk.

'As the beat officer was driving the old man to the

hospital, he tried to persuade him not to file a complaint. But the old guy, who's from Caltanissetta, dug in his heels.'

'I'm sorry, Fazio. But what is this policeman, anyway? A Franciscan monk? What's he want, peace on earth?'

'He wants peace all right, just not eternal peace.'

'Fazio, you and I have barely just met. But if you don't explain this whole business to me as clearly as possible within three minutes, I'm going to grab you and throw you out of this office. And you can report me to whoever you like, the union, the commissioner, or the pope!'

Very calmly, Fazio stuck a hand in his pocket and pulled out a piece of paper folded in four, unfolded it, smoothed it out, and began to read.

'Cusumano, Giuseppe, son of Salvatore Cusumano and Maria Cuffaro, was born in Vigàta on 18 October 19—'

Montalbano cut him off.

'Who's he?'

'The guy that punched the old man.'

'What the hell do I care about his personal particulars?'

'Chief, his mother, Maria Cuffaro, is the kid sister of Don Lillino Cuffaro, and Giuseppe is the favourite grand-son of Don Sisino Cuffaro. Get the picture?'

'Bright and clear.'

Now he understood everything. The beat officer was afraid to take sides against the scion of a Mafia family like the Cuffaros, and that was why he quite purposely wrote down the wrong licence-plate number. So that the assailant could never be properly identified.

'All right, thanks. You can go now,' he said curtly to Fazio.

*

On Friday morning he prepared his suitcase – actually three suitcases, and rather large ones at that – loaded them into the car, paid the bill, and headed off to his new home in Marinella. It didn't seem real to him. After Nicotra the barber had given him the keys the evening before, he hadn't been able to resist the temptation to go and look at the place once more before returning to the hotel for the last time. The little house was nicely furnished. There wasn't any heavy pseudo-aristocratic or pseudo-Arab Emirate stuff; only tasteful, modest pieces. The phone was already connected. Apparently the phone company had worked overtime because he was a police inspector. The empty fridge in the kitchen worked fine. The gas bottle was new. One reached the veranda — which was spacious enough for a bench, two chairs, and a small table — by means of French windows in the dining room. Three stairs led down from the veranda to the beach. Montalbano sat down on the bench and stayed for an hour, savouring the sea air. He would have liked to fall asleep right then and there.

Having dropped off the suitcases, he got back in the car and drove to headquarters to inform Fazio that he had some things to do and wouldn't be back until late morning. He went out, and in one shop he bought sheets, pillowcases, towels, tablecloths, and napkins. Then he went to a supermarket and bought up their stock of pots, pans, cutlery, dishes, glasses and everything else he needed. On top of this he bought some food to put in the fridge. When he headed back to Marinella, his car looked like a door-to-door salesman's. While unloading all the stuff he noticed that he was still missing a great number of things. And so he went shopping again. He didn't get back to the police station until after twelve.

'Any news?' he asked Fazio, who, while they awaited the arrival of a deputy inspector, had assumed those duties.

'None. Oh, yes, the Honourable M. P. Torrisi phoned twice from Rome asking for you.'

'And who's this Honourable Torrisi?'

'One of our local honourable representatives in the lower house of Parliament.'

'How many such honourables are there?'

'A lot, if you count the whole province. But the ones with the most votes from Vigàta are Torrisi and Vannicò.'

'Are they from two different parties?'

'No, Chief. They belong to the same parish: the Christian Democrats.'

To his displeasure, the words the commissioner had spoken to him during their sole encounter came back to him.

'Did he say what he wanted?'

'No, Chief.'

*

He spent that evening and part of the night putting the house in order and moving the furniture around a little. Before going home to Marinella he'd stopped at the Trattoria San Calogero to eat, as had already become his custom. He felt in good shape as he started his home-improvement jobs, but by the time he went to bed his legs and back felt broken. He had a leaden sleep, heavy and dense. Waking up just after daybreak, he prepared the *napoletana*, drank half its contents, put on his trunks, opened the French windows, and went out on the veranda. He nearly broke into tears. Month after month in Mascalippa, he had dreamt of a view like this. Now he could enjoy it whenever he pleased! He stepped down onto the beach and started walking along the water's edge.

The water was cold. There was no question of going for a swim yet. But his body and mind rejoiced. At last he decided to go back to the house and get ready for the day.

He got to work a little late. Just before leaving home, he'd taken general stock of the situation and written down what he still needed. Then he'd stopped at a carpenter's shop, recommended to him by Fazio of course, and made an appointment with him to come and cover an entire wall with shelves for the books that would soon be arriving from Mascalippa and those he intended to buy.

He'd been sitting at his desk for about an hour when Fazio came in to tell him that the Honourable Torrisi wanted to talk to him.

'Then put him on,' said Montalbano, picking up the receiver.

'No, Chief, he's here. He says he arrived in town from Rome last night.'

So the honourable had actually gone out of his way to annoy the inspector.

There was no escape, other than through a ground-floor window. He was tempted for a moment, then decided it would be undignified. And why all this aversion when he didn't even know the man and had no idea what he wanted from him?

'All right, then, show him in.'

The honourable was short and fat and looked about fifty, with a big face showing a smile but unable to camouflage the cold, snakelike look in his eyes. Montalbano stood up and came forward.

'*Carissimo! Carissimo!*' said the politician, grabbing the inspector's hand and shaking his arm up and down with such force that Montalbano feared his shoulder might be dislocated for the rest of his natural life.

He sat the man down in one of the two armchairs in a sort of sitting area in one corner of the office.

'Can I get you anything?' he asked.

'No, please don't bother, nothing at all! I can't drink for another two months: I've made a little vow to the Blessed Virgin. I just thought I would drop in to meet you and exchange a few words. You see, I've gathered such a good harvest of votes here in Vigàta that I feel that it's my moral duty to—'

'The Honourable Vannicò also did well in this area, didn't he?' Montalbano wickedly interrupted him, donning the expression of a born, incurable dolt.

The mood changed at once, as if a sheet of ice had formed on the ceiling.

'Well, yes, of course, Vannicò did . . .' Torrisi admitted in a soft voice.

Then, suddenly worried:

'Have you already met him?'

'No, I haven't yet had the pleasure.'

Torrisi seemed relieved.

'You know, Inspector, I take a keen interest in the problems of today's young people. And I have to admit, to my great regret and displeasure, that things are not going so well in that regard. Do you know what's missing?'

'No. What's missing?' the inspector asked with the face of someone expecting a life-transforming revelation.

'This,' said the politician, touching the lobe of his right ear with the tip of his index finger.

Montalbano hesitated. What did he mean? That we had to become gay to understand the malaise of our young people?

'I'm sorry, sir, I'm afraid I haven't understood what's missing.'

'Ears, my friend. We don't listen to the young, we don't lend them our ears. For example, we tend to judge them hastily and irrevocably for what might be just a mistake on their part . . .'

And then there was light! In a flash, Montalbano realized the purpose of the honourable's visit and what the man was getting at.

'And that's wrong,' he said, assuming a severe expression while laughing his head off inside.

'It is very wrong!' the politician laid it on, swallowing the bait. 'I can see that you, Inspector, are a man who understands! I think the Lord himself must have sent you here!'

The Honourable Torrisi kept on talking for a good half-hour, always keeping to generalities. But the gist of his argument was: when you testify before the court, try not to be too severe. Try to understand a young man's distress, even when he is wealthy, even when he comes from a powerful family, even when he punches an old man in the face. The Cuffaros had sent their plenipotentiary ambassador. Apparently the other honourable parliamentary deputy, Vannicò, was the plenipotentiary of the Sinagra family. The commissioner had been right.

*

The bad mood that had descended on him with the politician's visit lifted at four o'clock that afternoon, when Mery arrived. Unfortunately, she had to go back to Catania on Sunday evening, but that was more than enough time for her to set some order in the house and in the inspector's mind (and body).

4

Naturally, the bad mood returned on Monday morning, the moment he woke up, when he remembered he had to appear in court. He'd once known a person who was a supervisor of antiquities. The only problem was that this person suffered from a mysterious illness that made him scared to death of museums. He couldn't be left alone in one. Seeing a Greek or Roman statue nearly made him faint. Montalbano's case wasn't quite so extreme, but having anything to do with judges or lawyers made him upset. Even a walk along the beach failed to calm him down.

Montalbano drove there in his own car, for two reasons. The first was that he was appearing in court not as a police inspector but as a private citizen, and so if he'd had someone drive him there in a squad car, it would have been improper. The second was that the officer usually assigned driving duties for him was Gallo, a likeable man except for the fact that, no matter what kind of street or road he was on, even the most godforsaken unmade road in the country, he always drove as if he was on the track at Indianapolis.

The inspector hadn't yet had a chance to go to the Montelusa courthouse. It was a large, four-storey building, massive and graceless, which one entered through a vast portal. Inside, there was a sort of short corridor with an extremely high ceiling, mobbed with people shouting. It felt like a marketplace. To the left was the guard post of the carabinieri, and to the right was a rather small room, over the entrance to which was a sign saying 'Information'. And there, shouting confused questions and receiving equally confused answers from a single clerk, were five men ahead of him. The inspector waited his turn and then showed his summons to the clerk. The latter grabbed it, looked at it, checked a register, looked at Montalbano's card again, checked the register again, then looked up at the inspector and finally said:

'You should probably go to the third floor, courtroom five.'

Probably? Maybe they held mobile hearings in that courthouse, perhaps on roller skates? Or maybe the clerk simply believed that nothing was certain in life?

And that was when, coming out of the Information office, he saw her for the first time: a girl of about sixteen, an adolescent wearing a cheap-looking light cotton dress and carrying a large worn-out handbag. She was leaning against the wall beside the carabinieri's guard post. It was impossible not to look at her, with her huge, dark, wide-open eyes staring into space, and the strange contrast between her still little-girlish face and the already full, aggressive forms of her figure. She was so utterly still that she looked like a statue.

The entrance hall led to a sort of vast well-tended courtyard-garden. But how did one get to the third floor? Seeing a group of people to the left, Montalbano went towards them. There was a lift there. Beside it, however, handwritten with a marker pen, was a sheet of paper stuck to the wall which said: *The lift is reserved for judges and lawyers.* Montalbano wondered how many of the forty-odd people waiting there for the lift were judges or lawyers. And how many were slyboots pretending they were judges and lawyers. He decided to enrol in the second group. But there was still no sign of the lift, and people were starting to grumble. Then a man stuck his head out of a second-floor window and said:

'The lift's broken.'

Cursing, groaning, and muttering obscenities, everyone headed for a tall arch through which one saw the beginning of a broad, comfortable staircase. The inspector made it to the third floor. The door to courtroom five was open, but there was nobody inside. Montalbano looked at his watch: it was already ten past nine. Was it possible they were all late? It suddenly occurred to him that maybe the information clerk had been right to be doubtful, and perhaps the hearing was being held in another courtroom. The corridor was mobbed, with doors opening and closing continually, releasing gusts of lawyerly eloquence. After some fifteen minutes of confusion, he decided to ask a person pushing a cart overloaded with files and binders.

'Excuse me, could you tell me . . .'

And he handed him the little card. The man looked at it, gave it back, and resumed pushing his cart.

'Didn't you see the announcement?' he asked.

'No. Where?' the inspector asked, following behind him, taking short steps.

'On the bulletin board in the glass case. The hearing was postponed.'

'Till when?'

'Till tomorrow. Maybe.'

Apparently ironclad certainties were non-existent in that courthouse. Montalbano went back downstairs and queued up again in front of the information desk.

'Didn't you know that the hearing in courtroom five was postponed?'

'Oh really? Till when?' the information clerk queried.

Then Montalbano saw her again. About an hour had gone by, and the girl was still in exactly the same position as before. She must have been waiting for someone, of course, but her immobility was almost unnatural. It made one uneasy. For a moment Montalbano was tempted to approach her and ask her if she needed any help. But he changed his mind and left the courthouse.

*

The moment he got to the station he was told that the people from Mascalippa had called to say that the van with the boxes of his possessions would be arriving in Marinella at five-thirty that afternoon. Naturally, the inspector made sure he was at home by quarter past five, but the van was two hours late and didn't pull in until it was already getting dark. The driver, moreover, had hurt his arm and was therefore in no condition to help unload the boxes. Cursing like a Turk, Montalbano hoisted one box after another onto his shoulders, with the result that, when all was said and done, he felt like he had a dislocated shoulder and a double hernia. To top it all off, the driver demanded a ten-thousand-lire tip, it wasn't clear on what grounds, perhaps as a morale-booster for having been prevented from helping Montalbano unload.

Back inside, Montalbano opened only one box, the one with the television set. The house already had an aerial on the solarium roof, and cables leading indoors. He hooked it all up, turned on the set, and tuned in to Channel I. Nothing. Just snow and the sound of frying. He tried the other channels. The only difference was the density of the snowfall, and sometimes the frying sound became, variously, surf or blast-furnace. And so he climbed up onto the solarium roof and noticed that the antenna had moved, perhaps due to a gust of wind. With great effort, he managed to turn it a little. When he raced back down to check the television, the snowflakes had turned into ectoplasms, ghosts in a frying pan. Desperately zapping the remote control, he finally got the clearly defined face of a newscaster. He was speaking Arabic. Montalbano turned off the TV and went and sat on the veranda to try to calm down. He decided to eat something. Taking some bread from the freezer, he put it in the toaster, then ate a can of Favignana tuna dressed in olive oil and lemon.

He realized he absolutely had to find a woman to do the housekeeping, laundry, and cooking. Now that he had a house, he couldn't always do everything himself. When he lay down in bed, he discovered he had nothing to read. All his books were in two still unopened boxes, the two heaviest. He got up, opened one box and, naturally, did not find what he was looking for, a mystery novel by a Frenchman named Pierre Magnan, *The Blood of the House of Atreus*. He'd already read it, but he liked the way it was written. He opened the second box as well. The book was all the way at the bottom. Glancing at the cover, he put it down at the top of the last pile. He suddenly felt very sleepy.

*

He arrived at the courthouse slightly late, at ten past nine, because he'd had trouble finding a parking space. And there was the girl again, in the same light cotton dress, with the same purse, the same lost look in her big dark eyes – and in exactly the same spot where he'd seen her twice already, not one inch to the left or to the right. Just like alms-beggars, who choose their place of preference and stay there until they die or until someone gives them shelter. They're always there, come rain or shine, in summer as in winter. This girl, too, was asking for something. Not alms, of course, but what?

Today there was a sheet of paper on the lift door marked

in felt pen with the word: *Broken*. Montalbano climbed three flights of stairs and when he entered courtroom five, which was a rather small room, he found it packed with people. Nobody asked him who he was or what he was there for.

He sat down in the last row of benches, beside a man with red hair holding a notebook and ballpoint pen who every so often took notes.

'Has it been going on for long?' Montalbano asked him.

'The curtain was raised about ten minutes ago. He's performing the indictment.'

Strange rhetoric. The curtain! Performing! And yet, to judge by appearances, the man seemed rather down to earth and to the point.

'I'm sorry, but why did you say the curtain had been raised? We're hardly at the theatre.'

'We're not? But this is all theatre! Where are you from, the moon?'

'Montalbano's the name. I'm the new police inspector for Vigàta.'

'Pleasure. My name's Zito, I'm a journalist. Just listen to the indictment, then tell me whether it's all theatre or not.'

After the man in the robes had been talking for about ten minutes, Montalbano began to have his doubts.

'Are you sure that man is the public prosecutor?'

'What did I tell you?' the newsman Zito said triumphantly.

The statement of indictment had sounded just like a defence argument. It claimed that the assault by Giuseppe Cusumano had indeed occurred, but that one had to take into consideration the young man's particular emotional state at the time and the fact that the victim of the assault, Mr Gaspare Melluso, when getting out of his car, had called Cusumano a *cornuto*, a cuckold. He asked for a minimum sentence and a slew of allowances for extenuating circumstances. Then the beat officer was called to the stand.

What kind of a trial was this? What was its order of

procedure? The policeman said he'd hardly seen anything because he was busy talking to two stray dogs who'd seemed nice to him. He'd become aware of a problem when Melluso fell to the ground. He took down the licence-plate number of the car that later turned out to belong to Cusumano, and then drove Melluso to A&E. At the request of the defence counsel, who was none other than the Honourable Torrisi, the policeman admitted he'd clearly heard the word *cornuto* being uttered in the general vicinity, but in all good conscience could not say who had uttered it.

Then, to his extreme surprise, Montalbano heard his name called. After the customary ritual of generalities and pledges to tell the truth, he sat down and, before he could open his mouth, the Honourable Torrisi asked him a question.

'You, of course, did hear Melluso call Cusumano a *cornuto*, did you not?'

'No.'

'No? How can that be? The patrolman heard it, and he was much further away than you!'

'The patrolman may have heard it, but I did not.'

'Are you hard of hearing, Mr Montalbano? Did you suffer from otitis as a child?'

The inspector did not answer and was immediately dismissed. He was free to leave, but he wanted to hear Torrisi's harangue. And he was right, because he learned exactly what the youth's 'particular emotional state' was on that fateful day. As it turned out, some three years earlier, young Cusumano had married his beloved fiancée, Mariannina Lo Cascio. Unfortunately, when emerging from the church, right in the porch, he was handcuffed by two carabinieri for a conviction that had just been upheld. And on the very day of his scuffle with Melluso, Cusumano had just been released from prison and was literally flying into the arms of his bride to consummate the marriage, which, until that moment, had merely been 'formal'. Thus, upon hearing

himself called a *cornuto*, the young man, who still had not
plucked the flower that Mariannina Lo Cascio had dedicated to him alone, could not help but . . .

At this point Montalbano, who had been holding back
the urge to vomit, could not take any more, and so he bid
Zito the journalist a hasty goodbye and left. He was, after
all, quite certain that Cusumano was going to get off scot-
free and that it would already be a major achievement if old
Melluso wasn't sent to prison in his place.

Stepping into the corridor that led to the exit, the
inspector froze. The girl had moved two steps forward and
was talking to a skinny, thick-haired man of about forty
dressed higgledy-piggledy, with one of those thin little ties
that only lawyers wear. The man shook his head and headed
towards the garden. The girl returned to her usual place
and her usual immobility. Montalbano walked past her and
found himself outside. There was no point worrying about
it, racking his brains trying to work out the whys and
wherefores. It was highly unlikely he would ever see the girl
again, so he might as well forget about her.

When he went to start his car to drive back to Vigàta,
it refused to cooperate. He tried again and again, but in
vain. What to do? Call the station and have someone come
and pick him up? No, his court appearance in Montelusa
was a private matter. He remembered seeing a garage on the
same street as the courthouse. He went there on foot and
explained the situation to the shop foreman. The man was
quite polite and sent a mechanic back with Montalbano to
the car. Checking the engine, the mechanic discovered a
failure in the electrical system. The inspector could come to
the garage to pick it up later that afternoon, but not before.
Montalbano turned the keys over to him.

'Is there a bus that goes to Vigàta?'

'Yes. It leaves from the square in front of the station.'

He headed off on foot. It was a long walk, luckily all
downhill, then the whole length of the *corso*. At the station

square he read the board with the arrival and departure times and learned that a bus had just left. The next would leave in an hour.

He strolled down a tree-lined avenue from which one could see the entire Valley of the Temples, and, in the background, the line of the sea. Quite another thing from the quasi-Swiss landscapes around Mascalippa. When he got back to the station square, he saw that the next bus had arrived. On its side was a sign that said: *Montelusa–Vigàta*.

Its doors were open. He climbed aboard through the front door and on the first step, from which he could see the interior, he froze. What stopped him in his tracks was not the fact that the bus was empty but for one passenger, but that the one passenger was none other than the girl from the courthouse.

She was sitting in one of the two seats behind the driver, the one next to the window, but she wasn't looking outside; she was staring into the space in front of her and didn't even seem to notice the presence of another passenger frozen on the step. In fact Montalbano was wondering whether it might not be a good idea to do something provocative to shake the girl out of her absence and into the present, such as, for example, to go and sit down right beside her even though there were forty-nine other seats available in the bus.

But what reason would he have for acting that way? Was she doing anything wrong? No. And so?

He went and sat down in one of the two places in the row behind the driver. That way he could still see the girl's face, though only in profile. Still not moving, she was holding her bag on her knees with both hands.

The driver sat down behind the wheel and started the bus. At that moment a voice cried out: 'Stop! Stop!'

Forty or more Japanese tourists, all wearing glasses, all smiling, all with cameras slung over their shoulders and preceded by an out-of-breath woman who was clearly their guide, boarded the bus and occupied the empty seats.

No Japanese tourists, however, sat down beside either Montalbano or the girl. The bus drove off.

At the first stop, nobody got off and nobody got on. The Japanese were vying for the windows for photo opportunities in a no-holds-barred struggle fought with weapons of lethal courtesy. At the second stop, the driver had to get up from his seat to help a couple of hundred-year-olds get on.

'Come and sit over here,' the driver ordered Montalbano, pointing to the place next to the girl.

The inspector obeyed and the elderly couple could thus sit side by side and commiserate with each other.

The girl hadn't budged, however, and so Montalbano, to take his place, couldn't help but press up against her leg. But she didn't react to the contact, and left her leg where it was. Embarrassed, Montalbano oriented his body towards the aisle.

Out of the corner of his eye he saw her firm breasts under her cotton dress rise and fall with the rhythm of her breathing, and he attuned his hearing to that movement. It was a trick that Inspector Sanfilippo had taught him: increasing your auditory perception by linking your hearing with your sight. And in fact, little by little, he began to hear the girl's breathing more and more distinctly above the buzz of the Japanese voices and the sound of the engine. It was slow and regular, as when someone is asleep. But how to reconcile that breathing with the desperate plea that he saw in her eyes? Her hands holding the bag firmly on her knees had long, tapered, elegant fingers, but the skin was rough and chafed from heavy farm work; the fingernails were broken in spots but still bore traces of red polish. It was clear the girl had been neglecting herself for a while. Another thing the inspector noticed contradicting her apparent composure was that her right thumb started trembling every so often, without her realizing.

At the stop for the temples, the Japanese cohort got off noisily. The inspector could have changed places for greater comfort, but didn't move. Shortly after they passed the road sign indicating they'd entered the Vigàta municipal area, the girl stood up.

She remained slightly hunched to avoid hitting her head against the luggage rack. Apparently she was about to get off, but just stood there, staring at Montalbano and not asking if she could pass, not saying a word. The inspector had the feeling the girl was looking at him not as a man but as an object, an undefined obstacle. What could be going through her head?

'Would you like to get past?'

The girl didn't answer. And so Montalbano got up and went into the aisle to let her out. She got as far as the stairs and then stopped, one hand holding her bag, the other gripping the metal bar in front of the two seats in which the elderly couple were sitting.

After a short distance, the driver stopped the bus, opened the automatic door, and the girl got off.

'Just a minute!' Montalbano said in a voice so shrill that the driver turned around in surprise to look at him. 'Don't shut the door, I have to get off.'

He'd made the decision out of the blue. What the hell was he doing? Why was he so fixated on that girl? He looked around. He was on the older outskirts of town, where there were no new buildings or high-rises but only houses in ruins or still standing only with the support of the beams, houses inhabited by people who scraped by not by working at the harbour or doing business in town but by still farming the meagre land of the outlying municipality.

The girl was a short distance ahead of him. She walked slowly, almost as if she didn't want to go home. She hung her head, as though carefully studying the ground on which she trod. But did she really see the ground she was looking at? What did her eyes actually see?

The girl turned right, onto a narrow little street that at night would have made an ideal setting for a horror film.

On one side, a series of warehouses without doors and with caved-in roofs; on the other, a string of uninhabited, dying little houses. There was literally nobody about, not even a dog.

'What on earth am I doing here?' the inspector asked himself, as if waking up from a bad dream.

He was about to turn back, except that at that moment the girl staggered, seeming to lose her balance, then dropped her bag and was forced to lean against the wall of a house to keep from falling. At first Montalbano didn't know what to do, but then it seemed clear to him that the girl must have had a dizzy spell or something similar, since she hadn't stumbled or tripped over a rock. At any rate she needed help, and he was more than justified now in intervening. He went up to her.

'Are you all right?' he asked.

The ear-splitting scream the girl let out at the sound of his voice was so sudden and shrill that Montalbano, taken by surprise, leapt backwards in fear. The girl hadn't heard him approach and his words had suddenly brought her back to reality. She was now looking at Montalbano with bulging eyes and seeing him for what he was, a man, a stranger who had just said something to her.

'Are you all right?' he repeated.

The girl didn't answer. She began to fall forward, as if in slow motion, arm extended and hand open to pick her bag up off the ground.

But Montalbano was quicker than her and grabbed the bag first. Since it was an automatic gesture of courtesy on his part, he was stunned by the girl's reaction, as she suddenly grabbed the bag with both hands and tried to wrest it away from him.

He instinctively tightened his grip on it. When their eyes met, he read in hers an utterly wild desperation. And for a moment they engaged in an absurd, ridiculous tug of war. Then, as might be expected, a lateral seam broke open

and everything inside fell to the ground. A rather heavy
object struck the big toe on the inspector's left foot,
and he looked down and saw a large revolver. But the girl,
who meanwhile had become very quick in her movements,
grabbed it first. Montalbano seized her wrist and twisted it,
but the girl held fast to the gun. Then he pushed her with
all his body weight against the wall and pinned her there so
that her hand holding the gun and his hand holding her
wrist were both squeezed between the wall and the girl's
back. The girl reacted with her free hand, scratching Montalbano's face. He seized the wrist of that hand as well,
holding it high and pinning it against the wall. They were
both panting like two lovers making love. With his lower
body between the girl's spread legs, Montalbano pressed
hard against her stomach and breasts, and the slightly sour
smell of her sweat was not at all unpleasant, even in that
situation, which seemed without solution.

All at once the inspector heard a sound of screeching
brakes behind him, then a voice that shouted:

'Stop, you pig! Police! Let the girl go!'

And he realized that the policeman thought he was
witnessing a rape. An understandable mistake. Turning his
head around, he recognized one of his men, Galluzzo, who
also recognized him and froze.

'Mo . . . Mo . . . Mo . . .' he stammered.

He was trying to say, 'Montalbano,' but what came out
sounded like the intro to an old doo-wop song.

'Help me, she's got a gun!' Montalbano gasped.

Galluzzo was a man of quick decisions. Without a word,
he dealt the girl a swift punch to the chin. Her eyes closed
at once and she slid down the wall to the ground, unconscious. Montalbano delicately untangled himself from her,
but had trouble taking hold of the revolver. The girl's fingers
refused to release the weapon.

5

Her identity card, which had fallen to the ground with the other contents of her handbag, declared beyond the shadow of a doubt that Rosanna Monaco, daughter of Gerlando Monaco and Concetta Marullo, living at Via Fornace 37 in Vigàta, had become a legal adult just a few months earlier. The card was brand-new, which meant that the girl had had it made upon coming of age. In the eyes of the law she was therefore fully answerable for her actions. She was sitting in a chair in front of the inspector's desk, head down and staring at the floor, arms dangling. For two hours Montalbano had been unable to get a single word out of her.

'Can you tell me who the revolver belongs to?'

'Were you carrying it for self-defence?'

'Who did you want to defend yourself against?'

'Did you plan to shoot someone with it?'

'Who did you want to shoot?'

'What were you doing in the entrance hall of the court-house?'

'Were you waiting for someone?'

Nothing. After the strength, agility, and quickness she'd suddenly mustered during that silent scuffle that at moments had seemed to Montalbano like an intense sexual encounter, she had now returned to that sort of tormented impassivity that had aroused the inspector's curiosity from the moment he'd first seen her. Montalbano was, of course, well aware that 'tormented impassivity' was a stupid oxymoron, but he couldn't think of any other way to define what Rosanna's attitude evoked for him.

He made up his mind. They could not go on this way.

'Lock her up,' he ordered Galluzzo, who was at the type-writer to transcribe the interrogation but had so far written only the date. 'And get her something to eat and drink.'

Then, raising his voice: 'I'm going to go and talk to her parents.'

He had purposely stated his intentions out loud, but the girl seemed not even to have heard him. Before leaving the station, he had Fazio explain to him where Via Fornace was, gave him some things to do, went out, got in his car, and drove off.

The street was the second on the right after the street in which they'd struggled over the gun. It was unpaved and looked like a country road already. Number 37 was a two-storey house with a small storage building no larger than a kennel beside it, but it was less run-down than the others. The front door was open, and as Montalbano approached he heard some incoherent yelling. Standing in the doorway, he felt as if he was looking at a cross between a nursery and a primary school. Inside were half a dozen little children, ranging in age from one to seven years.

A woman of indeterminate age holding a new-born in one arm was working over a wood-fired stove. There seemed to be no telephone, or refrigerator, or television. But it wasn't a case of poverty, since the children were all well dressed and there were cheeses and salamis hanging from the ceiling. It had to be more a case of backwardness, of a lifestyle entrenched in ignorance.

'Whattya want?' the woman asked.

'Montalbano's the name, I'm a police inspector. Is your husband here?'

'Whattya want from my husband?'

'Is he here or not?'

'Nossir, he's not. He's in the fields working with the bigger kids, out in the country.'

'When will he return?'

'This evening when it gets dark.'

'Are you Mrs Concetta Marullo?'

'Yessir.'

'Do you have a daughter named Rosanna?'

'Unfortunately.'

'Listen, we've taken your daughter into custody because . . .'

'I don' care.'

'I don't understand.'

'Then I'll repeat it: I don' care. You can arrest 'er, put 'er in gaol, you can hang 'er for all I care . . .'

'Does she live here with you?'

'Nossir, I threw 'er out three years ago.'

'Why?'

' 'Cause she's a slut.'

'Why do you say that? What did she do?'

'She did wha' she did.'

'And where does she live now?'

'Here nex' door. My 'usband, who's a good-hearted man, let 'er 'ave the pigsty to sleep in. An' she likes it there, 'cause a pigsty's where she belongs.'

'Could I see it?'

'The pigsty? Sure. The door's unlocked.'

'Listen, do you know if your daughter harbours any ill-will towards anyone?'

'How the hell should I know? I tol' you I ain't talked to her for years. I don't know nothin'.'

'One last question. Does your husband own a gun?'

'Wha' kinda gun?'

'A revolver.'

'You kiddin'? My 'usband only got a knife for cuttin' 'is bread.'

'As soon as he gets home, tell your husband to come to the central police station.'

' 'E comes home late and tired, you know.'

'I'm sorry, but I'll be waiting for him.'

He left feeling a headache coming on. The whole conversation had taken place at high volume in order to be heard above the racket of the nursery.

Rosanna had cleaned up the pigsty rather nicely and

someone had given the walls a new coat of whitewash. There was barely enough room to fit a camp bed, a small table, and two chairs. Looking at it from another perspective, it could have been the cell of a Franciscan monk. The kitchen consisted of a single hollow-brick stove. To wash, Rosanna must have used the small basin on the table, getting the water from a well nearby, which Montalbano had seen on arrival. A cord stretching across the room served as a wardrobe, with two dresses and an inside-out overcoat hanging from it. Some underwear lay on a chair. It all spoke of extreme poverty but was very clean. Not a single photo anywhere, no newspapers or magazines. He looked around in vain for a letter or piece of paper, something written.

He went back to the station more confused than ever.

'I've done everything you asked,' Fazio said as soon as he saw the inspector come in, then followed him into his office.

'So?'

'So,' said Fazio, pulling from his pocket a piece of paper he glanced at every so often, 'the father, Gerlando Monaco, son of Giacomo Gerlando and Elvira La Stella, was born in Vigàta on—'

'Excuse me, Fazio,' Montalbano interrupted him, 'but why are you telling me these things?'

'What things?' Fazio asked, looking perplexed.

'The father, the mother, and all the rest . . . What the hell do I care about them? I asked you to see if Rosanna's father had a criminal record and to find out what people said about him around town. Nothing more.'

'He's got a clean record,' Fazio replied stiffly, putting the piece of paper back in his pocket. 'And in town, hardly anybody knows him, but the few who do, say he's a good man.'

'Does he have any grown children?'

Fazio was about to pull the piece of paper out again, but the inspector shot him a dirty look.

'Two sons. Giacomo, aged twenty-one, and Filippo, aged

twenty. They work with him in the country. And everybody says they're good boys.'

'So, the only one who's strayed appears to be Rosanna.'

The inspector told him that the mother considered her a 'slut', and that they made her sleep in a former pigsty.

'At any rate, tonight the girl's father is coming here, and we're going to try to find out a little more. Do you know if she's eaten anything?'

'Galluzzo bought her a panino, but she wouldn't touch it. And she hasn't drunk a drop of water either.'

'Well, sooner or later she'll collapse,' said Montalbano, 'and then she'll decide to eat and drink. And talk.'

'About that revolver . . .' Fazio began.

'Did you discover anything?'

'There wasn't anything to discover, sir. It's a Cobra, a gun that doesn't mess around. American. And that's not all: the serial number was filed off.'

'In short, you're trying to tell me it's a criminal's weapon.'

'That's right.'

'So somebody must have given it to Rosanna to shoot somebody with.'

'That's right.'

'And who would this somebody be?'

'Dunno.'

'And who was she supposed to shoot?'

'Dunno.'

'Fazio, you should try to find out everything there is to know about this girl.'

'It won't be easy, sir. From what I could gather, her family is rather isolated from everyone else in town. They haven't got any friends, just acquaintances.'

'Just try anyway. Oh, and one more thing. Send one of our men to tell the girl's mother to send a few changes of underwear for her daughter. She can give it to her husband to bring when he comes.'

He went and looked through the spy-hole of the holding cell. Rosanna was standing, head propped against the wall. The panino remained untouched, the glass of water too. It was a problem. He called Galluzzo.

'Listen, has she asked to use the toilet?'

'No, sir. I asked her myself, but she didn't even bother to answer. If you ask me, Inspector . . .'

'If I ask you?'

'If you ask me, she's having a tantrum.'

'A tantrum?'

'Yeah. She's got a grown woman's body, and her ID card says she's an adult, but she must have the brain of a child.'

'Are you saying she's retarded?'

'No, Chief. She is a child. She's angry because you prevented her from doing what she wanted to do.'

A totally insane idea flashed through Montalbano's mind.

'Let me into the cell. Then open the toilet door and leave it open.'

He entered the cell. She was still standing with her head against the wall. He went up beside her and yelled with all the breath in his lungs, like one of those Marine sergeants in American movies:

'Go to the toilet! Now!'

Rosanna gave a start and turned around in terror. The inspector cuffed her on the back of the head. The girl brought a hand to the spot on the nape of her neck where she'd been struck, and her eyes filled with tears. She shielded her face with her left forearm, as if she expected to be struck again. Galluzzo was right. She was a child. But the inspector didn't let this affect him.

'Go to the toilet!'

Meanwhile half the staff at the station had come running to see what was happening.

'What's going on? Who is it?'

'Out! Out of here, all of you!' Montalbano yelled, feeling

the veins on his neck ready to explode. 'And you, get moving!'

Like a sleepwalker, the girl began to move and went out the door.

'Over here,' Galluzzo said promptly.

Rosanna went into the toilet and closed the door. The inspector gave Galluzzo a questioning look. He'd never used that toilet before.

'There's no danger,' said Galluzzo. 'You can't lock it from the inside.'

A few minutes later they heard the flush, then the door opened and Rosanna walked past them as if they weren't there and returned to the holding cell, where she turned and faced the wall again. Face to the wall, as if being punished. Rosanna was punishing herself.

'Well, at least it worked,' Galluzzo commented.

'Gallù, I can't very well go through that whole rigmarole every time she has to use the loo!' Montalbano said in exasperation.

*

He'd spread out the contents of Rosanna's handbag across the top of his desk and studied them. A small fake-leather purse containing a ten-thousand-lira note, folded up several times over, plus three thousand-lira notes, five five-hundred lira coins, four of one hundred lire, and one of fifty.

But there was something else inside the purse that had nothing to do with money: a small piece of pink elastic. Maybe a sample to show to the dressmaker.

Rosanna had also kept her round-trip, Vigàta–Montelusa bus tickets. There were six of them, which meant that the girl had gone at least six times to stake out her post inside the courthouse entrance.

ID card; a small empty bottle of fingernail polish, traces of coagulated liquid inside the cap.

And something strange: an envelope with nothing

written on it but containing the skeleton of a rose whose petals had all fallen off. Though, when he really thought about it, there wasn't anything so strange about that rose. It was inside an envelope but it could easily have been between the pages of a book, where most people put that sort of thing. And so Rosanna, having no books, had put that rose – which surely had some sentimental value for her – in an envelope, which she always carried around with her. In conclusion, there was nothing that might seem out of place in a girl's handbag.

But then for a second, and only a second, a strange detail flashed in Montalbano's brain, making all those objects seem less obvious. But he was unable to bring into focus what it was.

This made him uneasy and nervous.

He was gathering Rosanna's things to put them away in a drawer when the switchboard operator appeared.

'Sorry to disturb you, sir, but there's a gentleman who says he's your father.'

'All right, put him on.'

'He's here in person.'

His father?! He suddenly remembered, with a sense of shame, that he'd never written to him to tell him about his promotion and transfer.

'Show him in.'

They embraced in the middle of the room with a touch of emotion and a touch of embarrassment. His father was, as usual, elegantly dressed and carried himself with equal elegance. Utterly unlike his own usually shabby self. They hadn't seen each other for over four months.

'How did you find me?'

'I read an article in the newspaper that sort of welcomed you to Vigàta. And so, since I was passing by anyway, I decided to come and say hello. But I'll be on my way in just a minute.'

'Can I get you anything?'

'No, that's all right, thanks.'

'How are you, Papà?'

'I can't complain. I'll be retiring in just a few years.'

'What do you think you'll do, afterwards?'

'I'm going to enter into a partnership with a friend who has a small wine-production company.'

'And what brings you this way?'

'I went this morning to see your mother, to tidy up the grave a little. Today's the anniversary, did you forget?'

Yes, he had forgotten. All he could remember about his mother was a colour, like spikes of ripe wheat.

'What do you remember about your mother?'

Montalbano thought for a moment.

'The colour of her hair.'

'It was a beautiful colour. Anything else?'

'Nothing.'

'Just as well.'

Montalbano hesitated.

'What do you mean?'

This time it was his father who hesitated.

'There were . . . misunderstandings, arguments, quarrels . . . between your mother and me . . . All my fault. I didn't deserve a wife like her.'

Montalbano felt awkward. He and his father had never confided much in each other.

'I was rather fond of the ladies.'

The inspector didn't know what to say.

'Are you busy with anything important these days?' his father asked, clearly trying to change the subject.

Montalbano felt grateful for it.

'No, nothing important. Though I do have a rather curious case on my hands . . .'

And he told him about Rosanna, stressing mostly the girl's indecipherable behaviour.

'Could I see her?'

Montalbano really hadn't expected such a request.

'Um, Papà, I don't know if it's allowed . . . Well, all right, come.'

He led the way and was the first to look through the spy-hole. The girl was standing with her back to the wall, staring straight at the door. The inspector stepped aside for his father, who looked through the hole for a long time, then turned around and said:

'It's really getting rather late for me. Would you walk me to my car?'

Montalbano went out with him. They embraced vigorously, no longer embarrassed.

'Come back soon, Papà.'

'Yes. And, Salvo, one thing: be careful.'

'About what?'

'About that girl. I wouldn't trust her.'

As he watched him leave, Montalbano felt a treacherous wave of melancholy come over him.

✳

It was already evening when Gerlando Monaco, the girl's father, appeared at the station carrying a plastic bag with a change of underwear for Rosanna. He too was of indeterminate age, hunched as he was from work and burnt red, cooked like a brick from the kiln. Contrary to his wife, however, he seemed nervous and troubled.

'Why'd you arrest her, eh?' was his first question.

'She had a revolver.'

Gerlando Monaco turned pale, staggered, and fell silent, hand groping for a chair, on which he plopped down heavily.

'*Madonna biniditta!* That girl's gonna bring my whole house down! A revolver! An' who gave it to her?'

'That's what we're trying to find out. You have any ideas?'

'Me?? Ideas?!'

He seemed quite sincere in his bewilderment.

'Listen, could you explain to me why you make your daughter sleep in a pigsty?'

Gerlando Monaco became defensive, his expression a cross between humiliation and offence, and stared at the floor. 'These is family matters and none o' your business,' he muttered.

'Look at me,' the inspector said sternly. 'If you don't tell me immediately what I want to know, tonight you're going to be keeping your daughter company.'

'OK. My wife don't want 'er about the house no more.'

'Why not?'

''Cause she got herself pregnant.'

'At fifteen? Who was it?'

'I dunno. An' my wife don' know neither. My wife beat 'er up pretty bad, but the girl din't wanna say who done it.'

'And the two of you didn't have any idea?'

'Mr Inspector, I wake up inna mornin' when iss still dark and I come home when iss dark again, an' my wife's always after the little kids. The girl, Rosanna, started cleanin' people's houses when she was ten . . .'

'So she's never gone to school?'

'Never. She don' know how to read or write.'

'What's the name of the family your daughter works for?'

'I don' know no names! She's changed families a hundred times! An' three years ago, when she got pregnant, the family she worked for was a couple of old folks.'

'And how does Rosanna get by now?'

'She still cleans people's houses when she can. Specially in summer when the foreigners come.'

'Who takes care of Rosanna's child?'

Gerlando Monaco gave him as astonished look.

'What child?'

'Didn't you just tell me Rosanna got pregnant?'

'Oh. My wife took 'er to a midwife woman. But then she had . . . a whatchacallit, when you lose a lot o' blood.'

'Haemorrhage.'

'Right. It was like she was dying. An' maybe it was better if she did.'

'Why did you make her abort?'

'Mr Inspector, try to think. Isn't it enough to have a whore for a daughter without having a bastard for a grand-child?'

When Gerlando Monaco left the room, Montalbano was unable to stand up. He had a sort of dull pain in the pit of his stomach, as if a hand were twisting his guts. A girl, barely ten years old, already a servant, illiterate, prob-ably raped at fifteen, made pregnant, beaten, subjected to a clumsy, illegal abortion, nearly killed by the butchery, now working again as a servant and forced to live in a former pigsty. Her holding cell must seem to her like a four-star hotel room. Now came the question: was it proper for a police inspector to want to free the girl, give her back her gun and tell her to shoot whoever she felt like shooting?

6

He couldn't very well go the whole day without eating just because the problem of Rosanna was gnawing at him. At the Trattoria San Calogero, he wolfed down fifteen different seafood antipasti for starters, but they were so light and delicate that they seemed to enter his mouth without being noticed. How could he resist, especially considering he hadn't eaten anything at midday? He suddenly had a bril-liant idea, and signalled to Calogero to approach.

'Listen, Calù. Now I want you to bring me a really fine sea bass, but in the meantime I want you to prepare three mullets *alla livornese*. With a lot of sauce, nice and fragrant. I mean it. Then have them delivered to the police station half an hour after I leave here. And also send along some bread and a bottle of mineral water. And knife, fork, glass, and dish, all plastic.'

'No sir, I could never do that.'

'Why not?'

'Because mullets *alla livornese* on a plastic dish would lose all their flavour.'

*

When he got back to the semi-deserted station, he went and had a look at Rosanna through the spy-hole. She was sitting on the straw mattress, hands on her knees. Her eyes had lost their stare, however, and she looked slightly more relaxed. The panino remained untouched. The water in the glass had gone down barely perceptibly. Maybe she'd wet her lips, which must have been not only dry but burning.

When the dish of mullets arrived, the inspector had the delivery boy set it down on his desk. Then he got the keys to the holding cell from the guard, took a chair, opened the door, put the chair right in front of the girl, and left, leaving the door open. The girl hadn't moved.

He returned with the dish of mullets and put it on the chair. Then he went out and came back with the plastic bag, which he tossed onto the straw bed.

'Your father brought you some clean underwear.'

He went out again and returned with another chair, which he set down next to the first one. There was a faint aroma of mullets *alla livornese* in the holding cell. He left and came back minutes later with the water, bread, and cutlery. The aroma had grown much more intense, a real provocation. Montalbano sat down in the chair and started staring at the girl. Then he began to clean the fish, putting the heads and bones in the plate that had served to cover the food.

'Eat,' he said when he'd finished.

The girl didn't move. And so the inspector took a small

piece of mullet on the fork and delicately rested it on Rosanna's closed lips.

'Shall I feed you?'

The way we do with very small children, perhaps accompanying the gesture with a little song.

'Now Rosanna's going to be a good girl and eat all this wonderful fish.'

How the fuck did he come up with that line? Luckily none of his men were anywhere nearby, or they would have thought he'd lost his mind.

The girl's lips opened just far enough to let the food in. She chewed and swallowed. And then Montalbano rested a little piece of bread soaked in sauce on her newly closed lips.

'And now Rosanna's going to eat some bread so she won't be hungry any more.'

Another ignoble line, which made him feel mortified, but he was no poet and, at any rate, it served its purpose. Rosanna chewed the bread and swallowed.

'Water,' she said.

The inspector filled a plastic cup and handed it to her.

'Think you can eat by yourself now?' he asked.

'Yes.'

Montalbano gently stroked her hair and went out, leaving the door still open.

He'd had the right idea. The girl was in touch with life again. And sooner or later, with the right amount of patience and delicacy on his part, she would make up her mind to tell him what she had wanted to do with the gun and, most importantly, who had given it to her. He let half an hour go by and then went back into the holding cell. Rosanna had eaten everything. The plate looked like it had been washed.

'Use the plastic bag,' he said.

The girl emptied the bag of her underwear, and put the dishes and cutlery in it. She kept the bottle, which was still half full, and a cup.

'Put the bread in too.'

'Can I go to the toilet?'

'Go.'

Montalbano took the bag, went out of the station, and threw it into a bin not far away. He killed a little more time smoking a cigarette in the quiet night. When he returned, he found Rosanna sitting calmly on the bed. She must have cleaned herself up quite thoroughly, since she smelled of soap. She had even washed her underwear and had spread it out to dry on the back of one of the chairs. But she had a strange, almost mischievous look in her eye.

'Rosanna is a lovely name,' said the inspector.

'Only the first part.'

'You only like the first part of your name? Rosa? Because it's a flower?'

He remembered the petalless flower in the envelope she kept in her purse.

'Nossir. Because it's a colour.'

'Do you like colours?'

'Yessir.'

'Why?'

'I don't know why. Colours make me remember things.'

He decided to change the subject. Perhaps the right moment had come.

'Do you want to tell me where you got the gun?'

The girl suddenly clammed up. Raising her knees to her chin, she wrapped her arms around her legs and squeezed. Her eyes started staring into space again. Montalbano realized he'd lost. Or lost only part of the battle, since he'd managed to make preliminary contact.

'Goodnight,' he said.

She didn't reply. He picked up the empty chair and took it away with him. He then locked the door, purposely making as much noise as possible.

Peering through the spy-hole, he had a surprise: big

round tears were falling from Rosanna's eyes. She wept silently, without sobbing, thus all the more desperately.

*

He sat out on the veranda for about an hour, smoking one cigarette after another, obsessing about Rosanna. He was about to go to bed when the phone rang. It was Mery.

'What do you say I come and see you on Friday?'

'Damn! I've been summoned to Palermo on Friday!'

The lie had come out by itself, without his brain being able to stop it. The fact was that he wanted to devote himself entirely, without any distractions, to Rosanna. Mery seemed disappointed. Montalbano consoled her by saying that maybe, in the coming week, he could get away to Catania for a day. He slept badly, tossing and turning all night.

The following morning he had just turned off the shower when a strange thing happened to him that had never happened before. He had the impression that someone, hidden somewhere, had taken his picture with a flash. And just as he was thinking of a specific statement the girl had made, 'Colours make me remember things,' a sort of fever came over him. Still naked, he went over to the telephone. It was seven o'clock in the morning.

'Montalbano here.'

'What is it, Inspector?'

Fazio sounded worried.

'Do you know anyone at the courthouse in Montelusa?'

'Yes.'

'I want you to be there the moment it opens. I want a list of all the judges and prosecutors. Right away. First and last names only. From both the criminal and civil courts. That'll be our first move.'

'What's the second?'

'If I'm wrong, you'll go back there tomorrow and get a list of everyone who works there, even the toilet cleaners.'

Then he started dawdling about the house. On purpose.

He wouldn't have been able to stand waiting at the station for Fazio to return with the list. Around half-past nine he decided to call in.

'Yes, Inspector, Fazio arrived just a few minutes ago.'

He dashed out of the door.

✳

He found the name: Emanuele Rosato, civil-court judge. Opening the drawer, he took out three things that had been in Rosanna's handbag and put them in his pocket. Then he called Fazio.

'Get the key to the holding cell and come with me.'

The girl was sitting as usual. She seemed calm and rested. Being incarcerated seemed to do her good. She first looked at the men without curiosity, but must have intuited at once from the inspector's face that there was some new development. And this made her tense up visibly. Montalbano pulled the little bottle of pink nail polish from his pocket and tossed it onto the bed. Then the little piece of pink elastic. Then the dried-up rose. Fazio didn't know what the hell was going on and looked first at the inspector and then at the girl.

'Colours make me remember things,' said Montalbano.

Rosanna was as tense as a bow.

'Wasn't the first part of your name enough to remind you that you were supposed to kill Judge Rosato?'

Taking both men by surprise, the girl sprang forth. Montalbano had guessed her intentions and shielded his face with his hands. But he still fell backwards, with Rosanna on top of him. And as Fazio grabbed her by the shoulders, trying to pull her off him, the inspector was rejoicing at all that unleashed fury the way the parched earth rejoices under a violent downpour, because he had been right on target.

✳

Since it would have been a waste of time to ask Rosanna why she wanted Judge Rosato dead, Montalbano decided at once to go to Montelusa and talk to him. Arriving at the courthouse, he got into the usual queue, and when he was in front of the information clerk, he asked:

'Excuse me, could you please tell me where I can find Judge Rosato?'

'You're asking me?' was his astonishing reply.

Montalbano immediately felt himself getting upset.

'Are you joking? I'm—'

'I'm not joking and I don't care who you are. Judge Rosato is with the civil court, if I'm not mistaken, right?'

'Right.'

'So go and ask for him at the civil courts.'

'They're not here?'

'They're not here.'

'So where are they?'

'At the old military barracks.'

Now, if he asked in turn where the old military barracks were, the man was liable to reply with the same mocking tone, and the whole thing would end in a row and maybe a few boxed ears.

Montalbano went out and saw a uniformed municipal policeman. The old military barracks were near the train station. He went there on foot. There were hundreds of people going in and out of the enormous main door. It looked like a station on the London Underground. Was it possible that half of these people were suing the other half? The inspector got the answer to his query when he read the shiny plaques on either side of the door: Civil Courts, State Corps of Forest Rangers, The Dante Alighieri Society, Municipal Tax Office, Provincial Draft Office, Giosuè Carducci Lyceum, Francesco Rondolino Charitable Association, Archaeological Heritage Administration, Protest Office, and the highly mysterious Bureau of Reimbursement. Who was reimbursing whom? And why? He went inside despairing

of ever being able to meet Judge Rosato. But then he immediately saw a sign that said that the civil courts were on the
second floor, which one reached by way of Stairway A. While
still on the stairs, he asked the first person he came across
where he could find the judge.

'Second door on the right.'

He shoved his way through the crowd and reached the
second door on the right, which was open. He realized he
was lost. The room must formerly have been the mess hall
of the barracks or some sort of exercise room. It was vast.
Every four or five yards there was a small table covered with
paper and surrounded by howling people, though it was
unclear whether they were lawyers, plaintiffs, or condemned
souls from some circle of Dante's hell. The judges were
invisible, hidden behind all the paper; at most one could see
the top half of their heads. There were dozens and dozens
of them, and just as many tables. What to do? Montalbano
walked with a military step – since he was in a barracks –
towards one of the tables closest to him and in a loud voice,
so that he could be heard above the yelling, which was worse
than at the fish market, he commanded:

'Stop! Police!'

It was his only hope. Everyone froze and looked at him,
turning into a sort of hyperrealist sculpture group that
could have been titled *At the Civil Court*.

'I want to know where Judge Rosato is!'

'I'm here,' said a voice practically between his legs.

He'd been lucky.

'What can I do for you?' the judge asked, invisible
behind the paper piled up on his table.

'I'm Inspector Montalbano of Vigàta police. I'd like to
speak to you.'

'Right now?'

'If possible.'

'The hearing is postponed until further notice,' the
judge's voice called out.

A chorus of curses, insults, obscenities, and prayers rang out.

'This has been going on for eight years!'

'This isn't justice!'

But the judge was not to be swayed. Lawyers and clients walked about, beside themselves with rage.

The judge, who had half stood up, sat back down and thus disappeared entirely from Montalbano's field of vision.

'Please go ahead,' he said.

'Listen, your honour, I don't feel like talking to a stack of file folders. Couldn't we go somewhere else?'

'Where?'

'I don't know, maybe to a nearby cafe.'

'They're all packed with lawyers. Wait. I have an idea.'

Montalbano saw the judge's hands grab files, folders, binders, and stacks of paper held together with strings and arrange it all on the table in such a way as to form a sort of barricade with a trench behind it.

'Find a chair and come back here with me.'

The inspector obeyed. Indeed they were completely hidden, so that nobody on the other side could see them. Their knees touched. Judge Rosato disappointed Montalbano. On his way there, he had imagined a scenario in which three years ago, Judge Rosato (tall, slender, elegant, a little grey at the temples, puffing on a long cigarette holder, a sort of photo-comic-book seducer) had taken advantage of Rosanna the maid, getting her pregnant, and the girl now wanted revenge. Yes, but why wait three years? The real Judge Rosato, not the one the inspector had fantasized, was over sixty, unkempt, short, completely bald, and wore glasses over an inch thick. Montalbano realized that to save time, the best approach was to use the technique of the ram – that is, to ram the point home from the start.

'We've arrested a girl who was planning to kill you.'

'Oh my God! Kill *me*?!'

The judge leapt out of his chair, provoking a small but

noisy landslide of binders at the western end of the trench. He was immediately drenched in sweat. Hand trembling, he took off his steamed-up glasses. He wanted to ask questions but was unable. His mouth was trembling too wildly. Justice Rosato was not the sort of hero that a trench called for.

'Do you have any male children?' asked the inspector.

This might be the solution.

'No. T . . . two g . . . girls. M . . . Milena lives in S . . . Sondrio, she's a lawyer. Giu . . . giuliana is a paediatrician in Turin.'

'How long have you been at the Civil Court of Montelusa?'

'Basically for ever.'

'Where do you live?'

'In Vigàta. I get around with my car.'

'Have you ever had a maid named Rosanna Monaco working for you?'

'Never,' the judge said at once.

'How can you say it so—'

'We've never had a maid. My wife hates them, for no particular reason.'

The judge had recovered a little and was now able to ask a question.

'Is this . . . Rosanna Monaco the girl who wanted to kill me?'

'Yes.'

'Did she tell you why, for Chrissake?'

'No.'

'But . . . does she even know me?'

'I don't think she's ever seen you.'

'Then somebody must have put her up to it!'

'I agree.'

'But who?'

Judge Rosato began to recite a litany, a sort of synopsis of his life.

'I have never quarrelled or argued with anyone. As a man

I prefer to get along with everyone. My wife is a saint except for a few little obsessions, my daughters love me, my sons-in-law respect me, and as a judge I have always dealt with minor civil cases, I have tried to be fair and use common sense. I have never sent anyone to gaol, and am now about to retire after a life of hard work . . . And now someone, for reasons unknown to me, wants me dead . . .'

The judge started weeping. Montalbano let the unhappy man cry.

✷

'Chief,' Fazio said after the inspector had told him of his talk with the judge, 'I've got some news. First of all, after you left, the girl calmed down. I guess she'd got it out of her system. And when I asked her what she had against Judge Rosato, she said the judge was a wicked man who had sent someone to gaol.'

'Rosato's never sent anyone to gaol.'

'I know, Chief, you just told me that. But someone made Rosanna believe he did.'

'The same person who gave her the revolver.'

Fazio screwed up his face.

'That's just it, Chief.'

'What do you mean?'

'While you were in Montelusa, we got a call from the commissioner's. The ballistics expert says he's absolutely certain that the weapon we sent him, Rosanna's revolver, can't shoot. It looks deadly, but it's basically scrap metal.'

'Rosanna didn't know that.'

'But in my opinion the person who gave her the gun did. Don't forget the serial number was filed off.'

'Let me get this straight, Fazio. I get a girl, I persuade her to kill someone who's got nothing to do with anything, somebody pulled right out of a hat, then I give her a gun that can't shoot?'

'Do you think the person who hired her for the murder was the same as the one who gave her the weapon?'

'Let's assume for a moment that it is. Why would I give her a useless firearm? Just to amuse myself behind Rosanna's back? No, it's too dangerous a game. To create a sensation? Much ado about nothing? And who would have benefited from it? One thing, however, is certain: that to understand anything about this we have to find out who the person behind the girl is. We absolutely must. She told you some things this morning; try to find out more. I won't show my face. You go and pay her a visit, win her trust, talk to her.'

'You know what Rosanna is, Inspector? She's a cat. One of those that lets you scratch her head, purrs and rubs against your legs, and then, suddenly, out of the blue, she scratches your hand.'

'I can only wish you luck. And we have to move fast. The clock is ticking. We can't keep the girl in custody any longer than the law allows. We either have to free her or inform the prosecutor.'

*

Around five o'clock that afternoon, Montalbano got a phone call he wasn't expecting.

'Inspector Montalbano? This is Judge Emanuele Rosato.'

'How are you, sir?'

'How do you expect? I'm a mess. At any rate, I wanted to let you know that I keep a notebook in which I note all the legal actions I handle, and their outcomes. I went back and looked at them, which took me a pretty long time. But I think I've found something. The girl's surname is Monaco, correct?'

'Yes.'

'Is her father's name Gerlando?'

'Yes.'

The judge heaved a long sigh.

'I don't fucking get it,' he muttered.

Realizing he'd used an obscenity, he excused himself, then made up his mind to say what he'd discovered.

'A certain Filippo Tamburello who owned a piece of land bordering that of Gerlando Monaco moved the property line forward when repairing a dry wall. It was only a couple of inches, but you know what these peasants are like. After endless arguments, Monaco decided to sue. And you know what? I settled the matter in favour of Gerlando Monaco. So can you tell me why Monaco's daughter would want to kill me?'

'Listen, your honour, when does this decision in Monaco's favour date from?'

'Over five years ago.'

✽

That evening, as he was watching television, Montalbano saw the face of the journalist he had met at the courthouse, Zito. He seemed to be saying sensible, intelligent things. The station he worked for was called the Free Channel. The inspector decided to ask him to lend him a hand. Wasting no time, he looked for the television studio's number and, as soon as the evening news report was over, he called them.

'Inspector Montalbano here, of Vigàta police. I'd like to speak to your newsman, Nicolò Zito.'

They put him on straight away.

'I remember you from the courthouse, Inspector,' said Zito. 'Is there anything I can do for you?'

'Yes,' said Montalbano.

7

The following morning, the start of a picture-postcard day, he got up early, took a long walk along the water's edge, washed, got dressed, and was already at headquarters by eight o'clock.

'What kind of night did Rosanna have?' he asked Galluzzo.

'She had company, Inspector.'

'Company? Did somebody sleep with her?'

'She talked all night, Chief. With Fazio. Now she's asleep in the holding cell, and Fazio's sleeping in the room with the beds. He left a note saying he wanted to be woken up as soon as you got in.'

'Let him sleep. I'll tell you when to wake him up.'

Nicolò Zito the newsman arrived punctually at half-past eight. When Montalbano told him Rosanna's story, Zito, who was a journalist born and bred, smelled a news story.

'What can I do for you, Inspector?'

Montalbano handed him the girl's ID card.

'I want you to . . . to have this picture enlarged and then, today if possible, have it broadcast on your news programme.'

'And what should I say?'

'You should say that all the families Rosanna Monaco has worked for over the last four years should contact the police for information. And please add that we'll be extremely grateful and very discreet.'

'All right. I'll try to get it on the midday broadcast.'

After Zito left, Montalbano told an officer to wake Fazio. Who came running without even bothering to comb his hair.

'The whole thing's rather complicated, sir.'

Fazio seemed upset and didn't know where to begin.

'Look, Fazio, just tell me what you don't know how to tell me. I think that's the best approach.'

'Well, this morning, at the break of dawn, after spending the whole night talking, Rosanna started crying and saying she couldn't take any more.'

'I'm sorry, but to be more precise: why did you stay behind with her?'

'I felt sorry for her.'

'All right, go on.'

'She sort of had an attack of nerves. She even fainted. And at one point she even told me the name of the person who told her to kill Judge Rosato and gave her the gun.'

'Who is it?'

'Her lover, Inspector. Giuseppe Cusumano.'

'And who's that?' Montalbano asked, confused.

'What do you mean, "who's that"? You testified at his court hearing over the accident!'

He suddenly remembered. The young tough who'd punched the old motorist in the face! The beloved grandson of Don Sisino Cuffaro.

Now they really did need to tread lightly!

'What should we do, Chief?'

'What would we have done if Rosanna had given you any old name and not that of the grandson of a Mafioso of the calibre of Don Sisino Cuffaro?'

'I would have gone and picked him up discreetly, brought him here, and asked him a few questions.'

'So what are you waiting for? Go and get him. But wait. Do you think it's a good idea for me to go and talk with the girl?'

'I dunno. You decide.'

*

There was absolutely no guarantee that Rosanna would be as well disposed towards him as she had been towards Fazio. But now, with the name Cusumano in the mix, things had changed. Montalbano couldn't afford to make even the slightest mistake. He went out of the station and into a little clothes shop, bought a light cotton dress, had it wrapped, returned to headquarters, and went into the holding cell.

'Good morning.'

'Good morning.'

She'd responded. She'd emerged from her silence. A good sign. The inspector found her intensely beautiful. Her eyes were powerfully alive, her lips fire-red with no need for lipstick. Montalbano tossed the package on the mattress.

'This is for you.'

She tried to untie the knot in the ribbon but couldn't, so she cut it with a single bite of her sharp, sparkling-white teeth, which looked almost like a wild animal's.

She unwrapped the package and saw the dress. Her movements, which were almost feverish at first, slowed way down. She picked up the dress, stood up, and held it against her body. The inspector felt a twinge of pride: he'd guessed the size perfectly.

'Want to try it on? I'll go outside.'

He'd never met a woman with the power to resist trying on a new present at once, whether a pair of earrings or a pair of panties.

'Yes,' she said.

When he returned, she was standing in the middle of the room, smoothing the dress down along her hips. In a single movement she saw him, ran up to him, and threw her arms around his neck.

She acts just like a little girl, he thought for a moment.

But only for a moment, because he immediately felt her pelvis press against his, remain there, then ever so gently rotate, while her embrace of his neck became tighter and her cheek pressed against his.

But that's not like a little girl, Montalbano noticed, freeing himself reluctantly from her embrace.

He was beginning to understand. That little bit of physical contact had been worth more than a thousand words for giving him a sense of things. She went back and sat down on the bed, leaning slightly forward to check the hem of the dress.

'I need to ask you a few questions,' he said.

'Go ahead.'

'When did Cusumano ... What do you call him, anyway?'

'Pino.'

'When did Pino tell you to kill Judge Rosato?'

'He wrote it to me in a letter a couple of weeks before he got out of prison.'

'Did you go and visit him in prison from time to time?'

'Just once. But not at first. They wouldn't let me in 'cause I was a minor. But Pino would send me messages.'

'But you don't know how to read!'

'That's true. But the person that brought me the messages would read them to me.'

'What's the name of the person who brought you the messages?'

'I dunno.'

'Where are these messages?'

'Pino asked me to burn them. And so I did.'

'When did he give you the gun?'

'He got the person that brought me the messages to give me the gun.'

'Have you seen Pino since he got out of prison?'

'Not yet.'

'Why not?'

'Because I was supposed to kill the judge first.'

'Wait a second: if you killed the judge, you wouldn't ever have seen Pino again.'

'Why not?'

'Because you would have been arrested. And do you know how many years in gaol you get for murder?'

She laughed a full-throated laugh, throwing her head backwards.

'They wouldna arrested me. There was two o' Pino's men ready to take me out of the courthouse as soon as I shot 'im.'

'Are you saying that as you were shooting the judge, two of Cusumano's men would create a diversion so you could escape?'

'Yeah, that kinda thing.'

'Do you know what they were going to do?'

Rosanna hesitated ever so slightly.

'They were gonna throw a bomb.'

Not a bad idea, a bomb in a crowd as a diversionary tactic.

'And naturally you don't know these men.'

'Nossir.'

Montalbano remained pensive for a moment.

'What's wrong? Fall under a spell?'

She'd taken a liking to answering questions.

'No,' the inspector said. 'I'm not under any spell. I was just thinking. Assuming that everything you've told Fazio and me is true—'

She shot to her feet, body tensed and fists clenched at her sides.

'But iss true! Iss true!'

'Calm down. I only wanted to know why you decided to tell us everything and pull your lover into this.'

'He din't keep 'is word.'

'How so?'

'He tol' me that if the cops caught me before I could shoot, I wouldn't spend a single day in gaol and they'd let me out right away. And instead . . .'

'Instead, he forgot all about you.'

She said nothing, and her eyes turned very dark.

'He's too busy,' said Montalbano.

She turned the black flame of her eyes onto the inspector's eyes. But said nothing.

'Too busy enjoying his fresh young wife, whom he hadn't been able to enjoy for three years.'

Rosanna clenched her fists so tightly they turned white.

'And he got you out of his hair with that rubbish about killing Judge Rosato.'

The girl was at the breaking point. One more word and something was certain to happen.

'And the proof that he wanted to screw you is that the revolver he gave you couldn't shoot. It was broken.'

He heard her exhale, which made a strange sound, exactly the same sound as when one is punched in the stomach. She didn't know the gun would never have worked. And something did indeed happen, though it wasn't what the inspector had expected. Rosanna stood up, bent forward, grabbed the hem of the dress, pulled it up over her head, threw it at Montalbano's feet, and remained there, absolutely beautiful, a ray of light in panties and bra.

'Take your dress back. I don't want nothing from you.'

And she started coming towards him. Slowly. Montalbano literally fled towards the door, went out, and locked it behind him. He'd once seen something similar at a circus, when the tamer ran away from a tigress that had rebelled.

*

Shortly before the midday bells, Fazio returned.

'Some definite news, Inspector. Giuseppe Cusumano is out of town. He'll be back late tonight or early tomorrow morning. And you needn't worry: I'm going to nab him sooner or later and bring him to you.'

'I'm not worried. I need to have something verified, but not through bureaucratic channels or we'll lose a whole month at the very least.'

'Let me try, if I can.'

'We need to find out if something the girl told me is true. That is, whether she went to see Cusumano at Montelusa prison a week before his release.'

'Well, if she went, it should be recorded in the register. I'll call them right now.'

Less than ten minutes later he was back in the inspector's office.

'They'll let me know within the hour.'

'Listen, do we have a TV here?'

'In the station? No. But there's one in the bar at the corner. We can ask them to turn it on, if you like.'

'Let's have a coffee.'

There was nobody in the bar. Fazio, who was one of the family there – like everyone else from police head-quarters – asked the barman to turn on the television and put on the Free Channel. The news programme had already started.

The usual stuff: two bank robberies in the province, a country house burnt down, an unidentified corpse found inside a well. Then there was an interview with an under-secretary who managed to speak for ten whole minutes without it being possible to understand what he was talking about. Afterwards, the face of Rosanna Monaco suddenly appeared, and Fazio, who knew nothing about this, nearly spilled the coffee in his demitasse. Off camera, Nicolò Zito diligently repeated what Montalbano had asked him to say, which was that any member of any of the families for whom Signorina Monaco had worked as a maid over the past four years should get in touch with police, etc.

'Brilliant move,' Fazio commented. 'But do you really think anybody will call?'

'I'm positive they will. Those who have nothing to hide will call. Just to show us how respectful of the law they are. Those with a dirty conscience will instead pretend they didn't know about our invitation. But we'll manage to get the names of those who didn't come forward. With a little luck, that is.'

Before going to lunch, he gave the officer at the switch-board precise instructions: if anyone called in reference to the girl, he should ask them to come to the station after four o'clock. And if anyone couldn't make it then, they should leave their telephone number.

*

With the taste of the sea still in his mouth – the mullets were a miracle of freshness – he took a long walk along the jetty, all the way to the lighthouse.

He had the troubling sensation that he was doing every-thing wrong, but he couldn't work out where the mistake was. Maybe the mistake lay precisely in the way he was conducting the investigation. He felt like someone floating on his back in the sea who notices that a gentle current is carrying him away and inertly abandons himself to that current.

✱

When he got back to headquarters, Fazio was out. In com-pensation the switchboard operator informed him that five people had called in reference to Rosanna Monaco. Of these five, four would be coming to the station as of 4 p.m., at half-hour intervals. The fifth, on the other hand, a Mr Francesco Trupìano, was ill with flu and didn't feel able to go out, but the inspector, if he wished, could come to his place whenever he wanted. Given that there was still almost an hour before the first appointment, and Mr Trupìano lived close by, Montalbano decided to pay him a call.

Trupìano came to the door himself. He was an elderly man, skinny as a rail, and wearing a *coppola* on his head, woollen gloves, and a shawl around his shoulders.

'Please come in,' he said, but in saying it he fled like a hare into the apartment. 'The draught! Please close the door! The draught!'

He yelled as if he was afraid he might be sent off to war. Montalbano closed the door and followed him into a sitting room with dark, heavy, but clean furniture. Mr Trupìano had run and sat down in an armchair in front of the TV set and put a blanket over his legs. At his feet was a brazier that gave off smoke. The inspector started to sweat, almost hoping he had nothing to tell him.

'And what can you tell me, sir, about this Rosanna Monaco?'

'What would you like to know?'

'Everything you can tell me.'

'And what can I tell you?'

'I don't know what you can tell me, Mr Trupìano. I'll try asking you a few questions, all right?'

'All right, but I'm only tangentially involved.'

'I don't understand.'

'You're interested in the people Rosanna worked for, from four years ago till now, is that right?'

'Correct.'

'So I'm involved only for the first five months of those four years.'

'So Rosanna worked for you for five months, four years ago?'

'No, sir, Rosanna worked for us for a year and five months. But you can't count that year, otherwise the number of years you're interested in becomes five. Make sense?'

'What was your profession, Mr Trupìano, accountant?'

'I was a watchmaker.'

That explained the man's precision.

'All right, then, let's talk about those five months that were part of the four years. What was Rosanna like?'

'Very pretty.'

'I don't want to know what she was like physically, but as a person.'

'What did she do, die?'

'Who?'

'Rosanna.'

'No, she's quite alive.'

'So why did you say "was"?'

'Would you please answer my question?'

'She was good. A good person. Worked hard. Never talked back. My wife, rest her soul, had no complaints.'

'You're a widower?'

'Since two years ago.'

'What sort of hours did Rosanna work?'

'She would arrive at eight in the morning and leave at six in the evening.'

'An excellent girl, in short.'

'For one year and four months.'

Montalbano, who was falling asleep from the heat he felt just from seeing Trupìano all covered up as he was, or perhaps from the poisoning of the noxious fumes rising from the brazier, at first didn't notice the time discrepancy.

'Thank you,' he said, starting to get up. But then he stopped, buttocks in midair. 'I'm sorry, what did you just say?'

'I said she was a good girl for one year and four months.'

'And what happened in the last month?' the inspector asked, pricking up his ears and sitting down again.

'During the last month, she changed.'

'How?'

'She became agitated, talked back all the time, turned up late to work and then didn't feel like working. Then, one day, she stopped coming. Some time after that, her mother came asking about her daughter, but I didn't tell her anything.'

'Why didn't you tell her anything?'

'Because she was rude and loud.'

'Could you tell me what you didn't tell Rosanna's mother?'

'Sure. There were phone calls.'

'Phone calls she made herself?'

'No, sir, she didn't make the phone calls, she received them. Every day, around five thirty – in other words, half an hour before she got off work – she would get a call. And she would race to the phone like someone had lit a fire under her bum, if you'll excuse the expression.'

'So you never had a chance to find out who—'

'Well, sometimes Rosanna didn't manage to pick up in

time and so either me or my wife would answer. It was always a young man, always the same one.'

'He never told you his name?'

'He did, all the time. He would say: "It's Pino . . ."'

'Cusumano!' the inspector yelled, hearing something like the triumphal march to the *Aida* strike up in his head.

Mr Trupìano gave a start in his armchair and got scared.

'*Matre santa!* What is it? Why are you shouting?'

'It's nothing, never mind,' said Montalbano. 'Calm down.'

'You calm down,' the old man said in irritation.

'So this Pino Cusumano would call . . .'

'Who ever said anything about Cusumano! Why are you fixated on this Cusumano? His name was Pino Dibetta!'

Very quickly the great orchestra in the inspector's head changed tune and started playing a requiem.

'Are you absolutely certain?'

'Of course I'm absolutely certain! I may be almost eighty, but my brain still works just fine!'

'A final question, Mr Trupìano. Do you own any weapons?'

'Do you mean knives, or firearms?'

A watchmaker's precision.

'Firearms.'

'I have a hunting rifle. I used to like to go hunting.'

✳

'Mr Corso, the first man on the list, arrived about ten minutes ago,' the guard informed the inspector.

'Is Fazio here?'

'No sign of him yet.'

'Call Gallo for me, would you?'

Gallo came running.

'You're from Vigàta, aren't you?' the inspector asked him.

'Yes.'

'Do you know anyone named Pino Dibetta?'

Gallo smiled.

'I certainly do.'

'Why are you smiling?'

'Because he's a friend of my younger brother, and he's staying at my place. They both work at Montacatini's.'

'Then listen. Tell him I want to see him in about two hours. And now bring me Mr Corso.'

8

Mr Corso owned a small grocer's shop. Based on what his wife said about the girl – since he himself was always at the shop, working from morning till night – Rosanna was a good kid. He'd always paid her well and contributed to her social-security fund. No, his wife said that nobody ever phoned for Rosanna. The girl hadn't left on her own. It was Corso's wife who asked her not to return, since they had a granddaughter of their own who needed work and they'd decided to help her by taking her on as a housekeeper. No, they didn't pay the granddaughter, just free room and board. No, sir, he owned no firearms whatsoever. Might he ask why the inspector was asking so many questions about the girl? No? Well, good day and thanks just the same.

Mrs Concetta Pimpigallo, née Currò, the seventy-year-old widow of ragionier Arturo Pimpigallo, former accountant for the Fruit & Vegetable Consortium, came in with her daughter Sarina, who looked about fifty and was unmarried and possibly mute, since she never once opened her mouth. Mrs Pimpigallo declared she had nothing whatsoever to say about Rosanna. In all good conscience she had to admit that the girl sometimes arrived a little late, but nothing serious, maybe five minutes late. And the signora would bring it to her attention by showing her the pendulum clock in the living room – 'a Swiss clock, my dear

Inspector, with split-second precision, the kind they don't make any more!' – and then would dock five minutes' worth from her pay. Why had Rosanna left? The girl said she'd met Mrs Siracusa at the market, and the bitch had offered to hire her for better pay. That's all. Why was Mrs Siracusa a bitch? Hadn't the inspector ever met her? No? Well, when he did, he should be so kind as to ring the widow Pimpigallo and then they could talk about it. No, nobody ever phoned for Rosanna. Firearms?! In her house?! Heaven forbid! Could they perhaps know why the police were . . . No? Oh, well . . .

Mr Giacomo Nicolosi was a nervous, grumpy man of about forty. He stated that since he was working in Germany at the time, he hadn't had a chance to meet the girl in person. Rosanna had been in his service for eight months during which time he hadn't been able to return to Italy. His wife told him to say that Rosanna Monaco had always worked well and had left of her own free will. They had no weapons in the house. Why had he come to the police station instead of his wife, who knew a great deal more about the girl than he did? Because never in a million years would he have allowed his beloved wife to appear in a police station like the commonest of whores.

Mrs Concita Filippazzo monologued against the current.

'I realized from the start that Rosanna was a strumpet. I got a sharp eye, you know. No sir, 's far 's the housework was concerned – cleanin', washin' floors, cookin', ironin' – no complaints. But she was a strumpet. First of all, she never went to church on Sunday and never took Communion. Secunnly, you just hadda see the way she would make my husban' and my son look at 'er. One time, Inspector, I went inna kitchen, where my husban' had gone to make hisself a cup a coffee. An' you know what? In one hand, my husban' was holdin' the little cup, and with the other he was strokin' the girl's bottom. No, I didn't raise hell, iss juss the way my husband is, he'd even stroke a mullet's bottom if he could. But a few months later, things got rilly serious. I got a son, Gasparinu, who was eighteen at the time. One time when Rosanna was makin' the bed in Gasparinu's room, I saw the girl bending forward wit' my son behind her stroking her bottom. So I ask you: was this girl's bottom made o' honey to have all the men's hands stuck to it alla time like that? After that happen, I threw 'er outta the house, the big slut. No, sir, when she was livin' wit' us nobody ever called for her onna phone. Weapons?! Wha'??'

*

'Why'd you ask them if they had weapons at home?' asked Fazio, who'd arrived a moment before Mr Nicolosi began his deposition and had stayed until the end.

'Rosanna told me that it was Cusumano who had the gun delivered to her through an intermediary whose name she didn't know. But what if this isn't true? What if she'd stolen the gun from one of the homes she'd worked at? And then told Pino about it, to show him that she was up to the task? It wouldn't change anything, in essence, but it would certainly compromise her own position.'

'Have all her former employers come in?'

'There's still one family that hasn't.'

'Can you tell me how you know that?'

'I just added up all the dates. Over these last four years, Rosanna has worked for Trupìano, Filippazzo, Nicolosi, Corso, and Pimpigallo, in that order. Between each of these periods of employment there were short intervals, the longest being between Trupìano and Filippazzo. And the explanation for this is the abortion and its consequences. But the last eleven months are still unaccounted for. Mrs Pimpigallo stated that Rosanna had told her she was going to work for a certain Mrs Siracusa, who offered her better wages. But neither of the Siracusas has shown up. Do you know anything about them?'

'No, Chief. But I can find out.'

'Get on it right away. Where've you been all afternoon?'

'This business of Pino Cusumano being unreachable seemed fishy to me. So I asked around. And I managed to get confirmation that he really is out of town. But that's all I know. Oh and, Inspector, I almost forgot. At Montelusa Prison they confirmed that Rosanna went to see Cusumano three days before he was released.'

'But doesn't one need to submit a written request before a visit?'

'Of course, and she'd done that a good month in advance.'

'But she can't read or write! How'd she sign it?'

'Somebody signed it as her trustee.'

'What's the person's name?'

'The signature's illegible, Chief.'

A few minutes after Fazio left, Gallo came in.

'Inspector, Pino Dibetta's here, I brought him in myself. Should I sit in on the conversation?'

'If you wish.'

'I'd rather not, actually. We're good friends, I don't want to make him feel uncomfortable.'

Pino Dibetta was just over twenty. A rather tall kid, naturally good-looking, and slightly worried about being summoned to the police station.

'Well, here I am,' he said, obeying Montalbano's invitation to sit down.

'Listen,' Montalbano began, 'do you know anything about—'

'I don't know anything,' the other blurted out.

But then he bit his lip, realizing he'd goofed. Trying to justify himself, he continued:

'I had nothing to do with slashing the foreman's tyres.'

'I don't care about any foreman's tyres!'

'Really?'

'Really.'

'So why did you call me in?'

'For something from a few years ago, concerning you and a girl called Rosanna Monaco.'

'What happened?'

'No, that's what I want to ask *you*. What happened?'

'I met her at the market, Inspector, when I used to help an uncle of mine who had a fruit and vegetable stall. I liked her. And I guess she liked me. She said she worked for some family . . . I don't remember their name . . .'

'Trupìano.'

'Ah, right. She gave me their phone number, which she'd memorized, but she didn't know how to read or write. Anyway, I started calling her up.'

'And the two of you would meet when she got off work.'

'Yes, sir.'

'Where would you go?'

'Out in the country. But we couldn't stay long, 'cause she had to be back home early.'

'What happened between the two of you?'

'What do you mean?'

'You know exactly what I mean.'

'Kids' stuff, you know: kissing, touching . . . nothing more than that.'

'She didn't want to?'

Pino Dibetta blushed.

'Inspector, Rosanna wasn't even fifteen at the time, but she already looked like a full-grown woman, a beautiful woman, but . . .'

'But?'

'Well, her head . . . I mean, she had the brain of a five-year-old. I was worried about the consequences. She was liable to tell everyone if we did it . . .'

'And so you left her.'

'No, sir, Inspector, I didn't want to leave her.'

'So what happened?'

'One night when I was coming home, I was jumped by

two guys I didn't recognize 'cause their faces were covered. They put a sack over my head and beat the shit out of me with clubs. Broke three of my ribs and two teeth. Look at this scar on my forehead: seven stitches. Before they left me for dead on the ground, one of 'em said: "An' forget about Rosanna Monaco."'

'So what did you do?'

'When I was in a condition to go out again, I phoned the Trupìanos. But someone answered that Rosanna didn't work for them any more and they didn't know how to reach her. I ran into her by chance about seven months later. But she was completely different, and really skinny . . .'

'Who do you think it was that attacked you?'

'At first I thought it was Rosanna's two brothers. But then I realized they didn't have any reason to . . . They wouldn't have had to cover their faces and all . . . Anyway I also realized her brothers wouldn't do anything like that . . . They would have talked to me if they had anything against it.'

'So, if it wasn't the two brothers, who could it have been, in your opinion?'

'Bah!'

'Could it have been that Rosanna maybe had another boyfriend when she was going out with you? Maybe some married man who . . .'

'Rosanna was a virgin. I lost a lot of sleep trying to work out who beat me up. But I never did find out.'

There wasn't much else to say. The inspector stood up, the youth as well. Montalbano held his hand out, and the other did the same. But when they shook hands, the inspector didn't let go.

'It *was* you who slashed the foreman's tyres, wasn't it?'

The youth looked at him, and they smiled.

*

'Inspector,' said Fazio, looking worried. 'About the girl, I think we're going to have to make a decision.'

'Why?'

'What do you mean, "why?" We've practically kid-napped the kid! Nobody knows we've even got her here – not the judge, not the commissioner, nobody.'

'Nobody's about to come asking for her.'

'With all due respect, Chief, that's not a good reason.'

'What do you think we should do?'

'Chief, she had a revolver in her handbag, didn't she? She told us she had planned to kill a judge, didn't she? She did. And so? We should play by the rules and—'

'And we'll never nab Cusumano. Actually, we'll be doing him a favour by getting Rosanna out of his hair. There is no contact between the two. Cusumano has been very clever.'

'What about the prison visit?'

'Do you know what they said to each other?'

'No.'

'Well, whatever Rosanna says about that conversation, Cusumano will deny it. And there's no way to prove other-wise. In short, Fazio, I need to keep the girl in custody for another couple of days.'

'Be careful, Inspector. You're gambling with your career.'

'I know. And that's why I've thought of something. You're married, aren't you?'

'Yes.'

'Don't you need a live-in maid? I'll pay for her myself.'

Fazio's jaw dropped.

'But you mustn't let her go outside. Nobody must know. Take her home with you right now, in fact.'

                                    *

Someone had told him that out by Racalmuto there was a restaurant, practically hidden in an out-of-the-way spot, where one ate in accordance with the laws of heaven. The same person had also explained to him how to get there, but he couldn't remember for the life of him the good

Samaritan's name. He made up his mind and headed off. It was a forty-five-minute drive from Vigàta to Racalmuto, if one took the road that went past the temples and towards Caltanissetta. The inspector, however, took an hour and a half to get there, because he twice made a wrong turn onto roads he thought led to the restaurant – which was called Da Peppino and was in a secluded spot deep within the almond groves. It consisted of one big dining room with ten or more tables, almost all of them taken. Montalbano chose a table near the entrance.

As he was inhaling the first course – *cavatuna* with a sauce of pork and pecorino cheese – two men who were sitting not far from him paid the bill, got up and left. As they walked past him, Montalbano thought he recognized one of them, the heavier of the two. Such is the policeman's eye: it takes snapshots and files them away in the brain. But that time, all that the inspector could think of was that he'd seen the man somewhere before.

For the second course, he had grilled sausages. But what most sent him into raptures were the restaurant's biscotti, which were simple, very light, and covered with sugar. Taralli. He ate so many he felt ashamed. Then he left and got back in the car. It was a dark night. Before turning off the track and onto the main road to Vigàta, he stopped, as there was some traffic. At last he saw an opening and gunned the engine. But at that same moment he heard a loud popping sound and the car began immediately to skid, going into a tailspin.

He was in the middle of the road, out of control, dazzled by the headlights of the cars coming from the opposite direction, then immediately from those coming from the same direction as him. Spinning like a top. Drenched in sweat, he raised his arms, letting the car do whatever it had in mind to do, as a pandemonium of screeching tyres, horn blasts, screams, yells, and curses broke out behind him. At that point the car decided to bear left and ended up in the ditch at the side of the road. End of race. The taralli had vaulted out of his stomach and into his throat and now remained there, waiting to slide back down or be thrown up and out of his body. Two or three people came running up to his car and opened the door.

'Are you hurt?'

'Jesus, what a scare you gave us!'

'What happened, eh?'

'Thank you, thank you,' the inspector said. 'I must have had a blowout.'

He took advantage of the kindness of a man who was headed for Vigàta with his wife and five extremely noisy children. Once back at the station, he had Fazio and Gallo summoned at once. With Gallo at the wheel, they took a squad car to the scene of the accident. Fazio bent down and studied a tyre in the beam of a bright torch.

'I think somebody shot at you,' he said darkly.

'I think so too,' said Montalbano.

'Who knew you were going to Racalmuto for dinner?'

'Nobody.'

They changed the tyre, pulled the car out of the ditch and went back to Vigàta. They studied the damaged tyre, but not for long, immediately finding a 7.65 mm bullet. As Fazio was working on this, Montalbano thought back on his time in the restaurant. A kind of movie began to play in his head. It was a long take. Customers eating. The owner bringing a bottle of wine. As the inspector had just finished ordering the first course, and the waiter was heading back to the kitchen, a corpulent man, one of two men at a table, got up and went to the wall telephone, put in a token, dialled a number, said very little, spoke in a low voice, laughed, hung up, and returned to his table. Fade-out and fade-in. Same scene, but the owner is absent. The waiter is carrying four plates; a young couple who were sitting at the table near the kitchen door are now gone. The inspector is finishing his *cavatuna*. The two men get up and head for the door, walking past his table. He notices the fat man, thinking he's seen him before. The camera zooms in on the man's face, bringing into focus a bluish birthmark from his nose to his ear. Jump cut to another scene. The square in Vigàta opposite the town hall. A policeman on his beat is talking to two dogs. A car approaches very slowly and is passed by a powerful sports car. It sideswipes the first car, both cars stop. An old man gets out of the slow car, a young tough gets out of the sports car and punches the old man. A fat man then steps out of the same car, grabs the young tough, and drags him back to the car. The camera zooms in on his face: he has a bluish birthmark from his nose to his ear. The lights come on in the theatre and in the inspector's head.

'Listen, Fazio, do you know any fat man who has a birthmark on his face and is probably part of Pino Cusumano's circle?'

'Absolutely! He's Ninì Brucculeri, an ex-convict and a kind of right-hand man.'

'Do you know where he lives?'

'Here in Vigàta.'

'Good. Round up as many men as you need and bring him to me. He's probably got a gun on him. Confiscate it. It's very important.'

'But we haven't got a warrant, Chief.'

'I don't give a damn. If we move fast enough, he'll be so surprised at having been identified that he'll flip out.'

'But why would Brucculeri want to kill you?'

'You're wrong, he didn't want to kill me. He wanted to give me a warning. It was pure chance. I came into a restaurant where he happened to be eating. So he phoned Cusumano to tell him. And Cusumano told him to give me a little scare.'

'OK, but what's Cusumano's reason?'

'Come on, Fazio, aren't you looking for him? He probably found out we were interested in him and decided to take a little preventive action.'

'Are you really so sure, Inspector? Because I've been proceeding very carefully. I've been asking around, it's true, but I've only talked to people who—'

'Trust me, there's no other explanation. Think about it. Cusumano surely knows by now that we've arrested Rosanna. Agreed?'

'Agreed.'

'Then you start going around asking about Cusumano. And what does this mean? It means that Rosanna has talked; she's told us that Cusumano wanted her to kill Judge Rosato. So he takes measures. It's as though he sent me a letter saying: "Be very careful about your next move." And you know what?'

'What?'

'Cusumano might be the grandson and son of Mafiosi, and himself a Mafioso, but he's mostly a great big dickhead.'

*

The birthmark on Ninì Brucculeri's face was starting to turn green. The fat man trembled with repressed rage.

'What is this? Why'd you wake me up at four in the morning and drag me in here like a common criminal? My wife nearly had a heart attack!'

'Because you are a common criminal,' said Fazio, who was standing beside him.

Montalbano, sitting behind his desk, raised a hand, as if to make peace. He'd decided to mess with him a little. He sometimes got the urge when dealing with obnoxious people.

'Mr Brucculeri, I have two simple questions for you. The first is: did you dine this evening at the restaurant Da Peppino in Racalmuto?

'Yes I did. What, is that a crime?'

'No. In fact, I ate there myself.'

'Oh, really?'

His intonation was false. Terrible actor, this Ninì Brucculeri.

'Yes. And I wanted to ask you what you had for your first course.'

It was the last thing Brucculeri expected him to ask. For a moment he lost his memory. How could he be arrested at four in the morning and dragged into the police station to answer such a stupid question?

'*Cavatuna* in pork sauce.'

'Me too. So here's the question: was it over-salted or not?'

Brucculeri started sweating. What was the meaning of this farce? And was it really a farce or only a trap? Better stick to generalities.

'To me it tasted just right.'

'Good. Thank you. The second question is: do you support Inter or Milan?'

Brucculeri felt lost. *C'mon, c'mon*, he thought. *This is a trap, I gotta be real careful how I answer.*

'I don't care about football,' he said.

'Very well. Have you recently shot your gun?'

'No. Yes. No, no. Yes, yes.'

'Did he have his gun on him?' Montalbano asked Fazio.

'Yessir. A Beretta 7.65. With one bullet missing from the magazine.'

'Oh,' Montalbano said neutrally.

He looked at Brucculeri and asked:

'Of course you have a licence to carry a gun?'

'No.'

By now the fat man's sweat was dripping onto his shoes.

'Oh,' Montalbano said, so neutrally he sounded Swiss.

'You've got that bullet we recovered from the tyre, haven't you?' he asked Fazio.

'Yes, sir.'

'This morning send the pistol and bullet to Forensics in Montelusa.'

'I don't feel so good,' said Brucculeri.
'Should I put this guy in a holding cell?' Fazio asked.
'Yeah,' said Montalbano.

9

Fazio came back after locking up Brucculeri. He was wearing a dark expression and Montalbano noticed.
'What's wrong?'
'Chief, what exactly do you intend to do with Brucculeri? According to the law, he should be facing a judge this very morning and being charged with attempted murder and all the rest so he can hire a lawyer. But from the little I know you so far, I have a feeling of what your intention is.'
'And what's that?'
'You intend to keep him in the holding cell without telling anyone.'
'What do you mean, without telling anyone? By now Brucculeri's wife has informed the people she needed to inform. All we can do is wait.'
'For what?'
'Their next move.'
'Look, Chief, I should inform you that we don't also need a butler at our house.'
Montalbano smiled and Fazio decided to let it drop. He changed the subject.
'Oh, Chief, while you went out to eat last night, I got some information on the Siracusa family.'
He was about to leave the office.
'Where are you going?'
'To get the piece of paper where I wrote it all down.'
'You've got to get rid of this records office complex of yours. Just tell me what you remember.'
Fazio sighed in disappointment, resigned.
'So. His name is Antonio Siracusa, son of, I think . . .'

'I told you to forget about mother, father, and that kind of thing.'

'Sorry, it just comes out that way. Anyway, this Siracusa is forty years old, originally from Palermo, and has been living in Vigàta for two years, working for Montedison as a chemist. His wife, thirty-five years old, is called Enza and is apparently very attractive. No children. He declared his collection with us some time ago.'

'Oh, yeah? What's he collect?'

'Handguns. He's got about forty, pistols and revolvers.'

'Jesus! Did you call them in for questioning?'

'No, Chief. They both left.'

'When? Do you know?'

'Yes. I talked to the lady next door. The Siracusas live in a small house that has only two apartments on each floor. The lady, a Mrs Bufano, who's about sixty and a gossip, told me they left in a hurry — or at least that was her impression — yesterday afternoon. Took the car.'

'Interesting. Mr Siracusa — or more likely Mrs Siracusa — hears on TV that we're interested in their maid, and instead of coming to talk to us they run away. Tell me exactly where they live. Then we can both go home and get a few hours' sleep.'

*

At eight-thirty in the morning, as fresh as if he'd had a full night's sleep and dressed like a fashion plate, the inspector searched the phone book for the number of the Montedison factory, dialled it, identified himself, and said he wanted to speak to the director.

'I'm Franzinetti, Inspector, what can I do for you?'

'You're the director?'

'No, he's not in yet, but if I can be of help, I'm happy to—'

'Who are you, exactly?'

'Head of personnel.'

'Then I can ask you. I need to talk to Dr Antonio Siracusa about a formality, but I'm told he's away. Has he gone on holiday?'

'No, absolutely not. Yesterday he went home for lunch, and a short while later he called in to tell us that he'd just learned that an uncle of his, to whom he'd been very close, had just died. So he's gone away for a few days.'

'Do you know when he'll be back?'

'No.'

'Do you know where he went?'

'I'm afraid not, sorry.'

In short, it was clear the Siracusas had something to hide. In fact they had so much to hide that they were forced to stay away from Vigàta for a few days, waiting for calmer seas. The only thing left to do was to talk to the woman next door.

The house was made in such a way that there were two garages and two patios on the ground floor, with two apartments with terraces above. Theoretically, the terraces were supposed to have a view of the sea, but one would have had to demolish the ten-storey high rise that had been built in front of them, on the other side of the street, for this to happen. The little garden that could be seen from the cast-iron entrance gate was well tended. There were two names on the intercom: Siracusa and Bufano. Montalbano pressed the buzzer for the latter.

'Who's there?' an old woman asked in a croaky voice.

'This is Dr Pecorilla.'

'What do you want?'

'Actually, signora, it's not you I wanted to talk to, but Mrs Enza Siracusa. But I keep ringing their bell and nobody answers.'

'They went away.'

'Oh, damn!'

Montalbano sensed the battle that was taking place in Mrs Bufano's mind between curiosity and the desire to gossip on the one hand, and the fear of opening the door to a stranger on the other.

'Wait just a minute,' the croaky voice said.

He heard some bustling, and the French windows on the right-hand side above opened and an elderly woman appeared, holding a pair of binoculars, which she trained on the inspector. He let her look at him. His appearance was more than reassuring: even his tie was muted in colour. The woman went back inside, and a minute later Montalbano heard the gate click open. He walked down the little path, pushed open the entrance door, and found himself in front of a staircase leading to a rather large landing. On the left was the locked door of the Sirucusas' apartment, and on the right, that of Mrs Bufano. It was open. Montalbano stuck his head inside.

'May I?' he asked.

'Come in, come in. Over here.'

Guided by her voice, he came to a sitting room in which Mrs Bufano was opening the window.

'Can I get you something?'

'Please don't bother, thank you.'

'Why were you looking for Mrs Siracusa, Doctor . . . ?'

'Pecorilla. I'm a medical doctor, and I work for Trinacria Insurance. I need to talk with Mrs Siracusa about a policy, and we'd made an appointment for this morning. I came all the way from Palermo.'

'Oh, I'm so sorry!' said Mrs Bufano cheerfully.

'It's certainly no way to do business,' said Montalbano, feigning irritation. 'And it doesn't reflect too well on Mrs Siracusa's character. Do you know her?'

'I certainly do!' Mrs Bufano said.

'Are you friends?'

'Hardly. Good morning, good afternoon, that's about it. But I do have eyes and ears, if you know what I mean.'

'Ah, yes. You said they've gone away. Do you know when they left?'

'Yesterday afternoon, around two o'clock. I saw them putting two big suitcases in their car.'

'So you're not in a position to tell me . . .'

'I can't tell you much, but . . . it was just an impression . . . but it seemed to me like they were running away.'

'My compliments,' Montalbano said, buttering her up. 'You seem to have keen powers of observation.'

'Oh, yes!' Mrs Bufano explained, rotating her right hand as if to mean that she could see not only what went on in this world but a few things from the next world as well.

'You said you have eyes and ears, so to speak. Have you ever seen or heard anything unusual next door? Insurance companies, you know, have an interest—'

'My good man, let me give you an example. Last month, the husband had to go to Rome for a week. He talks to me a little more than she does, and he told me himself. Well, every single night that week, his wife had guests. Two different men, one one night, and the other the next night.'

'But how did you know . . .'

'I could hear the gate opening! So I would get up out of bed and . . . Come with me.'

She led him into the entranceway. Beside the door was a window that let light into the vestibule. Mrs Bufano half-closed it.

'I can come here and see who goes in and out of the Siracusas' place.'

At that moment Montalbano thought that the honest thing to do would be to ring Mrs Concetta Pimpigallo and tell her she was right about Mrs Enza Siracusa being a tart.

They returned to the sitting room.

'And what's the husband like?' the inspector asked.

'Worse than her, when it comes to women.'

Montalbano was suddenly anxious to leave. He'd had a crazy idea. He said goodbye to Mrs Bufano then went out on the landing and had a look at what he was interested in.

Next to the Siracusas' door was a window identical to Mrs Bufano's. And it appeared not to be locked shut, but only pulled to. He absolutely had to test it. He descended the stairs, opened the front door, and then let it slam so that Mrs Bufano would hear it. Then he re-opened it and left it ajar. He retraced his steps down the path, opened the gate and left it ajar as well. At a glance it looked closed. As he was walking towards his car, he saw Mrs Bufano out of the corner of his eye going back inside from the terrace and closing the French windows. He started up the car, drove to the next street, braked, parked, got out, and walked back to the house. The cast-iron gate did not squeak. The front door made no noise. He started to climb the stairs on tiptoe when there was a sort of explosion, a cross between a bomb blast and a thunderclap. Montalbano froze in terror. Then it slowly dawned on him that the loud noise was music. Mrs Bufano was listening, at full volume, to a song that went: *Andiamo a mietere il grano, il grano, il grano* . . . How long did a song normally last? Three minutes? Three and a half? He dashed up the remaining stairs, pushed open the window to Siracusa's flat, got a firm grip of the lower rim with both hands, bounded up in what was supposed to have been an athletic leap, but his arms didn't hold up and he fell back down on the landing, cursing the saints. On the third try, however, he managed to get his buttocks on the lower rim and his upper body and head, bent backwards, through the window and into the vestibule, while his legs remained out-side, on the landing. Rotating on his buttocks, he managed to turn his whole body around, and as he was doing this his testicles got caught in his underpants, though he withstood the pain and managed to straddle the windowsill. The worst was over. Pulling the other leg inside, he dropped onto the floor and closed the window just as the last notes of the song finished rumbling. But immediately another one started up, more softly, singing: *Amore amor portami tante rose.*

The moment his feet touched the floor of the Siracusas'

apartment, Montalbano felt a sort of electrical current running up his legs, up his backbone, all the way to his brain.
And he understood what diviners must experience when
they feel a vein of water hundreds of yards under the
ground. Here, his body was telling him, was the gold mine,
the aquifer, the treasure to be found. And he proceeded as
though sleepwalking, barely glancing into the two bedrooms
– the master bedroom and guest room – the two bathrooms,
the kitchen, the dining room, the living room, and a sort of
boudoir equipped for developing and printing photographs.
At last he reached the place where his legs were leading him
to: the study, or whatever it was, of Antonio Siracusa, doctor
of chemistry. On his way he had noticed that the apartment
looked as if it had been cleaned out by burglars: open wardrobes, clothes thrown about, drawers half open, disorder
everywhere. But he knew these were the signs of a sudden
flight. In Dr Siracusa's study, on the other hand, everything
was in its proper place. A large desk, four chairs, a wall of
shelves filled with bottles, jugs, and jars full of different-
coloured powders. Against one wall was a sort of tall,
narrow wardrobe, shiny, clean, and locked. In one corner
was a metal filing cabinet, half open and full of folders.

Montalbano sat down at the desk. On it was a table
lamp, a typewriter in its case and, to the left, a great many
papers with chemical formulas on them. On the right were
three more sheets of paper: a request for a new telephone
line, a clinical report of a blood test, a letter from Commen-
dator Papuccio, the building's owner, in which he declared
himself under no obligation to fix the leaking roof, and,
lastly, a form to be filled out. A form that made Montalbano
literally jump out of the chair. It was the draft of a request
to visit a prisoner, the prisoner being none other than
Giuseppe Cusumano, and the petitioner, Rosanna Monaco.
Thus the person making the request for the illiterate
Rosanna, and acting as her guarantor, was Dr Siracusa.

But this still wasn't enough to justify their sudden

getaway. There had to be something else. The inspector opened the right-hand drawer on the desk: formulas, correspondence with Montedison, a licence granted by the Palermo Police Commissioner's Office to keep firearms at home for collection, another similar document with 'Montelusa Commissioner of Police' on the letterhead, and a list of the weapons owned, which the inspector set aside on the desktop. The left-hand drawer, on the other hand, was locked. The inspector forced it open with a letter opener. The first thing he saw was a key. He grabbed it, stood up, and went over to the wardrobe: the key turned in the hole. It was the right one. Montalbano didn't open the doors, however, but sat back down at the desk. In the drawer were also two large linen envelopes, one full to bursting, the other with so little inside that it looked empty. He opened the first one, turned it upside down, and at once the desk was covered with photographs. All in colour. All the same format. And all with the same subject: naked women. From fifteen to fifty years old, variously reclining on the same unmade bed. So Dr Siracusa didn't just collect guns. Apparently he was in the habit of immortalizing every one of his exploits *post coitum*, and then would develop and print the shots in his private darkroom. On the sly, far from prying eyes. Picking up one of the photos, Montalbano stood up and went into the master bedroom: the bed was the same as in the photographs. A rather open marriage, the Siracusas'. Maybe while the doctor was using the master bed, his wife kept the one in the guest room busy.

Montalbano returned to the study, put the photos back in the first envelope, then took the other one and emptied it. It contained three photos. Same subject as the other one: a naked woman posing, first on her back, then on her front, and then with her legs spread. The model was someone the inspector knew: Rosanna. But an affair between employer and maid wasn't enough to explain their sudden flight. The whole story had to be a lot more complicated than that. The inspector pocketed the photo of Rosanna lying on her back, put the other pictures back in the envelope, then put the envelope back in the drawer. He took the list of firearms and opened the wardrobe. The custom-made cabinet was entirely lined inside with light-blue velvet. Only handguns: revolvers and pistols of every kind, size and epoch. No carbines, no rifles. They were arranged in ten rows of four: three on the inside of the left-hand door, four at the back of the wardrobe, and three on the inside of the right-hand door. Each gun hung from three nails with golden plastic heads. A veritable exhibition. And there were forty of them, exactly as declared. Not one gun was missing. And there was room for another forty handguns. In the lower part of the cabinet there was a drawer, which the inspector opened. No ammunition of any sort, only holsters, swabs, and special oils. He closed the drawer and the cabinet, and was about to put the desk back in order when something began to nag at him, something to do with the gun cabinet. He went back and re-opened both doors, and the drawer as well. This time he noticed that the space between the bottom panel of the cabinet and the drawer was too wide, a good eight inches. There must certainly be a secret compartment there. But where was the mechanism for opening it? The light coming in through the closed shutter seemed sufficient. He grabbed a chair, sat down in front of the open cabinet, and lit a cigarette. After staring at it for a while, his vision started to blur. What if it was just a mistake in the design? No, impossible. Then all it once he realized he had solved the problem. Each gun was hung horizontally from three nails. Why, then, did the last gun on the back panel have four nails? He stood up, and pressed the three golden nail-heads with his index finger. Nothing happened. When he pressed the fourth, he heard a sort of click, and a flat drawer, hidden between the bottom panel and the drawer, right where Montalbano had suspected, sprang forth. He opened it all the way. There were a pistol and a revolver, held fast by an arrangement of nails so that they wouldn't move when the drawer was opened or closed. Next to the two guns was another set of three nails, also arranged as if to hold a gun, but empty. But the weapon's shape remained impressed in the velvet. Montalbano picked up the pistol: it was American, and apparently lethal. But only apparently, because he immediately noticed that it had been rendered inoperable: the firing-pin's spring had been released. The same little trick had been performed on Rosanna's revolver. And this serial number, too, had been filed off. He put the gun back. There were also three boxes of cartridges. One was open, and six were missing from it.

He put everything back in order and went into the entrance. Mrs Bufano was blasting her ears with 'Guarda come dondolo, guarda come dondolo, con il twist'. He spotted a providential stool, put it under the window, opened the window, climbed up, hoisted himself up, closed the window, jumped down, and went out. Olé! That, ladies and gentlemen, was Salvo Montalbano, known to friends as 'the acrobat'.

*

The first thing the switchboard operator told him was that the Honourable Torrisi had been calling since the morning. He urgently needed to talk to the inspector.

'Put him through to me when he calls back.'

Fazio turned up a minute later.

'How'd it go with Rosanna?'

'Fine, Chief. She and the wife seem to be getting along. But she asked me at least four times when we're going to decide to arrest Pino Cusumano. She's obsessed, just aching to see him behind bars. Strange, don't you think?'

'What's strange?'

'What do you mean, Chief? First the girl is willing to kill somebody just to please her lover-boy, and just a few days later she wants to see him rot in gaol?'

'She feels betrayed. She told us Cusumano was supposed

to get her out of the hot water, and instead he's abandoned her.'

'Hmph. You know what? It makes me think of the opera.'

'*La donna è mobile, qual piuma al vento?*'

'Yeah, that's the one.'

Without a word, Montalbano stuck a hand in his jacket pocket, pulled out the photo of Rosanna lying naked on her back, and handed it to Fazio. Who took it, looked at it, and then dropped it on the table as if it was poisonous.

'*Matre santa!*'

He sat down, flabbergasted.

'How did you get your hands on that, Chief?'

'I just took it. There are two more, but I took this one because it was the most presentable.'

'And where did you get it?'

'I searched the home of Dr Siracusa.'

'How did you get in?'

'Through a window.'

'Like a thief?'

'Like a thief.'

'Then you're wrong. "Search" isn't the right word.'

Fazio wiped the sweat from his brow with a large checked handkerchief.

'Chief, I'm telling you this dispassionately: one day or another you're going to end up in gaol. And I may be the one who has to put the cuffs on you. You took a really big chance, you know.'

'I know, but it was worth the risk.'

Fazio, a policeman born and bred, pricked up his ears.

'So tell me about it.'

The inspector told him everything.

'What do you think?' he asked when he'd finished.

'One question, Chief. Why did Siracusa keep those illegal guns hidden?'

'It's part of the collector's mentality. You see, those guns had almost certainly belonged to the Mafia, and may have even been used to kill people. He paid a lot of money for them. And every time he opened the secret door he felt a shudder of delight . . . So, what do you think of this new discovery?'

'What can I say, Chief? Siracusa's somebody who can't control himself in a woman's presence. So he loses his head over Rosanna. Brags about his guns, maybe shows them to her and explains how they work. Rosanna sleeps with him, but then starts demanding things. Like asking him to write the request for a visit to Cusumano in prison. So he does it for her. Then she asks him for a gun.'

'No, she didn't ask him for the gun. She just took it and then disappeared from the Siracusas' home. When our announcement appeared on the Free Channel, Siracusa went and checked, saw that a revolver was missing, realized what had happened – it didn't take much – that is, that Rosanna had screwed him, and so he flew into a panic and ran away.'

'And when Rosanna went to talk to Pino, she must have told him she had a gun,' said Fazio. 'But then why did she tell us she got the gun from the man who brought her Cusumano's messages?'

Montalbano was about to answer when the phone rang.

'It's the Honourable Torrisi on the line,' said the operator.

Before answering, the inspector said to Fazio:

'It's Torrisi. What did I tell you? Whoever was supposed to find out about Brucculeri's arrest has found out. Now they're trying to patch it up with flying colours. They realize that Cusumano has really fucked up.'

'Montalbano here,' he said, picking up the receiver.

'My dear Inspector! I'm so happy to hear your voice again!'

'What can I do for you, sir?'

'I've just come in from Rome, and I'm at the airport. I should be in Vigàta in an hour and a half at the most. Would that be too late for us to meet for lunch?'

'Actually, I've already got an engagement.'

'Dinner, then?'

'I'm so sorry, but I've got a friend coming.'

Not even after a month of fasting on a desert island would he eat a crust of bread with that man.

'Then shall I drop by around five this afternoon?'

'If you like, I could come to your office.'

Silence. The inspector realized what was going through the other's head. Torrisi was weighing his options. For his dignity as a member of parliament, it was better that Montalbano come to see him. But what would people think? If, on the other hand, he went to police headquarters, he could always say he simply wanted to inform himself as to the current state of local law enforcement. Montalbano was enjoying the honourable's embarrassment immensely. He decided to prod him a little.

'It's only a friendly chat we're talking about, correct?'

Torrisi hesitated for a second, then concluded:

'Thank you, Inspector, for your exquisite courtesy. But I think it's more convenient for me to come to you.'

'All right sir, as you wish. I'll see you later, then.'

He hung up.

'There are some papers that need to be signed,' said Fazio.

'Then sign them. Who's preventing you?'

'But, Inspector, it's you who's supposed to sign them!'

'Oh really? Well, let me tell you something, so we're on the same page. You have to tell me twenty-four hours in advance.'

'Tell you what?'

'That there are papers that need to be signed. It'll give me a little time to get used to the idea. Know what I mean? If you tell me out of the blue, it's traumatic.'

10

For the antipasti a small octopus, ever so soft, *a strascinasale*, followed by a little fried *nunnato*; for the first course, pasta in squid ink; for the second, two roasted bream of considerable size. A digestive-meditative walk along the jetty was in order. He started out in a cheerful mood. The honourable attorney-at-law Torrisi had rushed back from Rome, summoned by the Cuffaro family, who were alarmed mostly by the idiocy of their beloved scion, Pino, and so, around five o'clock that evening, there was going to be fun at the station. But when the inspector sat down on the flat rock under the lighthouse, his mood slowly changed. Perhaps it was the steady, monotonous background noise of the water lapping at the rocks that did it. But the fact was that he again had the uncomfortable feeling of being a puppet in the hands of a puppeteer. Someone who thought he was walking freely, with his own two legs, unaware that there were invisible strings pulling him forward. 'We are puppets . . .' Who'd written that? Ah, yes, Pirandello. Which reminded him, he wanted to buy the latest book by Borges. And once that name entered his brain, it refused to leave. *Borges, Borges*, he kept repeating to himself. And he suddenly remembered a half-page, perhaps less, by the Argentinian writer that he'd read some time before. Borges was telling the story of a mystery novel in which everything arose from the utterly chance encounter, on a train, of two chess players who had never met before. The two men organized a crime, carrying it out almost pedantically, successfully avoiding suspicion. It was a highly plausible plot, held together by logic, without a wrinkle. Except that at the end the writer adds a postscript in the form of a question. Namely: what if the encounter between the two men on the train was not a chance meeting? In the investigation the inspector was conducting, this sort of question hadn't even occurred to him. Those few lines of Borges were an invaluable lesson in how to carry out an investigation. And in this case, too, he had to ask himself questions that might turn everything upside down, cast everything into doubt. For example: why did Cusumano want Judge Rosato killed? (In fact the poor man had already phoned a couple of times to find out how the investigation was going.) In a flash, Montalbano realized that Judge Rosato was the weak link in the whole chain. Or rather, the link he hadn't understood. Or, better yet, the link he had taken for granted. He took a deep breath. At once the sea air entered his brain and blew away all trace of dust, cobwebs or dirt. With his head now clear and shiny, he could start to think properly.

✳

It was a quarter to four when he got up from the rock and hurried back into town. Fazio was undoubtedly already back at headquarters, but the inspector knew where he lived. Should he inform him first? He decided that it would be a waste of time. He could tell him all about it afterwards. Fazio lived in the upper part of town, in a horrendous high-rise of recent construction. Montalbano rang the buzzer. A woman's voice answered.

'This is Montalbano.'

'Hello, Inspector. My husband is—'

'At the station, yes, I know. But I need to talk to . . . the maid.'

'All right. Fourth floor.'

Fortyish and pleasant, Mrs Fazio was waiting for him in the doorway.

'Please come in.'

She showed him into a room that was both a dining and drawing room.

'As soon as she heard it was you, Rosanna went to change her clothes.'

'How's she been behaving?'

'Very well, actually. She's a good girl. She just lost her head over a bad apple.'

Rosanna appeared, seeming a little awkward, and stopped in the doorway.

'Hello,' she said.

She'd put on the dress the inspector had bought for her.

'Come in. I want to talk to you. Sit down.'

Rosanna obeyed. Mrs Fazio instead stood up.

'Would you like a coffee?'

'Thanks, but no.'

'I'll be in the kitchen, if you need anything.'

The girl seemed extremely tense, a rope stretched to the breaking point, her taut lips starting to uncover her teeth and gums. These few hours in the Fazio home certainly hadn't done her any good.

'You got good news for me?' was her first question.

'What kind of good news?'

'D'jou arrest Cusumano?'

He wasn't Pino any more. Now she called him by his last name.

'It's just a matter of hours now. We're going to arrest him, that's for sure, but not for the reason you told us.'

'An' wha'd I tell you?'

'That he wanted you to kill Judge Rosato.'

'So you don' think that's true?'

'No, I don't think it's true. Cusumano never gave you that name. You only remembered it because you'd heard it mentioned years ago in your home, when the judge was handling a suit your father had brought against a neighbour. And to prevent yourself from forgetting his name, you filled your purse with things that would remind you. You see, Rosanna, if Pino had really given you the judge's name, you never would have forgotten it, because you were in love with him, as you told us yourself. That name would have been burned into your brain with letters of fire, and you wouldn't have needed to resort to roses or strips of elastic.'

'So who'd I wanna kill, then?'

'Pino Cusumano.'

He heard a barely perceptible clang, the sound of something breaking or being suddenly released – perhaps a spring in the armchair the girl was sitting in, as it was utterly impossible the sound came from inside Rosanna's body, from her bundle of nerves taut as drums. Montalbano continued.

'But he found a way to avoid being seen by you when he went to court. He was afraid. Because you went to see him in gaol, thanks to that idiot Dr Siracusa, and you told him you would kill him. That was your big mistake.'

'It wasn't no mistake.'

Montalbano wasn't in the mood for arguing. He continued.

'A mistake because Cusumano got scared. He realized you meant it. The only problem was that if you had shot him, the revolver wouldn't have fired. Which you had no way of knowing. But, being a smart girl, you made allowances for the possibility that your plan might not work, and so you invented the story of Cusumano wanting you to prove your love for him by killing Judge Rosato. Which is what you told me. Therefore, if you carried out what you had in mind, Cusumano's fate was sealed regardless: either he died by your hand, or he would go to gaol for incitement to commit murder. Except that's not how things turned out. Now it's your turn to talk.'

Before she could manage to articulate any words, Rosanna opened and closed her mouth two or three times.

'Can you 'splain to me why I would wanna kill Cusumano?'

'Because he raped you.'

Rosanna screamed and leapt forward. Montalbano couldn't manage in time to get up. But this time the girl had no intention of harming him. She was on her knees, gripping his legs tight, her head on the inspector's lap and rocking back and forth, wailing. A wounded animal. Mrs Fazio appeared, having heard the scream. Only moving his lips, Montalbano said:

'Water.'

Mrs Fazio returned with a jug and a glass and immediately left again. Slowly the inspector put his hand on Rosanna's hair and started lightly stroking it. Then her wailing turned into weeping. They were not tears of despair, but of liberation. Only then did Montalbano ask her if she wanted some water. Rosanna nodded yes. But her hands were trembling too much, and she was able to drink only when Montalbano held the glass up to her mouth, as with a child.

'Stand up,' he said.

But Rosanna shook her head. She wanted to stay right where she was, perhaps because that way she wouldn't have to look Montalbano in the eye. Was she embarrassed to say what she had to say?'

'It wasn't 'cause o' what Cusumano done to me.'

The inspector felt lost for a moment. Did this mean he'd got it all wrong, and all his fine reasonings were already headed south on a one-way ticket?

'Why, then?'

''Cause o' what he made me do.'

And what did that statement mean? Because of something Cusumano had forced her to do when in his hands? Or because of what she'd been subjected to by others with Cusumano's consent? He decided not to ask any questions just yet, but to wait.

'They grabbed me one night after they seen me with a guy I went out with, whose name was—'

'Pino Dibetta.'

Surprised, the girl looked up for a moment, stared at him, then lowered her head again.

'. . . A car come, a guy got out – it was Cusumano – an' he grabbed my arm an' twisted it an' made me get in. The car drove off, it was driven by a fat man with a big spot on his face . . .'

'Ninì Brucculeri,' said the inspector. 'Just so you know, I've arrested him. He tried to kill me last night. Go on.'

'. . . An' they took me to a house in the country, an' then Brucculeri got out an' Cusumano punched me in the stomach an' face to make me take my clothes off, an' then he took his clothes off an' did everything he wanted to all night an' the nex' morning too. Then, around noon, Brucculeri showed up, an' Cusumano tol' him I was all his, got dressed and left. An' Brucculeri was worse than Cusumano. Nex' morning at dawn he left too, but before he left he tol' me that if I talked, if I tol' anyone what happened, they would kill me, an' then he punched me so hard I fainted. When I woke up I was alone. I washed myself 'cause there was a bad smell an' then I went home. It took me three hours to get there, 'cause I coun't walk. An' as I was walkin' home I swore to myself I would kill Cusumano, not 'cause he raped me, but 'cause he gave me away like a rag doll. But then four days later, when he was getting married—'

'He was arrested and sentenced to three years.'

'Yessir. An' the whole time I's thinkin' how I was gonna kill him. I coun't get him outta my head. You gotta kill him, you gotta kill him when he gets outta prison. The same words, day an' night. OK, but how? I was getting desperate, the years going by an' he's about to get out an' I ain't done nuthin'. Then, one day—'

'You meet Mrs Siracusa at the market and she makes you an offer. You accept and go to work at her house. And so you meet her husband.'

'Yessir. A skirt-chaser. He wanted to take advantage of me, an' at first I said no. Then he showed me his gun collection to impress me.'

'The illegal guns, too, the ones in the secret drawer.'

'Yessir. An' so I did what he wanted.'

'Did he give you the revolver himself?'

'Nossir. He just wrote me the request for the prison visit. But it wasn't a mistake, like you said. 'Cause I din't say nothin', when we met. He did all the talking.'

'What did he say?'

'He said, "What, you want another taste of my cock? Well, you can have some, soon as I get out of prison." An' he started laughing, but he was scared.'

'And so why did you go?'

'What, you understand everything so far but not that? I went 'cause if I wasn't able to kill him, I could say it was when I visited him in gaol that he tol' me to kill the judge. Paper talks.'

'Brilliant. Go on.'

'Meanwhile, Siracusa was getting more relaxed wit' me and showed me where he kept the key to the desk. So I stole a gun and loaded it, after he asplained me how to do it, just to show off.'

There wasn't much else to say. Montalbano leaned forward, took the girl by the arms, and made her stand up, as he stood up himself. Rosanna still had her head down.

'Look at me,' he said.

She looked at him. Oddly, her eyes seemed less dark and hollow. Before, they'd been a deep, murky well at the bottom of which one easily imagined poisonous snakes slithering. Now he could look into them without discomfort. Or, at most, with only the discomfort of sinking pleasantly into them.

'We have to make an agreement, you and me. I'm hoping to get you out of this mess without any charges against you. You'll walk away free, while Cusumano's going to do a few more years in gaol, I promise. But you have to be ready to testify that Cusumano raped you. I'll try to arrange things so it doesn't come to that, but I have to know that you're willing to do it.'

Without warning, Rosanna embraced him and held him tight. She clung to him with her whole body. Montalbano

sank into her warmth, her womanly scent. How good it felt
to drown in that body! Independently of his will, his arms
returned the embrace. They stayed that way, in silence, for
a few moments. Only their breathing spoke.

'I'll do whatever you want,' Rosanna's lips then said a
short distance from his right ear.

A little prayer in rhyme Montalbano had learned from
the priests in boarding school came into his head:

> St Anthony, St Anthony
> Who made the Devil flee from thee
> Let me be as hard as wood
> To fight his evil with good.

He wasn't quite sure whether the Devil had taken the
form of the girl, but he certainly was starting to turn hard
as wood, though probably not in the same sense as in the
prayer. The only hope was to call for help.

'Mrs Fazio!' he cried in the voice of a turkeycock.

Rosanna released him at once.

*

When he straggled back into the station, it was almost five.
Fazio shot into his office as fast as a cannonball.

'My wife called and said—'

'Yes. I talked for a long time to Rosanna, who finally
decided to tell me the truth. She led us around by the nose,
that girl, and took us exactly where she wanted us to go.'

He thought for a moment of his father, who after taking
one look at her had said: *Don't trust that woman.*

'But this afternoon,' he continued, 'I guessed right and
she couldn't deny it any longer. Quite the opposite.'

Fazio was dying to know.

'I'll just give a rough sketch, because we haven't got much
time,' said Montalbano.

When the inspector had finished talking, Fazio was pale

and in a daze. He had many things to say, but only asked the question that concerned him most.

'Are we sure Rosanna will respect her promise to testify against Cusumano for rape?'

'She swore to me she would.'

Montalbano went out of the station and stood in front of the entrance. Almost at once the chauffeur-driven car of the Honourable Torrisi pulled up. He raced to open the car door, face beaming with a broad smile.

'Your honour! How wonderful to see you again!'

Stepping out of the car, Torrisi gave him a perplexed look, confused by all this joviality. The man was a politician, after all, and certainly understood human nature. But this time he seemed not to know whether Montalbano was putting on an act or behaving sincerely. He didn't reply. It was better to see how the situation developed. The inspector, for his part, continued the performance.

'But why did you go out of your way, your honour? I meant it when I said I would gladly come to you!'

Then, once inside, he yelled to all within earshot and nobody in particular:

'Don't put any calls through to me! I don't want to be disturbed! I'll be with the Honourable Torrisi!'

But it wasn't until Montalbano had him sit down in his own chair behind the desk – there was no talking him out of it – that Torrisi became finally convinced that the inspector was someone who could not only be approached, but possibly even bought. And perhaps even cheaply. Thus he decided not to waste any time. There probably wasn't any point in wasting much breath over him.

'I've come to talk to you about an unpleasant affair – which, however, could, I believe, be resolved with a little good will.'

'Good will on whose part?'

'On everyone's part,' Torrisi replied ecumenically, gesturing broadly with his right arm as if to include the whole world.

'Then tell me what I can do for you, sir.'

'I'll get straight to the point. I was informed that the other evening your men burst into the home of a certain Antonio Brucculeri, known to his friends as Ninì. His home was searched and a firearm was found. And Brucculeri was brought here to the station. And all of this – as far as I know – without authorization, and without a warrant.'

'That's true. But we're talking about an ex-convict who—'

'Even ex-convicts have rights. An ex-convict is a human being like any other. He may have made some mistakes, but this doesn't give anyone, much less you, the right to treat him as if he's been branded for life and devoid of human dignity and rights. Have I made myself clear?'

'Perfectly clear,' said the inspector, visibly embarrassed and wringing his hands. 'Do you have any idea how we might get out of this sticky wicket . . . which I can only chalk up to my inexperience?'

Montalbano inwardly congratulated himself. Sticky wicket! How the hell did he ever come up with that? And perhaps Torrisi too was congratulating himself, convinced that he now had the inspector in the palm of his hand.

'I'm happy to see that you're a reasonable man. Given the fact that there are no written records of the search, the confiscation of the weapon, and Brucculeri's arrest, you can release him without worry. And in so doing, you will enjoy the tangible – and I mean tangible – gratitude of some people who matter around here. Besides, you yourself seem to realize that you did not act in accordance with the law.'

'Yes, and I take full responsibility, but there's still one thing I'm not sure about, which you, as a lawyer, might be able to help me with.'

'By all means.'

'When somebody shoots at me the way Brucculeri did

the other night, should that be considered attempted murder or just a warning?'

The politician shook his head, though smiling.

'Such big words! Attempted murder! Come now, Inspector. You were in your car and dri—'

'Let's stop right there, sir. Who told you I was in my car? Perhaps the other man who was with Brucculeri and eating with him at the restaurant?'

Torrisi became tongue-tied. The smile vanished. Ah, so with his great show of friendliness, this bastard was trying to set him up?

'Car or no car, that's an irrelevant detail.'

'That's true.'

Montalbano got up from his chair, went over to the window, and started looking outside.

'And so?'

'I was trying to think how we might set things right. You said there were no written records, but that's not true.'

'So what's been written?'

'I had the confiscated weapon sent to Montelusa Police Central, along with the bullet recovered from the tyre. There's a written request for a ballistics examination with Brucculeri's name on it as the owner of the gun.'

'That's unfortunate.'

'There may be a solution. You could persuade Brucculeri to admit to what he did, then you could defend him by saying he'd been drinking, he wasn't himself and just wanted to play a nasty trick on me . . . That way the thing would end there and go no further.'

The honourable politician's eyes narrowed to little slits, and his ears perked straight up like a cat's when it hears a slight rustle.

'Why, is there some chance it could go further?' he asked.

As though uncomfortable, the inspector – who was still

standing at the window – looked down at the tops of his
shoes.

'I'm afraid so.'

'Explain.'

'Were you aware that, in connection with another affair,
the telephone in that Racalmuto restaurant has been tapped
over the last few months?'

The inspector had blindly fired a great big whopper that
had come to him just then. In shock, Torrisi swallowed it
whole.

'What the fuck!'

And he leapt out of his chair, face beetroot-red, on the
verge of a heart attack.

'And so,' Montalbano continued, 'the order that Pino
Cusumano gave to Ninì Brucculeri when the latter informed
him of my presence at the restaurant was rec—'

'Recorded?!' sputtered the honourable politician, chok-
ing in the grips of an asthma attack.

'That young man is too impulsive,' Montalbano said
with magnanimous understanding. 'His father and grandfather ought to pay closer attention to him. One day he's
going to do something stupid and get himself in trouble.
Nothing irreparable, of course, but still unseemly and
shameful for the kind of family the Cuffaros are. Like what
he did three years ago, when he raped an under-aged girl.'

A sudden gunshot in the room would have had less
effect.

'What did he do?!' asked the red-violet pepper that was
once the Honourable Torrisi, loosening his tie and shirt-
collar.

'You didn't know?'

'No . . . We didn't know!'

He'd used the plural. Therefore even the family was
unaware of this brilliant move by their beloved Pino.

'The girl waited to become a legal adult before talking
about it,' Montalbano continued. 'She came here the other

day and told me she'd been kidnapped, held prisoner, beaten, and repeatedly raped by Pino Cusumano. Just three days before he got married.'

'Is the offence still actionable?'

'You're a lawyer, have you forgotten your jurisprudence? Of course it's still actionable, and officially prosecutable, since the victim was a minor at the time of the crime.'

'Has she filed an official complaint?'

'Not yet. But that's up to me. I'm trying to spare the Cuffaro family a public scandal. Just imagine: the member of so respected and honourable a family, behaving like some common criminal! They might lose face for ever! And the family's enemies, who are rather numerous, will have a field day. And I even took into account the poor wife . . .'

'What wife?' asked Torrisi, in a daze.

'What wife, sir? Why, Cusumano's wife! The one who hadn't been able to enjoy the marriage bed for three whole years because her husband had been arrested on the church steps on their wedding day. You yourself mentioned it at the trial where I was called as a witness, remember? You claimed that Cusumano was speeding in his car because, once he was out of gaol, he was in a rush to be with his wife, with whom he hadn't yet been able to consummate—'

'Yes, I remember,' Torrisi cut him off.

'Well, there you go! I told myself that if the poor woman ever found out that her husband, barely three days before their wedding, had decided to celebrate his goodbye to bachelorhood by raping a fifteen-year-old . . . well, she just might not accept it, she just might leave home, she just might create a scandal . . . The end of a family! What is this? Eh? What is this?' he concluded on a questioning note, bringing both hands, cupped like artichokes, to his forehead, and agitating them.

He'd played the part of shock and indignation superbly.

'What is what?' the politician asked.

'Don't you understand, sir? Please let me explain. When

the girl came to me and told me she'd been raped, I assigned one of my men to go with the utmost discretion and seek out Cusumano and make him talk to me. I wanted to hear his version of the story, don't you see? But all I got by way of reply, and as thanks for my deferential approach, was Cusumano ordering Brucculeri to shoot me. Now why was that? What kind of a way to act is that? The only explanation is that Cusumano lost his head when he found out that I was investigating the rape. Because if the story of the rape ever came out, Cusumano had more to fear from his family than from the law. He wanted me silenced. There is no other explanation. And this ill-advised gesture shows how untrustworthy, indeed how irresponsible Cusumano is. In fact, it might be best for the family if he goes to gaol, where he can't make any more trouble.'

'OK, OK. What do you intend to do?' Torrisi asked, in a sudden change of tone.

The inspector's intentions were now clear to him. He planned to shaft Pino, there was no getting around it. And he'd fallen for the inspector's little act like a fool.

'Me?!' said Montalbano. 'I don't intend to do anything. At the most, I could give you a choice. I won't combine the charges. Either attempted murder, or rape. The one or the other. Which is already a lot. It's your decision.'

He looked at his watch. It was six o'clock. He continued:

'You have until eight thirty this evening to tell me what you've decided. You correctly noted, earlier, that I haven't played by the rules. You will therefore understand my haste to get back on the right track. Careful, though. A deal's a deal. If Cusumano admits to the attempted murder in such a way as to give too many opportunities to the defence – to you that is – I will bring up the charge of rape.'

The Honourable Torrisi raised his hand.

'What is it?' asked Montalbano.

'If there's no mention of the rape investigation, what

motive would Cusumano have had to tell Brucculeri to shoot at you?'

'That, sir, is of no concern to me. You'll have to think of a motive yourself. And you'd better think of a serious one, because I want to see Cusumano . . .'

'. . . behind bars,' Torrisi concluded.

There was nothing left to say. Montalbano opened the window.

'I need to air this room. Goodbye, sir. It's been a great pleasure.'

And so saying, the inspector flashed a broad, apparently cordial smile. The Honourable Torrisi stood up, said nothing, and had to open the door himself, since Montalbano had not budged from where he was standing.

*

The Honourable Torrisi's phone call came in at eight twenty-five. Fazio was there too, waiting in the inspector's office, having been told the whole story.

'Inspector Montalbano? I hereby inform you that Pino Cusumano is ready to admit that he ordered Brucculeri to do what you already know.'

'Excellent. Then he should come to the police station at once.'

'Well, there's a slight problem. The poor boy quite unfortunately fell down a flight of stairs.'

'I'm so sorry. Did he hurt himself?'

'Apparently broke a couple of ribs, fractured his septum, and can't move one of his legs . . . We had to call an ambulance.'

'Which hospital is he at?'

'Santo Spirito, in Montelusa.'

They both hung up at the same time. Montalbano turned to Fazio.

'Did you get that? The Cuffaros beat the shit out of their beloved son and grandson. He's going to confess attempting to have me murdered. He's at Santo Spirito hospital now. You call Montelusa Central and tell them the whole story. They can take care of Pino Cusumano from here on.'

'And where are you going?'

'I'm suddenly hungry. I'm going to go and eat. Ah, and one more thing. When you go home, I want you to tell Rosanna I've kept my promise. Pino will go to gaol, and she won't have to testify. And give her my best.'

'All right,' Fazio said drily.

'What is it? Is there something wrong?'

'What are we going to do with Rosanna's handgun?'

'We'll file it away as found in the street.'

'And what about Judge Rosato? What'll we tell him when he calls?'

'We'll tell him that Rosanna turned out to be a mythomaniac and *non compos mentis*.'

'And what do we do about Dr Siracusa?'

'He'll be back in a few days feeling a lot more reassured, I promise. At that point you'll go to his house to check his gun collection. And, as if by chance, you'll discover the secret drawer. I'll tell you everything in due course. That way, he'll have other problems to think about.'

Fazio's face grew even longer.

'So everything's taken care of, then.'

'Yes.'

'But only by throwing the rules out of the window, Chief.'

'That's the same thing Torrisi said, Fazio. You're in good company.'

'If you want to insult me, sir, it can only mean one thing: that your conscience isn't clean.'

'Get it off your chest, if you want to.'

'Chief, we've behaved the way they do in American movies, the ones where the sheriff does whatever the hell he pleases because in those parts every man makes his own law. But things are different here. We've got rules that—'

'I know perfectly well that we've got rules! But you know what these rules of yours are like, Fazio? They're like the woollen sweater my Auntie Cuncittina made for me.'

Fazio gawked at him, utterly lost.

'A sweater?'

'You bet. When I was fifteen, my Auntie Cuncittina made me a woollen sweater. But since she didn't know how to knit, the sweater had some stitches so big they looked like holes, other stitches that were too small, and one arm that was too short, and the other too long. And so, to make it look right on me, I had to pull it out on one side, tuck it in on the other, squeeze it on one side and stretch it on the other. And you know why I could do it? Because the sweater lent itself to that kind of adjustment. It was made of wool, not iron. Do you understand?'

'Perfectly. So that's how you see things?'

'That's how I see things.'

✳

Around ten-thirty that evening he phoned Mery. They decided that he would come to see her the following Saturday. As he was about to say goodbye, Montalbano had an idea.

'Oh, and listen. I'd like to help set up an eighteen-year-old girl who—'

'Set up in what sense?'

'I dunno, as a housekeeper, caretaker of something or other, babysitter, that kind of thing . . . She's very neat, pretty – which never hurts – and is used to earning her keep, which she's been doing since childhood. And everyone she's worked for has only good things to say about her.'

'Are you serious about this?'

'Of course.'

'Doesn't she have anybody in Vigàta?'

'No. Nobody.'

'Why not?'

'I'll tell you the whole story when I come.'

'So she would be available to sleep at the home of her work-provider?'

'Yes.'

'Jesus, that's fantastic! My mother's been in despair . . . She called me just an hour ago saying she just can't manage any more . . . Listen, could you bring her with you when you come on Saturday?'

✻

He went out onto the veranda. Soft night, bright moonlight, surf gently washing the sand. There wasn't a soul on the beach. He undressed and dashed into the water for a swim.

FIFTY PAIRS OF HOBNAILED BOOTS

When the Americans landed in Sicily in 1943, they normally wore the ankle-boots that came with their standard equipment, and this spelled the end of the hard hobnail boots that had traditionally been worn by Italian foot soldiers as well as peasants. During the pandemonium of the Allied landing, a certain Michele Borruso, owner of a herd of goats at Castro, looted a hastily abandoned Italian military warehouse and brought home with him, among other things, fifty pairs of hobnail boots, enough to shoe a whole dynasty. When Borruso died, his son Gaetano inherited goats, pastures, and forty-eight pairs of hobnail boots. Many years later, Gaetano was robbed of some thirty goats, but the poacher appeared to get off easy, since not only did the goatherd not report the theft but, in conversations about town, he didn't even express any desire for revenge. And so the thieves, convinced that a second poaching would be taken in stride like the first, tried again, and this time they made off with a good hundred animals, since in the meanwhile business had been good for Gaetano Borruso. A couple of weeks after the second robbery, Casio Alletto, a violent man who everyone in town knew was the head of a gang that indiscriminately poached every kind of beast that walked on four or two legs, was found on the banks of the Billotta torrent, severely beaten by clubs, stones, kicks and punches. Rushed to Villalta hospital, he was dead on arrival. That the crime bore Gaetano Borruso's signature was beyond question: the marks made by hobnail boots on Casio Alletto's face spoke quite clearly.

Two days before the killing, the police commissioner of Villalta had learned that Inspector De Rosa, stationed in Castro, had fallen from his horse during a hunting party and could not take on the case. And so he sent Salvo Montalbano, who at the time had just turned thirty, to lend a hand to Sergeant Billè, upon whose shoulders had fallen the fairly light burden of the investigation, which actually appeared to be rather simple.

✳

But while the burden of the investigation may have been light, the same could not be said of the uphill climb that Montalbano and Billè had to make to reach the paddock in which Borruso had built himself a one-room dry-stone hut in which he normally lived. With the money he had, he could, of course, have afforded a more comfortable dwelling, but that would not have fitted with the family tradition of the Borrusos, who were not only goatherds, but were keen to appear as such. After driving over forty kilometres from Castro, Montalbano and Billè had been forced to leave the car behind and begin a gruelling ascent in single file, with Billè in front and Montalbano behind, along a footpath that even goats would have considered impassable. But while Sergeant Billè, who clearly concealed a satyr's physique under his uniform, easily negotiated the path nimbly and goatlike, with hops and leaps, Montalbano struggled, chest heaving like a pair of bellows. He used the first fifteen minutes of the climb to outline in his mind a subtle, tactical approach to questioning Borruso. During the second fifteen minutes, however, this strategy condensed into a very simple resolution: the moment the idiot contradicted himself, he would arrest him. The idea of looking for blood-stained hobnail boots in the man's hut didn't even cross

Montalbano's mind, since he had forty-seven extra pairs with which to shuffle the deck.

The morning was as limpid as a pane of glass just cleaned. The blue sky seemed to be shouting to the universe that it was twice as blue as usual, while the trees and plants answered back, as forcefully as they could, with the greenest of greens. One had to keep one's eyes half shut, so violent was the assault of the colours, while the crisp air stung the nostrils. After half an hour of climbing, Montalbano felt an urgent need to pause and catch his breath. Embarrassed, he said as much to the sergeant, who replied that he should be patient just a bit longer. They would get their chance to rest presently, at the halfway point, at the house of a peasant whom Billè knew personally.

*

When they got there, two men and a woman, seated outside around an old wooden table with a great big pile of wheat on top, were so busy removing the impurities from the grain that they hardly noticed the two outsiders. Instead a toddler about two years old ran clumsily towards Montalbano on legs as unsteady as those of a newborn calf and anchored himself solidly onto his trousers with two hands sticky with jam. The woman, apparently the mother, shot to her feet and took the little boy in her arms.

'This child is gonna bring the wrath of God down on our heads! Always making mischief!'

'Good morning, Sergeant,' said one of the men, standing up. The other remained seated and brought two fingers to his cap by way of greeting.

'Sorry to trouble you, Peppi,' said the sergeant, 'I'm just passing through with *Dottor* Montalbano. Would you give us a glass of water?'

'Water? Water's for drowning. Sit yourselves down and I'll get you some wine that'll pick you right up,' said Peppi, heading off to the house.

The woman followed him, with the child still in her arms.

'No, I'm sorry,' Montalbano said loudly, 'I really would like a little water.' Then, as if to justify himself: 'I never drink on an empty stomach.'

'Well, if that's the problem, there's a solution.'

'No, thanks, really. I only want some water.'

They sat down at the table. The man with the cap on his head kept on working.

'How's it going these days, Totò?' Sergeant Billè asked him.

'Better,' the other replied tersely.

'Have you been unwell?' Montalbano politely asked in turn, noticing that Billè looked confused.

'Yes, I've been unwell,' said Totò, suddenly looking Montalbano in the eye. 'Tell me, you're a doctor: how's a man supposed to feel after spending six months in gaol, knowing he's innocent?'

'The carabinieri sent our friend to gaol in a case of mistaken identity,' Billè attempted to explain. 'It was a—'

'And here's the water and wine!' Peppi interrupted, coming out of the door.

He hadn't brought a glass of water, but a whole jug. The ceramic receptacle was sweating, a sign that the clay had been well-fired. Montalbano brought his lips to the brim and took a long draught of water cooled to exactly the right temperature. Meanwhile, Billè had already knocked back his first glass of wine. When they got up to leave, the man in the cap stood up, shook Montalbano's hand, looked him in the eye again and said:

'Try not to do the same to Tano Borruso.'

*

'What did he mean by that?' Montalbano asked after they'd resumed their climb up to the paddock. The sergeant stopped and turned around.

'He meant what you think he meant. He doesn't think Tano Borruso killed Casio Alletto.'

'How can he be so sure?'

'The same way everyone in town is.'

'You too, Sergeant?'

'Me too,' Billè calmly confirmed.

Montalbano was silent for about five minutes before speaking again.

'I want you to explain your opinion.'

Again the sergeant stopped and turned around.

'Could I ask you something, Inspector?'

'Of course.'

'You see, Chief Inspector De Rosa would normally have told me to go get Borruso and bring him in. But you, when I asked you if you wanted me to go and get him, you said you preferred coming here in person, even though this involved a great deal of effort on your part. Why did you do it?'

'Well, Sergeant, maybe because I think it's helpful to see the people I have to deal with in their everyday environment. It seems that, unless I'm mistaken, this lets me get a slightly better sense of what they're like.'

'That's just it, Inspector. All of us, in town, know exactly what Tano Borruso is like.'

'And what's that?'

'The man would never cut down a nettle, let alone kill a man.'

He smiled, never taking his eyes off Montalbano.

'I hope you won't take it the wrong way,' he continued, 'if someone who's served in the police force for thirty years and is about to retire speaks his mind to you?'

'Not at all. Go ahead.'

'I really wish I could have worked under someone like you in my early days, when I was a kid.'

✻

Gaetano Borruso's home consisted of a single room, which was nevertheless rather large. Behind the house was an immense fold from which a deafening chorus of bleats rang out. In front of the house was an open space of beaten earth, at one corner of which stood a rather spacious pergola. Under the pergola Montalbano was amazed to find some twenty or so rustic stools made of branches. Three of the stools had peasants sitting on them, engaged in lively discussion. They lowered their voices when they saw the sergeant and Montalbano appear. The oldest of the three, who sat facing the other two, raised a hand to excuse himself, as if to say that at that moment he was busy. Billè got the message and went to fetch two stools, which he set down in the shade, but at a good distance from the arbour.

He and Montalbano sat down. The inspector took out a packet of cigarettes and offered one to Billè, who accepted it, then lit his own.

As he was smoking, Montalbano couldn't help but glance every so often at the three men, who were still discussing. The sergeant saw him looking over at them and at a certain point began talking.

'Administration,' he said vaguely.

'Do those two work for him? Are they employees?'

'Borruso has eight men who look after the goats and make cheese and other things. The goats you see here aren't the only ones he owns. There are a lot more. But these two men aren't part of his staff.'

'So what was that about administration? What's he administering?'

'Justice.'

Montalbano looked at him with surprise. In the sort of gentle manner one uses with children and the mentally handicapped, the sergeant explained.

'*Dottore*, it's known far and wide that Gaetano Borruso is a man of sound judgement and experience, always ready to lend a hand or put in a good word for someone. And so when there's a dispute or a quarrel, people have taken to coming to ask his advice.'

'And do they then do what he prescribes?'

'Always.'

'And what if they decide on another course of action?'

'If they find a more just solution, Borruso endorses it. He's always ready to admit when he's made a mistake. But if the dispute degenerates and people pass from words to deeds, Borruso doesn't want to see them any more. And when Borruso refuses to see someone any more, nobody in town wants to have anything more to do with him, and he's better off moving to another town. And by "another town" I don't simply mean Castro.'

'A splendid example of Mafia behaviour,' Montalbano couldn't help but comment.

The sergeant's satyr-like face hardened.

'Excuse me, but if that's the way you see this, it means you have no idea what the Mafia actually is. What on earth does Borruso get out of what he does?'

'Power.'

'Let me tell you something, from one policeman to another,' the sergeant said after a pause. 'What we've found out is that Borruso has used his power for only one purpose: to prevent violence. Did you know Inspector Mistretta, the one who died in a shootout six years ago?'

'I didn't have the pleasure.'

'He was like you. Well, after he'd frequented Borruso for a little while after meeting him by chance, you know what he said to me? That Borruso was a latter-day shepherd king, and he explained to me who the shepherd kings were.'

Montalbano turned around and glanced over at the pergola again. The three were now standing and taking turns drinking from a flask of wine that Borruso had kept on the ground near his stool. They weren't simply drinking, however. The slowness of their movements, the looks they exchanged each time the flask was passed, suggested a sort of rite. Each drank three times, and then they all shook hands. The two men who had come to talk to Borruso then walked away, after saying goodbye wordlessly, with only their eyes, to Billè and Montalbano.

'Come, gentlemen,' said Borruso, gesturing broadly for them to join him under the pergola.

'Inspector Montalbano and I are here about the murder of Casio Alletto,' Billè began.

'I've been expecting you. Do you want to arrest me?'

'No,' said Montalbano.

'Do you want to question me?'

'No.'

'What do you want, then?'

'To talk to you.'

Montalbano noticed a distinct change in the man before him. If at first Borruso had asked his questions with a certain indifference, he now had a keener, more attentive look in his eyes. And Montalbano was amazed at himself. During the climb up to the fold, had he not promised himself to arrest Borruso the moment the man contradicted himself? Why, then, was he now giving him so much time?

They sat down. And Montalbano noticed, as if through the eyes of another, that he and the sergeant were now in the same positions, on the same stools, as the two peasants who had come to demand justice from Borruso. Except that the perspective had changed. Until proved otherwise, it was he and the sergeant who represented justice. And Borruso, if not a defendant, was at least a suspect. But Gaetano Borruso simply sat there on his stool, with the ease, as well as the authority, of a natural-born judge.

'Would you like a little wine?' Borruso asked, holding out the flask.

Billè accepted and took a sip. Montalbano politely declined with a gesture.

'It wasn't me who killed Casio Alletto,' Borruso said

slowly and calmly. 'If I had, I would have already turned myself in.'

Every word that is ever spoken vibrates in its own, peculiar way; and truthful words have a different vibration from all the others.

'Why do you think it was me?' he continued.

'Because everyone knows that it was Alletto who stole your goats,' said Montalbano.

'I would never raise a hand even against the man who stole every goat I own.'

'And then there's the matter of the hobnail boots. Like the ones you're wearing right now.'

Gaetano looked at his boots as if he was seeing them for the first time.

'I've been wearing these for the past five years,' he said. 'They're solid shoes, good shoes. They say the ones the army gave our soldiers in Russia during the last war had soles made of cardboard. Well, these have leather soles, no doubt about it. In the years my father had remaining after he took them from the warehouse, he wore out only one pair. He was wearing them when he died in the field, turning the soil. And when I dressed him for the funeral, I gave him a new pair. That left me with forty-eight.'

'And how many do you have now?'

Gaetano Borruso half-closed his deep blue eyes.

'This is my second pair, and I've been wearing them for the past year. That would leave forty-six, except that I gave away five pairs to people who really needed them, poor things.'

He noticed something in Montalbano's expression.

'Don't get the wrong idea, *dottore*. The people I gave them to are alive and well and have nothing to do with your murder case. If you want you can always check. I'm not going to put the blame on anybody else.'

'So you have forty-one pairs left.'

'That's how many there should be, but I can only find forty.'

'So one pair's missing.'

'Yes, sir. When I heard this story about Casio having nail-marks on his face, I went and checked, 'cause I got a little worried.'

'About what?'

'That someone might've stolen a pair of my shoes and used them the way they did to make it look like I'd done the deed. Come with me.'

They all got up and went into the only room in the house. A little bed with a bedside table to the left, a table with four chairs in the middle, and a large chest of drawers against the wall opposite the entrance. On the wall to the right were two doors, through one of which a toilet could be seen. Borruso turned the knob on the other, opened it, and turned on the light. They found themselves in a large storeroom transformed into a pantry and cupboard.

'The shoes are there,' said Borruso, pointing to a rusty-looking set of shelves.

Montalbano could scarcely contain a feeling of nausea. From the moment he entered the little dispensary, a violent stench of rot had assailed his nostrils.

The shoes were lined up on four shelves, with each pair wrapped in newspaper. Borruso picked up one pair, unwrapped it, and showed the shoes to Montalbano. And the inspector finally understood where the sickening smell was coming from: On every shoe was a layer of fat half an inch thick.

'I covered them in fat a couple of weeks ago,' said Borruso, 'so they would stay like new.'

The sergeant started counting the pairs, and Montalbano took the opportunity to look at dates on the pages of newspaper. None of them were recent. There was a stack of about twenty on an empty part of one of the shelves.

'I got the newspapers from the tobacconist in Castro,'

Borruso explained, realizing what Montalbano was thinking.

'. . . and that makes forty,' said the Sergeant. 'I've
counted them twice, there's no mistake.'

'Let's go outside,' said Montalbano.

The fresh air immediately dispelled his nausea. He
breathed deeply and sneezed.

'Bless you.'

They sat back down under the pergola.

'In your opinion, how did the thief manage to enter your
house when you weren't there?'

'Through the door,' Borruso replied with an ever so
slight hint of irony. Then he added: 'I always leave everything open. I never lock the door.'

✳

The first thing Montalbano did when he got back to Villalta was to call the coroner, a polite little old man.

'Please excuse me, Doctor, but I need some information
about the body of Casio Alletto.'

'I haven't drawn up the report yet, but go ahead.'

'Aside from hobnail imprints, were there any traces of
dubbin on the man's face?'

'Traces?' said the doctor. 'There was half a ton!'

✳

The following morning Montalbano got to Castro rather
late. He'd had a flat tyre and was not only incapable of
changing a tyre, but didn't even know where to look for
the jack. When he finally walked into the police station, a
smiling Sergeant Billè came up to him.

'I really don't think Borruso had anything to do with
the murder,' said Montalbano. 'Things seem to have gone
the way he told us. Somebody stole his shoes to make it look
like he had some motive to kill Casio Alletto. We have to
start all over again.'

Billè kept on smiling.

'Well? What is it?' Montalbano asked.

'I've just arrested the killer, barely fifteen minutes ago. He's already confessed. I tried calling the commissariat to let you know, but you were already on your way here.'

'Who is it?'

'Cocò Sampietro, someone from Casio's band, a halfwit.'

'How did you do it?'

'At the market this morning, someone came in from the countryside selling broad beans. He was riding a mule. When I saw his shoes, I nearly fainted. But I didn't let on. I just took him aside and asked where he'd bought them. He told me straightforwardly that Cocò Sampietro had sold them to him the night before. So we staked out Cocò, and the moment he stepped out of his house, we slapped the handcuffs on him. He cracked almost immediately. He said the whole gang had rebelled against Casio because he never kept his word.'

'But if this guy's a halfwit, as you say, how could he have thought of a way to make it look like Borruso was the culprit?'

'He didn't. He told us the whole thing was organized by Stefano Botta, who was Casio's right-hand man.'

'Congratulations.'

'Thanks, Inspector. Want to come with us? We've still got another five people to arrest.'

Montalbano thought about this for a moment.

'No,' he said, 'you go on ahead. I'm going to go pay a call on the shepherd king. He'll be pleased to know that the whole thing is over.'

NECK AND NECK

When Montalbano arrived fresh to his appointed post as Chief Inspector of Vigàta police, his predecessor, when handing over the case files, informed him, among other things, that the territory of Vigàta and environs was a bone of contention between two Mafia 'families', the Cuffaros and the Sinagras, who, in their eagerness to put an end to their age-old dispute, resorted not to stamped sheets of paper but to murderous blasts of the *lupara*.

'What? They're still using the *lupara*?' Montalbano wondered aloud, since the method seemed, well, archaic, in an age when automatic weapons and Kalashnikovs were ten a penny at the local open-air markets.

'The rival bosses are traditionalists,' his colleague explained. 'Don Sisino Cuffaro is over eighty, and Don Balduccio Sinagra just sailed past eighty-five. They're very attached, you see, to their childhood memories, which include the *lupara*. But Don Sisino's son, Don Lillino Cuffaro, who's over sixty now, and Don Balduccio's fifty-year-old boy, Don Masino Sinagra, are champing at the bit. They're anxious to take over for their fathers and would like to modernize, but they're afraid to because their parents are still liable to slap them around in public.'

'Are you kidding me?'

'Not at all. The two old men – Don Sisino and Don Balduccio, that is – are very sensible. And they're always trying to keep up with each other. If someone from the

Sinagra family kills someone from the Cuffaro family, you can bet your last lira that in less than a week's time, one of the Cuffaros will kill one of the Sinagras. But only one, mind you.'

'So what's the score at present?' Montalbano asked sportingly.

'Six–all,' his colleague said in all seriousness. 'The next penalty kick goes to the Sinagras.'

*

By the end of the inspector's second year on the job, the score was momentarily stalled at eight–all. And since the Sinagras had the ball again, it so happened that on the 15th of December, following a phone tip from someone unwilling to identify himself, the dead body of one Titillo Bonpensiero was found in the district of Zagarella. Bonpensiero had apparently had the bad idea – despite his name – of going for a solitary morning walk along a desolate spur of sorghum, rocks, and sheer drops. A perfect setting in which to get killed.

Doubly bound to the Cuffaro family, Titillo was thirty years old, officially made his living as an estate agent, and had been married for two years to Mariuccia Di Stefano. The Di Stefanos, naturally, were hand in glove with the Cuffaros, since, in Vigàta, the story of Romeo and Juliet was taken for what it is, a pure and simple fairy tale. The joining of one of the Cuffaros in marriage to one of the Sinagras (or vice versa) was unimaginable, the stuff of science fiction.

During his first year as Chief Inspector of Vigàta police, Salvo Montalbano did not subscribe to the school of thought of his predecessor, which was: 'Don't get involved. Just let them kill each other off – so much the better for us and for the honest people in town.' Instead, he dived headlong into these Mafia murder cases, only to come up empty-handed.

Nobody had seen anything, nobody had heard anything,

nobody suspected anything, nobody imagined anything, nobody knew anyone.

'No wonder Ulysses, right here in Sicily, told the Cyclops his name was Nobody!' the inspector raved one day in the face of the pea soup his investigations had become.

This was why, when informed that one of the Cuffaro gang had turned up dead in the Zagarella district, he sent his second-in-command, Mimì Augello, in his stead.

Meanwhile, everyone in town began to wait for the next, inevitable murder of someone from the Sinagra family.

*

And indeed, on the 22nd of December, Cosimo Zaccaria, whose passion was fishing, went out with rod and worms to the tip of the western jetty before seven o'clock in the morning. After fishing for half an hour with reasonable luck, he must surely have been pissed off when a noisy motorboat out on the water began to approach the harbour at great speed. It was aiming not so much at the entrance between the two jetties, but directly at the tip of the western jetty, determined, to all appearances, to kick up such a row as to chase away all the fish Cosimo was waiting for. Ten yards before crashing into the breakwater, the motorboat put about and sped back out to the open sea, but by then Cosimo Zaccaria lay indecorously wedged face down between two rocks, his chest blown apart by a *lupara*.

When word got around, the whole town, including Inspector Montalbano, was flummoxed.

What? Wasn't Cosimo Zaccaria one of the Cuffaro family, just like Titillo Bonpensiero? Why had the Sinagras killed two Cuffaros in a row? Perhaps they'd got the score wrong? And if it wasn't a mistake, how come the Sinagras had decided to stop playing by the rules?

Now the score was ten—eight, and there was no doubt that the Cuffaros would waste little or no time tying it back up. The month of January promised to be cold and rainy,

with two Sinagras as good as dead for all intents and purposes. But it would have to wait until after the obligatory
Christmas holidays, since from the 24th of December to the
6th of January there had always been an unofficial truce.
Play would resume after the Epiphany.

*

The referee's whistle, heard not by the people of Vigàta but
only by the members of the two teams, must have been blown
on the evening of January the 7th. Indeed, the following
morning Michele Zummo, owner of a model chicken-farm
in the Ciavolotta district, was barely discernible, in his capacity as a corpse, from the thousand or more eggs either
shattered by the spray of the *lupara* or crushed by the weight
of Zummo's own body as it crashed to the ground in their
midst.

Mimì Augello reported to his superior that the blood,
brains, yolks and whites were so perfectly blended together
that one could have made an omelette for three hundred
people without anyone's being able to distinguish between
Zummo and the eggs.

Ten—nine. Things were returning to normal, and the
town began to feel reassured. Michele Zummo was a
Sinagra, and killed by a *lupara*, in keeping with tradition.

Now it was still the turn of someone from the Sinagra
team to go down, after which the families would once again
be neck and neck.

*

On the bitter, short second day of February, Pasqualino
Fichèra, a wholesaler fish merchant, took a glancing shot
from a *lupara* as he was returning home at one o'clock in the
morning. He fell to the ground, wounded, and would have
escaped with his life had he pretended he was dead instead
of yelling:

'Hey, boys! There's been a mistake! It's not my turn yet!'

People in neighbouring houses heard him, but nobody budged. Hit straight-on by a second shot, Pasqualino Fichèra departed, as they say, for his eternal reward with the cruel suspicion that there'd been a misunderstanding. Indeed, he belonged to the Cuffaro family. Order and trad-ition dictated that, to even things up, it was a Sinagra who should have been killed. That was what he'd meant to say when lying there wounded. Now the Sinagras had taken a sizable advantage: eleven–nine.

The town lost its head.

⁎

But this most recent murder, and Pasqualino Fichèra's last words, had the opposite effect on Montalbano, which was to fasten his head more securely to his neck. He got to thinking about things, based on a conviction that was, how-ever, merely instinctive: that nobody, on either side, had got the score wrong.

One morning, as he was thinking, he became convinced that he needed to chat for a good hour or so with Dr Pasquano, the coroner, whose office was in Montelusa. The doctor was moody, impolite, and getting on in years, but Montalbano got along well with him, and so Pasquano managed to free up an hour for him that same afternoon.

'Titillo Bonpensiero, Cosimo Zaccaria, Michele Zummo, Pasqualino Fichèra,' the inspector said, rattling off the names of the murder victims.

'So?'

'Did you know that three of them were from the same gang, and only one from the enemy gang?'

'No, I didn't. And I should add that I absolutely do not care. Political leanings, religious beliefs, professional affili-ations are not yet considered things to look for during a post-mortem.'

'Why did you say "not yet"?'

'Because I have no doubt that before long they'll develop

equipment so sophisticated that they'll be able to tell what a corpse's political ideas were. But get to the point, what do you want?'

'When you were examining those four bodies, did you find any anomalies, such as, I don't know—'

'What, you think I only have eyes and hands for *your* dead bodies? I've got the whole province of Montelusa on my shoulders! Did you know that the undertakers around here are building mansions in the Maldives?'

He opened a big metal filing cabinet, pulled out four sheets of paper, read them carefully, put three of them back, and handed the fourth to Montalbano.

'Mind you, I sent an exact copy of this file, at the proper time, to your office in Vigàta.'

Which meant: why don't you read the things I send you instead of coming all the way to Montelusa just to annoy me?

'Thanks. I'm sorry to have bothered you,' the inspector said after a quick glance at the report.

*

As he was driving back to Vigàta, Montalbano's anger at looking like a fool in the doctor's eyes had his nostrils fuming like those of an enraged bull.

'I want Mimì Augello in my office at once!' he shouted as soon as he entered the station.

'What is it?' Augello asked five minutes later, going on the defensive the moment he saw the expression on the inspector's face.

'Tell me something, Mimì. What do you do with the reports Dr Pasquano sends you? Do you use them to wrap fresh mullets from the market or to wipe your arse?'

'Why do you ask?'

'Do you at least *read* them?'

'Of course.'

'Then explain to me why you didn't tell me anything

about what the doctor wrote about the dead body of Titillo Bonpensiero.'

'Why, what did he write?' Mimì enquired, a seraphic look on his face.

'Listen, tell you what. You go back into your office now, find the report, read it, then come back to me. I, meanwhile, will try to calm down, because otherwise this is going to end badly between you and me.'

When he returned to his superior's office, Augello had a gloomy look on his face, while the inspector appeared a bit more serene.

'So?'

'So I'm an idiot,' Mimì admitted.

'That's something we can both agree on.'

Mimì Augello didn't react.

'Pasquano,' said Montalbano, 'had the strong suspicion that, given the very small amount of blood found at the scene, Bonpensiero was killed somewhere else and then brought to the rocky spur in the Zingarella district to be shot after he'd already been dead for a few hours. With a *lupara* blast between chest and chin, almost point-blank. A sham, in short, a put-on. Why? Because, again according to Pasquano, Bonpensiero was strangled in his sleep, and the wound of the shotgun blast didn't quite manage to obliterate all traces of the strangulation, as it was intended to do. And so, Mimì, what's your opinion, now that you've finally deigned to have a peek at the report?'

'Well, if that's how it went, then this murder doesn't follow the standard procedure.'

Montalbano shot an admiring glance at him, feigning astonishment.

'You know, Mimì, sometimes your intelligence frightens me! Is that all? It doesn't follow the standard procedure, full stop?'

'Maybe . . .' Mimì ventured, then stopped, mouth agape,

as if himself astonished by the thought that had just occurred to him.

'Go on, speak. I won't eat you.'

'Maybe the Sinagras have nothing whatsoever to do with the killing of Bonpensiero.'

Montalbano stood up, went up to Mimì, took his cheeks in his hands and kissed him on the forehead.

'You see? If someone tickles your bottom with a sprig of parsley, you *can* perform!'

＊

'Inspector, when you sent word that you wanted to talk to me one of these days, I didn't come running, but it wasn't because I have anything to fear from the law. It was because of the high esteem in which both my father and I hold you.'

Don Lillino Cuffaro – thickset, hairy, with one eye half shut, and dressed in a haphazard manner – had, despite his unassuming appearance, a sort of secret charisma about him. He was a man of authority, of power, and didn't manage to hide it very well.

Montalbano made no sign of acknowledgement, as if he hadn't heard the compliment.

'Mr Cuffaro, I know you're a very busy man, and so I won't waste your time. How is Signora Mariuccia?'

'Who?!'

'Signora Mariuccia, the daughter of your friend Di Stefano, the widow of Titillo Bonpensiero.'

Don Lillino Cuffaro opened his mouth as if to say something, but then closed it again. He was flustered. He hadn't expected an attack from that side. But then he pulled himself together.

'How do you think she's doing, poor woman? Married barely two years, only to have her husband killed like that . . .'

'Like what?' Montalbano asked, looking as innocent as a lamb at Easter.

'But I . . . I was told he was shot,' said Don Lillino, hesitating. He realized he was walking in a minefield. Montalbano was impassive as a statue.

'Wasn't he?' asked Don Lillino Cuffaro.

The inspector raised his right index finger and moved it back and forth from right to left and vice versa. Again he said nothing.

'Well, then, how was he killed?'

This time Montalbano deigned to reply.

'Strangled.'

'Who are you trying to fool?' Don Lillino protested.

It was clear, however, that he wasn't a very good actor.

'If I say so, you must believe me,' said the inspector, dead serious, even though he was having a ball.

Silence descended. Montalbano stared at the pen in his hand as if it was some mysterious object he was looking at for the first time in his life.

'But Cosimo Zaccaria made a big mistake, a very big mistake,' the inspector resumed after a spell. He set the pen down on the desk, giving up once and for all any hope of understanding it.

'And what's Cosimo Zaccaria got to do with it, rest his soul?'

'A lot. A lot.'

Don Lillino squirmed in his chair.

'And what, in your opinion, was his mistake, just for the sake of conversation?'

'For the sake of conversation, his mistake was trying to pin the murder he committed on the Sinagras. But the Sinagras made it known to those concerned that they had nothing to do with the whole story. And so the people on the other side, convinced that the Sinagras had no part in it, decide to conduct their own in-house investigation. And they discovered something which, if it were to be made public, would have covered them in shame. Please correct me if I'm wrong, Mr Cuffaro . . .'

'I don't see how I could correct you on something that—'

'Let me finish. Now, then, Mariuccia Di Stefano and Cosimo Zaccaria had been lovers for a while. In the early period they were so clever that nobody suspected a thing, neither at home nor outside the family. Then – but this is mere conjecture on my part – Titillo Bonpensiero begins to smell a rat and opens his eyes wide and pricks up his ears. Mariuccia becomes alarmed and talks about it with her lover. Together they concoct a plan to get rid of Titillo and have the blame fall on the Sinagras. One night, when the husband is fast asleep, the wife gets up out of bed and opens the door to let Cosimo Zaccaria in—'

'That's enough,' Don Lillino said suddenly, raising his hand. He found the story too painful to listen to.

To his surprise, Montalbano saw a different, changed person in front of him. Shoulders erect, eyes clear and sharp as a knife blade, face hard and decisive: a boss.

'What do you want from us?'

'It was you who gave the order for Cosimo Zaccaria to be killed, to restore order in the family.'

Don Lillino uttered not a syllable.

'So, I want Cosimo Zaccaria's killer to turn himself in. And I also want Mariuccia Di Stefano, the accomplice to her husband's murder.'

'Of course you have proof of everything you've just said.'

It was one last line of defence, and the inspector quickly demolished it.

'Yes and no.'

'So can you tell me why you inconvenienced me?'

'Only to tell you that I intend to do far worse than produce evidence.'

'And what would that be?'

'Starting tomorrow I will open an investigation into the murders of Bonpensiero and Zaccaria to the beat of a big bass drum. I'll have the TV and newspapers following it every step of the way and hold a press conference every other day. I'll drag your name through the mud. The Sinagras will piss themselves laughing every time you walk down the street. I'll embarrass you all so badly, you won't know where to hide. All I have to do is say what happened, and you'll lose the respect of everyone. Because I'll say there is no discipline in your family. I'll say that anarchy reigns, that whoever feels like it can fuck the first person to come along, whether it's married women or young girls, that everyone is free to kill anyone they want any time and any way—'

'That's enough for me,' Don Lillino said again. Then he stood up, made a half bow to the inspector, and left.

✻

Three days later, Vittorio Lopresti, of the Cuffaro family, turned himself in, saying he killed Cosimo Zaccaria because he had behaved badly as his business partner.

Early the following morning, Mariuccia Di Stefano, dressed all in black, left her home and walked with a hurried step to the tip of the western jetty. She was alone and seen by many. According to an eyewitness, Pippo Sutera, when she arrived at the foot of the lighthouse, the woman made the sign of the cross and threw herself into the sea. At once Pippo Sutera dived in to save her, but the sea was rough that day.

They persuaded her to kill herself because she had no other way out, thought Montalbano.

In town everyone was convinced that Mariuccia Di Stefano committed suicide because she could no longer bear the loss of her beloved husband.

FELLOW TRAVELLER

When the train pulled into Palermo station, Inspector Salvo Montalbano was in a dark mood. His gloom arose from the fact that, having learned too late that the airlines as well as sea-lines were on strike, the only thing he'd found that would get him to Rome was a bed in a two-person compartment in second class. Which meant, in short, spending a whole night with a stranger in a space so stifling that a solitary-confinement cell, by comparison, seemed like a luxury suite. Montalbano had never been able to sleep on trains, not even by popping sleeping pills till they were coming out of his oesophagus. To help the hours pass, he would normally enact a ritual that was only possible if he was completely alone. This consisted essentially of lying down, turning out the light, turning it back on barely half an hour later, smoking half a cigarette, reading a page of a book he had brought, putting out the cigarette, turning off the light, and then, after a five-minute pause, repeating the entire operation until he reached his destination. Therefore, if he was not alone, it was utterly indispensable that his fellow traveller have ironclad nerves or be blessed with a leaden sleep. In the absence of such requisites, the whole thing risked taking a bad turn.

The station was so mobbed with travellers that it looked like the first of August. And this darkened the inspector's mood even further. There wasn't the slightest chance the other bed would be unoccupied.

Standing in front of Montalbano's coach was a man dressed in dirty blue overalls with a little nameplate pinned to his chest. The inspector took him to be a porter, an endangered species. Normally all you get nowadays are the sorts of trolleys that make you lose an hour before you find one that works.

'Give me your ticket,' the man in the overalls ordered him threateningly.

'Why?' the inspector asked defiantly.

'Because the regular employees are on strike and I was told to do their job. I'm authorized to prepare your bed, but I'll warn you now, in the morning I can't make you coffee or bring you the newspaper.'

Montalbano's gloom increased. No problem about the newspaper, but without coffee, he was lost. He couldn't have imagined a less auspicious start.

He went into his compartment. His travelling companion hadn't arrived yet; there was no baggage to be seen anywhere. He barely had time to put away his suitcase and open the mystery novel he had brought, mostly for its length, when the train started moving. Perhaps the other had changed his mind and wouldn't be travelling after all? The thought cheered him up. After they'd been rolling for a while, the man in overalls appeared with two bottles of mineral water and two paper cups.

'Do you know where the other passenger will be getting on?'

'They told me he's reserved from Messina.'

The inspector took comfort in this. At least he could sit for three hours in peace, since that was how long it took to go from Palermo to Messina by train. He closed the door and started to read. The mystery story so absorbed him that when he happened to look at his watch, he realized there was only an hour left before they got to Messina. He called for the man in the overalls, had his bed made up – his was the one on top – and, once the attendant had finished, he undressed, lay down, and resumed reading. As the train pulled into Messina station, he closed the book and turned off the light. He would pretend to be asleep when his travel companion entered the compartment. That way there would be no need to make polite conversation.

Inexplicably, however, even after the train was finally loaded onto the ferry following an endless series of back-and-forth manoeuvres, the lower bunk remained empty. And as the ferry at last tied up to the quay with a jolt, Montalbano's mood was starting to turn to contentment. But then the door to the compartment opened, and the traveller made his dreaded entry. For a split second, in the faint light of the corridor outside, the inspector caught a glimpse of a short man with a crew-cut bundled up in a broad, heavy overcoat and carrying a briefcase. The passenger smelled of the cold. Apparently he had in fact boarded at Messina but had preferred to stay outside on deck while crossing the Strait.

The new arrival sat down on the lower bunk and stopped moving. Indeed he didn't budge at all, not even to turn on the little light that allows one to see without bothering the others in the cabin. And for an hour he remained that way, immobile. If not for the fact that he was breathing heavily, as though winded after a long run, Montalbano might have thought the bed below his was still vacant. To put the stranger at his ease, the inspector pretended to sleep and even started snoring lightly, eyes closed but not really, like a cat that looks asleep but is actually counting the stars in the sky.

But then, all at once, without realizing it, he fell asleep in earnest, as he had never done before.

He woke up with a cold shiver. The train was stopped in a station: 'Paola,' a helpful masculine voice called out over the loudspeaker. The compartment window was completely open, the station's yellow lights gently illuminating the cabin.

Montalbano's fellow traveller was now sitting at the foot of his bunk, still wrapped in his overcoat, the open briefcase lying on the lid over the washbasin. He was reading a letter, lips moving with the words as he read them. Once he'd finished, he ripped it up very carefully and placed the little scraps next to the briefcase. Taking a better look, the inspector noticed that the pile of scraps was quite high and must have consisted of several shredded letters. This had therefore been going on for a while, and he must have been asleep for two hours, or almost.

The train began to move, gained speed, and when they were out of the station the man stood up wearily, gathered some scraps of paper into his cupped hands, and let them fly out of the window. He repeated the gesture with the remaining half, and then, after a moment of indecision, he grabbed the briefcase, which still contained many letters to be read and shredded, and hurled it out the window. From the way the man was sniffling, Montalbano realized he was crying. A moment later, in fact, the stranger rubbed his eyes with his coat-sleeve to dry his tears. The man then unbuttoned the heavy overcoat, pulled a dark object out of the back pocket of his trousers, and flung it forcefully out of the train.

The inspector was certain the man had just got rid of a gun.

Buttoning his coat up again, the stranger closed the window and drew the curtain, then collapsed onto his bunk with a thud. He began sobbing uncontrollably. Embarrassed, Montalbano turned up the volume of his phony snoring. It was quite a performance.

Little by little, the sobbing subsided. Fatigue, or whatever it was, got the upper hand, and the man fell into a troubled sleep.

When he realized they would soon be pulling into Naples, the inspector climbed down the little ladder, fumbled about for the coat-hanger with his clothes, then started carefully to get dressed. The stranger, still in his overcoat, was turned away from him, but from the way he was breathing, Montalbano had the impression he was awake but didn't want him to know, a bit the same way the inspector had done during the first part of their journey.

When bending down to tie his shoes, Montalbano noticed a white paper rectangle on the floor. He picked it up, opened the cabin door, and immediately went out into the corridor, closing the door behind him. In his hand he had a postcard, which had an image of a red heart surrounded by white doves in flight against a blue sky. It was addressed to Ragionier Mario Urso, Via della Libertà 22, Patti (Messina prov.). It had only seven words on it: 'I think of you always with love', and was signed 'Anna'.

The train hadn't yet come to a stop under the station canopy before the inspector was already running along the platform, desperately in search of someone selling coffee. Finding nobody, he was forced to go all the way to the main hall, where he scorched his mouth with two demitasses in a row, then raced to the kiosk to buy a newspaper.

He had to break into a run to get back on the train, which had already started moving. Standing in the corridor for a few moments to catch his breath, he started reading, beginning with the national news, as he always did. And at once his eyes fell upon a news item from Patti (Messina province). Only a few lines, as many as the story required.

A well-respected ragioniere of fifty, Mario Urso, had surprised his young wife, Anna Foti, in a compromising situation with a certain R.M., aged thirty and with a criminal record, and killed the wife with three shots from a pistol. R.M., the lover, who had publicly mocked the betrayed husband on several occasions, had been spared, but was nevertheless hospitalized and in a state of shock. The police and carabinieri were still looking for the killer.

The inspector did not go back into his compartment, but remained in the corridor, smoking one cigarette after another. Then, after the train had already slowed to a crawl and went under the canopy of Roma Termini station, he decided to open the door.

Still bundled up, the man was sitting on his bunk, arms wrapped around himself, body shaking with the shivers. He neither saw nor heard anything around him.

The inspector plucked up his courage and entered that dense atmosphere of palpable desolation and visible despair, which filled the compartment with a rotten yellow smell. He grabbed his suitcase and then delicately laid the postcard on his fellow traveller's knees.

'Good luck, ragioniere,' he whispered.

And he fell in line behind the other passengers queuing up to get off the train.

DRESS REHEARSAL

It was a really nasty night, with gusts of angry wind alternating with fast-moving, ill-intentioned sheets of water that seemed they would slice right through the rooftops. Montalbano had come home just a short while before, weary from a day of hard work that was especially trying on the brain. He opened the French windows giving onto the veranda. No, it was out of the question. The only thing to do was to have a shower and go to bed with a good book. Fine, but which one? Choosing a book with which to spend the night, sharing his bed and last thoughts with it, could easily cost him a good hour. First he had to select a genre, the one that best fitted the mood of the evening. A historical essay on the events of the past century? Careful: with all the revisionism currently in fashion, he might end up with a book that would tell him that Hitler was in fact someone paid by the Jews to make them into victims just to win sympathy across the world. And he would get upset and then not sleep a wink. How about a mystery, then? Fine, but what kind? Perhaps most appropriate for the occasion was one of those English mysteries, preferably written by a woman, consisting entirely of interwoven states of mind — which, however, after three pages begin to get boring. He reached out to take one he hadn't read yet, and at that moment the telephone rang. Christ! He'd forgotten to call Livia. That must be her calling, worried. He picked up the receiver.

'Hello, is this the home of Inspector Montalbano?'

'Yes, who is this?'

'This is Orazio Genco.'

And what could Orazio Genco, the nearly seventy-year-old burglar, possibly want at this hour? Actually Montalbano rather liked the old thief, who'd never committed a violent act in his life, and the old man knew it.

'What's up, Orà?'

'I need to talk to you, Inspector.'

'Anything serious?'

'I don't know how to explain it, Inspector. It's something strange that seems suspicious to me. But I think it's better if you know about it.'

'Do you want to come to my house?'

'Yessir.'

'How will you get here?'

'On my bicycle.'

'Your bicycle? Aside from the fact that you'll catch pneumonia, you won't get here till tomorrow morning.'

'So what should we do?'

'Where are you calling me from?'

'From the phone booth near the monument to the fallen.'

*

He got there a little later than expected because before going out, he'd had a good idea: to fill a thermos with piping-hot coffee. Sitting beside the inspector in the front seat of his car, Orazio Genco gulped down an entire plastic cup of it.

'I got a li'l chilled out there.'

He clucked his tongue in joy.

'And now I could use a nice cigarette.'

Montalbano handed him the packet and then lit his cigarette for him.

'Need anything else? Orà, did you make me drive all the

way here just because you wanted a cup of coffee and a cigarette?'

'Inspector, tonight I went out to rob a house.'

'Then I'm putting you under arrest.'

'Let me rephrase that: tonight I was planning to rob a
house.'

'Did you change your mind?'

'Yes, I did.'

'Why?'

'I'll tell you. Until a few years ago, I used to work the
little houses along the seashore, after the owners went away
when the weather turned bad. But now things have changed.'

'How?'

'The houses aren't empty any more. Nowadays people
spend the winters there too, since they can still get to work
in their cars. An' so, now, burgling in town or by the seashore makes no difference to me any more.'

'So, where'd you go tonight?'

'I went to town, right here. You know Giugiù Loreto's
garage?'

'The one on the road to Villaseta? Yes.'

'Well, right above it, there are two apartments.'

'Come on, those are poor people's apartments! What are
you going to steal there? A broken black-and-white television?'

'I beg your pardon, Inspector, but do you know who
lives in one of those apartments? Tanino Bracceri, that's
who. Whom you certainly must know.'

He certainly did know Tanino Bracceri. A fifty-year-old
made up of two hundred and twenty pounds of shit and
rancid lard. A pig fatted for slaughter looked like a fashion
plate compared to him. The man was an obscene loan shark
who sometimes accepted payment in the form of little boys
or girls, the unfortunate children of his victims. The sex
made no difference. Montalbano had never been able to get
his hands on him, as he would have liked very much to do,

since nobody had ever levelled specific charges against him. Orazio Genco's idea of burgling Tanino Bracceri's home therefore met with the unconditional approval of that guardian of law and order, Inspector Salvo Montalbano.

'So why didn't you do it? It's likely that if you had I wouldn't have arrested you.'

'I knew that Tanino goes to bed every night at ten o'clock sharp. The other apartment, which shares a landing with his, is lived in by an old couple who never go out. They keep to themselves. Both retired, husband and wife. Mr and Mrs Di Giovanni. So I felt pretty safe, also 'cause I know Tanino stuffs himself with sleeping pills before he goes to bed. Anyway, when I got to the garage, I waited a little. With this weather, there wasn't a soul about, and so I opened the front door next to the garage and was inside in a flash. The staircase was dark. I turned on my torch and went upstairs on tiptoe. When I got to the landing, I pulled out my tools. And I noticed that the Di Giovannis' door was ajar. I figured the two old folks had forgotten to close it. It got me worried. With the door open like that, those two might hear something. And so I went up to the door, intending to close it softly. There was a piece of paper on the door, or at least I thought it was a piece of paper, like when you go out and write "Back soon", or something like that.'

'And so what was written on it?'

'I don't remember now. All I can think of is one word: *general.*'

'And the guy that lives there, Di Giovanni, is he a general?'

'I don't know, I guess he could be.'

'Go on.'

'So I was about to close it nice and softly, but the temptation of that half-open door was too strong. The entrance hall was dark, as were the living and dining room. But I could see a light on in the bedroom. So I went up to it and nearly had a heart attack. There, lying on the double bed, all dressed up, was a dead woman. An old woman.'

'How could you tell she was dead?'

'Inspector, the lady had her hands folded over her breast with a rosary wrapped around her fingers, and she had a kerchief knotted over her head to keep her mouth shut. Her eyes were closed. But the best is yet to come. There was a chair at the foot of her bed with a man sitting in it, with his back to me. The poor guy was crying. He must have been her husband.'

'You were unlucky, Orà, what can I say? The man was keeping vigil over his dead wife.'

'Of course. But then, at a certain point, he picked up something he'd been holding in his lap and pointed it at his head. It was a gun, Inspector.'

'Good God! And what did you do?'

'Fortunately, as I was standing there not knowing what to think, the man seemed to change his mind and lowered the hand holding the gun. Maybe he chickened out at the last minute. And so I started walking backwards without making a sound and returned to the entrance hall and went out, slamming the door so hard it sounded like a cannon blast. That way he could forget about killing himself for a while. An' then I called you.'

Montalbano didn't speak right away. He was thinking. By that point the widower had probably already shot himself. Or else he was still sitting there, wavering between staying alive and taking himself out of the game. The inspector made up his mind and turned the key in the ignition.

'Where are we going?' Orazio Genco asked him.

'To Giugiù Loreto's garage. Where did you leave your bike?'

'Don't worry about that, Inspector, it's chained to a pole.'

Montalbano pulled up in front of the garage.

'Did you close the front door yourself?'

'Yes, when I went to call you.'

'Can you tell if you can see any light behind the shutters?'

'I don't think so.'

'Now listen, Orazio. I want you to get out of the car, open the front door, go inside and see what's happening in that apartment. Don't let anyone hear you, no matter what you see.'

'An' what about you?'

'I'll be your lookout.'

Orazio laughed so hard he started coughing. When he'd calmed down, he got out of the car, crossed the street, opened the building's front door in a flash, and closed it behind him. It had stopped raining, but the wind had picked up. Montalbano lit a cigarette. After just ten minutes Orazio came back out, closed the door behind him, hurried across the street, opened the car door, and got in. He was trembling, but not from the cold.

'Let's get out of here.'

Montalbano obeyed.

'What's wrong?'

'I got really scared.'

'So speak!'

'The door was closed, an' so I opened it an' . . .'

'Was the piece of paper still there?'

'Yes. An' so I went in. Everything was the same as before. The light was still on in the bedroom. I went up to it . . . Inspector, the dead lady wasn't dead!'

'What do you mean?'

'I mean what I mean. This time, *he* was dead. The general. Laid out on the bed like his wife was before, with the rosary and the kerchief round his head.'

'Did you see any blood?'

'No, the man's face looked clean.'

'And the wife, the dead lady who wasn't dead, what was she doing?'

'She was sitting in a chair at the foot of the bed, pointing a gun at her head and crying.'

'You wouldn't be putting me on, Orazio, would you?'

'Why would I do that, Inspector?'

'All right, let's go. I'll drive you home. Forget about the bike for tonight, it's too cold.'

*

Are an elderly couple, husband and wife, free to do whatever comes into their heads in the privacy of their own home at night? To dress up as Indians, run around on all fours, or hang upside down from the ceiling? Of course they are. So what? If Orazio Genco hadn't become concerned, he, Montalbano, wouldn't have known a thing about any of this and would have slept soundly and peacefully for the three hours remaining, instead of tossing and turning in bed as he was now doing, cursing the saints and growing more and more agitated. There was no getting around it: faced with a situation that didn't add up, he was like Orazio Genco in front of a door ajar. He had to go inside, to discover the whys and wherefores. What did that sort of ceremony mean?

*

'Fazio! Come to my office at once!' he yelled upon entering the station. The morning was worse than the night before, cold and gloomy.

'Fazio's not in, Chief,' said Gallo, coming into his office.

'And where is he?'

'There was a shootout last night, and a member of the Sinagra family got killed. It was predictable, you know how it is: first it's someone from one family, then it's the turn of someone from the other family.'

'Is Augello with Fazio?'

'Yes, sir. The only people here are me, Galluzzo, and Catarella.'

'Listen, Gallo, do you know where Giugiù Loreto's garage is?'

'I certainly do.'

'Above the garage there are two apartments. Tanino Bracceri lives in one, and an elderly couple lives in the other. I want to know everything there is to know about them. Now get moving.'

*

'All right, Chief. The husband's name is Andrea Di Giovanni, eighty-four years old, retired, a native of Vigàta. The wife is Emanuela, née Zaccaria, born in Rome, eighty-two, also retired. No children. They keep to themselves, but I don't think they have such a bad time of it, in that the whole building belongs to Di Giovanni, who inherited it from his father. He sold one apartment to Tanino Bracceri but hung on to the one he lives in, as well as the garage, which he rents to Giugiù Loreto. They used to live in Rome, but they moved here about fifteen years ago.'

'Was he a general?'

'Who?'

'What do you mean, who? This Di Giovanni guy, was he a general?'

'Where'd you get that idea? They were actors, both of them. Giugiù told me their living room is full of photos from the theatre and the movies. They told Giugiù they've worked with some of the biggest stars but always as . . . wait, let me look, I wrote it down here . . . always as *character actors*.'

*

Apparently they practised to stay sharp. And they would rehearse old scenes they'd played long before. Maybe they were repeating the scene that had been the biggest success of their careers, the one that had won the loudest applause . . .

No, no way. That wasn't possible; the switching of the roles made no sense. There had to be an explanation, and Montalbano wanted to know what it was. Whenever he butted up against an enigma, there was no way out. He would have to find an excuse for going and talking to the Di Giovannis.

*

The door crashed violently against the wall, giving the inspector a start and inspiring overwhelming murderous desires in him.

'Cat, I've told you a thousand times . . .'

'I'm rilly, rilly sorry, Chief, my 'and slipped.'

'What is it?'

'Orazzio Genico's 'ere, the thief, sayin' as how 'e wants a talk t'yiz poissonally in poisson. Iss possible 'e wants a toin 'isself up.'

'You mean turn himself *in*, Cat. Show him in.'

Orazio Genco came in.

'You know I didn't sleep a wink last night, Inspector?' he said immediately.

'Me neither, as far as that goes.'

'Well, just half an hour ago I was having a coffee with an old friend who got arrested by the carabinieri and put away for three years, and at one point he said to me: "They didn't even catch me red-handed! I was only rehearsing!" And the sound of that word, *rehearsing*, made me remember what was written on the piece of paper taped to the old couple's door. Now I can see it clearly: the sign said *General rehearsal*. And that was why I thought the guy might be a general.'

Montalbano thanked Orazio Genco and sent him off. A few minutes later Fazio appeared.

'You were looking for me, Chief?'

'Yes. Apparently you were out with Mimì, looking into a murder. There's just one thing I want to know: how come neither you nor Inspector Augello deigned to inform me that there'd been a murder?'

'What are you talking about, Chief? Do you know how many times we tried to call you at home? There was never any answer. Had you unplugged the telephone?'

No, he hadn't unplugged the telephone. He'd been out with a burglar, acting as his lookout.

'Tell me about this little killing, Fazio.'

*

The matter of the murder kept him busy until five o'clock that evening. Then the Di Giovanni business came back to him. And it worried him. They'd written on the door that they were doing a general rehearsal: a dress rehearsal. Which meant that the following day was opening night, when they would perform in earnest. But what, for the Di Giovannis, would the real performance be? Perhaps the enactment of what they'd rehearsed the night before – in other words, a real death and a real suicide? In alarm, he grabbed the telephone directory.

'Hello, is this the Di Giovanni home? I'm Inspector Montalbano.'

'Yes, I'm Andrea Di Giovanni, what can I do for you?'

'I would like to talk to you?'

'But what are you an inspector of?'

'The police.'

'Oh. And what do the police want from me?'

'Nothing of any importance. I'm just personally curious about something.'

'Curious about what?'

He had an idea.

'I found out entirely by chance that you were both actors.'

'That's right.'

'Well, I have a personal passion for the theatre and the cinema. I would like to know—'

'You're quite welcome to come and see us, Inspector. There isn't a single person in this town, not one, who understands the theatre.'

'Can I come to your place in about an hour, no later?'

'Whenever you like.'

※

The wife looked like an unfledged baby bird fallen from the nest, the husband like a sort of hairless, half-blind St Bernard. The apartment sparkled, and was in perfect order. They sat him down in a small armchair, while they themselves settled in one right next to the other on the sofa, their normal position when watching the television in front of them. Montalbano's eyes fell on one of the hundred or so photographs covering the walls.

'Isn't that Ruggero Ruggeri in Pirandello's *The Pleasure of Honesty*?' he asked.

And as of that moment came an avalanche of names and titles: Sem Benelli in *The Jesters' Supper* and *Six Characters in Search of an Author*, also by Pirandello, Ugo Betti in *Corruption in the Courthouse*, together with Ruggeri, Ricci, Maltagliati, Cervi, Melnati, Viarisio, Besozzi . . . The parade lasted an hour or more, by which time Montalbano was in a daze and the elderly couple delighted and rejuvenated.

There was a pause, during which Montalbano gladly accepted the glass of whisky offered him from a bottle that had apparently been bought in a hurry by Mr Di Giovanni for the occasion. When they resumed the conversation they changed the subject to movies, which the elderly couple did not hold in high regard, television even less.

'Don't you ever see what they broadcast, Inspector? Pop songs and quiz shows. It's once in a blue moon if they ever show a play, and when they do, it makes us want to cry.'

And now that the subject of performance had been exhausted, Montalbano had to ask the question for which he had come to their home.

'Last night,' he said smiling, 'I was here.'

'Here where?'

'On your landing. I'd been called by Mr Bracceri concerning a matter that turned out to be of no importance. You'd forgotten to close your door and I took the liberty of closing it.'

'Ah, so it was you.'

'Yes, I'm sorry if I made too much noise. But there was something I was curious about. There was a piece of paper attached to your door with a drawing pin, if I recall, with the words: *General rehearsal.*'

He smiled and assumed a distracted expression.

'Were you rehearsing anything interesting?'

They both became suddenly very serious and drew even closer to each other. And with the most natural of gestures, one they must have repeated thousands of times, they held hands and looked at each other. Then Andrea Di Giovanni said:

'We were rehearsing our death.'

And as Montalbano sat there, frozen, he added:

'But we're not working from a script, unfortunately.'

And now the wife spoke up.

'When we got married, I was nineteen and Giovanni was twenty-two. We've always been together and never accepted jobs with different companies. And for that reason we sometimes went hungry. Then, when we got too old to work any more, we retired here.'

The husband continued.

'For some time now we haven't been well. We're just getting old, we thought. But then we went to the doctor's. Our hearts are a shambles. When it comes time to part, it will be sudden and inevitable. And so we decided to start rehearsing. Whoever goes first will not be alone in the afterlife.'

'The best thing would be to die together, at the same

instant,' she said. 'But it's unlikely we'll be granted that favour.'

*

She was wrong. Eight months later, Montalbano read two lines in the newspaper. Mrs Di Giovanni died peacefully in her sleep, and Andrea, realizing this upon awakening, had rushed to the phone to call for help. But halfway between the bed and the phone, his heart stopped.

AMORE

Born to parents who had trouble making ends meet – her mother washed the stairs at the town hall, while her father, a seasonal worker in the countryside, was blinded by a hand grenade left over from the war – Michela Prestìa got more and more beautiful as she began to grow up. The threadbare clothes she wore, little more than rags but very clean, couldn't hide the gift from God that lay beneath them. A brunette with dark eyes always shining as if happy to be alive despite her poverty, she had learned only to read and write. She dreamed of becoming a salesgirl in one of those great department stores she found so fascinating. At fifteen, already fully developed, she ran away from home with a man who wandered from town to town in a small truck selling kitchenware: glasses, dishes, cutlery. When she returned a year later, her father and mother acted as if nothing had happened, or rather, they acted as if they had another mouth to feed. In the five years that followed, many were the men in Vigàta, single as well as married, who went with her and then dropped her, or were dropped by her, though always without fuss or quarrels. Michela's vitality was able to accommodate change, to make it seem natural. At twenty-two she moved in with the elderly Dr Pisciotta, who made her his mistress, showering her with gifts and money. But the good life lasted only three years for Michela. After the doctor died in her arms, the young widow got mixed up with lawyers who took away everything the old man had given her, leaving her destitute and crazy. Less than six months later, Michela met an accountant named Saverio Moscato. At first it seemed an affair like all the rest, but soon it became clear around town that things were very different this time.

Saverio Moscato, a clerk at the cement works, was a good-looking man of thirty, the son of an engineer and a Latin teacher. Though very attached to his family, he didn't hesitate to leave the fold the moment his parents let him know what they thought of his relationship with a girl who was a favourite subject of the town gossips. Without a word, Saverio rented a flat by the harbour and moved in with Michela. They were happy. Saverio had not only his salary to live on, but some land and shops an uncle had left to him. Yet what surprised people most was Michela's behaviour. Having always shown herself to be free and independent, she only had eyes for Saverio now. She hung on his every word, did everything he said, and never rebelled. And Saverio repaid her in kind, attentive to her every desire, even those expressed not aloud but with a mere glance. When they went out for a stroll or to the movies, they walked together so tightly embraced that it looked as if they were saying goodbye and would never see each other again. And they would kiss whenever they could, and even when they couldn't.

'No doubt about it,' said Smecca, the land surveyor, who had briefly been Michela's lover. 'They're in love. And if you really want to know, I'm glad. I hope it lasts. Michela's a good girl, she deserves it.'

*

Having done everything humanly possible not to absent himself from Vigàta and leave Michela's side, Saverio Moscato finally had to go to the cement works at Milan and stay there for about ten days. Before leaving, he went to see his only friend, Pietro Sanfilippo, who found him desperate.

'First of all,' his friend comforted him, 'ten days is not eternity.'

'For me and Michela it is.'

'Then why not take her with you?'

'She doesn't want to come. She's never been outside Sicily. She says a big city like Milan would only frighten her, unless she stayed with me the whole time. But I can't have that. I have to go to meetings, see people . . .'

*

During Saverio's stay in Milan, Michela never left the house and wasn't seen about town. But the strange thing was that when Saverio returned, the girl no longer appeared at his side. Perhaps the time her love was away had made her unwell or depressed.

A month after Saverio Moscato's return, Michela's mother came in to see Inspector Salvo Montalbano of Vigàta police. But it wasn't maternal concerns that had brought her there.

'My daughter Michela missed the monthly payment she usually gives me.'

'She gives you money?'

'She certainly does. Every month. A hundred euros, two hundred, depending. She's always been a responsible daughter.'

'And what do you want from me?'

'Well, I went to see Saverio Moscato, the man she lives with. He said Michela doesn't live there any more. Says she was gone when he got back from Milan. He even showed me the rooms. Her things are all gone. There's nothing, no clothing, not even a pair of panties.'

She blushed.

'What did Moscato say? How did he explain her disappearance?'

'He had no explanation for it. He said maybe Michela,

being the way she was, had run away with another man. But I don't believe it.'

'Why not?'

''Cause she was in love with Moscato.'

'And what do you want me to do?'

'Oh, I dunno . . . Go and talk to him, maybe he'll tell you what really happened.'

*

To avoid giving an official cast to the questions he wanted to ask him, Montalbano waited until he ran into Moscato by chance. One afternoon he saw him sitting alone at a table at the Castiglione cafe, drinking a mint tea.

'Hello, I'm Inspector Montalbano.'

'I know.'

'I'd like to talk with you a minute.'

'Please sit down. Would you like anything?'

'I wouldn't mind some cassata ice cream.'

The accountant ordered the ice cream.

'What can I do for you, Inspector?'

'I feel a bit awkward mentioning this, Mr Moscato, but the other day Michela Prestìa's mother came to see me. She says her daughter has disappeared.'

'That's exactly right.'

'Could you explain a little better?'

'For what reason?'

'You live, or used to live, with Michela Prestìa, didn't you?'

'I wasn't referring to myself. I was asking why you, Inspector Montalbano, were interested in the matter.'

'Well, since her mother came to see—'

'Michela's an adult, I think, and free to do whatever she feels like. She left. It's as simple as that.'

'Well, I'm sorry, but I'd like to know more about it.'

'I had to go to Milan for business, and she didn't want to come with me. She claimed that big cities like Milan frightened her, made her feel uneasy. Now I think it was just an excuse to be left alone so she could prepare her escape. Whatever the case, the first week I was away, we spoke every day, in the morning and at night. On the morning of the eighth day, she said she was in a bad mood. She said . . . she couldn't stand to be away from me any more. When I called back that night, she didn't answer. But I didn't worry. I assumed she'd taken a sleeping pill. The next morning the same thing happened, and I started to worry. I called a friend of mine, Pietro Sanfilippo, and told him to go and have a look. He called me back a little while later and said the house was locked up. He said he knocked a long time but nobody answered. I thought she must be ill or something. So I called my father, who I'd given an extra set of keys before leaving. He unlocked the door, but found nothing. Not only was there no trace of Michela, but all her belongings were gone. Even her lipstick.'

'And what did you do then?'

'Do you really want to know? I started to cry.'

*

But why, then, as he was talking about his beloved's disappearance and his tears of despair, was there not only no sadness in his eyes, but something rather like a glimmer of contentment? He was trying, of course, to assume the proper expression for the occasion, but he wasn't entirely succeeding. Out of the ash he was trying to spread over his gaze, a flame of joy leapt treacherously forth.

*

'My dear Inspector,' said Pietro Sanfilippo, 'what do you want me to say? I'm at a loss. Just to give you an idea, when Saverio came back from Milan, I requested a three-day leave from work. You can ask at the office, if you don't believe me. I thought he'd be desperate after Michela ran away, so I wanted to be at his side every minute. I was afraid he might do something stupid. He was too much in love. So I went to Montelusa station, but when he got off the train, he was cool as a cucumber. I was expecting to see him wailing and weeping, and instead . . .'

'Instead?'

'As we were driving back to Vigàta from Montelusa, he started singing softly to himself. He's always liked opera and actually has a pretty good voice. He was singing "*Tu che a Dio spiegasti l'ali*". It sent chills down my spine. I thought it must be shock. That evening we went out for dinner together, and he was perfectly calm and untroubled as he ate. I decided to go back to work the next day.'

'Did you talk about Michela?'

'Are you joking? It was as if the woman had never existed!'

'Do you know if they'd had some sort of quarrel?'

'Are you joking? They were always in love, always in agreement.'

'Were they jealous of each other?'

'She wasn't. He was, but in his own kind of way.'

'What do you mean?'

'I mean he wasn't jealous of Michela's present life, but of her past.'

'Nasty stuff.'

'Yeah. It's the worst kind of jealousy. There's no cure for it. One evening, when he was in a particularly bad mood, he came out with something I'll never forget: "Everyone's always got everything they wanted from Michela," he said "There's nothing new, nothing pure, left for her to give me." I wanted to tell him that if that's how he felt, he'd really picked the wrong woman. She had too much of a past. But I decided it was better to keep quiet.'

'Mr Sanfilippo, you were Saverio's friend even before he met Michela, weren't you?'

'Of course. We're the same age; we've known each other since elementary school.'

'Think hard. If we look at the time with Michela as an interlude, do you notice any difference in your friend before and after?'

Pietro Sanfilippo thought hard.

'Saverio's never been very open about his feelings. He's the quiet type, and often moody. The few times he's looked happy to me were when he was with Michela. Now he's more closed than ever. He avoids even me. At the weekend he goes out to the country.'

'Does he have a house in the country?'

'Yes, around Belmonte, in Trapani province. His uncle left it to him. Until now, he never wanted to set foot in the place. But tell me something.'

'If I can . . .'

'Why are you so interested in Michela's disappearance?'

'Her mother asked me to look into it.'

'That woman doesn't give a damn. She's only interested in the spare cash Michela used to pass on to her!'

'Don't you think that's a good reason?'

'Look, Inspector, I'm not stupid. You're asking more questions about Saverio than about Michela.'

'You want me to level with you? I have a suspicion.'

'About what?'

'I have the strange impression that your friend Saverio was expecting it. And that maybe, just maybe, he even knew the man Michela ran off with.'

Pietro Sanfilippo took the bait. Montalbano congratulated himself for improvising a convincing reply. How could he tell him that what bothered and perplexed him was a bright flame in Saverio Moscato's eyes?

*

The inspector didn't want any of his men to get involved in this. He was afraid to look ridiculous. And so he went through the effort of interrogating all the tenants in Moscato's building himself. Everything about this investigation

— which wasn't even an investigation — was tenuous, if not downright non-existent, and the starting point for all his questions was as airy as a spider's web. If what Saverio Moscato told him was true, Michela had answered his phone call that morning, but not that night. Therefore, if she *had* run away, she'd done so during the day, and somebody may have noticed something.

The building had six floors, with six apartments per floor. The inspector dutifully began on the top floor. Nobody had seen or heard anything. Moscato lived on the second floor, in apartment 8. Discouraged, Montalbano rang the doorbell to apartment 5. The name-plate outside said 'Maria Costanzo, Widow Diliberto'. And it was she who answered the door, a little old lady, neatly dressed, with sharp, penetrating eyes.

'What do you want?'

'Montalbano's the name, I'm with the police.'

'What do you want, please?'

She was impossibly deaf.

'Is there anybody home?' the inspector yelled.

'Why are you shouting?' the old lady asked, indignant. 'I'm not *that* deaf!'

Hearing the commotion, a fortyish man appeared from the one of the back rooms.

'You can talk to me; I'm her son.'

'May I come in?'

The man showed him into a small living room. The old woman sat down in an armchair in front of Montalbano.

'I don't live here; I just came to see Mamma,' the son said, just to be safe.

'As you must know by now, Michela Prestìa, who lived in apartment number eight with Saverio Moscato, disappeared without a word when Moscato was away in Milan, between the seventh and the sixteenth of May.'

The old woman gave a look of impatience.

'What's he saying, Pasqualì?'

'Wait,' Pasquale Diliberto said in a normal voice. Apparently his mother was accustomed to reading his lips.

'What I'd like to know is whether your mother, during this period, saw or noticed anything that—'

'I've already asked her. Mama doesn't know anything about Michela's disappearance.'

'But I *do!*' said the old woman. 'I saw him. I even told you. But you say it's not true.'

'Whom did you see, ma'am?'

'Inspector, I should warn you,' said the son. 'My mother is not only deaf, she's not really right in the head.'

'Oh, so I'm not right in the head, eh?' said Maria Costanzo, widow of Augusto Diliberto, springing to her feet. 'You horrible, wretched son! How dare you insult me in front of strangers like that!'

And she left the small living room, slamming the door behind her.

'*You* tell me about it,' Montalbano said sternly.

'The thirteenth of May is Mamma's birthday. That evening, my wife and I came to see her. We had dinner together, then some cake and a few glasses of Spumante. At eleven we went home. Now, my mother claims, maybe because she sort of overdid it with the cake – she's a bit of glutton, you know – that she couldn't sleep that night. Around three o'clock in the morning, she actually remembered that she forgot to take the rubbish out. When she opened the front door, she noticed that the hall light was burnt out. She says that in front of apartment number eight, which is opposite ours, she saw a man with a big suitcase. And she thought he looked like Moscato. But I said: "Do you realize, woman, what you're saying? Saverio Moscato didn't come back from Milan until three days later!"'

*

'Inspector,' said Angelo Liotta, manager of the cement works, 'I checked all the things you asked me to. Our accountant Moscato duly presented me with his plane tickets and lists of out-of-pocket expenses. So here's what I've got: he left Sunday, from Palermo airport, at 6.30 p.m., on a flight for Milan. He spent that night at the Hotel Excelsior and stayed there until the morning of the seventeenth, when he returned on the 7.30 a.m. flight out of Milan's Linate Airport. And it looks like he attended all the meetings and made all the contacts he went to Milan for. If you have any other questions, I'm at your service.'

'Thank you, you've been very thorough.'

'Moscato's a good, hard-working man, I admire him for that. I hope he's not in any kind of trouble.'

'I hope so, too.'

As soon as the man left, the inspector picked up the envelope with all the receipts from Moscato's business trip, which the manager had left for him on his desk. Without opening it, he put it in a drawer.

With this gesture, he signed off on an investigation that had never been an investigation.

*

Six months later, he got a phone call. At first he didn't recognize the man at the other end.

'What was the name, sorry?'

'Angelo Liotta. Remember? I'm the manager of the cement works. You called me into the station to ask—'

'Ah, yes, of course I remember. What can I do for you?'

'Well, we're closing the books for the financial year, and I need the receipts I left with you.'

What was he talking about? Then Montalbano remembered the envelope he'd never opened.

'I'll get them back to you by the end of the day.'

Fearing he might forget it, he immediately took the envelope, put it on the desk, and looked at it. For reasons that were never clear to him, he opened it. He studied the receipts one by one, then put them back in the envelope. Leaning back in his chair, he closed his eyes for a few minutes, thinking. Then he took the receipts out again and put them in order on his desk, one after the other. The first one on the left, which was dated 4 May, was for filling up the petrol tank; the last slip of paper on the right was a train ticket, dated 17 May, from Palermo to Montelusa. It didn't add up. This meant that Saverio Moscato must have driven from Vigàta to the airport in his car and, when his business trip was over, returned to Vigàta by train. And Pietro Sanfilippo's testimony in fact confirmed that he'd returned by train. The question, then, was very simple: who brought Moscato's car back to Vigàta when he was away in Milan?

✶

'Mr Sanfilippo? Montalbano here. I need some information. When your friend Moscato drove to the airport to catch his flight for Milan, were you in the car with him?'

'Is that still on your mind, Inspector? Did you know that since we spoke, several different people have come to town claiming they've seen Michela in Milan, Paris, even London? Anyway, no, I wasn't in the car with him, but I think you're on the wrong track. If he came back on the train, how could he have gone there in his car? And Michela couldn't have driven him there, either, since she didn't know how to drive.'

'How's your friend doing?'

'Saverio? I haven't seen him for a long time. He left his job at the cement works and gave up his apartment in town.'

'Do you know where he went?'

'Of course. He's living in the country, in that house in Trapani province around Belmonte. I wanted to go visit him, but he made it clear that . . .'

But the inspector was no longer listening. Belmonte, Sanfilippo had said. And indeed, printed in the upper

left-hand corner of the filling-station receipt were the words:
'Pagano-Belmonte Service Station (TR).'

*

He stopped at that very same service station to ask what
road to take to Saverio Moscato's house, and was duly
informed. It was a small, modest house, but well-maintained
and completely isolated. The man who came to the door
only vaguely resembled the Saverio Moscato he had met.
Poorly dressed, in haphazard fashion, and wearing a long
beard, Moscato barely seemed to recognize the inspector.
And his eyes, which Montalbano studied closely, had
entirely lost their flame. Now there was only black ash. The
man showed him into a very modest dining room.

'I was just passing through,' Montalbano began.

But he didn't go on. The other had practically forgotten
about him and just stood there staring at his hands. Through
the window Montalbano could see the back garden: a rose
bed, flowers, and plants, contrasting strangely with the rest
of the stark landscape. He stood up and went into the
garden. Right in the middle was a big white stone, hemmed
in by countless rosebushes. Montalbano bent over the little
enclosure and touched the stone with his hand. Moscato, too,
had come outside. Montalbano could sense him standing
behind him.

'This is where you buried her, isn't it?'

He asked the question softly, without raising his voice.
And just as softly came the answer he hoped for and feared.

'Yes.'

*

'That Friday, in the afternoon, Michela wanted us to come
here, to Belmonte.'

'Had she ever been here before?'

'Once, and she liked it a lot. I could never say no to her,
no matter what she asked. We decided to spend all day

Saturday here, then on Sunday I was going to drive her back to Vigàta in the morning and take the train to Palermo in the afternoon. Saturday was a fantastic day, better than any we'd ever spent together. In the evening, after dinner, we went straight to bed and made love. Then we had a cigarette and started talking.'

'What did you talk about?'

'Well, that's just it, Inspector. She brought up a certain subject.'

'What subject was that?'

'It's hard to explain. I used to reproach her . . . No, "reproach" isn't the right word . . . I used to regret the fact that, because of the life she led before we met, she was no longer able to give me anything she hadn't already given to someone else.'

'But as far as Michela was concerned, the same was true of you!'

Saverio Moscato gave him a blank look, speechless, ashen-eyed.

'Me?! I'd never slept with a woman before Michela!'

Strangely, without knowing why, the inspector felt embarrassed.

'After a while she went into the kitchen, stayed there five minutes, then returned. She was smiling. Then she lay back down beside me. She held me very tight and said she was about to give me something that she'd never given anyone else, and that no one else could ever have again. I asked her what it was, but she wanted to make love again. Only afterwards did she tell me what this thing was. It was her death. She'd poisoned herself.'

'And what did you do?'

'Nothing, Inspector. I held her hands in mine. And she never once took her eyes off me. It was over quickly. I don't think she suffered much.'

'Don't kid yourself. And don't underestimate what

Michela did for you. Death by poison is a painful thing, I assure you!'

'That very night I dug a grave and put her where she is now. Then I left for Milan. I felt desperate and happy all at once, do you understand? One day, work was over early. It wasn't even five in the afternoon, so I got on a plane to Palermo, then got in my car, which I'd left at the airport, and drove to Vigàta. I took my time, since I didn't want to get into town until late at night. I couldn't risk anyone seeing me. I stuffed her clothes and things into a suitcase and brought it here. I've got them all upstairs, in the bedroom. When it came time to drive back to Palermo airport, my car decided not to cooperate. I hid it among those trees over there and called a taxi from Trapani to take me to the airport. I made it barely in time for the first flight out to Milan. Once my work was finished, I came back by train. For the first few days I was in a kind of daze, overjoyed that Michela had the courage to give me what she did. That's why I moved here, so I could enjoy my happiness alone with her. But then . . .'

'Then?'

'Then, one night, I woke up with a start. I couldn't feel Michela beside me any more. And to think that when I'd shut my eyes, I thought I could hear her breathing in her sleep. I called out to her, looked for her all over the house. But she wasn't there. And that's when I realized that her tremendous gift had really cost a lot. Too much.'

He started crying, without sobs, silent tears running down his face.

Montalbano stared at a lizard that had climbed to the top of the white tombstone. It basked in the sunlight, motionless.

THE ARTIST'S TOUCH

The ringing of the telephone was not the ringing of the telephone, but the sound of a drill being applied by a crazed dentist bent on boring a hole in Montalbano's head. He opened his eyes with great effort and looked at the alarm clock on the bedside table: five-thirty in the morning. It must surely be one of his men at the station trying to reach him to tell him something important. It couldn't be anyone else, given the hour. He got up out of bed, cursing the saints, went into the dining room, and picked up the receiver.

'Salvo, do you know Potocki?'

He recognized the voice of his friend Nicolò Zito, the newsman for the Free Channel, one of the two private television stations that broadcast in Vigàta. Nicolò wasn't the type to play stupid jokes, and so Montalbano didn't get angry.

'Do I know who?'

'Potocki, Jan Potocki.'

'Is he Polish?'

'Apparently, to judge by the name. He's supposedly the author of a famous book, but out of all the people I asked, not one was able to tell me anything. If even you don't know him, then I can just stuff it.'

Fiat lux. Maybe the inspector could answer his friend's unlikely question after all.

'Do you know by any chance if the book's title is *Manuscript Found at Saragossa*?'

'That's it! Shit, Salvo, you're a god! And have you read the book?'

'Yes, many years ago.'

'Can you tell me what it's about?'

'But why are you so interested in it?'

'Alberto Larussa, whom you knew well, has committed suicide. His body was found around four o'clock this morning and I was dragged out of bed to cover the story.'

The inspector felt upset. He wasn't particularly close to Alberto Larussa, but still he used to go and see him every now and then, when invited to his house in Ragona, never missing an opportunity to borrow a few books from his friend's vast library.

'Did he shoot himself?'

'Who? Alberto Larussa? Do you think he would choose such a banal way to kill himself!'

'So how did he do it?'

'He turned his wheelchair into an electric chair. In a sense he executed himself.'

'So what's the book got to do with it?'

'It was right there beside the electric chair, on a stool. It's probably the last thing he read.'

'That's right, we spoke about it. He liked it a lot.'

'So who was this Potocki?'

'He was born in the late eighteenth century to a military family. He himself was a scholar and a traveller. I think he went from Morocco to Mongolia. The Tsar made him an adviser. He published some ethnological studies. There was a group of islands, I forget where, that were named after him. The novel you asked me about he wrote in French. And that's about all I know.'

'So why was he so into this book?'

'I told you, Nicolò: he liked it, so he read and reread it. I think he considered Potocki a sort of kindred soul.'

'But he never set foot outside his house!'

'A kindred soul in terms of eccentricity and originality. And at any rate, Potocki also committed suicide.'

'How?'

'He shot himself.'

'That doesn't seem very original. Larussa topped that.'

*

Given Alberto Larussa's notoriety, the morning news was reported by Nicolò Zito, who usually limited himself to the more widely watched evening edition. He devoted the first part of his report to the circumstances that led to the discovery of the body and to the manner in which the suicide was carried out. At around 3.30 a.m. the previous night, Martino Zìcari, a hunter, had noticed smoke coming out of a small basement window of Larussa's house when passing by. Since it was well known that that was Alberto Larussa's workshop, Zìcari at first was not alarmed. When a gust of wind let him get a whiff of the smoke, however, he did grow alarmed. And so he called the carabinieri, who, after knocking with no results, broke down the door. In the basement they found the half-charred, lifeless body of Alberto Larussa, who had quite cleverly turned his wheelchair into a perfect electric chair. Later a short circuit occurred, leading to the fire that devastated part of the house. Escaping the flames unscathed, however, was a stool beside the body, with the novel by Jan Potocki on it. At this point Nicolò Zito mentioned some of the things Montalbano had told him, then he apologized to viewers for giving only outside shots of Larussa's house, since the marshal of the carabinieri had forbidden all filming inside.

The second part of the report was used to give the suicide victim's background. Alberto Larussa was fifty years old and wealthy, but had been paralysed thirty years earlier when he fell from a horse. He never ventured beyond the walls of his native city of Ragona and had never married. He had a younger brother who lived in Palermo. A passionate reader, he possessed a library of over ten thousand books. After his fall, he'd discovered, entirely by chance, his true vocation: that of jeweller. But a very particular kind of jeweller: he used only cheap materials – iron and copper wire, coloured glass of various hues. And yet the design of this cheap jewellery was always highly inventive and elegant, so that the articles became veritable works of art. Larussa didn't sell them, but gave them away as presents to friends and people he liked. To help himself in his work, he had turned his basement into a highly equipped workshop – where, in the end, he killed himself, leaving no explanation whatsoever.

Montalbano turned the TV off and called up Livia, hoping to find her still at home in Boccadasse, a suburb of Genoa. She was there, and he told her the news. She had known Larussa, and they were fond of each other. Every Christmas Alberto would send her one of his creations as a present. Livia was not a woman who cried easily, but Montalbano could hear her voice cracking.

'But why did he do it? He never seemed like the kind of person who would do anything like that.'

*

At around three o'clock that afternoon, the inspector rang Nicolò.

'Any new developments?'

'Well, yes, quite a few. Larussa's workshop had a 380 tri-phase electrical system. He took all his clothes off, strapped bracelets around his ankles and wrists, a large metal band around his chest, and a kind of headset to his temples. And to increase the effect of the electrical charge, he stuck his feet into a basin full of water. He wanted to be sure. Naturally, he'd made all these gadgets himself with saintly patience.'

'Do you know how he managed to turn on the current? I'm under the impression he was bound hand and foot.'

'The fire chief told me there was a timer. Brilliant, no? Oh, and he'd also downed a bottle of whisky.'

'Did you know he was a teetotaller?'

'No.'

'I want to tell you something that occurred to me just now as you were telling me about the gadgets he'd created to conduct the electrical current. There's an explanation for why he'd left the novel by Potocki beside him.'

'So, will you finally tell me what's in this damn book?'

'No, because it's not the novel itself that's of interest to our case, but the author.'

'Meaning?'

'I remembered how Potocki killed himself.'

'But you've already told me! He shot himself!'

'Yes, but in those days they used muzzle-loading pistols, only one bullet at a time.'

'So?'

'Three years before checking out, Potocki had unscrewed the ball from the lid of a silver teapot of his. He spent a few hours each day filing it down, and it took him three years to give it the right circumference. Then he had it blessed, stuffed it into the barrel of his pistol, and killed himself.'

'Christ! This morning I'd declared Larussa the winner in terms of originality, but now I'd say he and Potocki are about even. So that book, in short, was left there as a sort of message, as if to say, "I've killed myself in extravagant fashion, like my teacher Potocki."'

'Let's say that might be the meaning of it.'

'Why do you say "might be"?'

'Because I honestly don't know.'

*

The following day it was Nicolò's turn to call him. He had something interesting to show the inspector on Larussa's suicide, which continued to spark curiosity because of the imaginative way it was carried out, and so Montalbano went to the Free Channel studios to see what it was. Nicolò had interviewed Giuseppe Zaccaria, who was the administrator of Larussa's holdings, as well as Carabinieri Lieutenant Olcese, who was conducting the investigation. Zaccaria, a Palermo businessman, was surly and rude.

'I'm under no obligation to answer your questions.'

'Of course you're not. I was simply asking whether you'd be so kind as to—'

'Oh, just fuck yourself, you and your television station!'

Zaccaria turned his back and was about to leave.

'Is it true that Larussa had an estate estimated at fifty billion lire?'

It was clearly a bluff on Zito's part, but Zaccaria fell for it. He turned around in a huff, enraged.

'And who fed you that pile of crap?'

'According to my sources—'

'Listen, the late Mr Larussa was rich, but not that kind of rich. He owned stocks and other investments but, I repeat, nothing like the figure you just blurted out.'

'And who will get the inheritance?'

'Don't you know he has a younger brother?'

Lieutenant Olcese was a six-foot-five beanpole. Polite but cold as ice.

'The only new information that has emerged, all of it, points to a suicide. Certainly a very elaborate, fanciful suicide, but a suicide nonetheless. Even his brother—' Lieutenant Olcese suddenly broke off. 'That's all, thank you,' he said.

'You were saying that his brother . . .'

'That's all, thank you.'

Montalbano looked at his friend Nicolò.

'Why did you ask me to come here? Those two interviews don't seem to reveal anything!'

'I decided to keep you abreast of everything. Anyway, you don't convince me, Salvo. This suicide doesn't smell right to you, I can feel it.'

'It's not that it doesn't smell right; it just makes me uneasy.'

'You want to talk about it?'

'Sure, we can talk. At any rate, the case isn't in my hands. But you have to promise me that you won't just use what I say for your news reports.'

'Promise.'

'When I talked to Livia about it on the phone she said that she didn't think Larussa was the type to commit suicide. And I have a lot of faith in Livia's sensitivity.'

'Good God, Salvo! The ingeniousness of the makeshift electric chair has all the hallmarks of an eccentric like Larussa! It's practically got his trademark on it!'

'And that's exactly what makes me uneasy. Are you aware that after the rumour of the wonderful works of art he created began to spread, he never once agreed to give an interview to any of the fashion magazines that were pressuring him?'

'He wouldn't give me one either, the one time I asked him. He was unsociable.'

'Right, he was unsociable. And when the Mayor of Ragona wanted to sponsor an exhibition of his work for charity, what did he do? He refused, but sent the mayor a cheque for twenty million lire.'

'That's right.'

'And then there's that novel by Potocki he left out for everyone to see – another touch of exhibitionism. No, none of this stuff fits with his usual way of doing things.'

They looked at each other in silence.

'You should try to interview this younger brother of his,' the inspector suggested.

*

On the eight o'clock news report, Nicolò Zito broadcast the two interviews of which he'd given Montalbano an advance screening. When the Free Channel newscast was over, the inspector switched to the evening news report of TeleVigàta, the other local station, which began at eight-thirty. The opening story was, naturally, the suicide of Alberto Larussa. There again was Carabinieri Lieutenant Olcese, being interviewed by Simone Prestìa, Galluzzo's brother-in-law, who worked for the television station.

'The only new information that has emerged,' the lieutenant declared, using exactly the same words as in his interview with Nicolò Zito, 'all of it, points to a suicide. Certainly a very elaborate, fanciful suicide, but a suicide nonetheless.'

Damn, what an imaginative guy this lieutenant is! thought the inspector, but then the officer continued.

'Even his brother . . .' and then he suddenly broke off, before adding, 'That's all, thank you.'

'You were saying that even his brother . . .'

'That's all, thank you,' said Lieutenant Olcese. And he walked stiffly away. Montalbano sat there with his mouth open. Then, since the footage had shown only the lieutenant, with Prestìa's voice coming from off-camera, he began to suspect that Zito had passed his interview on to Prestìa. Journalists sometimes did each other these sorts of favours.

Montalbano rang Zito.

'Did you give Prestìa your interview with Olcese?'

'Not on your life!'

He hung up, pensive. What did that bit of play-acting mean? Maybe the towering Lieutenant Olcese wasn't as stupid as he was trying to appear.

But what could be the purpose of this scenario?

There could only be one: to put the journalists onto the suicide victim's brother. To what end? Whatever the case, one thing was certain: the suicide didn't smell right to the lieutenant, either. There was no getting around it.

*

For three whole days Nicolò, Prestìa, and a host of other journalists were on the trail of Larussa's brother in Palermo, whose name was Giacomo, but never once managed to track him down. They took up positions outside his house and in front of the school where he taught Latin. No luck. He seemed to have become invisible. Then the school's headmaster, besieged with requests, made up his mind to announce that Mr Larussa had taken a ten-day leave. He didn't even appear at his brother's funeral (which was held in a church: rich people who commit suicide are always considered insane and therefore absolved of their sin). It was a funeral like any other, which triggered a hazy memory in Montalbano's brain. He phoned Livia.

'I think I remember that one day, when we went to visit Alberto Larussa together, he spoke to you about the kind of funeral he would like to have. Do you remember?'

'Of course! He was kidding, but not entirely. He took me into his studio and showed me the drawings he'd made.'

'Drawings of what?'

'Of his funeral. You wouldn't believe the hearse, with weeping angels six feet tall, cherubs, and stuff like that. All mahogany and gold. He said that when the time was right, he would have it specially made. He'd even designed the uniforms that the wreath-bearers would wear. And I can't even begin to describe the casket: something probably on a par with the pharaohs.'

'How odd.'

'What?'

'That somebody so reclusive as him, practically a loner, would dream of having a funeral fit for a pharaoh, as you put it, something so exhibitionistic.'

'Yeah, I thought it was strange at the time too. But he said that death was such a total transformation that, after we die, we might as well show ourselves as the exact opposite of what we were when we were alive.'

✲

A week later Nicolò Zito broadcast a veritable scoop. He'd managed to video the objects that Alberto Larussa had created in his workshop for the purpose of killing himself: four bracelets, two for the ankles and two for the wrists; a copper band a good three inches wide, which he'd strapped around his chest; and a sort of headset where instead of earphones there were two rectangular metal plates to be placed at the temples. Montalbano saw it on the midnight edition of the news. He immediately called up Nicolò; he wanted a copy of the tape. Zito promised to get him one by the following morning.

'But why are you so interested in those things?'

'Did you get a good look at them, Nicolò? Those are things that you or I could make, except that we don't know how. Those objects are so crude that not even the *vo' cumprà* would bother to peddle them on the beach. An artist like Alberto Larussa would never have used anything like that, not in a million years – he would have felt ashamed to be found dead with such poorly made objects attached to his body.'

'So then what does it mean, in your opinion?'

'In my opinion, it means that Alberto Larussa did not commit suicide. He was murdered, and whoever killed him set things up to look like the manner of his suicide was consistent with Larussa's eccentricity and originality.'

'Maybe we should inform Lieutenant Olcese.'

'You know what?'

'What?'

'Lieutenant Olcese knows more about this than you and me put together.'

*

In fact, Lieutenant Olcese knew so much about it that exactly twenty days after the death of Alberto Larussa, he arrested his brother, Giacomo. That same evening, the Free Channel newscast featured an interview with the assistant prosecutor Giampaolo Boscarino, a man who was keen to look good when he appeared on the air.

'Dr Boscarino, what are the charges against Giacomo Larussa?' asked Nicolò Zito, who had rushed to Palermo to cover the story.

Before replying, Boscarino smoothed out his blondish moustache, touched the knot of his tie, and ran a hand over one of lapels of his jacket.

'He is charged with the brutal murder of his brother, Alberto, which he tried to pass off as a suicide by staging a macabre spectacle.'

'How did you arrive at this conclusion?'

'Sorry, but the proceedings of investigations are sworn to secrecy.'

'Can you tell us anything at all?'

Boscarino ran his hand over his lapel again, touched the knot of his tie, and smoothed out his blondish moustache.

'Giacomo Larussa clearly contradicted himself several times. The investigation brilliantly carried out by Lieutenant Olcese also brought to light a number of elements that further compromise Mr Larussa's position.'

He smoothed out his blondish moustache, touched the knot of his tie, and then the face of Nicolò Zito appeared.

'We were also able to interview Mr Filippo Alaimo, of Ragona, a pensioner of seventy-five whose testimony has been considered crucial by the prosecution.'

The screen filled with a full shot of a very thin peasant with a large dog curled up at his feet.

'I'm Filippo Alaimo, that's right. You should know, Mr Newsman, that I have insomnia an' can't sleep at night. I'm Filippo Alaimo—'

'You've already told us that,' said Zito's voice off-camera.

'So what the hell was I sayin'? Ah yes. So, since I can't sleep, when I don' feel like stayin' inside no more, I wake up the dog an' take 'im out for a walk, no matter what time o' the night. An' so the dog, whose name is Pirì, when 'e's woke up inna middle o' the night, well, 'e gets a li'l annoyed.'

'What does the dog do?' Nicolò asked, still off camera.

'I'd like t' see whachoo'd do, Mr Newsman, if somebody woke you up inna middle o' the night and made you go out an' walk fer two hours! Woun't you get annoyed? Well, so does the dog. An' so Pirì, soon as 'e sees somp'n move – don' matter if iss a man, anamal, or car – well, 'e goes after it.'

'And that's what happened on the night of the thirteenth, is that correct?' Nicolò cut in, probably fearing that if he let the man go on, viewers wouldn't understand a thing any more. 'You were near the home of Alberto Larussa, the deceased, when you saw a car come out of his gate at high speed . . .'

'Yessir, 'ass right. Juss like you say. So the car come out, Pirì wen' after it, an' that idiot behind the wheel run over my dog. Look at this, Mister Newsman.'

Filippo Alaimo bent down, grabbed the dog by the collar and lifted him up. The animal's hind legs were wrapped in bandages.

'What time was it, Mr Alaimo?'

'Le'ss say it was roundabout two-thirty, three o'clock inna mornin'.'

'And what did you do?'

'I started yellin' after the car an' sayin' 'e was a fuckin' idiot. An' I took down 'is licence plate.'

Nicolò Zito's face reappeared on screen.

'According to reliable sources, the licence plate number jotted down by Mr Alaimo corresponds to that of Giacomo Larussa. The question now is: what was Giacomo Larussa doing at his brother's house in the middle of the night, especially since it was well known that relations between the two siblings were not good? Let us put the question to Gaspare Palillo, the lawyer who has taken on the task of defending the suspect.'

Fat and pink, Palillo looked exactly like one of the three little pigs.

'Before answering your question, I would like to ask you one myself. May I?'

'Please go ahead.'

'Who advised the supposed witness Filippo Alaimo not to wear the glasses he usually wears? This seventy-five-year-old pensioner has a myopia of minus eight in both eyes and very limited vision. And at two-thirty in the morning, by the faint light of a streetlamp, he's able to read the licence-plate number of a fast-moving car? Come on! Now, as for your question, it should be pointed out that over the last month of the deceased's life, relations between the two brothers had improved, so much so that my client went to his brother's house in Ragona no less than three times over the course of that month. And I should further point out that it was the suicide victim himself who had initiated this reconciliation, telling my client on several occasions that he could no longer stand the loneliness, that he felt very depressed and in need of his brother's comfort. It's true that my client went to Ragona on the thirteenth, stayed for a few hours with his brother, who seemed even more depressed than usual, and then headed back for Palermo before supper-time, around 8 p.m. He learned of his brother's suicide the following day, when he heard it reported on a local radio station.'

*

In the days following Alberto's death, the sort of things that usually emerge in cases like these began to emerge.

Michele Ruoppolo of Palermo declared that as he was heading home around 4 a.m. on the morning of the four-teenth, he saw Giacomo Larussa's car pulling in. Normally it takes two hours at the most to drive from Ragona to Palermo. If Giacomo Larussa had left his brother's house at 8 p.m., how did it take him eight hours to get home?

Palillo the lawyer retorted that Giacomo Larussa had returned home at 10 p.m. but had been unable to fall asleep because he was so worried about his brother. And so around 3 a.m. he'd gone out again, got in his car, and gone for a drive along the seafront.

Arcangelo Bonocore of Ragona swore by all that was holy that around 6 p.m. on the evening of the thirteenth, as he was passing by near the home of Alberto Larussa, he'd heard yelling and loud noises inside, as if from a violent altercation.

Palillo the lawyer said that his client remembered the moment well. There was no altercation. At one point Alberto Larussa had turned on the television to watch a programme he liked called *The Marshal*. In that episode there was a violent brawl between two characters. Palillo could even produce a video recording of that broadcast episode, if need be. Mr Bonocore was mistaken.

*

Things went on in this fashion for another week, until Lieutenant Olcese pulled out the ace he'd been keeping up his sleeve, something that Prosecutor Boscarino had already hinted at. Right after they'd found the body – the lieutenant said – he'd ordered his men to look for a sheet of paper, anything written that might explain the motivation for such a gruesome act. But they didn't find anything, because Alberto Larussa had nothing to explain, inasmuch as the idea of committing suicide never even passed through his mind. To make up for this, in the first drawer on the left-hand side of his desk – unlocked, Olcese emphasized – they found an envelope in plain view, on which was written: *To be opened after my death.* And since Mr Larussa was dead – the lieutenant explained with a logic worthy of Monsieur La Palisse – they opened it. Just a couple of handwritten lines: *I leave everything I own, stocks, shares, land, houses, and other properties to my beloved younger brother Giacomo.* Followed by his

signature. There was no date. It was precisely the lack of
date that aroused the lieutenant's suspicion, and so he submitted the testament to both chemical and graphological
tests. The chemical examination revealed that the letter had
been written one month earlier at the most, given the particular type of ink used, which was the same as the one
normally used by Alberto Larussa. The graphological test,
conducted by the court of Palermo's handwriting expert,
gave an unequivocal result: that the handwriting of Alberto
Larussa had been skilfully falsified.

This business of the fake testament did not go down
easy with Palillo the lawyer.

'I know the scenario the people conducting the investigation have in their heads. My client pays a call on his
brother, somehow knocks him unconscious, writes up the
will himself, goes to his car and gets the stuff for the mock
self-execution, which he's had made by someone in Palermo,
carries his unconscious brother into the workshop (which he
knows well and has even admitted so, since Alberto often
received him there), and sets up the whole macabre *mise en
scène*. But I ask myself then: what need was there to write
up a false testament when a will already existed, duly registered, which said the same things? Let me state that as
clearly as possible: the last will and testament of Angelo
Larussa, father of Alberto and Giacomo, went as follows:
"I leave all my possessions, movable and immovable, to
my eldest son Alberto. Upon his death, all possessions will
pass on to my younger son, Giacomo." So I ask myself: *Cui
prodest?* Who stood to gain anything from that pointless
second testament?'

Montalbano heard Olcese's and the lawyer Palillo's
statements on the midnight news broadcast, when he was
already in his underwear and about to go to bed. They upset
him and he no longer felt like sleeping. It was an exceptionally quiet night, and so, still in his underpants, he went for
a walk along the water's edge. The second testament made

no sense. Though he considered Larussa's brother guilty, he
sensed something excessive in the concoction of that text.
Actually everything about this whole story seemed excessive.
But the phony testament was like an extra brushstroke on a
canvas, one colour too many. *Cui prodest?* Palillo the lawyer
had asked. Who stood to gain? And the answer came spon-
taneously, unstoppably, to his lips. He saw a sort of blinding
burst of light, as if a photographer had just popped a flash
in his face, and he suddenly felt his legs go weak. He had to
sit down on the wet sand.

✳

'Nicolò? Montalbano here. What were you doing?'

'Well, given the time, I was going to bed, if you don't
mind. Did you hear what Olcese said? You were right all
along: Giacomo Larussa is not only a self-interested murderer, he's a monster!'

'Listen, have you got something to write with?'

'Wait while I go and get a pen and paper. Here we are.
OK, go ahead.'

'Let me preface this, Nicolò, by saying that these are
sensitive matters that I can't let my men get involved in,
because if the carabinieri ever found out, there would be hell
to pay. Therefore, I too should be left out of it. Is that clear?'

'Crystal clear. It's my baby.'

'Good. First of all, I want to know why Alberto Larussa
didn't want anything to do with his brother for so many
years.'

'I'll try to find out.'

'Second, I want you to go to Palermo right away —
tomorrow, in fact — and talk to the handwriting expert
that Olcese consulted. You need to ask him only one question. Be sure to write this down: is it possible for someone
to successfully write something so that it appears falsified?
That's all for today.'

Nicolò Zito was a highly intelligent man, and it took

him about ten seconds to grasp the meaning of the question he was supposed to ask the expert.

'Christ!' he exclaimed.

*

The monster was plastered, as they say, all over the front pages. Most of the newspapers – since the story by now had gone nationwide – dwelt on the personality of Giacomo Larussa, an impeccable teacher, according to the school's headmaster, fellow teachers, and pupils, and at the same time a ruthless killer who like a snake had insinuated himself back into his brother's life at a moment of weakness and regained his trust only to murder him in hideous fashion, motivated by the most squalid self-interest. The mass media had already reached their verdict – at this point a trial would seem like a pointless ritual.

The inspector could feel his liver gnawing away at him as he read these articles of conviction without appeal, but he still had nothing in hand that might enable him to affirm the incredible truth that he had intuited the night before.

Late that evening, Nicolò Zito finally called.

'I just got back. But I've got a bombshell.'

'Let's have it.'

'I'll go one step at a time. Palillo knows the reason for the hatred between the two brothers – because that's what it was. His client, as he likes to call him, told him all about it. It goes like this: Alberto Larussa never fell from a horse thirty-one years ago, as everyone in town thinks. That's just a rumour that their father, Angelo, put into circulation to hide the truth. Apparently the brothers had a terrible argument and came to blows, and Alberto fell down a flight of stairs, injuring his spine. He said Giacomo pushed him. Giacomo for his part said that Alberto had slipped. The father tried to sweep the whole thing under the rug with the story of the horse, but he punished Giacomo in his will by subordinating him, in a sense, to Alberto. To me the story rings true.'

'To me too. And what did the handwriting expert say?'

'The handwriting expert, whom I had trouble approaching, was baffled, mystified by my question and actually started stammering. But to cut a long story short, he said that one could, in fact, answer the question in the affirmative. And he added something very interesting. He said that no matter how much one tried to falsify one's own handwriting, a very careful examination would, in the end, expose the deception. And so I asked him whether he'd conducted such a careful examination, and he answered, quite frankly, no. And do you know why? Because the question put to him by the assistant prosecutor was whether Alberto Larussa's handwriting had been falsified, and not whether Alberto Larussa had falsified his own handwriting. Do you see the subtle difference?'

Montalbano didn't answer. He was thinking of another task to assign his friend.

'Listen, you absolutely have to find out the exact date when Alberto fell down the stairs.'

'Why, is it important?'

'Yes, or at least I think so.'

'Well, I already know it. It happened on the thirteenth of April . . .'

He suddenly fell silent. Montalbano could hear Nicolò breathing heavily.

'Oh, Christ!' Nicolò muttered.

'So, have you done the maths?' Montalbano asked. 'The incident occurred on the thirteenth of April thirty-one years ago. Alberto Larussa died – whether by his own hand or another's – on the thirteenth of April thirty-one years later. And the number thirty-one is simply the number thirteen backwards.'

*

'Larussa left the book by Potocki next to the electric chair as a challenge – challenging people to understand,' said Montalbano.

He was at the Trattoria San Calogero with Nicolò, savouring super-fresh mullets in tomato sauce.

'To understand what?' asked Nicolò.

'You see, when Potocki first started filing the ball from his teapot, he was calculating time: I will go on living until the ball is small enough to fit into the pistol's barrel, he said to himself. Alberto Larussa wanted to have his revenge exactly thirty-one years later, on the same day, the thirteenth of April. A calculation of time, just like Potocki. An allotment. You look perplexed. What is it?'

'Well, I'm just wondering,' said Nicolò. 'Why didn't Alberto Larussa take revenge thirteen years after his fall?'

'I was wondering the same thing. Maybe something made this impossible, maybe their father was still alive and would have known the truth. We can investigate it, if you like. But the fact remains that he had to wait all these years.'

'So how do we proceed now?'

'In what sense?'

'What do you mean, "in what sense"? Are we just going tell each other all these stories and let Giacomo Larussa rot in gaol?'

'What do you want to do?'

'Oh, I dunno . . . Go and tell Lieutenant Olcese everything. He seems like a good person.'

'He would laugh in your face.'

'Why?'

'Because what we say are just words – wind, hot air. What's needed is evidence to bring to court, and we don't have any. Get that through your head.'

'And so?'

'Let me think it over tonight.'

*

Wearing his usual television-viewing outfit – that is, Guinea-T, underpants and barefoot – he slipped the cassette Nicolò had made for him the previous day into the VCR, lit a cigarette, got comfortable in the armchair, and pressed play. When he'd reached the end, he rewound the whole thing and ran it again. He repeated the procedure three times, carefully studying the objects that had been used to turn the wheelchair into an electric chair.

When his eyelids started drooping from tiredness, he turned off the TV, got up and went into the bedroom, opened the top drawer of the chest of drawers, took out a box, and went and sat back down in the armchair. In the box was a splendid tie-pin poor Alberto Larussa had given him. He looked at it a long time, holding it in his hand all the while, then started the video again. Then suddenly he turned the VCR off, put the box back in the drawer, and looked at his watch. It was three o'clock in the morning. It took him twenty seconds to overcome his reluctance. He picked up the phone and dialled a number.

'*Ciao, amore.* Salvo here.'

'Oh my God, Salvo, what is it?' a worried Livia asked in a voice thick with sleep.

'I need you to do me a favour. I'm sorry, but it's very important. What do you have of Alberto Larussa's?'

'A ring, two brooches, a bracelet, and two pairs of earrings. They're magnificent. I took them out the other day when I learned that he'd died. My God, how terrible! To be killed in that gruesome way by your own brother!'

'Things may not be what they seem, Livia.'

'What do you mean?!'

'I'll explain later. What I want you to do is describe to me the objects you have – not so much their form, but the materials used. Got that?'

'No.'

'Come on, Livia, it's perfectly clear! For example, how thick is the iron or copper wire or whatever it is?'

*

It wasn't even seven in the morning when Montalbano's phone rang.

'So, Salvo, what did you decide to do?'

'Look, Nicolò, we can only move in one direction, but it'll be like walking a tightrope.'

'Which means we're in deep shit.'

'Yes, but only up to our chests. We have at least one move we can make before we're completely submerged in it. The only person who can tell us anything new concerning what we suspect is Giacomo Larussa. You should phone his lawyer and tell him to have Giacomo tell him in minute detail what happened during his three visits with Alberto. Everything that happened. Even if a fly flew past. What rooms they went into, what they ate, what they talked about. Even the minutiae, even stuff that seems irrelevant. I mean it. Let him get a brain hernia from the effort.'

*

'Dear Mr Zito,' began the letter from Palillo the lawyer to Nicolò, 'I am sending you an exact transcription of my client's account of his three visits to his brother, which took place on the 2nd, the 8th, and the 13th of April of the current year.'

The lawyer was an orderly, precise man, despite an appearance that made him one of Disney's three little pigs.

On the first visit, on the 2nd of April, Alberto had done nothing but apologize and express regret for having so stubbornly kept his brother away for so long. There was no point any more in going over the mishap, no point in trying to determine calmly whether he had slipped or Giacomo had pushed him. Let's bury the hatchet, he said. On top of everything else, he said he was as lonely as a dog and had no one to love, and he was getting sick and tired of the situation. And he suffered from bouts of depression – which had never happened before – where he would sit in his wheelchair for entire days without doing a thing. Sometimes he would close the shutters and just sit there thinking. Thinking of what? Giacomo asked him. That my life is a failure, Alberto replied. And then he took him into his workshop for a visit, showing him the things he was working on and giving him a magnificent watch chain. The visit had lasted three hours, from 3 to 6 p.m.

The second meeting, on the eighth of the month, was almost a carbon copy of the first. This time, the present was a tie-pin. But Alberto's depression had clearly worsened, and at moments Giacomo had the impression that he was struggling to hold back his tears. Duration of the visit: two and a half hours, from 4 p.m. to 6.30. They parted with the agreement that Giacomo would return on the thirteenth at lunch time and stay at least until eight o'clock.

The account of the last visit, which took place on the thirteenth, contained some differences. Giacomo arrived a bit early and found his brother in a terrible mood and quite agitated. He'd taken it out on the maid in the kitchen and had even thrown a frying pan on the floor in rage. He was muttering to himself the whole time and hardly said a word to Giacomo. Just before noon, somebody came to the door and Alberto shouted at the maid for not going to see who it was. Giacomo went to the door instead: it was a delivery man for a private courier with a very large parcel. Giacomo signed for his brother and managed to read the printed address of the sender on the form glued to the package. Alberto practically tore the parcel out of his hands and then clutched it to his chest as if it was some cherished living thing. When Giacomo asked him what it was that could be so important, Alberto didn't answer, saying only that he'd given up hope that it would arrive in time. In time for what? 'In time for something I have to do before the day is over,' was the reply. Then he'd gone down to his workshop to put the package away, but didn't invite his brother to join him. Giacomo was keen to underscore the fact that that time he didn't go into the workshop. From the moment the parcel arrived, Alberto's attitude had changed completely. Back in a more normal mood, he apologized profusely to his brother and even the maid — who, after serving them lunch, cleared the table, cleaned up the kitchen, and left around 3 p.m. During lunch neither brother drank even so much as a drop of wine — a point that Giacomo was keen to emphasize, as they were both teetotallers. Alberto invited his brother to lie down for about an hour and had had a bed prepared for him in the guest room. He would do the same and have a nap. Giacomo got up around four-thirty, went into the kitchen, and found Alberto already there, having made coffee for him. Giacomo found him quite affectionate but almost melancholy, as if his thoughts were elsewhere. He never once made any reference to the misfortune of thirty-one years earlier, as Giacomo had feared. They spent a nice afternoon together, talking about the past, their parents, their relatives. Whereas Alberto had distanced himself from everyone, Giacomo had maintained relations with all, especially their mother's very elderly sister, Zia Ernestina. Alberto suddenly took a keen interest in this aunt, who he'd literally forgotten about, asking how things were going, how her health was, and going so far as to offer to give her substantial financial assistance through Giacomo himself. And so they'd gone on until 8 p.m., when Giacomo got back in his car to return to Palermo. When saying goodbye they'd agreed to meet again later that month, on the twenty-fifth. As for the name and address of the sender of the parcel, Giacomo had tried hard to recall it, but wasn't able. It might have been something like Roberti (or maybe Goberti, or Foberti or Romerti, or maybe even Roserti) Inc., Seveso. That it was sent from Seveso, Giacomo was absolutely certain. In his early years as a teacher he'd had a brief relationship with a colleague from that town.

*

Worried that news of his parallel investigation might leak out, the inspector went in person to the post office, which, as a public telephoning centre, had phone books for the entire country. So . . . in Seveso, there was a Fausto Roberti, dentist; Giovanni Roberti, a dermatologist; and there was a certain Ruberti Inc., which looked promising. He gave it a try. A woman answered in a sing-song voice.

'Ruberti's. What can I do for you?'

'I'm calling from Vigàta, Sicily. I'm Inspector Montalbano, police, and I need some information. What line of business is Ruberti, Inc. in?'

The woman had a moment of hesitation.

'Do you mean what do we produce?'

'Yes.'

'Electrical conductors.'

Montalbano pricked up his ears. Maybe he'd guessed right.

'Could I speak with the director of your sales department?'

'Ruberti is a small company, Inspector. I'll put you through to our engineer Tani, who also handles sales.'

'Hello, Inspector? Tani here. What can I do for you?'

'I'd like to know whether there's been any recent purchases of materials of yours on the part of a certain Mr—'

'Just a second,' Tani interrupted him. 'Are you talking about a private individual?'

'Yes.'

'Inspector, we don't sell to individuals. Our products aren't sent to electrical shops because they're not intended for domestic use. What did you say this man's name was?'

'Larussa. Alberto Larussa, from Ragona.'

'Oh!' said Tani.

Montalbano said nothing, waiting for the other to recover from his surprise.

'I heard about it on TV and in the newspapers,' said

Tani. 'What a terrible, insane way to go! Yes, Mr Larussa did call us to buy some Xeron 50, which he had read about in a magazine.'

'I'm sorry, I don't understand. What is Xeron 50?'

'It's a hyperconductor, our very own patent. In a few words, it's a sort of energy multiplier. And very expensive. Larussa was so insistent, he was an artist and all, and so I sent him the fifty metres he'd asked for – which, you realize, is a derisory amount. But it never reached its destination.'

Montalbano gave a start.

'It never arrived?'

'Not the first time, no. He called us a few times asking about it. He even went so far as to send me a wonderful pair of earrings for my wife. So I had another fifty metres sent via Pony Express. And they, unfortunately, did reach their destination.'

'What makes you so sure?'

'Because on TV I saw all the macabre images of how he'd set up his electric chair. I'm referring specifically to the bracelets for the ankles and wrists, and the chest strap. One look was all I needed. He'd used our Xeron 50.'

*

He went into his office and got his second-in-command, Mimì Augello, to take over for him. Then he went home, undressed, put on his TV-viewing clothes, slipped in the cassette he'd already seen again and again, sat down in the armchair equipped with a pen and a few sheets of graph paper, and set the tape going. It took him two hours to finish his task, either because it was objectively so hard to calculate or because he'd never been too good with numbers. He managed however to work out how many loops of Xeron Larussa had needed to make the ankle braces, wrist bracelets, chest strap, and headset. By dint of cursing, sweating, crossing out, adding again, and rewriting, he convinced himself that Larussa had used about thirty metres of Xeron 50. Then he got up and summoned Nicolò Zito.

*

'You see, Nicolò, he absolutely needed that special wire for two reasons. The first was that it was very large in circumference – for his art objects he used wire that was almost as fine as spider's webs, and so anyone who knew him would say that the makeshift electric chair could not have been made by him because it was too crude in design and the materials too thick. I fell for it, too. The second reason is that he wanted to be absolutely certain he would be killed, and not just burned, by the electric chair. So he had to cover himself, and Xeron 50 was exactly what he needed. That was why his brother Giacomo found him in such a nervous state when he went there on the morning of the thirteenth: the package hadn't arrived yet. Because he didn't want to sit down in his electric chair without the Xeron. When Giacomo finally left around 8 p.m., he worked like mad to set the whole scene up. And I'm convinced that he succeeded in killing himself before midnight.'

'So what should I do? Go to Lieutenant Olcese and tell him the whole story?'

'At this point, yes. Tell him everything. And tell him also that according to your calculations – *your* calculations, mind you – Alberto Larussa must have used about thirty metres of Xeron 50. Therefore there must still be another twenty or so metres of the same cable – probably charred from the fire, but still there. And I mean it: my name must not be mentioned. I have nothing to do with this; I don't exist.'

*

'Salvo? Nicolò here. We did it. As soon as I left you, I phoned Ragona. Olcese told me he had no statements to make to the press. I replied that I wanted to see him in my capacity as a private citizen. And he consented. An hour later I was in Ragona. I'll tell you straight off that it's more congenial talking to an iceberg than to that man. I told him everything, and I told him to go into the workshop and see if the twenty metres of Xeron were still there. He replied that he would look into it. I didn't tell you about this first discussion because I didn't want you to get annoyed.'

'Did you mention my name?'

'Are you serious? I wasn't born yesterday. Anyway, around four o'clock this afternoon, he summoned me to Ragona. The first thing he said to me — though without seeming the least bit ruffled, since, after all, what he was about to tell me meant he'd got the investigation completely wrong — the first thing he said was that twenty metres of Xeron were found in Alberto Larussa's workshop. Not one word more or one word less. He thanked me with the same human warmth as if I had told him what time it was, and he shook my hand. And as we were saying goodbye, he said: "Have you ever thought about joining the police force?" I hesitated in surprise for a second, then said: "No, why do you ask?" And you know what he replied? "Because I think your friend Inspector Montalbano would be very happy if you did." The bastard!'

*

Giacomo Larussa was released, Lieutenant Olcese garnered heaps of praise, Nicolò Zito got a memorable scoop, and Salvo Montalbano celebrated with such a feast that he was ill for the next two days.

MONTALBANO'S RICE BALLS

The first to begin the litany, or novena, or whatever it was, on that 27th day of December was the commissioner.

'Montalbano, naturally you will be spending New Year's Eve with your Livia, I assume?'

No, he would not be spending New Year's Eve with his Livia. They'd had a terrible spat, one of the dangerous ones that begin with the statement 'Let's try to reason calmly' and invariably end up in the gutter. And so the inspector would be staying in Vigàta while Livia went off to Viareggio with her friends from the office. The commissioner noticed that something wasn't right and was quick to spare Montalbano from having to give an embarrassed reply.

'Because otherwise we'd be delighted to have you at our place. My wife hasn't seen you for a long time, and she's always asking about you.'

The inspector was about to launch into a reply gratefully in the affirmative when the commissioner continued.

'Dr Lattes will also be there. His wife had to rush to Merano to be with her mother, who's unwell.'

Montalbano also felt unwell at the idea of spending an evening with Dr Lattes, the chief of the commissioner's cabinet, known as 'Lattes e Mieles' for his unctuous manner. No doubt after the meal the doctor would start talking endlessly about the 'problems of public safety in Italy', which would have made a good title for his long monologues.

'Actually I'd already made—'

'Listen,' interrupted the commissioner, familiar with Montalbano's feelings about Lattes, 'if you can't make it, perhaps you could come for lunch on New Year's Day.'

'I'll be there,' the inspector promised.

✢

Then it was Mrs Clementina Vasile-Cozzo's turn.

'If you haven't got anything better to do, why don't you come to my place? My son will be there with his wife and child.'

And what would his role be at such a nice little family gathering? He reluctantly declined.

Next it was the turn of Burgio the headmaster. He and his wife were going to Comitini, to a niece's house.

'They're very nice people, you know. Why don't you tag along?'

They might be nicer than nice, but Montalbano didn't want to tag along. Burgio hadn't used the right expression. If he'd said 'join in the fun' or something similar, there might have been a chance.

✢

Right on cue, the litany or novena or whatever it was began again at the station.

'What are you doing for New Year's Eve, Salvo? Want to come with me?' asked Mimì Augello, sensing that he'd had a quarrel with Livia.

'And where are you going?' Montalbano asked in turn, defensively.

Being unmarried, Mimì would surely take him to a noisy party at the house of friends or in some anonymous, pretentious restaurant thundering with voices, laughter, and music at full volume.

He himself preferred to eat in silence. That sort of racket risked ruining his appreciation of any dish whatso-ever, even if prepared by the best cook in creation.

'I've reserved a table at the Central Park,' Mimì replied.

He should have known. The Central Park! A great big restaurant out by Fela, ridiculous in name and furnishings, where they'd managed to poison Montalbano with the simplest of cutlets and some steamed vegetables.

He stared at his second-in-command but said nothing.

'OK, OK, forget I ever mentioned it,' concluded Mimì, leaving the room. But then he poked his head back in. 'The truth of the matter is that you prefer to eat alone.'

Mimì was right. The inspector recalled reading a short story, surely by an Italian author whose name he couldn't remember, that told of a country where eating in public was considered an affront to common decency. Whereas in reality it was the most normal thing in the world to eat in front of everybody. Deep down, however, he agreed with the concept. To savour a dish properly cooked, as God would have it, is one of the most exquisite solitary pleasures known to man, and not to be shared with anyone, not even the person you love most.

When he got home, he found a message from Adelina, his housekeeper, on the kitchen table.

> *Im sorry but I teke tamarro off cuz its New Years an botha my boys are free an I gonna meck arancini rice balls wich they lika so much. If you wanna do me the onner an come an eat some, you no the adress.*

Adelina had two delinquent sons who were always in and out of gaol. It was a lucky conjunction, as rare as Halley's comet, that they were both out at the same time. One to be solemnly celebrated, therefore, with arancini.

Good God, Adelina's arancini! He'd tasted them only once — but the memory had surely entered his DNA.

Adelina would take two whole days to prepare them. He knew the recipe by heart. On the first day you make a stew of bullock's beef and pork in equal parts, which you cook on a very low flame for many hours with onions, tomatoes, celery, parsley and basil. The following day you make a risotto, the kind they call *alla milanese* (but without saffron, for Christ's sake!), and then you spread this out on a table, fold in some fresh eggs, and then let the whole thing cool. In the meantime you cook the peas, make a béchamel, take a few slices of salami, break them up into little pieces, and knead this all together with the stewed meat, which you will have chopped finely with a mezzaluna (no blenders, for heaven's sake!). The meat juices will blend in with the risotto. At this point you take a bit of risotto, wedge it into your cupped hand, put a spoonful of the kneaded mixture inside it, and cover it with more rice until you've formed a nice round ball. As you make each ball, you roll it around in flour, then in egg white, and then in breadcrumbs. When they're ready, you put all the balls in a pan with boiling olive oil and fry them until they take on the colour of old gold. Then you blot them on absorbent paper. And finally, giving thanks to the Lord, you eat them!

There was no doubt in Montalbano's mind as to who he should dine with on New Year's Eve. Only one question still nagged him before he fell asleep: would both of Adelina's delinquent sons manage to stay out of gaol until tomorrow?

*

On the morning of the 31st, as Montalbano was entering his office, Fazio restarted the litany or novena or whatever it was.

'Listen, Chief,' he said, 'if you got nothing better to do tonight—'

Montalbano interrupted him and, since Fazio was a friend, told him how he would be spending his New Year's Eve. Contrary to what he'd expected, Fazio frowned.

'What's wrong?' the inspector asked, alarmed.

'Is your housekeeper's surname Cirrinciò?'

'Yes.'

'And her sons are Giuseppe and Pasquale?'

'Of course.'

'Wait just a second,' said Fazio, and he left the room.

Montalbano started getting nervous.

Fazio returned a few minutes later.

'Pasquale's in trouble.'

The inspector felt a chill run down his spine. Goodbye, arancini.

'What do you mean, he's in trouble?'

'I mean there's an arrest warrant out for him. The Montelusa Flying Squad. For robbing a supermarket.'

'Burglary or armed robbery?'

'Burglary.'

'Listen, Fazio, try to find out a little more. But not officially. Do you have any friends on the Flying Squad?'

'As many as you like.'

Montalbano really didn't feel like working any more.

'Chief, somebody torched the car of Salvatore Jacono, the engineer,' said Gallo, running in.

'Tell Inspector Augello about it.'

Then Galluzzo came in.

'Inspector, Ragioniere Pirrera's house was broken into last night and they cleaned the place out.'

'Tell Inspector Augello about it.'

That way Mimì could kiss goodbye to his New Year's Eve at the Central Park. He should actually thank him for it, since he was being spared a certain case of food poisoning.

*

'Chief, it's just like I said. On the night of the twenty-seventh and twenty-eighth, they burgled a supermarket in Montelusa and loaded all the stuff onto a truck. The Flying Squad's sure that Pasquale Cirrinciò was part of the gang. They've got proof.'

'What kind of proof?'

'They didn't say.'

There was a pause, then Fazio grabbed the bull by the horns.

'Chief, I'm going to talk to you straight. You can't go and eat at Adelina's tonight. I won't say anything, you can count on that. But what if the arrest team gets the bright idea of going to look for Pasquale at his mother's place and finds him eating arancini with you? I don't think it's advisable.'

The telephone rang.

'Is that you, Inspector Montalbano?'

'Yes.'

'Pasquale here.'

'Pasquale who?'

'Pasquale Cirrinciò.'

'Are you calling me from your mobile phone?' Montalbano asked.

'Nossir, I ain't that stupid.'

'It's Pasquale,' the inspector said to Fazio, covering the receiver with his hand.

'I don't want to know anything!' said Fazio, leaving the room.

'What is it, Pasquà?'

'Inspector, I need to talk to you.'

'I need to talk to you too. Where are you?'

'On the main road to Montelusa. I'm calling from a phone booth outside Pepè Tarantello's bar.'

'Try not to let anyone see you. I'll be there in forty-five minutes, max.'

✻

'Get in the car,' the inspector ordered, the moment he spotted Pasquale near the phone booth.

'Are we going far?'

'Yes.'

'Then let me take my own car and I'll follow you.'

'You're going to leave your car here. What do you want to do, make a convoy?'

Pasquale obeyed. He was a good-looking youngster, just over thirty, with dark hair and lively, dark eyes.

'Inspector, I wanna explain . . .'

'Later,' said Montalbano, starting the car.

'Where you takin' me?'

'To my place, in Marinella. Try to slouch down and keep your right hand on your face, as if you have a tooth-ache. That way nobody outside will recognize you. Do you know there's a warrant out for your arrest?'

'Yeah, that's why I called. I found out from a friend this morning, on my way back from Palermo.'

*

Settling in on the veranda, with a glass of beer in front of him, courtesy of Montalbano, Pasquale decided the time had come to explain.

'I ain't got nothin' to do with this Omnibus supermarket thing. I swear on my mother's head.'

Pasquale would never have sworn falsely on his beloved mother's head. Montalbano was immediately convinced of his innocence.

'Swearing's not going to help much. We need proof. And the Flying Squad say they've got some solid stuff in their hands.'

'Inspector, I can't even guess wha' they got in their hands, since I wasn't there when the supermarket was robbed.'

'Wait a second,' said the inspector.

He went into the bedroom and made a phone call. When he came back out, he was frowning darkly.

'What's wrong?' Pasquale asked nervously.

'What's wrong is that the Flying Squad's got evidence to nail you.'

'What evidence?'

'Your wallet. They found it near the cash register. There was even your ID card in it.'

Pasquale turned pale, then shot to his feet and slapped himself in the forehead.

'So that's where I lost it!'

He sat back down immediately; he felt weak in the knees.

'So how'm I gonna get outta this now?' he wailed.

'Tell me what happened.'

'On the evening of the twenty-seventh, I went to that supermarket. They were just closing. I bought two bottles of wine and a bottle of whisky, then some savoury snacks an' cookies, stuff like that. An' I brought it all to a friend's house.'

'Who's this friend?'

'Peppe Nasca.'

Montalbano grimaced.

'And I'll bet that Cocò Bellìa and Tito Farruggia were there too, right?'

'Yeah,' Pasquale admitted.

The whole gang, all with criminal records, all comrades in burglary.

'So why'd you get together?'

'To play cards.'

Montalbano's hand flew through the air and struck Pasquale's cheek.

'Now start talking. That's the first.'

'Sorry,' said Pasquale.

'So: why did you guys get together?'

Unexpectedly, Pasquale started laughing.

'You find this funny? I don't.'

'No, Inspector, it really *is* funny. You know why we got together at Peppe Nasca's place? We were planning a robbery for the night of the twenty-eighth.'

'Where?'

'A supermarket,' said Pasquale, laughing until the tears started rolling down his face.

Montalbano finally understood why he was laughing so hard.

'The same one? The Omnibus?'

Pasquale nodded in affirmation, choked with laughter. Montalbano refilled his glass.

'And somebody beat you to it?'

Another nod.

'Look, Pasquà, you're still in hot water. Who's going to believe you? If you tell them who you were with that evening, they'll lock you up and throw away the key. Good God! Four offenders like you, serving as each other's alibis! Now there's something to split your sides over!'

He went back into the house and made another phone call. When he returned, he was shaking his head.

'You know who they're looking for, besides you, in connection with the supermarket heist? Peppe Nasca, Cocò Bellìa, and Tito Farruggia. The whole gang.'

'*Madunnuzza santa!*' said Pasquale.

'And you know what's amazing? That you and your friends are going to gaol because you, like a stupid idiot, went and lost your wallet in that very same supermarket. It's like you put your name on the whole caper, like you were there casing the joint.'

'When the other three are arrested and find out why, they're going to shaft me the first chance they get.'

'I can see why,' said Montalbano. 'So you'd better get ready for it. Fazio also told me they've already got Peppe Nasca at the station. Galluzzo arrested him.'

Pasquale buried his face in his hands. While staring at him, Montalbano got an idea of how he might save the arancini dinner. He dashed inside, and Pasquale heard him rummaging about, opening and closing drawers.

'Come in here.'

Montalbano was in the dining room, waiting for him

with a pair of handcuffs. Pasquale gawked at him in disbe-
lief.

'I couldn't remember where I'd put them,' said the
inspector.

'What are you going to do?'

'Arrest you, Pasquà.'

'Why?'

'What do you mean, why? You're a thief and I'm a
policeman. You're wanted by the law, and I've found you.
Don't make a fuss.'

'Inspector, you know perfectly well that with me there's
no need for handcuffs.'

'There is this time.'

Resigned, Pasquale approached him, and Montalbano
put a handcuff around his left wrist. Then he led him into
the bathroom and locked the other cuff around the U-bend.

'I'll be back shortly,' said the inspector. 'If nature calls,
you can relieve yourself without any trouble.'

Pasquale couldn't even manage to open his mouth.

*

'Have you informed the Flying Squad that we've arrested
Peppe Nasca?' he asked as he entered the station.

'You asked me not to, and I didn't,' Fazio replied.

'Bring him into my office.'

Peppe Nasca was about forty and had a huge nose. Montalbano sat him down and offered him a cigarette.

'You're fucked, Peppe. You, Cocò Bellìa, Tito Farruggia,
and Pasquale Cirrinciò.'

'We didn't do it.'

'I know.'

Peppe looked stunned.

'But you're fucked anyway. And you know why the
Flying Squad had no choice but to issue a warrant for you
and the rest of your gang? Because Pasquale Cirrinciò lost
his wallet at the supermarket.'

'The stupid bastard!' Peppe Nasca exploded.

And he began a coda of curses, damnations, and blasphemies. The inspector let him get it out of his system.

'And there's worse,' Montalbano finally said.

'What could be worse than that?'

'The moment you four go behind bars, your prison mates will regale you with boos and jeers. You've lost face. You're a bunch of clowns and puppets. You're going to prison for something you didn't do. Typical losers.'

Peppe Nasca was an intelligent man. And he showed this by the question he asked.

'Would you please explain to me why you're so convinced it wasn't us?'

The inspector didn't answer, but only opened a drawer on the left-hand side of his desk, took out an audio cassette, and showed it to Peppe.

'See this? This is a recording from a bugging device.'

'Does it involve me?'

'Yes. It was made at your house, on the night of the twenty-seventh. All four of your voices are recorded. I had you put under surveillance. In it, you can be heard planning the supermarket heist. But for the following night. Some people a little sharper than you lot beat you to it.'

He put the cassette back in the drawer.

'That's how I'm so sure you guys didn't do it.'

'But then all you've got to do is play the tape for the Flying Squad and they'll realize we had nothing to do with it.'

Imagine the look on their faces if he played the tape for them! It contained a special performance of Beethoven's First Symphony that Livia had recorded in Genoa.

'Peppe, try to think for a second. The tape might exonerate you, or it might constitute further proof against you.'

'Please explain what you mean.'

'There's no date on the recording. Only I can make that claim. And if I suddenly decided to claim that the bugged conversation took place on the twenty-sixth, the night before the burglary, you four would end up in prison and the more intelligent burglars would be free to enjoy their money in peace.'

'And why would you ever do something like that?'

'I'm not saying I would. It's just a possibility. In short, if I play this tape, not for the Flying Squad, but for some of your friends, I'll disgrace you for ever in their eyes. Nobody'll ever want to buy your stolen goods from you. Nobody'll want to lend you a hand. You won't have any accomplices. Your career as a thief would be over. Follow?'

'Yeah.'

'So you have no choice but to do what I ask of you.'

'What do you want?'

'I want to offer you a way out.'

'All right, so tell me what it is.'

Montalbano told him.

*

It took him two hours to convince Peppe Nasca that there was no other solution. Then Montalbano handed Peppe back to Fazio.

'Still don't tell the Flying Squad anything.'

He went out of the office. It was two o'clock, and the streets were almost empty. He went into a phone booth, dialled a Montelusa number, and pinched his nose with his free hand.

'Hello? Is this the Flying Squad office? You're making a mistake. That supermarket was robbed by a gang from Caltanissetta, the one headed by Filippo Tringàli. And don't ask who this is or I'll hang up. I can even tell you where the loot is, 'cause it's still in the truck. It's in the Benincasa warehouse, on the Montelusa–Trapani road, in the Melluso district. But you better get there fast, 'cause I think they plan to take the stuff away tonight in another truck.'

He hung up. To avoid any unfortunate encounters with

the Montelusa police, he decided it was best to keep Pasquale at his house, perhaps without handcuffs, until nightfall. Then they would go together to Adelina's. And he would savour the arancini – not only for their heavenly goodness, but also because he would feel perfectly at peace with his conscience as a policeman.

AS ALICE DID

The worst thing that could happen (and inevitably did happen at more or less regular intervals) to Salvo Montalbano, in his capacity as the Chief Inspector of the Vigàta Police Commissariat, was to be given the chore of signing papers. These hated papers consisted of reports, briefings, memos, surveys, and bureaucratic minutes first simply requested and later menacingly demanded by the 'offices in charge'. At times Montalbano would suffer a strange paralysis in his right hand that prevented him not only from writing up such documents (in which case Mimì Augello took care of them), but even from putting his signature on them.

'Your initials, at least!' Fazio would plead.

Nothing doing. His hand refused to function.

And so the papers would pile up on Fazio's desk, the stacks growing taller by the day, until they grew so tall that, with the slightest draught, they would totter and fall over, fluttering down to the floor. The folders, as they opened, would briefly create a lovely effect of snowfall. When this happened, Fazio, with saintly patience, would pick the papers up one by one, put them back in order, create a stack that he could carry in his arms and, kicking his superior's office door open, he would lay his burden down on the desk without saying a word.

Montalbano would then start yelling that he didn't want

to be disturbed and, amidst a flurry of curses, would begin his drudgery.

One morning Mimì Augello, on his way to Montalbano's office, didn't run into anyone who could have warned him that the inspector was 'signing papers' and not to be disturbed, and so he walked right in, hoping Salvo might console him over a recent disappointment. As he entered, he had the impression the office was empty, and was about to leave when the angry voice of the inspector, hidden behind the stacks of paper, stopped him in his tracks.

'Who's that?'

'It's Mimì. But I don't want to disturb you, I'll come back later.'

'Mimì, you're a disturbance no matter when you come. Now or later makes no difference. Take a chair and sit down.'

Mimì sat down.

'Well?' said the inspector after some ten minutes.

'Listen,' said Augello, 'I don't really feel like talking to you if I can't see you. Let's forget about it.'

And he started to stand up. Montalbano must have heard the sound of the chair moving, because his voice immediately grew even angrier.

'I said to sit down.'

He didn't want Mimì to slip away. He needed him there so he could vent his spleen while he was signing papers and the ache in his hand grew worse and worse.

'So, tell me what's happening.'

By now it was too late to back out. Mimì cleared his throat.

'We weren't able to catch Tarantino.'

'Got away again?'

'Got away again.'

As if the window had suddenly opened and a powerful gust of wind had blown in, the papers scattered everywhere.

But the window was closed, and it was the inspector, now visible to Mimì's frightened eyes, who had scattered them.

'Bloody hell! Bloody fucking hell!'

Montalbano seemed blind with rage. He stood up, started pacing back and forth across the room, and stuck a cigarette between his lips: Mimì handed him a box of matches, Montalbano lit the cigarette, threw the still-burning match onto the floor, and a few sheets of paper immediately caught fire as if they'd been waiting for that all their lives. They were very light, onion-skin paper. Mimì and Montalbano broke out into a kind of American Indian dance, trying to stamp out the fire with their feet, but then, seeing that it was a losing proposition, Mimì grabbed a bottle of mineral water that was on his boss's table and emptied it onto the flames. Once the fire was out, they both realized they couldn't remain in the now unusable office.

'Let's go and get a coffee,' the inspector suggested, his anger momentarily subdued. 'But first tell Fazio about the damage.'

✳

It took them half an hour to have their coffee. When they returned, the office was in perfect order. All that remained was a slight smell of burning. The papers were all gone.

'Fazio!'

'At your service, Chief.'

'What happened to all the papers?'

'I'm putting them back in order in my office. They're soaking wet, on top of everything else, and so I'm also drying them out. So cheer up, you can forget about signing them for today.'

Visibly reassured, the inspector turned to Mimì and smiled.

'So, my friend, you got screwed again, eh?'

This time it was Mimì whose face darkened.

'That man is a devil.'

Giovanni Tarantino, sought by the law for the past couple of years for fraud, bad cheques and forged bills of exchange, was a distinguished-looking fellow of about forty with a rather open and cordial manner who inspired sympathy and trust. So much so that during her deposition against Tarantino, the widow Percolla, whom he'd fleeced for over two hundred million lire, couldn't help but repeat disconsolately:

'But he was so distinguished!'

As time went by, capturing the fugitive Tarantino had become a sort of point of honour for Mimì Augello. Over the past two years he'd burst into Tarantino's home no less than eight times, sure of nabbing him by surprise, and each time there was neither hide nor hair of the swindler.

'But why have you got it into your head that Tarantino's going to see his wife?'

Mimì answered with another question.

'But have you ever seen Mrs Tarantino? Her name's Giulia.'

'No, I don't know Giulia Tarantino. What's she like?'

'She's beautiful,' Mimì said decisively, knowing a thing or two about women. 'But not only beautiful. She belongs to that category of women that, around here, they used to call "women for bedding". She has a way of looking at you, of giving you her hand, of crossing her legs, that gets your blood pumping. She lets you know that under the covers, or on top of the covers for that matter, she can catch fire as quickly as that paper did just now.'

'Is that why you always go and search the place at night?'

'You're wrong, Salvo. And you know I'm telling you the truth. I'm convinced that woman is tickled pink that I can never manage to nab her husband.'

'Well, that's understandable, isn't it?'

'In part, yes. But from the way she looks at me as I'm about to leave, I can tell she's also delighted that I, as a man, as Mimì Augello – not as a policeman – have been defeated.'

'So you're turning the whole thing into a personal matter?'

'Unfortunately, yes.'

'Ugh!'

'What's that supposed to mean: "ugh"?'

'I mean that that's the best way to end up doing something stupid, in our line of work. How old is this Giulia?'

'She must be just a little over thirty.'

'But you still haven't told me why you're so sure the guy goes to see his wife every so often.'

'I thought I'd given you a good idea why. She's not the kind of woman who can go for very long without a man. But she's not a flirt, mind you. And her neighbours say she hardly ever goes out or has family or friends over. She has everything she needs delivered to her at home. Oh, but I forgot to mention: every Sunday morning she goes to the ten o'clock Mass.'

'Tomorrow's Sunday, isn't it? Let's do this: let's meet at the Castiglione Cafe at a quarter to ten, and you can point her out to me when she passes by. You've piqued my curiosity.'

*

She was more than beautiful. Montalbano watched her attentively as she walked towards the church, well dressed but tastefully so, with nothing too ostentatious. She held her head high, responding with a slight nod to a few rare greetings. There was no affectation in her gestures; everything about her was natural and spontaneous. She must have recognized Mimì Augello standing there stiff as a poker beside Montalbano. She changed her route, moving from the middle of the street towards two men and, now right in front of them, she responded to Mimì's awkward greeting with her usual nod of the head. But this time a hint of a smile played on her lips. It was, beyond the shadow of a doubt, a mocking, teasing sneer. And she went on her way.

'Did you see that?' Mimì asked, pale with rage.

'I did,' said Montalbano. 'I saw enough to put her out of bounds. From this moment, you're off the case.'

'Why?'

'Because by this point that lady's got you in the palm of her hand. She gets your blood boiling and you're no longer able to tell what's what. And now we're going back to the office, and you're going to give me a report on your visits to the Tarantino home. And the address, too.'

*

At Via Giovanni Verga 35, a road on the edge of town, stood a small two-storey house, recently renovated. Behind it passed Vicolo Capuana, which was too narrow for cars. The plate on the intercom said: G. TARANTINO. Montalbano buzzed. Three minutes went by with no reply. The inspector rang again, and this time a woman's voice answered.

'Who is it?'

'It's Inspector Montalbano.'

A brief pause, then:

'Inspector, it's ten o'clock at night on a Sunday, and it's not polite to disturb people at this hour. Do you have a warrant?'

'For what?'

'A search warrant.'

'But I don't want to search anything! I just want to have a little chat with you.'

'Are you the gentleman who was with Inspector Augello this morning?'

A keen observer, Mrs Giulia Tarantino.

'Yes, ma'am.'

'I'm so sorry, Inspector, but I was in the shower. Could you wait five minutes? I'll be quick.'

'You can take your time, ma'am.'

Less than five minutes later, there was a buzz and the door unlocked with a click. Montalbano went in and found himself in a large entrance hall with two doors on the left, one on the right, and in the middle a wide staircase leading upstairs.

'Please come in.'

Signora Giulia was fully dressed.

The inspector came in, looking her up and down. She seemed serious, composed, and not the least bit worried.

'Will this take long?' she asked.

'That's up to you,' Montalbano said, playing tough.

'We'd better go and sit in the living room,' the woman said.

Turning her back to him, she started climbing the stairs, with the inspector following behind her. They came out in a large, spacious room with modern but reasonably tasteful furnishings. The woman gestured for the inspector to sit on the sofa and sat down herself in an armchair with, beside it, a small table holding an imposing Twenties-style telephone clearly made in Hong Kong or somewhere similar. Giulia Tarantino lifted the receiver from the golden forks and set it down on the table top.

'That way nobody will disturb us.'

'Thank you for the courtesy,' said Montalbano.

He sat there without speaking for a good minute under the questioning but always beautiful eyes of Mrs Tarantino, then took the plunge.

'It's very quiet here.'

Giulia seemed momentarily puzzled by the observation.

'It's true there aren't many cars on this street.'

Montalbano fell silent for another whole minute.

'Do you own this house?'

'Yes, my husband bought it for me three years ago.'

'Do you own any other property?'

'No.'

'How long has it been since you last saw your husband?'

'Over two years, ever since he went into hiding.'

'Aren't you concerned for his well-being?'

'Why should I be?'

'Well, to go for that long without any news . . .'

'Inspector, I said I haven't seen him for two years, not that I hadn't heard from him. He calls me on the phone every now and then. Which you should already know, since my phone is tapped. I worked it out, you know.'

This time the pause lasted two minutes.

'How strange!' the inspector said suddenly.

'What's strange?' asked the woman, immediately on the defensive.

'The layout of your house.'

'What's so strange about it?'

'Well, for example, the living room is up here, on the first floor.'

'Where do you think it should be?'

'On the ground floor. Which is where your bedroom must be, am I right?'

'Yes, that's right. Why, is that not allowed?'

'I didn't say it wasn't allowed, I was just making an observation.'

Another silence.

'All right, then,' said Montalbano, standing up. 'I'll be on my way.'

Signora Giulia likewise stood up, apparently bewildered by the policeman's behaviour. Before heading for the stairway, Montalbano saw her put the phone back on the hook. When they got downstairs, before she was about to open the front door, the inspector said softly:

'I need to go to the toilet.'

Signora Giulia turned and looked at him, now smiling.

'Do you really have to go, Inspector, or do you just want to play cat and mouse? Anyway, follow me.'

She opened the door on the right, showing him into a spacious bedroom, also furnished rather tastefully. On one of the two bedside tables there was a book and a normal telephone. That must have been the side she slept on. She pointed to a door on the left, next to a large mirror.

'The bathroom's in there,' she said. 'I'm sorry if it's a little messy.'

Montalbano went in, closing the door behind him. The bathroom was still warm with steam; so she really had been having a shower. On the glass shelf over the sink, alongside the bottles of perfume and jars of cream, he noticed a razor and a can of shaving cream. He peed, pushed the button to flush, washed his hands, and opened the door.

'Signora, could you come here for a minute?'

Signora Giulia came into the bathroom. Without saying a word, Montalbano showed her the razor and shaving cream.

'So?' asked Giulia.

'Do those look like women's things?'

Giulia Tarantino gave a brief, full-throated laugh, sounding like a dove.

'I guess you've never lived with a woman, Inspector. That's all mine, for hair removal.'

*

By now it was late, and so he went directly home to Marinella. Once there, he went and sat out on the veranda, which faced the sea. First he read the newspaper, then a few pages of a book he liked a great deal, *Tales of St Petersburg* by Nikolai Gogol. Before going to bed, he phoned Livia. As they were saying goodnight, it occurred to him to ask her a question.

'Tell me something. To remove body hair, do you use a razor and shaving cream?'

'What a question, Salvo! You've seen me do it a thousand times!'

'No, no, I just wanted to know—'

'And I'm not going to tell you!'

'Why not?'

'Because I can't believe you can be in an intimate relationship with a woman for years and not know what she does to remove body hair!'

He hung up feeling angry. Then he rang Mimì Augello.

'Mimì, how does a woman normally remove body hair?'

'Is this some erotic fantasy of yours?'

'Come on, don't be a nuisance.'

'I dunno, they use creams, plasters, body wax . . .'

'How about razors and shaving cream?'

'Razors, sure, and maybe even shaving cream. But I've never seen it. Normally I don't frequent bearded women.'

Come to think of it, Livia didn't use razors either. But, then again, was it really so important?

※

The following morning, as soon as he got to the office he called Fazio.

'Do you know what Giovanni Tarantino's house is like?'

'Yes, I went there once with Inspector Augello.'

'It's at Via Giovanni Verga 35, and it doesn't have a back door. Right? The back of the house faces Vicolo Capuana, which is very narrow. Do you know the name of the street after that, the one parallel to Via Verga and Vicolo Capuana?'

'Yes, it's another narrow alleyway. It's called Vicolo De Roberto.'

Made sense.

'Listen. As soon as you're free, I want you to go to Vicolo De Roberto, survey the whole street, and then give me a detailed list of every house.'

'I don't understand,' said Fazio.

'I want you to tell me who lives at number one, who at number two, and so on. But try not to call any attention to yourself, don't go up and down the street. You're very good at that sort of thing.'

'Why, am I not any good at other things?'

After Fazio left, he called Augello.

'You know what, Mimì? Last night I paid a call on your friend Giulia Tarantino.'

'Did she mess with your head the way she did with me?'

'No,' Montalbano said firmly, 'not with me, she didn't.'

'Were you able to work out how the husband gets into the house? The only entrance is the front door. The Fugitives Brigade have lost many nights of sleep over it. They've never managed to see him. And yet I would bet the family jewels that every now and then he goes and sees her.'

'I think so too. But now you have to tell me everything you know about the husband. Not his scams and bad cheques, I don't give a damn about that. I want to know about his obsessions, his tics, what he was like when he lived in town.'

'Well, first of all, he's extremely jealous. I'm convinced that whenever I go and search the house he goes crazy, imagining that his wife is taking advantage of the situation to cheat on him. Then there's the fact that being a violent man despite appearances, and being a fan of Inter Milan, he was always getting in fights on Sunday evenings, or whenever his team would play. Another thing about him is . . .'

Mimì went on for a good while, describing Giovanni Tarantino's life from the cradle to the present. By now he seemed to know the man better than himself.

Montalbano then wanted to know in minute detail how Tarantino's house had been searched.

'The usual way,' said Mimì. 'Since we were looking for a man, I and the guys from the brigade looked everywhere a man could hide: the attic, under the staircase, places like that. We even searched the floors for some kind of trapdoor. But everywhere we knocked, it rang solid, not hollow.'

'Did you try looking in the mirror?'

'But the big mirror is screwed to the wall!'

'I didn't ask if you looked *behind* the mirror, but *in* the mirror. You do that by opening the front door and looking at its reflection in the mirror.'

'Have you gone crazy?'

'Or else you do as Alice did: you imagine the glass is a kind of gauze.'

'Seriously, Salvo, are you OK? Who's this Alice?'

'Haven't you ever read Lewis Carroll?'

'Who's that?'

'Never mind, Mimì. Listen, tomorrow morning, using whatever excuse you can think of, go and pay a visit to Mrs Tarantino. Make sure she invites you into the living room, and then you must tell me whether or not she does a certain thing.'

'What kind of thing?'

Montalbano told him.

*

After receiving Fazio's report on Wednesday, the inspector gave him until the following day to gather further details concerning the other houses on Vicolo De Roberto. On Thursday evening, before going to visit Mrs Tarantino, Montalbano went into Bevilacqua the chemist's, which was the one open that day. There was a flu bug going around, and the shop was full of people.

One of the two female employees noticed Montalbano and asked him out loud:

'What can I do for you, Inspector?'

'I can wait,' said Montalbano.

Hearing the inspector's voice, Bevilacqua raised his head, looked over at him, and saw that he seemed embarrassed. Dispatching the customer he was attending to, he went over to a shelf, took a small box, came out from behind the counter, and with a conspiratorial air put it in the inspector's hands.

'What's in here?' Montalbano asked in bewilderment.

'Condoms,' the chemist said in a low voice. 'You asked for them, didn't you?'

'No,' said Montalbano, handing the little box back to him. 'I want the pill.'

The chemist looked around and lowered his voice to a breathy whisper.

'Viagra?'

'No,' said Montalbano, starting to get nervous. 'The one that women take. The most common one.'

Out on the street, he opened the packet the chemist had given him, threw the birth-control pills into a rubbish bin, and kept only the piece of paper with the instructions for use.

*

Except for the fact that this time Giulia Tarantino hadn't just come out of the shower, everything happened the same way as the previous Sunday. The inspector sat down on the sofa, Mrs Tarantino sat in an armchair, and the receiver of the old-fashioned phone was taken off the hook.

'What is it this time?' she asked, a hint of resignation in her voice.

'First of all, I wanted to inform you that I've taken the case away from my second-in-command, Inspector Augello, who came to see you a few mornings ago and whom you know quite well.'

He'd stressed the word *quite*, and the woman had given a start.

'I don't understand . . .'

'You see, when relations between the investigator and the person being investigated become, as in your case, rather close, it's always better . . . In short, starting today, I'll be handling your husband's case personally, myself.'

'As far as I'm concerned . . .'

'It makes no difference? Ah, but it does, my friend. I'm better, a lot better.'

He'd managed to give the last part of the statement an obscenely insinuating suggestiveness. He didn't know whether to congratulate himself or spit in his own face.

Giulia Tarantino had turned a little pale.

'Inspector, I . . .'

'Let me do the talking for you, Giulia. Last Sunday, when we went first into the bedroom downstairs, and then into the bathroom . . .'

The woman turned paler than ever, raising a hand as if to make the inspector stop talking, but Montalbano continued.

'I found this little piece of paper on the floor. It came with Securigen, which it says are birth-control pills. Now, if you haven't seen your husband for two years, what could you need them for? I can make a few conjectures. My second-in-command—'

'Please!' cried Giulia Tarantino.

And she did what the inspector was hoping she would do: she picked up the receiver and put it back in its forks.

'You know what?' said Montalbano. 'I've known from the start that that phone's a fake. Whereas the one on the bedside table in the bedroom is real. This one only lets your husband listen to what people say in this room. I have a very keen sense of hearing. When you pick up the receiver, I should be able to hear a dialling tone, but I don't. Your telephone is silent.'

The woman said nothing. She looked as if she might faint at any moment, but she resisted with all her might, taut as a wire, as though expecting something terrible to happen.

'I also found out,' the inspector resumed, 'that your husband owns a small garage in Vicolo De Roberto, less than thirty feet away from here, as the crow flies. He dug a tunnel that almost certainly comes out behind the mirror downstairs. Which the police never look behind when they search the place. They always think there's nothing behind a mirror.'

Realizing that she'd lost, Giulia Tarantino recovered her
air of detachment. She looked straight into the inspector's
eyes.

'Tell me something. Don't you ever feel ashamed of what
you do and how you do it?'

'Yes, now and then I do,' Montalbano confessed.

At that moment they heard a loud crash of broken glass
downstairs, and a furious voice cried out:

'Where are you, you filthy slut?'

Giovanni Tarantino then started climbing the stairs in
a rush.

'And here's the idiot himself,' sighed his wife, resigned.

THE PACT

Dressed all in black, wearing high heels and an unfashionable little hat, with a small patent-leather purse hanging from her right arm, the lady (since it was immediately clear she was a lady of ancient class) advanced in small but decisive steps at the side of the road, looking down all the while, oblivious to the infrequent cars grazing past her.

Even in the daytime the woman would have attracted Inspector Montalbano's attention for her old-fashioned distinction and elegance; all the more so at two thirty in the morning, on a road outside town. Montalbano was on his way home to Marinella after a long day at the station. He was tired but driving slowly. Through the open windows came the scents of a mid-May night, gusts of jasmine from the gardens of the houses on his right, wafts of brine from the sea to his left. After driving behind the woman for a brief stretch, the inspector pulled up beside her and, leaning over the passenger's seat, asked her:

'Need any help, signora?'

The woman didn't even look up. She just continued on her way, making no gesture at all.

The inspector turned on the emergency lights, stopped the car, got out, and planted himself in front of her, stopping her from going any further. Only then did the lady, who was not the least bit frightened, decide to look at him. In the glare of the lights Montalbano saw that she was very old, but her eyes were an intense, almost phosphorescent blue whose well-preserved youth clashed with the rest of her face. She was wearing precious earrings and a fine pearl necklace.

'I'm Inspector Montalbano,' he said to reassure her, even though the woman gave no sign of being nervous.

'Pleased to meet you. I am Miss Angela Clemenza,' she said, stressing the word *Miss*. 'Can I help you?'

'No, you can't,' the inspector snapped at her. 'Does it seem normal to you to be out alone in that get-up at this time of the night? You're lucky no one has robbed you and thrown you into a ditch. Please get in the car, I'll drive you home.'

'I'm not afraid. And I'm not tired.'

It was true. Her breathing was regular, and there wasn't a trace of sweat on her face. Only her shoes, whitened with dust, indicated that she had been walking for a long time.

Montalbano delicately took her arm with two fingers and nudged her towards the car.

Angela Clemenza kept looking at him for a moment, the blue of her eyes as though mixed with violet. She was clearly angry, but said nothing and got in the car.

Once inside the car, she laid the little bag on her knees and gently massaged her right forearm. The inspector noticed that the bag was swollen and looked heavy.

'Where shall I take you?' he asked.

'Gelso district. I'll tell you how to get there.'

The inspector heaved a sigh of relief. Gelso wasn't very far out of town, in the country only a few miles from Marinella. He would have liked to ask the lady how she happened to be walking home alone at night, but felt intimidated by her reserve and self-possession.

For her part, Signorina Clemenza didn't say a word except to tell him what road to take. He went through an open cast-iron gate and down a perfectly tended drive, then stopped in the parking space in front of a three-storey nineteenth-century villa, smart and freshly stuccoed, with a front door and green shutters that looked as if they'd just been freshly painted. They got out of the car.

'You are so kind,' said the lady. 'Thank you ever so much.' And she held out her hand. Surprised at himself, Montalbano bent down and kissed it. Turning her back to him, Miss Clemenza rummaged through her bag, pulled out a set of keys, opened the door, went inside, and locked the door behind her.

*

It wasn't yet seven o'clock in the morning when a call from Mimì Augello woke him.

'Sorry to bother you at this hour, Salvo, but there's been a murder. I'm already at the scene. I've sent a car to pick you up.'

Montalbano barely had time to shave before the car arrived.

'Do you know who was killed?' he asked the officer at the wheel.

'Some retired schoolteacher, Corrado Militello's the name. He lives past the old train station.'

The late Mr Militello's house stood just past the old train station, but already in the open country. Before Montalbano got through the doorway, Mimì Augello, who apparently wanted to be first in the class that morning, filled him in.

'Militello was already over eighty. He lived alone and had never married. He hadn't even left the house for about ten years. A housekeeper used to come every morning to look after him, the same one for thirty years, and it was she who found him dead and called us. Here's how the house is laid out: upstairs there are two large bedrooms, two bathrooms, and a walk-in cupboard. The ground floor consists of a living room, a small dining room, a bathroom, and a study, which is the room he was killed in. Pasquano's already at work in there.'

Seated at the edge of a chair in the anteroom outside the study, weeping in silence and rocking back and forth from the waist up, was the housekeeper. The body of Mr Militello lay on its back on the desk in the study. Dr Pasquano, the coroner, was examining it.

'The killer,' said Mimì Augello, 'had some sadistic desire to terrorize the victim before killing him. Have a look here: he shot at the lamp, the bookcase, and that painting, which looks to me like a reproduction of *The Kiss*, by Velazquez—'

'You mean Hayez,' Montalbano wearily corrected him.

'And he also shot at the window, but left the last bullet for him. A revolver, since there are no cartridge cases.'

'Let's not get caught up in counting the shots,' Pasquano chimed in. 'There were five, I agree, but he also shot at the bust of Wagner, which is made of bronze, and the bullet ricocheted and hit the victim square in the forehead, killing him.'

Augello said nothing.

In the fireplace was a mountain of incinerated paper. Montalbano was curious and cast a questioning glance at Augello.

'The housekeeper said he'd been burning letters and photographs for the last two days,' Mimì replied. 'He kept them in this trunk here, which is now empty.'

Apparently Mimì Augello was having one of those days where, once he started talking, there was no stopping him, not even with cannon-fire.

'The victim must have opened the door for the killer; there's no trace of forced entry. Clearly he knew him and trusted him. Like family. You know what I say, Salvo? That at some point some little grandson will pop up who'd long been waiting for the inheritance and ran out of patience. Got fed up. The old man was rich, owned houses, land suitable for building, the works.'

Montalbano had stopped listening, lost in memories of British detective films. That was why he ended up doing something he'd seen in one of these films: he bent down before the fireplace, stuck his fingers into the pile of ashes, and felt around. He was lucky. His fingers found a small, square piece of heavy paper. It was a fragment of a photograph, about the size of a postage stamp. He looked at it and felt a jolt of electricity run through him. Half of a woman's face, but how could he not recognize those eyes?

'Find anything?' Augello asked.

'Nah,' said Montalbano. 'Listen, Mimì, you take care of everything. I've got stuff to do. Give my best to the judge, when he gets here.'

✻

'Do sit down and make yourself comfortable,' said Miss Angela Clemenza, clearly pleased to see him again. 'Come over here. The house has become too big for me, ever since my brother the general died. I've kept just three rooms for myself on the ground floor, to save myself the trouble of going up and down the stairs.'

Nine thirty in the morning, and Signorina Angela looked impeccable. Next to her, the inspector felt dirty and unkempt.

'Can I get you a coffee?'

'Please don't trouble. I only need to ask you some questions. Did you know Corrado Militello, the teacher?'

'I've known him since 1935, Inspector. I was seventeen at the time, and he was one year older.'

Montalbano looked her straight in the eye. Nothing, no emotion, eyes a lake high in the mountains, without a ripple.

'I'm very sorry, really, but I have some bad news for you.'

'But I already know, Inspector! I shot him myself!'

The ground opened up under Montalbano's feet, exactly the same way it had felt to him during the earthquake at Belice. He collapsed into chair that luckily was behind him. Signorina Clemenza also sat down, perfectly composed.

'Why . . . did you do that?' the inspector managed to articulate.

'It's an old story, old as the hills . . . It would only bore you.'

'I assure you it wouldn't.'

'You see, from the mid-nineteenth century onwards, for reasons I don't know and have never wanted to know, my family and Corrado's family had always hated each other. There were deaths, duels, injuries. Like the Capulets and the Montagues, remember? Whereas the two of us, instead of hating each other, we fell in love. Just like Romeo and Juliet, in fact. Our families managed to separate us, and for that one time they were allied. I was sent to live in a convent, and he was packed off to a boarding school. My mother, on her deathbed, made me swear I would never marry Corrado. Either him or nobody, I said to myself. And Corrado did the same. For years and years we wrote to each other, phoned each other, did everything we could to find ways to meet. By the time the two of us were the only ones left, the sole survivors of our families, I was sixty-two years old and he was sixty-three. We both agreed that it would be ridiculous to get married at that age.'

'All right, then, but why . . . ?'

'Six months ago, Corrado phoned me and we had a very long talk. He said he couldn't stand living alone any longer. He wanted to marry a widow, a distant relative of his. And I asked: how can that be? You thought it ridiculous at sixty, and now at eighty you don't?'

'I understand. And is that why you . . . ?'

'Are you joking? As far as I was concerned, he could have married a hundred times over! As a matter of fact, he called me again the next day. He said he hadn't slept a wink all night. He confessed he'd lied to me. He wasn't marrying because he was afraid to be alone, but because he had actually fallen in love with that woman. So, you see, that changed things.'

'Why?'

'Because we'd made an agreement. We had a pact.'

She stood up, went over to small low table, opened the little bag she'd had the night before, extracted a tiny yellowed piece of paper, and handed it to the inspector.

We, the undersigned, Angela Clemenza and Corrado Militello, swear in the eyes of God the following: that should either one of us fall in love with a third person, he or she shall pay for this betrayal with his life. In witness whereof,

Angela Clemenza, Corrado Militello
Vigàta, 10 January 1936

'Did you read it? All in order, no?'

'But he'd probably forgotten about it!' said Montalbano, nearly yelling.

'I certainly hadn't,' said the lady, her eyes turning a dangerous violet colour. 'And yesterday morning, you see, I phoned him to make sure. "What are you doing?" I asked him. "I'm burning your letters," he said. And so I went and reread our pact.'

Montalbano felt something like an iron ring squeezing his head. He was sweating.

'Did you get rid of the weapon?'

'No.'

She opened her little bag, extracted a huge Smith & Wesson Centennial, and handed it to Montalbano.

'I had a little trouble hitting him, you know. I'd never fired a gun before. Poor Corrado, he got so scared!'

What was he supposed to do now? Stand up and declare her under arrest?

He sat there looking at the revolver, undecided.

'Do you like it?' Miss Angela Clemenza asked him, smiling. 'You can have it. I don't need it any more.'

MORTALLY WOUNDED

1

The blame for the sleep he was losing, tossing and thrashing in bed almost to the point of strangling himself with the sheet, could hardly be laid on his dinner that night, since he'd eaten only light stuff. No, the fault lay probably with the book he'd brought to bed with him and the irritation he'd felt upon reading the insipid, humdrum pages of a novel that reviewers had praised to the skies as one of the loftiest pinnacles attained in world literature over the past fifty years. The discovery of the latest pinnacle usually occurred every six months or so, and the cries of ecstasy always came from a somewhat snobbish newspaper which all the other dailies fell in with immediately. If you added it all up, the panorama of world literature over the past fifty years looked a great deal like a satellite photograph of the Himalayas. But, the inspector reasoned, it wasn't really the book's fault. Once he'd had enough, he could very easily have shut it, thrown it on the floor, turned off the light, and good-night. But he had a defective personality, one aspect of which was that once he started reading something – an article, an essay, a novel – he was utterly incapable of break-ing off halfway; he had to continue all the way to the end.

When the phone rang, it was like a liberation. He hurled the book against the wall and looked at the clock. It was three.

'Hello?'

'Halloo?'

'Cat!'

'Chief!'

'What is it?'

'Summon got shat!'

'Who got shot?'

'Some guy.'

'Dead?'

'Dead.'

A splendid dialogue, worthy of Alfieri.

'The dississed ginnelman, 'oo wint by the name o' Gerlando Piccolo, was shat in 'is own 'ome, which'd be the one belongin' to 'im,' Catarella continued prosaically.

'Gimme the address.'

'Iss not so easy t' fin', Chief, this place. Y'oughter come 'ere foist, cuz Gallo's waitin' f'yiz an' 'e awriddy knows the way.'

'Have you informed Inspector Augello?'

'I tried, but 'e wasn't home.'

'Fazio?'

''E's awriddy on 'is way to the scene o' the crime.'

'OK, I'll be straight over.'

*

The darkness outside was so dense you could cut it with a knife. As far as he could gather, the home of the dississed, as Catarella called him, must have been totally isolated, in the open countryside. As he and Gallo pulled up at the house, their headlights lit up the patrol car parked right outside the front door, which was wide open. He went inside, with Gallo following, and entered a large salon that was at once a living room and dining room. All clean, orderly, and dignified. Out of one of the three doors leading to the salon came Galluzzo with a glass of water in his hand. The inspector briefly glimpsed a kitchen behind him.

'Where are you going?' he asked.

Galluzzo pointed to the door in front of him.

'Into the niece's room. Poor thing! I laid her down on the bed.'

'Where's Fazio?'

Galluzzo gestured towards the staircase leading to the floor above.

'You stay here,' Montalbano said to Gallo.

'An' what am I supposed to do?'

'You can review your times tables.'

The bedroom in which the murder had taken place was in a post-earthquake state of disorder. Open drawers, clothes and underwear scattered across the floor, both doors of the wardrobe flung open. Jarring with the whole scene were two small paintings that had once hung on the walls but had been removed and smashed in with a heel, and the remains of a small statue of the Blessed Virgin that had been thrown violently against the wall. What did such vandalism have to do with a burglary? The late Gerlando Piccolo, who until now had been a ruddy, stocky man of about sixty, lay on a double bed with his upper body resting against the headboard, a large red stain in the middle of his chest. Apparently he'd managed just in time to sit up in bed before the killer's bullet laid him out once and for all. His eyes were open – not gaping wide, but a little more open than normal – in an expression of shock. But there wasn't much to speculate about. When you see death standing before you, you're either stunned or frightened; there is no third way. Despite the fact that it was rather cold in the bedroom, the man had gone to bed bare-chested, without so much as a tank top or T-shirt on. Fazio, who was standing beside the bed looking like a travelling salesman displaying his merchandise, intercepted the inspector's gaze.

'He's completely naked. Isn't even wearing underpants.'

'How do you know?'

'I stuck my hand under the covers and poked around.

What should I do, call Forensics and inform the prosecutor?'

'Wait.'

Something didn't add up. Montalbano bent down to look under the bed on the side where the body lay, and saw that that the underpants and tank top had ended up there. When getting back up, he froze as though he'd thrown his back out. On the floor, between the bedside table and the foot of the bed, lay a revolver.

'Fazio. Did you see that?'

'Yeah, Chief.'

'The killer must have left it there.'

'No, Chief. It was in the drawer of the bedside table. It was the niece who took it out and fired it. She told me herself.'

'Who'd she fire at?'

'The killer.'

'I'm not understanding a damn thing here. Maybe I'd better go and talk to this niece.'

'Maybe you'd better,' Fazio said enigmatically.

The niece was a seventeen-year-old girl, with dark skin, big black eyes reddened with tears, and great mass of black hair. She was reed-thin, and the way she looked at the inspector and leapt straight out of the bed on which she'd been not lying but sitting revealed something wild, something animal about her. She was wearing a sort of light dressing gown and was trembling from the cold and shock.

'Go and make something hot for her to drink,' the inspector said to Galluzzo.

'There's some camomile in the kitchen,' the girl said.

'And make me some coffee while you're at it,' Montalbano ordered.

'With cream? Or *corretto*?' Galluzzo asked ironically as he walked out.

'We need to talk,' the inspector said to the girl. 'But you

can't go on like that. Tell you what: I'll go in the other room for five minutes, and in the meantime you get dressed. OK?'

'Thank you.'

'What's your name?'

'Grazia Giangrasso. I'm the daughter of one of Uncle Gerlando's sisters.'

He went into the living room. Gallo was sunk deep in one of the armchairs.

'What's seven times seven?' he asked the inspector.

'Forty-nine,' Montalbano replied automatically. 'Why do you ask?'

'Didn't you tell me to review my times tables?'

How very witty his men were that morning! He went back upstairs. Fazio had changed position in the master bedroom. Now he was looking all around, with his back against the closed window.

'Find anything?'

'Some things don't make any sense to me.'

'Give me an example.'

'Gerlando Piccolo's wife died two years ago.'

'Oh, really? I didn't know.'

'So what I'm wondering is—'

'Who was sleeping in the bed with him when the killer came in?'

Fazio looked at him in astonishment.

'So you also noticed that both sides of the bed had been used? Look at the pillow, the placement of the sheet and blanket on the other side . . .'

'Fazio, just because you notice something, does that mean I'm not supposed to notice it too, at a glance? Keep looking around, then you can talk to me.'

Fazio frowned, as though offended.

'Shall I call Forensics?' he asked frostily.

'Set your watch for ten minutes from now. Then you can call them without me telling you to.'

Next to the dead man's bedroom was another bedroom,

unused. A pair of bare mattresses lay on the bed frame, and a film of dust covered all the furnishings. Then there was a locked door. Montalbano tried to force it open, thrusting his shoulder into it, but it resisted. Opposite the locked door was a bathroom in fairly decent order. Another door gave onto a tiny room used for storage.

He went downstairs.

'Coffee's ready,' Galluzzo called from the kitchen.

Before going, he knocked on Grazia's door. There was no answer.

'She went into the bathroom,' said Gallo, still slouching deep in the armchair.

Montalbano was drinking his coffee when the girl came into the kitchen.

She had washed and dressed and had regained a little colour. Galluzzo handed her a cup of camomile. She started drinking it standing up.

'Why don't you sit down?' Montalbano asked amicably.

She sat down. But on the edge of the chair. Ready to jump up and run away. She definitely gave the impression of a hunted animal. One could easily imagine the muscles tensed under her clothes – the blouse, the light red shawl around her shoulders, the broad skirt, all low-quality stuff. Then Galluzzo did something unexpected.

'There's a good girl, let's calm down now,' he said, patting the girl's head as though she were indeed an animal to be tranquillized and tamed.

And Grazia reacted just like an animal, heaving a deep sigh.

'Before we start talking, I have to ask you what's in that locked room upstairs,' Montalbano began.

'That's . . . that was Uncle Gerlando's office.'

'His office?'

'Well, it was where he would receive people.'

'What people?'

'The people who came to see him.'

'And what did they come to see him for?'

'To borrow money.'

A loan shark! What good news! It meant a hundred potential murder suspects among Piccolo's clients.

'Did he receive a lot of people?'

'I don't know. They didn't come through here.'

'Where did they come in, then?'

'There's a staircase outside the house at the back. The office has a French door.'

'And where's the key?'

'My uncle always kept it in his pocket.'

The victim's clothes were on a chair in the bedroom.

'Galluzzo, go upstairs and get the key, then have a look around his office with Fazio. When you've finished, put everything back in place.'

After Galluzzo left, the girl looked at Montalbano.

'Where should we go?'

'To talk, you mean? Does it get any better than this?' Montalbano replied, gesturing broadly with his arm to mean the kitchen.

'I'm always in here anyway,' the girl said, shrugging.

The inspector noticed that her voice sounded more self-assured. She probably felt less insecure with the questioning take place in her most familiar environment. He poured himself another cup of coffee and sat down.

'How long have you been living here with your uncle?'

He was purposely giving her a wide berth. He didn't want to broach the subject of the murder until the girl was in a condition to talk about it without breaking into hysterics.

And so he learned that Grazia was the only child of Gerlando Piccolo's sister Ignazia, who had married a small-time grain merchant by the name of Calogero Giangrasso. At the age of five Grazia became an orphan after her parents both died in a car accident. She was also in the car, which collided with a truck, and broke her head pretty badly, but they'd set it right again at the hospital. And thus Uncle Giurlanno and his wife Titina, having no children of their own, took her in.

'Did they love you?'

'They needed a maid.'

She said it plainly, with no hint of rancour or contempt. A simple statement.

'Did they send you to school?'

'No. They always needed me at home. I don't know how to read or write.'

'Do you have a boyfriend?'

'Me?!'

'OK, go on.'

Then, when she was fifteen, her Aunt Titina died.

'What did she die of?'

'The doctor said it was her heart. She had a bad heart.'

But after that, things got better.

'Did your aunt mistreat you?'

'All the time. And she was conceited.'

Her uncle treated her rudely, but was also a little fond of her and didn't demand, say, that she wash a pan five times over. And every now and then he would give her some money to go into town and buy something she liked.

'Now I want you to tell me what happened. Do you feel up to it?'

'All right.'

As she was about to start talking, Galluzzo appeared in the doorway.

'Chief, we opened the room. You want to go and have a look? I'll stay here.'

As Grazia had said, the room was fitted out to look like an office. There was a desk, two armchairs, a few chairs, and a filing cabinet. On the wall behind the desk was a safe that looked rather solid.

'Is it locked?' Montalbano asked Fazio.

'Yeah.'

The inspector opened the French windows, which were
protected by an iron rod. It gave onto the external staircase
the girl had mentioned. Clients could come inside without
having to go through the front door.

'Tell you what. Open the filing cabinet; I'm sure it contains the names of Uncle Giurlanno's clients.'

'Galluzzo told me he lent money.'

'Write down four or five names, no more. Then put
everything back in place. It has to look like we never set foot
in here.'

'You think the case will be assigned to the Flying
Squad?'

'Of course, don't you? Speaking of which, did you make
those calls?'

'All of 'em. But it'll be another half-hour before any of
'em get here.'

In the kitchen, Galluzzo and Grazia were talking nineteen to the dozen. They fell silent as soon as the inspector
came in.

'Can I stay?' Galluzzo asked.

'Sure. But let's pick up where we left off.'

As he did every night, at ten o'clock sharp, Uncle
Gerlando turned off the television, even at the tragic climax
of a miniseries, and went upstairs to bed. This was also a
specific signal for Grazia. She cleaned up the kitchen, washing the things that had been used for dinner, then got
undressed in the downstairs bathroom and retired to her
bedroom.

'Wait a second,' said the inspector. 'Who locked the
front door?'

'My uncle did, before coming in to eat. He always did it
that way. He would lock the door and then hang the keys
from a nail beside it.'

Montalbano looked at Galluzzo.

'The keys are still there. And there's no sign of a
break-in. So he probably used duplicate keys to get in.'

'Why are you speaking in the singular? The gunman might not have been alone.'

'No, Chief.'

'He was alone,' the girl confirmed.

Grazia said she'd fallen asleep immediately, but then was woken up by a loud noise she didn't understand. She pricked up her ears but, hearing no other sound, she convinced herself that the noise had come from outside, where it was open country. But no sooner had she closed her eyes again than she heard loud noises coming from her uncle's bedroom. She immediately thought that he must not be feeling well, since this had happened before.

'What do you mean?'

Her uncle loved to eat. One time he'd eaten three-quarters of a suckling goat. During the night he'd got up to go to the kitchen and take a little bicarbonate of soda, but hadn't made it there, falling down in the throes of a violent dizzy spell.

'What did you do this time?'

She got up, slipped on her dressing gown, and ran up the stairs in her bare feet. The light was on in the bedroom. The first thing she saw was her uncle sitting up in bed, shoulders against the headboard. She approached him from the side, calling him, but he didn't respond. Only then did she notice the blood on his lips and the stain on his chest. She turned suddenly around and saw a figure of a man running out the door. Then she remembered that her uncle kept a revolver in the drawer of the bedside table, and so she grabbed it, ran after the man, and shot at him from the top of the stairs as he was about to go out through the front door and escape. She gave chase, but couldn't see anything outside. It was too dark. She'd only heard the sound of a small motorbike. So she went back upstairs to the bedroom, knowing there wasn't anything more to be done for her uncle. Dropping the revolver to the floor, she went back downstairs to call the police.

Grazia had started trembling again, swaying like a tree in the wind. Galluzzo stroked her hair again.

'It all tallies,' he said. 'Even the bloodstain.'

'What bloodstain?'

'The one in front of the house. I saw it with my pocket torch. Now that the sun's up, you can see it for yourself. It could only be the killer's blood. The girl must have hit him square in the back.'

At that moment Grazia gave an animal-like scream, thrust her head backwards, and fainted.

2

Two days earlier, Commissioner Bonetti-Alderighi had gone over the instructions repeatedly for him.

'Now, I mean it, Montalbano, don't forget that your responsibility is one of temporary command and nothing more.'

'I don't quite understand, sir.'

'Jesus Christ! I've already said it at least three times! If you are summoned to the scene of a crime, you mustn't do more than take temporary command while you wait for those assigned the investigation to arrive. No one should move.'

'Do I have to say it?'

'Say what?'

'Police! Nobody move!'

The commissioner gave him a suspicious look. The inspector was standing in front of his desk, body leaning slightly forward, face expressing only a humble yearning to understand.

'Do whatever you think best!'

So now 'those assigned the investigation' were about to arrive and he, Montalbano, had no desire to see them. He went into Grazia's bedroom. The girl had pulled herself together a little and was lying, fully dressed, on the bed.

Galluzzo was sitting in a chair.

'I'm going to go,' said Montalbano.

The girl shot to her feet.

'What? Is it over?'

'No, it hasn't even begun. Galluzzo, come with me.'

From the living room, the inspector called Fazio. Gallo was asleep, sunk deep into the armchair. The inspector gave him a glancing kick in the calf.

'What is it? What happened?'

'Nothing, Gallo. Go and start up the car, we're heading back.'

'Did you call me?' Fazio shouted from the top of the stairs.

'Just to tell you I'm leaving. You wait here for the others.'

Heading for the door, he took Galluzzo's arm.

'Would you explain to me why you're so interested in the niece?'

Galluzzo blushed.

'I feel sorry for her. She's just a kid, all alone and dejected.'

Outside it was light.

'Show me where you saw the bloodstain.'

Galluzzo looked down at the ground and looked puzzled. Then he smiled.

'It's right under your car.'

He signalled to Gallo to reverse, and the stain emerged. Luckily the tyres hadn't run over it. Montalbano crouched down for a better look, and then touched it with his forefinger. It was blood, no doubt about it.

'Put something around this to protect it. Otherwise when all those idiots arrive from Montelusa, they'll turn it into dust. You stay here with . . . with Fazio. See you later.'

'Thanks,' said Galluzzo.

*

He made Gallo get out in front of the station, slid over into
the driver's seat, and continued home. As he was shaving,
he thought again of the dead man's bed. If both places had
been slept in, this meant that someone was lying beside
Gerlando Piccolo either before or during the killing. So,
aside from Grazia the niece, who had entered the room after
the deed, there must be another eyewitness to the murder.
He'd forgotten to ask the niece what she knew about Uncle
Gerlando's nocturnal encounters. Grave mistake, which he
would never have made if he hadn't already been certain that
the case would be handed to 'those assigned the investigation'. Let those morons deal with it.

*

When Fazio straggled in wearing a dark expression, it was
already time for lunch.

'Where's Galluzzo?'

'Well, after they sealed the place off, Galluzzo called his
wife and told her the niece didn't have anywhere to go. He
asked if he could take her home with him, and his wife said
OK. And then he called a doctor, since after Prosecutor
Tommaseo and Inspector Gribaudo had finished questioning her, the poor kid couldn't think straight any more.
They're going to continue the interrogation tomorrow.'

'Are they going to take her to Montelusa?'

Fazio looked embarrassed.

'No, they're bringing her here. Gribaudo told me to ask
you to get a room ready for him.'

'So get one ready for him.'

'Where? We don't even have room for—'

'No, no, no! Stop right there. Have you forgotten the
proverb? "A house is as big as its master wishes." Prepare
the little room next to the bathroom.'

'But it's hardly any bigger than a broom cupboard! And
there are papers scattered all over the place!'

'Just make a little space for them in there, OK? Listen,

tell me something. Did they ask Grazia whether she had an explanation for why both sides of the bed had been slept on?'

Fazio started laughing.

'Chief, you know what Tommaseo's like, don't you? In his opinion – and these are his exact words – we are looking at "a classic crime hatched in murky homosexual circles". In plain speech: Gerlando Piccolo brought someone home, probably a coloured immigrant, and after having relations, the guy shot him and robbed him.'

'Was Gribaudo of the same opinion?'

'Inspector Gribaudo says it doesn't matter whether the person sleeping with him was male or female, immigrant or no; what matters, according to him, is that the person was definitely an accomplice. That is, after having relations, he left the door open to the murderer and thief.'

'And what about Grazia?'

'The girl says that sometimes, when making his bed, she would realize that her uncle had had company. There were also noises that would come from her uncle's room at night that didn't leave any room for doubt. She also didn't have any doubt that they were women, not men. But she claimed that never in a million years would he have had anyone come through the front door. The women that came to see him would always come in from the external staircase. The uncle would leave the French windows to his office open, and the deal was done. When they were finished, the visitor would leave by the same route. And the uncle would put the iron rod back in place.'

'Exactly the way we found it ourselves.'

'Right. But Grazia also said something else.'

'What?'

'That the fact that both places in the bed looked used didn't necessarily mean her uncle had had company. He guy ate like a pig and there was hardly a night when he wasn't unwell with indigestion and heartburn. So he would thrash about in bed, going from one side to the other.'

'Just like me last night,' said the inspector.

'Because of what you ate?'

'Because of what I'd been reading.'

'Just to cover all the bases,' Fazio went on, 'Tommaseo and Gribaudo advised Dr Arquà to have the lab carefully examine the other side of the bed.'

'And what did Arquà say?'

'He was pissed off. He said he didn't need any advice. At any rate, they were clearly leaning in one direction: that of a robbery that ended badly, in a murder.'

They exchanged a glance and smiled. They understood each other perfectly. That direction was a dead-end road full of cracks and potholes.

✼

Back at the station after eating at the Trattoria San Calogero and taking the customary meditative-digestive stroll to the end of the jetty, the inspector was finally able to talk to Galluzzo.

'How's Grazia?'

'She's sleeping. The doctor gave her an injection. He says she'll be all right when she wakes up. My wife also feels sorry for the kid.'

'What time did Gribaudo order her to appear?'

'Nine o'clock tomorrow morning, here.'

'But doesn't the girl have anyone — any relatives, any friends?'

'Nobody, Chief. Based on what she told me, the Piccolos practically kept her chained up. Only after her aunt died did she have a little more freedom, but only in a manner of speaking. Her uncle would allow her to go into town once a week, and the most she could ever stay out was two hours.'

'What's she going to do when this is all over?'

'No idea. When Gribaudo told her she would have to

live somewhere else for a few days, she went nuts. She didn't want to move. It took some doing just to convince her to come with me.'

'Listen, just out of curiosity, did you ask her about the revolver?'

'I don't understand, Chief.'

'Well, a girl like that . . . by the way, exactly how old is she?'

'Just turned eighteen.'

'She looks a bit younger. Anyway, as I was saying, doesn't it seem a little strange to you that a young girl who's woken up in the middle of the night and finds herself faced with a stranger who has just murdered her uncle would have the courage and composure to open a drawer, grab a gun, and start shooting?'

'Of course it's strange.'

'And so?'

'You know, Chief, I asked her exactly the same question. And her answer was that, first, she's never scared of anyone or anything. And second, it was her Uncle Gerlando himself who taught her how to use a gun. And he would get her to practise every now and then.'

'Apparently Piccolo, who was a blood-sucker, a loan shark in common parlance, was afraid that one of his victims might want to take revenge. He was covering his back. And his niece could help him protect himself.'

'That revolver wasn't the only weapon in the house, either.'

'Oh no?'

'No. Remember that armchair Gallo was sleeping in? There was a hunting rifle behind it, and he kept a Beretta in a drawer of his desk. At Gribaudo's request, Grazia showed us how she handled a pistol. She cocked it like it was nothing.'

*

Around 6 p.m. the situation suddenly changed.

'Chief? Iss Dacter Latte wit' a ess at the end an' 'e wants a talk t'yiz poissonally in poisson. Whattya wan' me to do?'

Dr Lattes was the chief of the commissioner's cabinet, nicknamed 'Lattes e Mieles' because he was unctuous, obsequious, and perfectly capable of smiling affectionately while twisting the knife in your back.

'*Carissimo!* Dear, dear Montalbano, how are you? And the family?'

'We're all fine, thanks.'

'I wanted to tell you, on the commissioner's behalf, that you're going to have to handle this Piccolo murder case yourself. It seems to me a pretty routine case, after all, no?'

Depending on your perspective. For the murder victim Gerlando Piccolo, to take one example, you couldn't exactly define the case in those terms.

'Highly routine, Doctor. A routine robbery that turned into a routine murder.'

'Quite right! That's exactly what I meant.'

'Excuse me for being so bold as to . . .'

Montalbano congratulated himself. This was precisely the right tone to use to get Lattes to talk.

'Go ahead and be as bold as you like, my friend.'

'Why can't Inspector Gribaudo handle the case any more?'

Lattes lowered his voice to a circumspect whisper.

'His honour the commissioner doesn't want them to be distracted, neither him nor his second-in-command, Inspector Foti.'

'Forgive me for prying, but "distracted" from what?'

'From the Laguardia case,' Dr Lattes sighed, hanging up.

Alessia Laguardia, a good-looking, discreet woman of thirty, plied her trade in Montelusa at the highest levels, paying house calls or receiving clients in her secluded house built up against a Greek temple, illegally of course, with a view of the 'great African sea', as Pirandello, who was from the area, once called it. In this same house, a week earlier, Alessia had been found dead, with her throat slashed and some sixty stab wounds. Up to that point it could be considered a routine murder, to use Dr Lattes's terminology. But then the police found a notebook that the killer had looked for in vain, in which were kept, in perfect order – it was said – the ever so secret telephone numbers and names of some of the most prominent male inhabitants of Montelusa and its province: politicians, businessmen, professors, magistrates, and even, apparently, a monsignor with a reputation for sainthood. The sort of thing over which you could get your hide thrashed, if you didn't proceed with extreme caution. And apparently his honour the commissioner wanted to keep his hide intact.

'Fazio! Galluzzo!'

They both came running.

'I just got a call from Lattes. We have to handle the Piccolo murder case ourselves.'

Fazio made a gesture of contentment; Galluzzo sighed and said:

'That's a relief!'

'Why do you say that?'

'Because the chief of the Flying Squad got off on the wrong foot with Grazia. That's all the poor kid needs, to be pursued by a rabid dog like Gribaudo,' Galluzzo concluded.

'All right, then, listen to me . . . Jesus Christ!'

Fazio and Galluzzo both gave a start at the sudden, loud curse.

'Would somebody please do me the favour of telling me where the fuck Mimì has disappeared to? He hasn't shown up all day! Do you two have any news of him?'

'No,' the two said in unison.

'Catarella!'

Catarella arrived like a rocket, miscalculated the turn he had to make to come through the doorway, and very nearly broke his nose against the jamb. He was shaken.

'*Beddra Matre*, wha' a scare!'

'You got any news of Inspector Augello?'

'From 'im poissonally in poisson? Nossir.'

The inspector dialled Mimi's home phone number. After a few rings Beba, his girlfriend, answered and immediately recognized Montalbano's voice.

'Is that you, Salvo? Thanks for calling, he's feeling a little better. The doctor's been here to see him.'

'Why, what's wrong with him?'

'He had a renal colic. I told Catarella this morning.'

He hung up and glared at Catarella.

'Why didn't you inform me that Signora Beba had called you to tell me that Mimi was ill?'

Catarella looked genuinely distressed and surprised.

'So 'e's ill? All's the lady said to me was somethin' 'bout a renaholic an' I din't unnastan' nothin'.'

'Renal colic, Cat, not "renaholic". Anyway, why didn't you tell me when I asked you just now?'

''Cause you axed me if Isspecter Augello talked t' me poissonally in poisson. An' in fack i' was 'is goilfriend 'at called.'

Montalbano buried his face in his hands. Catarella looked on the point of tears.

'I swear, Chief! She din't say nothin' bout bein' sick, but only 'bout a renaholic!'

'For heaven's sake!' the inspector shouted. 'Go back to your post.'

'So, how should we proceed?' asked Fazio.

'Have you written down those names from Piccolo's office like I asked you?'

'Yes, Chief.'

'How many of them are there?'

'Five. I've got them in my office. Should I get them?'

'There's no need. See if you can talk to any of them. Try to find out what rate Piccolo charged, what kind of person he was, how he behaved when somebody didn't pay up. Then report back to me tomorrow morning.'

'What about me?' asked Galluzzo.

'Listen, there's no point, for now, in continuing Gribaudo's interrogation of Grazia. I'll let you know when I think I need further clarification from her. Meanwhile try to win as much of the girl's trust as you can. It's possible that, just chatting in a casual manner with someone she considers a friend, she'll remember some important details. We'll meet up again tomorrow. I'm going to go and see how Augello is doing.'

Left to himself, the inspector realized he didn't really feel like seeing Augello. Mimì was the type to start wailing like a man at death's door over an ingrown toenail, so imagine for colic! And when Mimì acted that way, Montalbano couldn't stand it. He redialled the number. Beba answered.

'Mimì's resting.'

'No need to disturb him. I'm just calling to let you know I won't be able to come and see him. Tell him to get well soon. I need him. We've been assigned a murder case.'

'The loan shark?'

'Yes. How did you know?'

'A local TV station mentioned it.'

＊

As he was leaving the station he was overcome by a sudden and overwhelming desire for pasta in Trapanese pesto sauce, a dish that Adelina, for inscrutable reasons, refused ever to make. When he got to the supermarket, the rolling metal shutters were lowered halfway. He squatted, went in, and found the manager, Mr Aguglia, standing right in front of him.

'Inspector! What can I do for you?'

'I'd like a jar of *pesto alla trapanese*.'

'Wait right here and I'll go and get it for you.'

The lights in the supermarket were turned down three-quarters, and there was nobody left at the cash registers. The manager returned with a jar in hand.

'Here you go. You can pay for it next time. Today's been a bad day. I was on the phone the whole time, dealing with complaining customers.'

'What were they complaining about?'

'Dindò didn't come in to work today, and so none of the deliveries were made.'

Dindò was a lanky youth of about twenty with the brain of a ten-year-old, who was always running about in Vigàta and the neighbourhood making home deliveries of groceries.

'But he's going to hear from me tomorrow!'

3

Back home, he boiled the pasta, drained it, put it in a dish, poured the entire jar of sauce onto it ('Serves four,' it said on the label), sat down at the kitchen table, and had a feast. In the fridge he found mullet in tomato sauce prepared by Adelina, warmed it up, and wolfed it down. After eating he washed the dishes very carefully so as not to leave any signs of the pesto alla trapanese. If Adelina happened to notice the following day, she was likely to make a stink. He even made sure to stuff the empty jar deep towards the bottom of the rubbish. Then he sat down in front of the television as pleased as a murderer who is certain he has got rid of every trace of the crime. The opening story on the Tele-Vigàta evening news was naturally the murder of Gerlando Piccolo. After showing various shots of the house from the outside, the reporter, who was Galluzzo's brother-in-law, said he'd managed to get his hands on a brief amateur video of Grazia, the brave niece of the victim. He added proudly that it was a scoop, since no other images of the girl were known to exist. Montalbano gave a start. Where did he get that video? There was no sound. You could only see the girl working in a kitchen that was not the kitchen of Piccolo's house. Grazia was wearing a rather elegant dress and was tastefully made up. She moved the way she always did, however, like a cat made nervous by the presence of an extraneous element that might prove dangerous. The camera then zoomed in on her face, and the inspector realized how beautiful she was — secretly, dangerously beautiful. For a brief instant, the video camera seemed to have the power to reveal mysterious things not visible to the naked eye. She had the same qualities as the heroines of American Westerns: a woman who knew how to defend herself with a rifle. Someone off-camera told her to smile, and she tried, but only managed to stretch her lips over her bright white teeth, which were small and sharp. Like a tigress hissing menacingly.

Another news item followed, and the inspector changed the channel. But if anyone had asked him what his eyes were watching, he certainly would not have been able to answer. A question at the back of his mind was nagging him too insistently: how did the TeleVigàta crew get their hands on that material? He could have answered the question at once by ringing Galluzzo's brother-in-law directly. But he didn't want to give him the satisfaction. Then, all at once, the answer occurred to him, simple, clear, and linear, the only one possible. And it got him all worked up.

✳

Before going to bed, he picked up the phone and told Livia about his day. The snag came as he was describing his surprise at seeing how different Grazia looked on television, compared to when he'd seen her that morning.

'Well,' said Livia, 'if the video was shot before the murder, it's perfectly natural that the girl looked serene and tranquil in it.'

'No, that's not it,' Montalbano retorted. 'It was . . . I don't know . . . a strange, unexpected sort of beauty . . .'

'So you're saying she's very photogenic,' Livia cut in.

'No, I'm not talking about being photogenic.'

'So what are you talking about?'

'It was as though the camera had X-ray vision . . . I can't really explain it because I don't have a clear sense of it myself. It was as though . . .'

'Are we going to have to talk about this at length?'

'Well, by talking about it I can get a clearer sense—'

'Can I ask a question?'

'Of course.'

'Do you notice a woman's beauty only in photographs?'

'What's that got to do with it?'

'It's got everything to do with it. Because if it's true, I'm going to have a video taken of me and then send you the tape.'

'Do you always have to bring everything back to yourself?'

And so began the squabble.

*

For no apparent reason, as soon as he opened his eyes onto a day that, based on what he could see out of the open window, promised to be dark and windy, two lines of verse that his father used to recite when he first got out of bed in the morning came back to him: *Accominzamo, con nova promissa, / sta gran sulenni pigliata pi fissa.* 'Let us begin, with promises boding, / another day's royal railroading.' Though he didn't realize it till much later, the 'railroading', the *pigliata pi fissa* his father was referring to, was life itself – everyday life. Well, his father was a serious man, and the 'promises' meant the commitments he renewed and maintained each day. But he himself, that morning, as he got up to shower and put his hand on his heart, did not feel up to maintaining any renewed commitments either to himself or most of the world. All he wanted to do was to get back under the covers, curl up, close his eyes, sink into the warmth of the still-warm sheets, and submit his formal resignation from everything, because he'd reached every sustainable limit of fatigue, boredom, and tolerance.

In the bathroom he looked at himself in the mirror and didn't like what he saw. How on earth could certain people stand him and even manage to love him? He certainly didn't love himself. One day he'd considered himself with ruthless lucidity.

'I'm like a photograph,' he'd said to Livia.

Livia gave him a confused look.

'I don't understand.'

'I exist in so far as there's a negative.'

'I still don't understand.'

'I'll explain what I mean. I exist because there's a negative made up of crimes, murders, and acts of violence. If that negative didn't exist, I, the positive image, wouldn't exist either.'

Livia, curiously, started laughing.

'I don't buy it, Salvo. The negative of a murderer, when developed, doesn't show a policeman, but the murderer himself.'

'It was just a metaphor.'

'It doesn't work.'

The metaphor might not work, but there was a grain of truth in it just the same.

＊

As soon as he got to the office, he called Galluzzo.

'Congratulations.'

'For what?'

'For your stinking charity. I've had enough of your compassion for Grazia and saying you brought her to your house because she had nowhere to go. You did it just so your brother-in-law would have a scoop.'

'Chief, that's not true.'

'Do you deny that she was filmed in your kitchen?'

'No.'

'And that the clothes she was wearing were your wife's?'

'No.'

'Well? At the very least you're a hypocrite, somebody who abuses people's trust.'

'No, Chief. The truth of the matter is that I couldn't say no to my wife. She told her brother I'd brought the girl home, and he couldn't believe it, and he did everything in his power . . . At one point my wife threatened that if I didn't do her brother this favour, Grazia couldn't stay with us any more and I—'

'Get out of here and find me Fazio.'

'Yes, sir. I'm sorry.'

But instead of Fazio, it was Catarella who appeared.

'Chief, Fazio ain't onna premisses insomuch as he ain't onna premisses yet. But there's a Mr Cuglia 'at wants a talk t'yiz poissonally in poisson.'

'All right, put 'im on.'

'I can't put 'im on, Chief, insomuch as Mr Cuglia's 'ere in poisson.'

'Then send him in.'

Mr Cuglia was of course Mr Aguglia, the manager of the supermarket.

'Inspector, do you remember how I said just last night that Dindò hadn't come into work? Well, he didn't come in this morning, either.'

'I don't see how we could be of any—'

'Wait. Seeing that he wasn't coming in, I went to his home. He lives alone in a squalid room under a staircase because he doesn't want to be with his father, who lives on the floor above. I knocked at the door, but nobody answered. So I went up to see the father, who has a key to the place. We opened it up, and it was empty. A real pigsty, I'm telling you. The father hasn't seen Dindò for three days. I even asked some of the neighbours, but nobody could tell me anything. So you tell me: what should I do now?'

Montalbano felt irked. Why did Aguglia come to him with a problem that he, as a police inspector, didn't care two hoots about?

'Just hire another assistant,' he said coldly.

'Well, the fact, is, Dindò disappeared with the shop's moped. I'd been letting him use it to come to work.'

'Is this the first time Dindò has behaved this way?'

'Yes. He thinks and sometimes acts like a child, but as far as his work goes, I've never had any complaint.'

'Listen, I suggest you wait another day before filing an official report. You yourself said Dindò is like a child. Maybe he got lost chasing a butterfly.'

Upon saying this, he had a moment of doubt. Were there still little kids capable of getting lost chasing butter-flies?

✻

'So it turns out,' said Fazio, sitting down in front of Montalbano's desk, 'that Gerlando Piccolo was a poor excuse for a human being — when he was alive, that is.'

'Meaning?'

'Chief, the voices I heard in town all sing the same song. Whoever it was that shot Piccolo ought to have a statue erected for him in the town square. If you were unlucky enough to borrow a hundred from him, after six months he'd already taken back a thousand from you. He wasn't just a bloodsucking leech, but a pig as well.'

'In what sense?'

'He took advantage of women in need. Apparently he didn't miss a single chance. Even before lending the money, he would demand a down payment in services on the interest.'

'Did you manage to talk to the people on the list?'

'You think that's so easy? The poor bastards who fall into the clutches of someone like that feel ashamed on the one hand, and afraid on the other. I was only able to talk to two of them. One was a widow by the name of Colajanni, who told me she wouldn't answer any of my questions because she wouldn't want to do anything to harm the killer. Get the picture? The other was a lady named Raina, who had a greengrocer's shop before Piccolo ate up her fruit, vegetables, the walls, and her panties.'

'So, if he took advantage of the women, then we have to add to the list of suspects not only the ladies he plucked, but also some husbands and brothers who might have wanted to avenge their family honour.'

Fazio's eyelids drooped halfway.

'If you say that, it means you're not convinced that it was a burglary that degenerated into a murder.'

'Why, do you think it was a burglary that degenerated into a murder?'

'No.'

'Me neither. Do you think I'm a bigger idiot than you?'

'I wouldn't dare.'

'Did you find out how Piccolo would react when some-one rebelled and didn't want any more of his blood sucked?'

Fazio grimaced.

'He would send someone to collect, and they would pay up. They didn't have any choice.'

'And who was this someone?'

'Nobody wanted to tell me, Chief. They're afraid. It must be someone who doesn't mess around. But give me another twenty-four hours and, you'll see, I'll manage to find out everything there is to know about him.'

'I don't doubt it for a second. Has Montelusa sent you the house keys?'

'Yeah, I've got them in my office. But I have to tell you, there's no point in going to have a look at Piccolo's bedroom. First Forensics, then Dr Pasquano, then the men who came to pick up the corpse . . . Everything's been moved around.'

'Do you yourself remember how it was when you first got there?'

'Absolutely.'

'Have Forensics send you the photos they took before they turned the place upside down. They might be of help.'

'I'll call them right away.'

'While you're at it, first call Jachino, the locksmith.'

'Why?'

'I want to open the safe that's in Piccolo's studio.'

'We don't need Jachino. Inspector Gribaudo found the keys himself. But he didn't use them. Said he'd open the safe the following day. He didn't have time. He sent those to us too.'

'But isn't it a combination safe?'

'What are you talking about, Chief? That strongbox must be at least two hundred years old! I'll go and call Forensics for those pictures.'

He returned after a short spell, deflated.

'I talked to Scardocchia, Arquà's second-in-command, who said he had to ask his boss. When he came back he said they were sorry, but they still needed the photos themselves.'

Montalbano started cursing under his breath. He picked up the phone.

'Montalbano here. Let me talk to Arquà.'

Since he hadn't spoken to the man for a long time, he couldn't remember whether they used the familiar or polite form of address. The problem — if it was indeed a problem — was resolved by Arquà.

'What can I do for you, Montalbano?'

'Did you know that I've been assigned the Piccolo investigation?'

'Yes.'

He admitted it reluctantly, between clenched teeth.

'I know you're disappointed, but that's just the way it is. Now it just so happens that Prosecutor Tommaseo, who'll be directing the investigation, is here in my office. He's the one who wants those photos, and he wants them now. If you want to hang on for just a minute, I'll put him on so you can talk to him as soon as he gets back from the toilet. But I should tell you he's pretty pissed off at the response you just gave. Ah, here he is now. Let me put him on.'

'There's no need. Just give Dr Tommaseo my regards. I'll send the photos over straight away by car. Scardocchia misunderstood me.'

'You mean you didn't need the photos?'

'No, we do, but we can make copies.'

'Excellent idea,' said the inspector, hanging up.

'What if the bluff hadn't worked?' Fazio asked.

'What do you mean?'

'What if Arquà asked to talk to Tommaseo?'

'Just to be shouted at? No way. Don't you know what Arquà rhymes with? *Quaquaraquà*.'

The photos arrived about half an hour later. Montalbano had an idea spinning around in his head, and so he was quick to take them out of their envelope and examine them carefully. The forensic photographer had been meticulous, capturing all the slightest details. Montalbano handed a photo to Fazio that showed the whole bedroom, with Gerlando Piccolo lying dead in the middle of the bed.

'Does this match your recollection of the scene?'

Fazio took a long hard look at the photo.

'I think that's exactly the way it was.'

Montalbano handed him another photo. This one showed the two paintings that had been torn off the walls, thrown to the floor, and stamped on with somebody's heel on the narrow strip of floor between the chest of drawers and the foot of the bed. The open drawers further reduced the space. The photograph highlighted hundreds of tiny shards of the glass that had once covered the little paintings in their frames.

'When you went up to the bed, did you step on those paintings?'

'No, sir. I stepped over them, in fact. I'd seen the pieces

of glass. You stepped over them too when you came into the room.'

'I did?'

'Yes, sir, you did it instinctively, which is why you don't remember. But why are you so interested in those paintings?'

'It's not the paintings I'm interested in, but all the broken glass. In your opinion, if someone stepped on it barefoot without realizing, would they get cut or not?'

'Of course they would get cut.'

'Grazia told me she went upstairs to see what was happening without putting her shoes on. She went upstairs barefoot.'

Fazio remained pensive. Then he said:

'It might not mean anything. Grazia's a peasant girl who's used to walking barefoot. It's possible the bottoms of her feet are so callused that you couldn't stick a knife in them.'

'Go and find Galluzzo for me, and come back with him.'

Galluzzo came in with his eyes downcast, still feeling embarrassed at what Montalbano had said to him earlier.

'I need to ask you a question. Does Grazia limp, by any chance?'

'What are you, Chief, some kinda magician or something? She doesn't exactly limp, as far as that goes, but yesterday afternoon she started complaining about shooting pains on the bottom of her feet. My wife had a look. The soles of her feet weren't bleeding, but they were stuck with all these little pieces of glass. My wife pulled them all out with a pair of tweezers.'

'Thanks, you can go.'

After Galluzzo left, the inspector and Fazio made no comment.

'How soon should we get moving?'

Montalbano looked at his watch.

'This afternoon, I'd say. Now it's time to go to lun—'

The door, which Galluzzo had closed, flew open with a crash. Catarella appeared.

'Beckin' yer pardon, my 'and slipped. I jess got a nominous phone call. Summon foun' a dead body in Pizzutello districk. An' they tol' me azackly where.'

4

For once, Catarella had understood and correctly reported the information provided by an anonymous caller as to the exact location where a murder victim could be found. Pizzutello was an area barely five hundred yards away from Piccolo's house, thick with Mediterranean scrub still untouched by concrete, and a favourite haunt of furtive couples. Indeed the traffic of these couples had formed a complex web of trails and clearings through the brush, a labyrinth which, despite the wealth of information, made finding the right path a real conundrum. The two vehicles – a patrol car and the inspector's car – were twice forced to make complicated manoeuvres in order to turn around and try another path. In the end they managed. The dead man lay face down, arms spread. It was hard to tell what colour his jacket was, so soaked was it with the blood, now clotted, which had come out of a small but visible hole just below his right shoulder blade. Not far away from the body was a moped equipped with an ample parcel rack on the back.

'Even without seeing his face,' said Fazio, 'I think I know who this is.'

'It's Dindò,' said Montalbano, 'the kid who used to make deliveries for the supermarket. Already last night Aguglia, the manager, told me he hadn't come in to work that day. And this morning he came and reported the theft of the moped by Dindò.'

'But he was just a poor halfwit!' exclaimed Germanà,

who was part of the squad on duty with Tortorella and
Imbrò.

'We have to find the weapon,' said Montalbano.

'You mean the one he was killed with?' Tortorella asked
in surprise.

'No,' replied Fazio, after a quick glance at Montalbano,
having immediately understood his thoughts. And he added:
'The one Dindò had with him and fired.'

He looked back at Montalbano as if seeking confirmation that what he'd said was correct. The inspector nodded
in assent.

'Jesus Christ! I haven't understood a thing!' Germanà
complained.

'Never mind understanding and just start looking,'
Fazio ordered him.

They looked and looked, going as far as Piccolo's house,
but didn't find anything.

'Maybe the gun's under the body,' Tortorella suggested.

They raised the body up on one side, enough to see what
they needed to see.

'If Arquà saw what we're doing, he'd have a heart attack,'
Fazio commented.

The weapon wasn't there. In compensation, they discovered that his flesh and jacket had been literally torn apart
around the exit wound.

'Maybe he threw it away while crawling to this secluded
spot,' said Fazio.

Montalbano suddenly felt a lump of sorrow in his
throat. Poor Dindò, a mortally wounded man-child coming
here to die unseen, exactly the way animals do . . . Wasn't
Mortally Wounded the title of a beautiful book by Raffaele La
Capria he'd read and loved many years ago?

'He bled to death,' said Fazio, as if he'd been reading
Montalbano's mind.

'Inform whoever you need to inform,' said the inspector.
'But let me speak to Dr Pasquano.'

Moments later, Fazio passed the phone to him.

'Doctor? Montalbano here. Were you able to have a look at Gerlando Piccolo?'

'Yes indeed. Inside and out.'

'Can you tell me anything?'

'There's nothing to tell you. He was killed by a single shot that cut him right down. The details are in the report. He was a picture of health. If they hadn't shot him, he would have lived to be a hundred. He'd just finished having sex.'

This was something Montalbano hadn't expected.

'Before they shot him?'

'No, after. He started fucking after he died. What kind of stupid fucking question is that? Are you sure you feel OK?'

'Doctor, I've got another corpse for you.'

'What, have you decided to go into mass production?'

'Fazio will explain to you how to get here. Have a good day.'

When Fazio had finished speaking to Pasquano, Montalbano called him aside.

'Listen, I'm going to go. You and the others stay here. There's no point in me wasting a whole day looking at a corpse knowing who he is, who shot him, and why.'

'All right,' said Fazio.

'Oh, and listen. You must tell Arquà that I want the dead man's fingerprints compared with those found in Piccolo's bedroom. Just to double-check. And then, to go for broke, I want him to compare Dindò's blood with the dried blood in front of Piccolo's house.'

*

He blew into the station like a bullet. Only Catarella was there.

'Where's Galluzzo?'

"E's at home in 'is house, eating.'

'Get him on the line for me.'

He went into Fazio's office, found the keys to Gerlando Piccolo's place, then went into his own office as the telephone was ringing.

'Have you finished eating, Galluzzo?'

'No sir, we're just starting.'

'I'm sorry, but I'll be outside your front door in five minutes. You and Grazia have to come with me.'

'OK, Chief. Who was the dead man?'

'I'll tell you later.'

They were so punctual that when he arrived outside the front door of Galluzzo's building, they were already waiting outside.

'Where are we going?' asked Galluzzo.

Montalbano answered him indirectly.

'Grazia, do you feel like going back to your house for an hour or so?'

'Sure.'

They were all silent for the rest of the drive. As soon as they entered the house, they were overwhelmed by a dense, musty smell that turned one's stomach.

'Open some windows.'

When the house was aired out, Montalbano explained what he had in mind.

'Now listen to me. I want us to enact a precise reconstruction of what happened the other night. We'll go through it several times, until I'm convinced of certain things. You, Grazia, said you were in your room, sleeping.'

'Yessir.'

'You, Galluzzo, go upstairs into the bedroom, and when I tell you, I want you to start making noise.'

'What kind of noise?'

'How should I know? Throw stuff on the floor, open and close some drawers, stamp your feet.'

Galluzzo headed towards the staircase.

'The two of us will go instead into your bedroom.'

'I was lying down in bed,' Grazia said as soon as they entered.

'Then lie down.'

'I was undressed.'

'There's no need for that. Just take off your shoes.'

Grazia lay down on the unmade bed.

'Was this door open or closed?'

'Closed.'

Before closing it, the inspector shouted:

'OK, Galluzzo, you can start!'

The noise he started making could be heard loud and clear. There was no way Grazia could not have become alarmed.

'Now do what you did.'

The girl got up, took a dressing gown hanging from a nail, and opened the door.

'OK, stop. You stop too, Galluzzo.'

They exited the bedroom and went into the living room. Galluzzo came out at the top of the stairs.

'When you left your room, was the light in the living room on or off?'

'Off.'

'So you ran in the dark.'

'I know the house by heart.'

'Did you notice whether the front door was open or closed?'

'I didn't pay any attention. But it must have been open because when—'

'We'll get to that later. Galluzzo, go back to your room.'

'Should I start making a racket again?'

'Not for the moment. Just get out of here. You, Grazia, go back to your bedroom and close the door. As soon as I tell you, I want you to run out of your room and up the stairs to your uncle's room the way you did that night.'

He closed the windows, shutters, and doors, almost succeeding in making the house totally dark inside.

'Come, Grazia.'

He heard the door opening, then saw a slightly more visible shadow move quickly through the darkness and become a human figure as it climbed the stairs, in the light shining through the bedroom window, which they had left open.

'What should we do?' Galluzzo's voice called from above.

'Wait.'

The inspector left the doors and windows closed, opened the front door, and climbed the stairs.

'Are you sure the door was open when you got to the top of the stairs?' he asked Grazia.

'Absolutely. I could see from the stairs that the light was on. If it was closed, I wouldn't have seen the light.'

'What was the first thing you noticed when you went in?'

'My uncle.'

'Did you see blood?'

'Yes.'

'And what did you think?'

'That he was bleeding from the mouth because he was ill. It was only when I leaned over him that I realized he'd been shot.'

'Galluzzo, go out into the hall. And you, Grazia, go back to your room and come out again, reclimb the stairs, come into this room, and show me the exact moment when you realized that someone had killed your uncle.'

Montalbano went over and stood by the window, to avoid getting in Grazia's way. The girl came up a minute later, panting from the run and her excitement. She passed between the chest of drawers and the foot of the bed, turned around, and when she reached the side where Gerlando Piccolo's body had lain, she leaned slightly forward. Only the bare mattresses remained atop the bedsprings. Forensics had taken everything else away.

'And what happened next?'

'I looked up, because I heard a sound.'

'And what did you see?'

'I saw someone come out from behind the door, where he hid when he heard me coming.'

'Heard you coming? But you were barefoot!'

'I might've been calling my uncle when I was coming up the stairs.'

'Did the man still have the gun in his hand?'

'I don't know, I can't say,' the girl said after thinking about it for a moment.

'All right. Galluzzo! I want you to do what Grazia tells you.'

The girl treated Galluzzo the way a window dresser treats a mannequin. In the end she said:

'OK, when I saw him, he was just like that.'

'If he was just like that, then you couldn't have seen his face. He already had his back to you.'

'And that's why I didn't see his face.'

'Now go back to your place beside the bed. As soon as I say go, you, Galluzzo, run down the stairs and go out of the front door, which is open. And you, Grazia, show me how you grabbed your uncle's gun and pursued the killer. Ready? Go!'

Galluzzo was off, Grazia stood up, opened the drawer of the bedside table, grabbed an imaginary revolver, and dashed after Galluzzo.

'Stop! OK, come back, we're going to do it all over again.'

For a second he felt like one of those legendary hard-to-please film directors.

'This time we're going to add something. You, Grazia, are going to shoot at him like you did that night. And when you do, you're going to shout: "Bang!" And you, Galluzzo, as soon as you hear that, you're going to stop right where you are.'

They repeated the scene three times, and each time, Grazia's 'Bang!' stopped Galluzzo right in the doorway. The timing coincided perfectly.

'All right, now let's all go and sit down in the kitchen.'

Galluzzo gulped down two glasses of a water, one right after the other.

'Shall I make you a little pasta with tomato sauce?' Grazia suggested.

'Sure, why not? While you're doing that, Galluzzo and I'll go outside for a breath of air. Call us when it's ready.'

'Satisfied?' was the first thing Galluzzo asked him.

'Fairly. There's still one detail to be clarified.'

'Which?'

'I'll ask Grazia when we're eating.'

Galluzzo looked miffed and remained silent for a spell. Then he couldn't resist any longer and asked again a question for which he hadn't received an answer.

'So who was killed?'

'Dindò.'

Galluzzo looked shocked.

'The kid from the supermarket?'

'Yes.'

'What could the poor guy have possibly done?'

'Well, he could have done any number of things.'

'Like what?'

'Like killing Gerlando Piccolo.'

To keep from falling to the ground, as his legs had turned to mush, Galluzzo had to lean against the house.

'Are . . . are you kidding me?' he stammered.

'I'm not in the mood.'

Galluzzo ran his hand over his face. Then his eyes opened wide, as he finally understood that two plus two makes four.

'So it was Grazia who shot Dindò!' he said.

'Exactly. And we came back here because I wanted to make sure the girl was telling the truth.'

There was a well beside the house. Montalbano went up to it, followed by Galluzzo, who looked like a puppet whose strings had broken. He lowered the bucket, filled it with water, and hauled it up.

'Come here and wash your face. And don't say anything to Grazia.'

As Galluzzo was splashing water on his face, Montalbano noticed that the window in front of him looked out from the kitchen, and he could see the girl bustling about inside. He went a few steps closer. There was nothing of the beauty that had so struck him the previous evening. Now she just looked like a perfectly normal eighteen-year-old girl, neither beautiful nor ugly, laying the table. If Livia had seen her at that moment, she would certainly have thought that Salvo had been telling her his personal fantasies and passing them off as reality. Grazia, sensing that she was being watched, looked up and smiled at him.

'You can come in now, it's ready.'

They sat down and ate in silence. When they'd finished, the inspector said:

'Excellent sauce. Where did you buy it?'

'I didn't buy it. I made it myself.'

'My compliments. Listen, Grazia, I need to ask you a few more things.'

'OK.'

'How were you able to tell that the man was in the doorway – in other words, still inside the house – and that therefore you could still get off a shot at him?'

She didn't hesitate.

'He was running away and his shoes made a lot of noise. I just fired the gun blindly, and whatever happened, happened. It never occurred to me I actually hit him.'

'Why didn't you follow him outside?'

'I was afraid he would shoot me first. He had a gun.'

'A short while ago you said you didn't know whether the man had a gun in his hand.'

'But he killed my uncle, didn't he?' Grazia said resentfully. 'Anyway, I didn't know if I'd a managed to go down the stairs. My legs were shaking.'

'OK, so you fired blindly, but you shot him beneath one shoulder blade. He went off and hid and was later found dead from loss of blood about half a kilometre from here. With that gunshot wound, he couldn't get very far.'

Grazia turned pale.

'What are they going to do to me?'

'They can't do anything to you.'

'Did you identify him?'

'Yes. It was Dindò, the kid from the supermarket.'

Quite unexpectedly, Grazia gave a hint of a smile.

'Dindò? I don't believe it. Come on, tell me. Who was it?'

'Dindò,' Galluzzo confirmed.

'Did you know him?' Montalbano asked.

'Of course I knew him. He used to bring us stuff at least twice a week. But we never got to know each other. Dindò! But why'd he do it? What for? He was just some unhappy jerk! Some poor guy! And I killed him!'

She started crying desperately. Galluzzo got up and stroked her hair gently.

✼

Barely able to remain standing, Grazia asked for permission to go and lie down on the bed. Montalbano for his part went upstairs into Piccolo's office and handed the keys to the wall-safe to Galluzzo, who opened it. Inside was only a little money in cash, not even two hundred thousand lire; a large enveloped misshapen from the papers it contained; and a small metal file box that looked like a drawer, full of index cards in alphabetical order. At the top of each card were the first and last names of the client, the date of the loan, the due dates, and the payments received. The loans all involved large sums from fifty million lire upwards. The filing cabinet in the room, for its part, contained an infinity of similar cards but for smaller loans, from one hundred thousand lire up to twenty or thirty million. Gerlando Piccolo's volume of business, so to speak, must have been almost as much as that of a small bank. And the papers in the envelope confirmed this for the inspector: they were all account statements from banks in Vigàta and Montelusa amounting to figures in the billions of lire.

It didn't add up.

'Did they find any money in the clothes Piccolo had taken off before going to bed?'

'Yes, sir. Over three hundred thousand lire.'

'Which Dindò didn't touch.'

'Maybe he didn't have time to.'

Why did Gerlando Piccolo keep less than two hundred thousand lire in his safe and carry more than three hundred thousand on his person?

5

Three days later, the initial findings of the crime lab came in. They'd taken only three days! Enough to give one a heart attack. The bureaucracy, the inspector reflected, is a labyrinth in which lie the blanched bones of millions of files that never had the chance to come out. Fallen to the ground for not having been pushed hard enough, the files are overwhelmed by thousands of famished rats that devour them. He'd glimpsed these rats on occasion as packs of them raced through the file-stuffed cellars of various courthouses. Ever so rarely, and for utterly inexplicable reasons, one file in ten thousand would manage to travel the labyrinth with the speed of an Olympic hundred-metre sprinter and reach its destination. As in the present case. Fingerprints aplenty, belonging to Dindò, whose real name was Salvatore Trupìa, had been found in Gerlando Piccolo's bedroom; and it was

Dindò's very own blood that had formed the little puddle as he tried to start up his moped after killing 'u zu Giurlanno. The murder weapon had never been found. Most likely Dindò got rid of it while fleeing to his death. And then there were the statements made by Mr Arturo Pastorino, shop owner, who said that while driving down the provincial road at the time the crime had taken place, he'd seen the light in front of Gerlando Piccolo's house come on and, a second later, a moped speed away from Piccolo's house and onto the same provincial road, very nearly crashing into Mr Pastorino's car.

✼

Grazia repeated her story of that night some ten times to Prosecutor Tommaseo without ever changing so much as a syllable. But for the prosecutor this wasn't enough.

'You see, Montalbano, I would like to re-enact the event at the scene of the crime. I want that girl to stand naked before me.'

He was practically foaming at the mouth. But since he caught a glint of irony in the inspector's glance, he reached for a fig-leaf:

'Figuratively speaking, of course.'

The re-enactment at the scene of the crime brought out nothing new. As for the light that was on in front of Piccolo's house, which the witness Pastorino had seen, Grazia forcefully maintained that that light was off. The prosecutor called it a negligible detail; the witness probably mistook the moped's headlight for the light that normally illuminated the area in front of the house.

Before reaching this conclusion, however, Tommaseo wanted to verify something that he had got into his head at the very start of the case.

'Miss, was your uncle a homosexual?'

Grazia gave a hearty laugh.

'No, he didn't go with men. He liked women.'

'Even in town they say he took advantage of women,' the inspector interjected.

'*Vox populi* isn't always *vox Dei!*' Tommaseo fulminated. Then, turning back to the girl: 'So you would rule that out?'

'I never saw any of his night-time visitors.'

'So you don't know whether they were men or women?'

'No, I don't.'

'Therefore you can't rule out that they might have also been men.'

'What do you mean, "also"?'

'Haven't you ever heard of bisexuality?' the prosecutor said ironically, licking his bottom lip.

As far as that went, Montalbano had even heard of tri-sexuality, quadrisexuality, and so on down the line, but he thought it better to let it slide.

Grazia, too, let it slide.

'I don't know what to say,' she said.

And so the prosecutor had an open road before him.

'I have two hypotheses,' he declared once he was left alone with the inspector. 'The first is that Piccolo had an appointment in the middle of the night with Trupìa, whom he knew from having stuff delivered to his home from the supermarket. At the appointed hour, Piccolo gets up, goes downstairs, opens the front door carefully so as not to wake his niece up, lets Trupìa in, and closes the door but doesn't lock it. After having relations, the two men quarrel. Perhaps Piccolo doesn't want to pay Trupìa what he wants. And so the young man loses his head and shoots him, then tries to grab what he can. The unexpected intervention of the brave girl, however, forces him to flee. He manages to open the front door, but is shot by Grazia. And so Trupìa lets himself bleed to death. He can't go to any hospital, since he would have to explain what happened, which he can't do because he would then be immediately identified as Piccolo's mur-derer.'

He drank half a glass of the bottle of mineral water he'd sent for, then continued.

'Now for my second hypothesis, which will surely be the more appreciated, given your obstinate refusal to admit that Piccolo was also a homosexual. So, Piccolo has an appointment that night with a woman. He opens the front door for her, brings her upstairs into his room. They have sexual congress. When they're finished, the woman leaves and Piccolo tells her to be sure to close the door behind her. He'll lock it as soon as he finds the strength to get out of bed. Apparently the woman has . . . well, never mind. The woman, however, opens the door, lets Trupìa in, and then leaves. Trupìa thinks Piccolo won't react when he threatens him with a gun, but in fact he makes a move and Trupìa shoots him. And we know what happens next. But now we need to find . . .'

'Waldo?' the inspector asked in the most serious of tones.

'What? I didn't get that,' said Tommaseo, flummoxed.

'Sorry, I was distracted. You were saying we had to find . . .'

'The woman who was his accomplice. But how? Where should we look?'

'It would be like looking for a needle in a haystack,' said Montalbano, knowing that clichés have a tendency to impose a full stop heavier than a boulder.

'Right. Which do you prefer?'

'Which of what?'

'My two hypotheses.'

'The second one.'

'But the second one forces us to keep the investigation open to look for the mysterious female accomplice!'

'Then let's take the first one instead.'

After all, why bother to waste one's time and breath on Tommaseo?

*

When, years later, he happened to think back on the Piccolo
case, he was never able to explain why, that same afternoon,
he went to see Dindò's father. Perhaps it was to ease his
conscience of the fact that he'd allowed Tommaseo to write,
in the conclusion to his report, that the poor youth 'was in
the practice of prostituting himself for money'. He'd got the
father's address from Aguglia, the supermarket manager,
who'd asked him, as soon as he'd seen him:

'When will I get the scooter back?'

Reassured that it would be returned to him in the
coming days, Mr Aguglia saw fit to express an opinion he
had about Dindò.

'Inspector, with all due respect to law enforcement, this
whole business seems fishy to me.'

'How?'

'Just to make things clear, I'm talking based on what I've
been hearing in town. Dindò didn't go with men *or* with
women. And he wasn't capable of stealing so much as a
toothpick. Here at the supermarket he could take whatever
he liked, and yet every time he needed something he would
say so and pay for it. He was an honest kid.'

Dindò's father's house was near the harbour. It was a
tiny construction so rickety that one wondered how it ever
remained standing without the help of outside supports.
The ground floor used to be a large warehouse but was now
closed, with a large plank of wood nailed over the doorway.
And just in front of the front door leading upstairs was
another door, also closed, which led into a space under the
staircase. Above, on the first and only floor, lived Antonio
Trupìa. Montalbano knocked. A decrepit old man with a
hunched back and no teeth, even more rickety than the
house, came to the door.

'Inspector Montalbano, police. Are you the grandfather
of Salvatore Trupìa, known as Dindò?'

'Grandfather? I'm his father.'

Jesus! So how old was he when he sired Dindò? The old man seemed to realize what the inspector was thinking.

'I had m'boy Dindò pretty late in life, maybe tha'ss why he came out a little off in the head.'

The man showed him into a room that was a jumble of filth and disorder and sat him down in a wobbly straw chair.

'Ya gotta 'scuse me, Isspector, fer receiving you this way. But I'm ill, I'm a widower, I live on the minimum pension, an' I got no one to help me.'

'I wanted to know something about Dindò.'

'An' what do you want to know, Inspector? Alls I know is they killed 'im. But the history of us poor folk's never told by us, iss told by them that write in the papers.'

Deep down, the inspector thought, the man was absolutely right: lately the journalists were passing themselves off more and more as historians.

'Why didn't he want to live any more in your house? Did you quarrel?'

'Nah, never! You couldn't quarrel with Dindò! How do you quarrel with a little kid? No, 'bout four years ago, when he started getting' paid at the supermarket, he tol' me he wanted to go live alone. An' so I gave him the key to the cubbyhole under the stairs, which belongs to me.'

'Did you see him often?'

'Nossir. But if that's what you wanna know, over the past couple o' months he'd changed.'

'How can you say that if you never saw him?'

'I could hear it. He'd started singing, last couple o' months.'

'Singing?'

'Yessir. At the top of his lungs. In the morning, when he woke up, and in the evening when he came home.'

'And he never sang before then?'

'Never.'

'Listen, I'd like to have a look at his room under the stairs.'

'Here, take the key.'

'I'll bring it back when I'm done.'

'There's no need. Just leave it in the door. Nobody comes here anyway.'

'Would you tell me something? Why was he called Dindò?'

'He liked the sound of the bells. Whenever they rang, he would go *dingdong* with his head, rockin' it from side to side.'

The cubbyhole under the stairs was about ten feet by ten, with a sloping ceiling and a tiny window about ten inches square and barred, which let in some air but no light. The furnishings consisted of a rusted bedstead with a mattress on top, a blanket riddled with holes, a pillow without a pillowcase, a tiny little table, and a wicker chair. A stack of cardboard boxes served as a dresser. In a sort of recess there was a toilet bowl and a small sink with a continually running tap. A pigsty, Mr Aguglia had called it. But in fact it was somewhat worse, more like an abandoned prison cell in an underdeveloped country. Dirty socks, underpants, and vests, newspaper pages, comic books, and old issues of *Topolino* covered the floor. The inspector felt heartsick, and decided to close the door and leave. But, as sometimes happened to him, his body refused to obey the order. And so he cleared off the chair and sat down in it. How was it possible that one fine day joy had entered this stinking cell, a happiness so great as to make Dindò, who had never done so before, suddenly start singing at the top of his lungs and not stop until the moment he was shot? Until he was mortally wounded like a bird in flight cut down by a hunter? Again the title of that novel came back to him. He couldn't see inside that little space under the stairs and would have had to get up and turn on the little light bulb hanging from the ceiling, but he didn't feel like it. He wanted to stay a little longer in the dark amidst the stench, hoping to coax the answers to his questions from that stench. The first and

certainly most important question was: why had Dindò
killed Gerlando Piccolo? That was the kid's intention when
he entered the room in which Piccolo was lying. Everything
else, the rifled drawers, the smashed paintings pointing to a
breathless search for something to steal, was all theatre,
stage decor. And somebody'd put a revolver in his hands –
Dindò would never have been able to get one on his own
– and convinced him that the loan shark deserved to die.
And Dindò had done what he'd been talked into doing. And
since he was the way he was, when he found himself confronted with Grazia, he hadn't shot her, which would have
been easy as pie, not to mention inevitable, because it had
never even remotely occurred to him that the girl might
react or, if he was arrested, could become a damning witness. No, these were all considerations that Dindò's childlike
brain was unable to work out. He'd simply tried to run
away, just as someone had told him to do.

The second question was: how did he get inside the
house? The front door showed no signs of having been
forced. He'd probably used duplicate keys. But for the keys
to be copied, someone would have had to make impressions
of them, which meant that there had to be, aside from the
niece, someone who could go in and out of the house at will
and freely. Who could that be? There was no housekeeper,
not even a daytime cleaning lady. Grazia saw to everything.
Piccolo's clients were made to climb the outdoor staircase
and had no idea what the house was like inside. And so?
Montalbano racked his brains, and soon a figure of a man,
with no face or name, began to surface in his head. A person
everyone in town was afraid of, and whom Fazio had been
unable to identify: the man who used to go and shake down
clients for Piccolo. His collector. Now everything began
hesitantly to acquire logic and reason, even if it was still ever
so faintly outlined.

He got up to go back to the station, and when moving
about in the dark, he ran into the little table and knocked

it over. Cursing the saints, he turned on the light and noticed that the little table had a drawer which had come open. Inside was a comic book called *Zorno, the Masked Avenger*. Zorno? He thumbed through it. It was a porn version of Zorro.

In the margin of each page, Dindò had written the same word with a red ballpoint: *JUSTICE!*

He put the comic in his jacket pocket, turned off the light, and went out.

*

Instead of going to the station, he went to Galluzzo's. When he rang the buzzer, Grazia's voice answered at once.

'Who is it?'

'Montalbano.'

When the girl opened the door for him, he noticed immediately that she was pale and her eyes were red. At that moment you certainly couldn't say she was pretty.

'Are you alone in the house?'

'Yes. Amelia's out shopping.'

'What were you doing?'

'Nothing.'

'Do you feel bad?'

'Yes.'

'What's wrong? Would you like to see a doctor?'

'No, it's nothing for a doctor. It's just that . . . I haven't been able to sleep since I found out I killed that poor guy . . . An' . . . An' I wish I could go home.'

'Don't you like it here?'

'I do, but home is home.'

'Aren't you afraid to go and live there alone?'

'I'm not afraid of anything.'

'Just a few more days – three, at the most – and you'll be able to go home. But I came to ask you something that could be extremely useful to us in investigating your uncle's murder.'

Grazia, alarmed, opened her eyes wide.

'Why, is the investigation still going on? Didn't Dindò do it?'

'Of course Dindò did it. But haven't you ever wondered how Dindò got inside the house that night? Either someone opened the door for him or he had a duplicate key. In either case it means that he had an accomplice. And the accomplice was someone who was free to go in and out of the house whenever he liked. So my question for you is this: was there anyone your uncle saw often? Someone he also spent a lot of time talking to? Whom he would sometimes invite to stay for lunch?'

The girl's face lit up.

'There certainly was! A guy called Fonzio. An' sometimes 'u zu Giurlanno would ask me to bring them coffee when they were talking in the office.'

'Do you know his surname?'

'No.'

At that moment they heard the front door open. It was Galluzzo's wife, returning with the groceries.

'Signora Amelia, Grazia's coming with me to the station. Your husband'll bring her back with him later. And you, Grazia, will you need to change before coming out?'

'Yessir, it won't take more than five minutes.'

*

Montalbano sat Grazia down beside Catarella, who showed her, on the computer monitor, mug shots of every convicted criminal in Vigàta and environs. He barely had time to sit down at his desk before Catarella streaked into the room, halted in his mad dash by Fazio, who grabbed him on the fly. He was panting.

'Chief! The goil idinnified 'im!'

They went into Catarella's cupboard. Grazia was sitting in one corner, face buried in her hands and crying.

'Galluzzo! Take the girl back home, would you?'

The file said that Alfonso Aricò, born forty years earlier in Vigàta, was the kind of person you wouldn't want to break bread with. He was a gambler. And when he wasn't gambling, stuff like burglary, extortion, assault, rape, vandalism, and battery was his daily fare. The photo showed a good-looking man with the face of a born criminal.

'Fazio, spread the word around. I want this cretin in my office first thing tomorrow morning.'

6

He ate listlessly, with no appetite, sitting at the table and looking at the album of comics he'd taken from Dindò's hovel. There had been a good ten or so such albums scattered across the floor, but this one the half-wit had given special importance, keeping it in the drawer of the little table so that he could read and reread it, as was visible from the sullied and worn-out pages. Then at a certain point Dindò had started writing that single word, *justice*, in the margins. A word that, in itself, did not explain whether Dindò intended to administer justice himself or to demand it. The inspector started reading the comic book's story with saintly forbearance. It was about a dirty old man of the upper classes who plots to kidnap a beautiful young girl and make her yield to his desires. After a number of vicissitudes, the kidnapping is pulled off successfully, and the dirty old squire can finally contemplate Alba (that was the girl's name) naked and imploring, in his very own bedroom. Her teary entreaties and laments only serve to enflame the old man's passions, and he grabs her and possesses her in every manner possible. Then he has her thrown into a cell, promising himself a repeat of the whole business after a restorative sleep. But Zorno, having managed to enter the nobleman's house on the sly, kills him after a series of intense duels with his henchmen. He frees the girl, and in her happiness and gratitude she sets about doing even nastier things with the masked avenger than were done to her by the old man. An idiotic pretext for making pornographic drawings. But why had Dindò felt the obsessive need to keep writing that comment: *justice*? Maybe he was like one of those common movie-goers who get so engrossed in the plot that they shout out comments, advice, and suggestions to the unhearing shadows on the screen who irremediably follow the path marked for them by fate and the screenwriter. The inspector became almost convinced of this explanation. He went and sat down in his usual armchair and turned on the TV. Onscreen appeared a political debate, already in progress, on the question 'Is it legitimate for an undersecretary still in office to start making paid advertisements on television?'. About halfway through he turned it off, feeling depressed. He rang Livia and talked about Dindò, describing to her the filthy cell the kid had lived in. And he asked her:

'But can you tell me why a poor wretch like that would suddenly start singing, amidst all that squalor?'

Livia gave a simple answer that, in its very simplicity – indeed, in its very obviousness – had the force of absolute truth.

'Why, Salvo? He was in love.'

There was a flash. He staggered, barely managing to remain standing, and grabbed the table with one hand. In dizzying fashion, all the pieces of the puzzle fell into place, forming a logical, perfect picture.

'Salvo? Salvo! Why don't you answer?'

He was unable to open his mouth and tell her he was still on the line. He hung up.

*

Over the course of the morning, his men came into the station one by one, dejected and empty-handed. They hadn't succeeded in tracking down Fonzio Aricò, the ex-con who worked as Gerlando Piccolo's enforcer. His neighbours hadn't seen him for a week, saying he often did that, staying away for many days at a time without coming home. And each of them, expecting a scene of furious rage when reporting the negative results of his search, was shocked at the inspector's placid, courteous reply.

'OK, thanks.'

Indeed they were so astonished that they asked each other whether their superior hadn't perhaps grown stigmata on his hands and feet in the meantime.

That same morning, Montalbano made two phone calls, the first to Prosecutor Tommaseo, which turned out to be quite long, as the prosecutor demanded a great many explanations. The second call was to the captain of the Flying Squad, who didn't ask for any explanations at all. But he said there was just one problem. For how long would the inspector need the equipment? Montalbano replied that the whole matter would be settled within forty-eight hours. And so they came to an agreement.

At four o'clock that afternoon, an officer of the Flying Squad came and brought him the keys to Gerlando Piccolo's house. Half an hour later, Montalbano summoned Galluzzo and told him, as he gave him the keys, that Grazia could go back home if she wanted.

'Actually, call her right now, from here.'

After hanging up, Galluzzo told him the girl wanted to go home straight away, while there was still light. Not that she was afraid or anything, but she would be less impressionable this way.

'If you'll allow me, I'll take her home in my car. I should be able to get there and back in an hour, max.'

'Listen, there's no need for you to come back to the station. After helping Grazia get settled, go straight home. At the most you can give me a ring and tell me how she reacted, and whether there were any problems. And tell her she can call me for any reason at all if she starts to get worried.'

Galluzzo smiled.

'Inspector, that girl never worries about anything. She's got courage to burn. What is there for her to get worried about anyway?'

'There's Fonzio Aricò, for one. We've been unable to track him down, but that doesn't mean he isn't waiting around for the right moment to reappear.'

Galluzzo's smile vanished.

'And what could Fonzio want from Grazia?'

'I don't know. Maybe Gerlando Piccolo's papers. If he knows how to play them right, he could make some serious money.'

'You're right. Do you want me to stay with her tonight?'

'Who's to say Fonzio's going to come tonight? Listen, you can tell Grazia that tomorrow I'll get authorization to confiscate all of Piccolo's papers, so she can rest easy. So, no, just do as I said.'

Galluzzo rang at seven-thirty. He had just got home after dropping off Grazia, who was happy to be back in her own world. The other phone call that Montalbano was waiting for, the one that he hoped would confirm that his castle of conjectures was made not of sand but of stone and mortar, came barely an hour later.

'Inspector Montalbano? She called. As soon as a man's voice answered, she said she was finally back home and there was no surveillance. She added that she had two things to give him. And the man answered that he would come to her place shortly after midnight. So what do we do now?'

'That's all, thanks.'

After this phone call confirming that he'd been right on the mark, he should have felt something other than the wave of nausea that gripped his stomach.

'Fazio! Gallo!'

'Yessir.'

'I want you both to go home and eat and then come back

here. Inform your families that you're going to be busy tonight.'

The two looked at each other in consternation, then looked at the inspector as if asking a question.

'I'll explain everything when you get back. There's no hurry. But don't say anything to anyone. I mean it.'

'How can we say anything if we don't know anything?' asked Fazio.

Montalbano also left the station. He felt as if he couldn't breathe. When he reached the Trattoria San Calogero, he had a moment of hesitation. Should he go in or not? Then the nausea returned, stronger than before. And so he headed for the harbour, stopping to watch the tourists boarding the ferry for the islands. They were almost all young foreigners wearing backpacks. They certainly weren't going to enrich the islands with their money – but with the beauty of their youth, yes. He sighed and began his customary walk to the end of the jetty.

*

'They're all just conjectures of mine, mind you, but they're starting to be confirmed. At the Piccolos' house, where she was taken in at the age of five after both parents died, Grazia was always treated like a slave. She told me this herself, and I don't think she was exaggerating. And I'm also convinced that Uncle Gerlando, who was who he was, took advantage of his niece when she was still a little girl. Then, as soon as the aunt dies, Grazia becomes her uncle's steady mistress when he can't find anything better. For years – first in confused fashion, but then more and more clearly and strongly – the girl develops a hatred for the man, but can't rebel. She has no way out. Until the day when an understanding, a passion, or whatever you want to call it, is born between her and Fonzio Aricò, the enforcer. The uncle doesn't notice anything. He stays in his office upstairs, sucking people's blood, while Grazia and Fonzio do what they please downstairs. One day Grazia and Fonzio get an idea, and we'll clarify this later: they decide to free themselves of Gerlando Piccolo and start out on their own, while carrying on his practice. Piccolo's inheritance was certainly going to go to Grazia anyway, since he didn't have any other relatives. But how would they pull the thing off without arousing suspicion? The ideal scenario would be for some third person to kill Gerlando. And this is where Grazia – and I'm sure she was the one to come up with the idea – remembers Dindò, the supermarket delivery boy who's about twenty with the brain of a four-year-old. She starts being nice to him, tries to win his trust, and every time she sees him she shows him more and more affection. And Dindò falls for it. He falls in love, in fact. And so Grazia confesses to him that she can never be his, because she's imprisoned by her uncle, who sates his base desires on her and forces her to do repugnant things. Dindò gets all worked up, feels like a knight of yore, and promises to free the girl and kill the man keeping her prisoner. He vows up and down to do right by her. At first Grazia pretends to try and talk him out of it, but then finally says that if he's really so determined, she could slip him one of the firearms that are in the house. But after he uses it, he'll have to take it away with him.'

'But we've recovered all the firearms that were in the house,' Fazio cut in, 'and none of them fired the shot that killed Piccolo.'

'Because in fact that weapon belongs to Fonzio Aricò. But let me continue. On the appointed night, Grazia, once she's finished her work in the kitchen, quietly opens the front door and leaves the revolver Aricò gave her on the first step of the staircase.'

'Can I interrupt? Where's Fonzio in the meantime?' Fazio asked.

'He's working on an iron-clad alibi. Undoubtedly in a gambling den, with fifty other people who can testify for him. Grazia wants to be certain that Dindò will fire the gun. So the ideal situation would be for him to come in just as her uncle is forcing her to do those things she finds so repugnant, as she's already told the kid. And in fact that's exactly what happens.'

'Wait a second,' said Gallo. 'The position of the corpse—'

'I know what you're thinking. But you, Gallo, are enough of a grown-up to know that to make love you don't always have to do it in the traditional position.'

Gallo blushed and said nothing.

'Dindò is late in arriving, and so Grazia remains glued to Piccolo, even afterwards. When Dindò finally gets there, Grazia screams and breaks away, the kid fires, sets the gun down and starts turning the room upside down to make it look like a burglary. But at this point Dindò's rage suddenly subsides and he looks over at Piccolo's dead body and realizes what he's done. He goes completely berserk, smashing the paintings and the little statue of the Madonna, then races out of the room. Grazia realizes she's screwed. She thinks, or probably guesses, that sooner or later Dindò will cave and spill all the beans. So she opens the drawer to the bedside table, grabs her uncle's gun, runs after the kid and fires, mortally wounding him.'

'And that's something I don't understand,' said Fazio. 'If he was really planning to spill the beans and turn himself in, and if he had the strength to get to the spot where he finally died, why didn't he just go to any house whatsoever, say the one closest to Piccolo's, and ask for help?'

'Because the moment he's wounded by Grazia's bullet, Dindò becomes an adult.'

'I don't understand,' Fazio muttered.

'Before that he was a little boy in love who didn't know what he was doing. One second later he realized he was a murderer who'd been manipulated like a puppet. The bullet didn't mortally wound just his body, but also, and above all,

his soul, because it meant that Grazia had betrayed him. He
wanted to let himself die.'

'But even if the girl hadn't shot him, Grazia and Fonzio
must already have made plans for Dindò,' said Fazio.

'Of course. They would have got rid of him quickly,
maybe making it look like an accident. But let me continue.
When she sees Dindò is still running away, Grazia chases
after him, turns on the light in front of the house – a witness already reported this detail, though the prosecutor had
a different interpretation for it – but the kid has already
started up his scooter and is gone. Grazia sees the blood on
the ground, but doesn't know how serious the wound is.
And this worries her, it makes her nervous, and so she makes
a mistake. Her only one, in an otherwise perfect plan. She
goes back up to her uncle's room – to see if there's anything
that can still be done for him, or so she tells us later – and
she drops the revolver she shot Dindò with, grabs the keys
to the safe, goes into the office, takes the money she finds
in it – and there must've been a lot – leaves two hundred
thousand lire behind, closes and locks it, puts the keys back,
and at this point she realizes that the gun that Dindò used,
the one given him by Fonzio, is on the bed, or somewhere
else in the room. She doesn't know what to do. According
to the plan, Dindò was supposed to take it away with him
and Fonzio would get it back later and dispose of it. Grazia,
fearing that the gun could lead back to Aricò, hides it in the
house together with the money. The house that we never
searched, since, aside from the bedroom and office, there
wasn't any reason to.'

'But how do you know all this about the weapon?' asked
Gallo.

'I don't; I'm just assuming it. To be honest with you, it's
the weakest point of my reconstruction. But if Dindò had a
crisis when still at the Piccolo house, the first thing he
would have done was to throw the gun as far away from him
as possible. At any rate, after hiding the money and the gun,

Grazia calls us, saying that her uncle's been murdered. And she's scared to death because she doesn't know anything about Dindò, whether or not he's strong enough to report the crime and turn her in, but she manages to control herself quite well. I was the one who gave her the news of the kid's dead body being found, and she played her part well.'

'Chief, you said that this reconstruction of yours was starting to be confirmed,' said Fazio. 'How?'

'The minute Grazia was left alone in the house, she called Fonzio.'

'How do you know?'

'I had her phone tapped. She told him to come to her place because she had two things to give him. If you ask me, she's talking about the gun and the money. Fonzio replied that he'd come by to see her after midnight.'

'So what are we going to do?'

'We'll take up position in the vicinity. We'll steel our nerves for a few hours in the cool night air. Because there's going to be a lot of kisses, hugs, a little fuck in celebration, and then some mutual storytelling. Then, when Aricò comes back out, we'll arrest him. If we find the money and the gun on him, he's screwed. He can probably defend himself about the money, saying it's his, that he won it in some gambling den, but the gun will hang him, because there's nothing he can say about that. It won't take much to prove that it's the weapon that fired the shot that killed Piccolo. How's he ever going to explain how we found it in his pocket?'

'What about Grazia?'

'You two'll have to go and arrest her yourselves. I don't want to get my hands dirty.'

*

Montalbano was right on the money. Fonzio Aricò arrived at half-past midnight. The house was all dark, the door opened, Fonzio went in, and the door closed. After an hour of waiting, Montalbano, Fazio, and Gallo were beginning to get cold and started swearing. They couldn't even warm themselves up with a cigarette. At ten past three in the morning, the first to notice that the door had opened and a shadow had come out was the inspector. Fonzio headed for his car, which he had left on the main road. He was carrying a package in his hand. When he went to open the car door, Fazio and Gallo jumped on him, threw him to the ground, and handcuffed him. It all happened without any noise. In Fonzio's pocket was a revolver, which Fazio took and handed to Montalbano.

'You know that you're fucked now, with this?' the inspector asked him.

Aricò smiled unexpectedly.

'Of course I know,' he said.

Inside the cardboard box was eight hundred million lire in bills of varying size. Fonzio Aricò was a good gambler who understood when he'd lost a game, and didn't even try to claim that the money was his.

In the car he spoke only once.

'For what it's worth, Inspector, I wasn't really the one who set this whole thing up. It was that nasty little bitch.'

Montalbano didn't have much trouble believing him. He had Gallo drop him off at the station, then got in his car and drove home to Marinella.

An hour later, the telephone rang. It was Fazio.

'We've arrested the girl,' he said.

'What was she doing?'

'What do you expect? She was sleeping like an angel.'

＊

The following week, the whole department was busy consoling Galluzzo, who had grown fond of Grazia and didn't want to believe the whole story. Indeed every five minutes he would poke his head into Montalbano's office, a sorrowful expression on his face, and ask:

'Can it really be true, Inspector?'

After an hour of this, Montalbano couldn't take it any more and got up, stepped out, and went to see Mimì Augello, who'd had a relapse.

'How can this be, Mimì? Before, you never used to even catch cold, and now you get every bug that's in circulation!'

'I can't explain it, Salvo.'

'Want me to explain it for you? It's psychosomatic.'

'I don't get it.'

'It's the fact that you're going to get married soon, and so you come down with every illness imaginable to try and postpone your wedding day for as long as you can.'

'Oh, don't be so silly! Tell me instead about the murder of that loan shark — what was his name? — oh, yeah, Piccolo.'

So Montalbano told him. And he also told him about the strange thing that happened to him when Grazia appeared on TV and she'd looked to him like an exceptionally beautiful girl, which in reality she wasn't.

'Well,' said Mimì, 'apparently the video camera revealed Grazia's true face to you. Based on your description of her, the girl seems like a real devil. And people who know about these things are always talking about the devil's beauty.'

Montalbano didn't believe in the devil, let alone clichés, commonplaces, or truisms. But this time he didn't object.

CATARELLA SOLVES A CASE

'How did I get into this?' Montalbano asked himself as he got out of the car and looked around. It was 6 a.m. and the morning was shaping up to be clear and pleasant. After a half-hour's drive on the road to Fela and another fifteen minutes on an impassable track, he still had another fifteen minutes to go, at the very least – but all on foot, because the track had turned into a little trail negotiable only by goats. He looked up. At the top of the hill he wanted to reach, the old bunker wasn't visible, hidden as it was amidst clumps of wild plants. He cursed the saints, took a deep breath as if about to dive underwater, and began to climb.

*

An hour and a half earlier, he'd been awakened by the telephone.

'Hullo, Chief? Izzatchoo poissonally in poisson?'

'Yeah, Cat.'

'What wuz ya doin', Chief, sleepin'?'

'Until a moment ago, yes, I was sleeping.'

'An' now y'ain't sleepin' no mores?'

'No, I'm not sleeping any more, Cat.'

'Ah, good.'

'Why is that good, Cat?'

'Cuzzit means I dint wake yiz up, Chief.'

Either shoot him in the face at the first opportunity, or pretend it's nothing.

'Cat, if you don't mind too much, would you please tell
me why you're calling me?'

'Cuz Isspecter Augello's gotta a col' an' fever.'

'Cat, what the hell do I care if Augello is ill at four-
thirty in the morning? Don't call me, call a doctor for him
and then call Fazio.'

'Fazio in't in neither. 'E's onna stakeout wit' Gallo 'n'
Galluzzo.'

'All right, Cat, what is it?'

'A shippard called. Sez 'e foun' a kiddaver.'

'Where?'

'In Passo di Cane districk. From isside an ol' banker.
Do y'rimimmer, Chief, you wint 'ere roundabouts tree years
ago to—'

'Yeah, Cat, I know where it is. And it's called a bunker.'

'Why, wha'd I call it?'

'Banker.'

'Iss the same ting, Chief.'

'Where was this shepherd calling from?'

'Where djy'aspeck 'e's callin' from? From the banker,
Chief.'

'There's no telephone there! It's in the middle of nowhere.'

'The shippard called from 'is mobble phone, Chief.'

He should have known! A few more years and anyone in
Italy caught without a mobile phone would be arrested
immediately.

'All right, Cat, I'll go there myself. But as soon as anyone
gets back to the office, send them to me at the bunker.'

'But 'ow 'm I gonna know, Chief?'

'How are you going to know what, Cat?'

''Ow'm I gonna know 'oo gits back to the affice? I'm 'ere.'

The inspector felt a sudden chill.

'Do you mean to tell me you went to the bunker yourself?'

'Yessir, Chief. Seein' as how there's nobody around . . .'

'Wait for me right there and don't touch anything, I mean it. By the way, where are you, in fact?'

'I tol' yiz. I came ousside cuz inside there's no recession. I'm callin' wit' my mobble phone.'

'Well, since you've got your mobble phone, mobble phone a call to Pasquano and the prosecutor.'

'Beckin' yer pardin an' all, Chief, ya don' say "mobble phone a call", even if ya gotta mobble phone, you jess make a call like wit' a reggler phone.'

✱

As soon as he spotted the inspector in the distance, Catarella started waving his arms in the air like a castaway on a deserted island who's just seen a ship on the water.

'Over 'ere, Chief! Over 'ere!'

The bunker was built right at the edge of a very steep cliff. Below lay a narrow strip of golden-yellow beach and the sea. Montalbano noticed a car stopped on the beach.

'What's that car doing there?'

'I c'n tell yiz, Chief.'

'Then tell me.'

'Iss cuz I came 'ere innat car. It b'longs t'me, so iss mine.'

'And how did you get all the way up here?'

'I climbed up the rock's face. I'm better 'n' a Alpist.'

Around his neck Catarella was wearing a large battery-powered lamp. For once he'd done something right, as the bunker would certainly be completely dark inside. They went down a staircase that had once been made of cement and was now a sort of rubbish dump. They found more rubbish inside the bunker. By the light of Catarella's lamp, the inspector walked on a thick layer of shit, plastic bags, cans, bottles, condoms, and syringes. There was even a rusted baby walker. The dead body lay on its back, the lower half immersed in waste. It was a woman, bare-chested and in jeans half open over her stomach. Rodents and dogs had devastated her face, making her unrecognizable. Montalbano asked for the lamp and had a close look at the body.

'Chief, if ya don' mind, I'm goin' ousside,' said Catarella, who could no longer stand the sight.

There were no visible traces of firearm injuries. But the victim might have been strangled or stabbed from behind with a knife. All he could do was wait outside for Dr Pasquano, since, among other things, the air in there was irrespirable, and the stench seized you by the throat.

'Tink I c'd 'ave a cigarette?' Catarella asked him, looking jaundiced.

They smoked for a while in silence, looking out at the sea.

'What happened to the shepherd?' the inspector asked.

''E left 'cuz 'e 'adda go an' take care o' 'is sheep. But I writ down 'is name an' addriss.'

'Did he tell you why he'd gone into the bunker in the first place?'

''E 'adda relief 'isself.'

*

'I have a vague hunch as to who this poor woman might be,' said Fazio, back from his stakeout of a fugitive, which had come to nothing.

Montalbano had returned to the office after Dr Pasquano had the body taken away for the post-mortem. The doctor promised to let him know the results the following day.

'Who do you think she is?'

'Her name is probably Maria Lojacono, wife of a certain Salvatore Piscopo, street vendor by trade.'

The inspector showed clear signs of irritation. Fazio's mania for people's personal particulars got on his nerves.

'And how do you know that?'

'Three months ago, the husband reported her missing.

I've got a photo of her in my office. Wait just a second. I'll get it for you.'

Maria Lojacono was a beautiful girl, with an open, smiling face and big dark eyes. She looked to be barely over twenty.

'So when did she disappear?'

'Exactly three months ago today.'

'And did the husband give any personal details?'

'Yes, sir. This Maria got married when she was just eighteen. Nine months later a little girl was born. She died two months later. A horrible misfortune: choked on her vomit. After that, Maria started to lose her head – said she wanted to kill herself, saying she was responsible for the baby's death. The husband took her to Montelusa to be treated, but there was nothing to be done. She just got worse and worse. To the point that Piscopo, her husband, didn't want to leave her alone when he went out on his rounds, so he would take her to her sister, who would look after her. One night the sister went to bed and before falling asleep she heard Maria going into the bathroom. Since she was very tired, she went right to sleep. But when she woke up, around four o'clock in the morning, she had a sort of pre-monition and got up. Maria's bed was empty and cold. And the bathroom window was open. Maria had escaped over five hours before. The husband came home in less than an hour and started looking for her nearby. Then he called us and the carabinieri. And there's been no more news of the girl since then.'

'Did Piscopo describe how his wife was dressed?'

'Yes, sir. I looked at the report when I went and got the photograph. She was wearing jeans, a red blouse, a black sweater, and shoes . . .'

'When we saw her, she wasn't wearing any bra or black sweater.'

'Ugh.'

'Well, that doesn't necessarily mean anything. Do me a

favour. Get a good torch, take Galluzzo, and both of you go to the bunker. Put on some heavy gloves and be very careful not to hurt your hands. And look around for any articles of clothing that might have belonged to her.'

'As far as you know, was she wearing panties?'

'Yes. You can see them under the half-open jeans.'

*

Fazio came back about four hours later with a clear plastic bag in his hand. Inside was what must have once been a black sweater.

'Sorry I'm late. But after Galluzzo and I'd been searching around in the shit for over an hour, I felt contaminated, so I went home to wash and change my clothes. All we found was this sweater. It's black, like the husband said. But it was the sister who'd told him what his wife was wearing.'

'Listen, Fazio. The poor thing, when we found her, was wearing a wedding ring. Take a spin up to Montelusa and ask Pasquano to give it to you. Then take the sweater and ring and show them to this Piscopo. If he recognizes them as hers, bring him here to me.'

*

Salvatore Piscopo, who looked about forty, immediately seemed to the inspector like a man in the throes of a deep, genuine grief. He was a diminutive man, with a very thin moustache.

'It's definitely my wife,' he said in a choked voice.

'I'm sorry,' said Montalbano.

'We loved each other. That baby girl who died, innocent thing, she ruined our lives.'

And he could no longer contain his terrible sobs. Montalbano stood up, walked around the desk, sat down beside the man, and squeezed one of his knees.

'Be brave. Would you like a little water?'

Piscopo shook his head. The inspector waited for him to regain control of himself.

'Listen, Mr Piscopo. When you found out that your wife was missing, where was the first place you looked for her?'

Despite his pain and bewilderment, the man looked the inspector straight in the eye.

'Why are you asking me that?'

'Because I can see that your grief is sincere, Mr Piscopo. Exactly three months to the day have passed since your wife disappeared. Were you hoping all this time that your wife was alive? And, if so, where did you think she'd gone to hide? With a relative? A girlfriend? That's why I'm asking you.'

'No, Inspector, already by the day after her disappearance, I was convinced I would never see her alive again.'

'Why?'

'Because she didn't have any family or friends, or even acquaintances. She had no place to go. There was only her sister. And if you can see the state I'm in, Inspector, it's because it's one thing to imagine the worst, and it's another thing to know the worst has happened.'

'How come your wife didn't have any friends?'

'Well, to start, they were orphans, she and her sister Concetta, who's four years older and quickly got married. I lived near them and had known them since they were little girls. There was a twenty-year difference between me and Maria. But that didn't matter. After we got married, she didn't have any chance to form new friendships. You know what happened to us.'

'So where did you go to look for your wife?'

'I dunno . . . I looked all around the house outside . . . asked the neighbours if they'd seen her . . . Among other things, it was cold and raining that night. On top of that, it was late and there was nobody out on the streets any more. Nobody could tell me anything. So first I went to the carabinieri, then I came here. I started looking in the hospitals of Vigàta, Montelusa, and towns nearby, in the monasteries, convents, charitable organizations, churches . . . Nothing.'

'Was your wife religious?'

'She only went to Mass on Sundays. But she never confessed or took communion. She didn't trust anyone, not even priests.'

Then, with a visible effort, and in a low voice, he forced himself to ask the inspector a question.

'Did she kill herself? Or did she freeze to death? There was a frost three months ago . . .'

Montalbano threw up his hands.

*

'No, she didn't freeze to death or die of hardship,' said Dr Pasquano. 'Somebody killed her. Or else she killed herself.'

'How?' Montalbano asked.

'Common rat poison. I talked with the doctor whose patient she was, here in Montelusa. She suffered from terrible bouts of depression and tried many times to take her own life, in a variety of ways.'

'So suicide would be the most plausible scenario?'

'Not necessarily. Only apparently the most plausible, as you call it.'

'Why only apparently?'

'Because I found . . . Look, Montalbano, I know I'm right: she'd been tied up with rope around the wrists and ankles.'

The inspector thought about this for a minute.

'It's possible that someone in the family — I dunno, maybe the husband or her sister — tied her up when they had to leave her alone, just to prevent her from killing herself or hurting others. They used to use straitjackets in insane asylums for the same purpose, no?'

'I don't know whether or not it was for her own good

that she was tied up. That's for you to investigate. I'm only telling you what I found.'

'All right, Doctor, thanks,' said Montalbano, standing up.

'I haven't finished.'

Montalbano sat down again. His pathologist didn't exactly have the most cordial relationship with humanity, and if on a sudden whim he decided to stop talking, the inspector would have to wait for ever for the written report.

'There's something suspicious.'

The inspector held his breath.

'When did you say she disappeared from her sister's place?'

'Over three months ago.'

'There's one thing I'm absolutely sure of, Inspector. She didn't die three months ago. The body was in terrible shape, but that was only because every kind of animal had taken a piece of her. The process of decomposition was very slow. But it didn't start three months ago.'

'When did she die, then?'

'About two months ago. Maybe less.'

'And what could she have done during her last month alive? Where did she go? Apparently nobody saw her!'

'That's your fucking business, Inspector,' said Dr Pasquano, in all politeness.

☀

'So, shall I explain the situation to you?' said Mimì Augello, still pale from his bout with the flu. 'Maria Lojacono's sister is called Concetta. She seemed like a nice girl to me. Her husband too, whose job is freezing fish. They have three children; the oldest is six. Mrs Concetta rules out the possibility that her sister could have found the poison at home. They've never had any in the house. She says the kids are so restless they'd be liable to eat it themselves. Which seems to me like a convincing argument. When I asked her outright

whether they'd ever, out of necessity, been forced to tie
Maria up, she looked at me disdainfully. I really don't think
they ever did. And so I asked if it could have been Piscopo,
Maria's husband. Concetta ruled that out: if Salvatore had
done it, she would have known straight away, the same with
any other kind of violence. She explained to me that sometimes her sister would fall into a state of abulia, of complete
apathy – she would turn into a kind of rag doll. Those were
her exact words. And in those cases she, Concetta, was
forced to take all her clothes off to wash her. If anybody
bound Maria hand and foot, that's not where we should be
looking for them. Oh, and she asked me about a little ring.'

'What little ring?'

'Maria's husband told her that to identify the body he
was shown a sweater and a wedding ring. Is that right?'

'Yes, that's true.'

'Was she wearing any other rings?'

'No.'

'Mrs Concetta told me Maria used to wear a small
worthless ring on her little finger that she was very attached
to. It was the first present anyone ever gave her when she was
a little girl.'

'There definitely was no ring of that sort. Pasquano
would have told me. Unless it was in one of her jeans
pockets.'

Just to be sure, he rang Pasquano. He hadn't found anything at all in her pockets.

*

Montalbano had copies made of the photo of Maria Piscopo, then called Gallo and Galluzzo. He wanted them to
go, picture in hand, and ask around if anyone had seen her
or thought he'd seen her, along a sort of zigzagging line that
ran from the dead woman's sister's house to the bunker at
Passo di Cane.

'It's going to take at least three or four days,' said Montalbano. 'Proceed in parallel lines, starting from Vigàta. That way you'll be sure not to skip any houses.'

They'd just left when Catarella came in with a face fit for the Day of the Dead.

'What's wrong with you?'

'I jess now foun' out about the 'signment ya gave Gallo 'n' Galluzzo.'

'Do you have some objection?'

'Yer the boss 'ere, Chief, an' don' haff to asplain whatcha do.'

'OK, so?'

'Beckin' y' pardin, Chief, but it don' seem right to me.'

'Speak more clearly, Cat.'

'I's the one told yiz 'bout the poor goil's kiddaver. An' so I tought iss only right f'me t' have a same 'signment as Gallo 'n' Galluzzo.'

'But, Cat, you're needed here! You're a precious asset! With you away, the whole station'll go to the dogs!'

'Chief, I know my importancy here. Bu' still, it jess don' seem right.'

'OK, then. Here's a photograph. But I want you to go to Passo di Cane and start your search from the area around the bunker.'

'Chief, yer great an' moissyfull!'

Like Allah. But it was a subtle form of revenge, since Catarella would certainly feel obliged to scale the vertical rock face again.

*

Gallo and Galluzzo returned towards evening, empty-handed. Nobody they'd interviewed and shown the photo to had seen the girl. Catarella, on the other hand, never came back. As it was already dark outside, the inspector began to get worried.

'Want to bet he got lost?'

He was about to send out a rescue team when Catarella finally called in.

'Chief, izzatchoo poissonally—'

'In person, Cat. What happened to you? I was starting to get worried.'

'Nuttin' happen a me, Chief. I jess wannit a tell yiz I'll be back atta station in about half a hour, max — actually I'm about to be on my way to come. Will ya wait f'me? I gotta talk t'yiz.'

Catarella appeared exactly half an hour later, tired and seeming strangely perplexed, something the inspector had never seen before in him.

'I'm bewillered, Chief.'

'Why's that?'

'Cuz o' the tots in my 'ead, Chief.'

Ah, so that was it. Catarella's bewilderment was the result of the few thoughts courageously venturing into the desert of his brain.

'And what are you thinking, Cat?'

Catarella didn't answer his boss's question directly.

'Well, Chief, a' Passo di Cane 'ere's a lotta villers an' a lotta li'l pheasant 'ouses, an' 'a fact is, they's so far away from one anutters an' 'ass why I'm late. After I'd a been already to fourteen of 'em — an' I counted 'em — I says, less do 'em all!'

'Well done. But tell me something. How'd you get up to Passo di Cane? Did you climb the rock face again?'

'Nah, Chief. I did like you did lass time.'

Catarella was wising up.

'Anyways, Chief, so I knock atta door odda fifteenth li'l house, an' iss really li'l, I mean, teeny weeny, wittout no plasser onna walls. But 'ere was a lotta sheeps an' goats an' chickens, an' a cage full o' rabbits, an' a big fat pig . . .'

'Forget about the zoo, Cat, just get on with the story.'

'Well, who comes an' answers the door but Scillicato hisself!'

'Really?' the inspector asked in amazement.

'Rilly an' trully, Chief!'

'OK, Cat, now that I've shown the amazement you wanted me to show, could you please tell me who the hell Scillicato is?'

'Wha', din't I tell yiz? Pasquale Scillicato's the shippard 'at founna dead body, the one 'at called!'

'Didn't you already know that? Didn't you tell me he gave you his address?'

''Ass right, Chief, 'e gave me 'is addriss, but I din't know where th'addriss was localized. Anyways, Chief, Scillicato's li'l house's jest a li'l over a half miles away from the banker.'

'Interesting.'

''Ass what I tought too. Diss Scillicato's a wile man, Chief.'

'What do you mean?'

'Well, iss true 'e gotta TV in 'is li'l house, an' iss true 'e gotta refritcherator in 'is li'l house, an' iss true 'e's gotta mobble phone, an' iss true 'e goes aroun' on one o' them motor cooters . . .'

'Scooters, Cat, scooters . . .'

'Oh, right, well, iss true 'es got one of them scooters—'

'Cat, just tell me what's wrong with the man, or tell me what isn't wrong with the man . . .'

'Chief, bessides from the fack 'e drisses like summon beggin' for alms, an' bessides from the fack 'e 'itches up 'is britches witta piece o' string, an' bessides from the fack 'e keeps a salami in one pocket an' 'is bread in annutter, an' besides . . .'

He was launching into another litany.

'Cat, just get to the point.'

'The point, Chief, izzat 'ere's a' least tree points. The foist point izzat when as 'ow I shewed 'im the pitcher o' the goil, 'e tol' me 'e only saw 'er after she's already dead, which is when 'e foun' her isside the banker and called the station.'

'So?'

'Ah, Chief, Chief! Atop of everyting eltz, when 'e seen the kiddaver i' was dark ousside, so jest immagine wha' i' wuz like inside the banker! He couldna seen much assept fer the kiddaver bu' not the face! An' anyways, the poor ting's face wuz all et up by dogs 'n' rats! If 'e idinnified 'er, iss cuz 'e seen 'er foist!'

'Go on!' said Montalbano, extremely attentive.

'The seckin' point is I had to go.'

'You had to leave?'

'No, Chief, I had to pee. 'N' so I axed 'im where the bat'room wuz, an' he answered 'at 'ere waren't none inna house. If I 'ad to go, I c'd go right ousside, like 'e done.'

'Well, Cat, I don't see anything wr—'

'Beckin' y'pardin, Chief, bu' if summon is useta doin' 'is bidness ousside, whass 'e doin inna banker when 'is bidness is to do 'is bidness?'

Montalbano gawked at him. Catarella's reasoning made perfect sense.

''N' so the toid point, Chief, izzat dis Scillicato went into the banker at tree-toity inna mornin' when there in't nobuddy roun' Passo di Cane, not e'en a dog. 'Oo's gonna see 'im anyways, at 'at time o' the night?'

Catarella chuckled, pleased with his witticism. Montalbano shot to his feet, embraced Catarella, and kissed him noisily on both cheeks.

*

'In my opinion, Mimì, here's how it went. Maria Lojacono runs away from her sister's house and, to her misfortune, crosses paths with Scillicato, who is driving by on his scooter. The shepherd stops – maybe Maria asked him for a lift. It doesn't take long, however, for Scillicato to realize that the girl isn't right in the head. So he decides to take advantage of her and takes her home. Maria is almost certainly going through a period of abulia, as happens after days of being in a useless frenzy, which drove her to flee.

The situation suits Scillicato just fine, and he carries on for a good month. Whenever he has to go out, he ties the girl up with rope. He sees her the same way he sees his chickens and sheep. But one day Maria wakes up, frees herself, and runs away. Before doing this, however, she's tempted to kill herself, as in the past, and she grabs the rat poison that Scillicato surely has in his house. When the shepherd comes home and finds her missing, he doesn't get too worried. Maybe he thinks the girl went back to her family. In fact she's gone and hidden in the bunker, where she poisons herself. Much later, Scillicato finds out that they're still looking for Maria. And so he starts to look for her himself, fearing perhaps that she might tell about being repeatedly raped for a whole month. In the end he finds the body and calls us.'

'What I don't understand,' said Mimì, 'is why did he want to get involved at all? If he hadn't told us he'd found the body, who knows how long it would have stayed there in the bunker without anybody knowing?'

Montalbano shrugged.

'No idea,' he said. 'Who knows. Maybe he thought she died of hardship and felt reassured that she couldn't talk any more. And so he wanted to look like a law-abiding citizen. He must have thought he was throwing us off the trail.'

'So what do we do now?'

'Get yourself a search warrant and pay Scillicato a visit.'

'What should we look for?'

'I don't know. We haven't found either the bra or the red blouse of the victim, and by now they've probably been burned. Decide for yourself. I mostly want you to put Scillicato under pressure.'

'All right.'

'Ah, one thing. Bring Catarella along with you. If Scillicato is to be arrested, let Catarella put the handcuffs on him. He deserves that small satisfaction.'

*

They searched the cottage for hours without finding anything. They'd already given up hope when, in the dark corner of a windowless cupboard that stank so bad you wanted to throw up, Catarella noticed something shining amidst the filth. He bent down to pick it up. It was a cheap little ring. The very first present a little girl had been given a long time ago.

BEING HERE . . .

The moment the man walked into his office, Montalbano thought he was hallucinating. The visitor was a dead ringer for Harry Truman, the decidedly deceased former President of the United States, as he had appeared in the photographs and documents that the inspector had seen from that era. The same double-breasted pin-striped suit, the same light hat, the same gaudy tie, the same spectacle frames. But when you looked closely, there were two differences: the first was that the man was pushing eighty, if he hadn't already reached that milestone, but wore his years extremely well. The second was that while the former president was always laughing, even when doing things like ordering the atomic bombing of Hiroshima, the present man not only wasn't smiling, but had an air of composed melancholy about him.

'Excuse me for bothering you, sir. My name is Charles Zuck.'

He spoke textbook Italian, with no trace of regional accent or dialect. Or, more precisely, he did have an accent, and a rather clear one.

'Are you American?' the inspector asked him, gesturing to him to sit down in the chair in front of the desk.

'I'm an American citizen, yes.'

A subtle distinction, which Montalbano correctly interpreted to mean: I wasn't born an American, but became one.

'What can I do for you?' the inspector asked.

He took a liking to the man. It wasn't just his melancholy air; he seemed out of his element, lost in an alien
land.

'I arrived in Vigàta three days ago, intending to make a
very brief visit. In fact I'm flying out of Palermo the day
after tomorrow to go back to Chicago.'

So what? Anyone other than Montalbano might have
lost patience.

'And what's the problem?'

'The Mayor of Vigàta won't see me.'

And what did this have to do with the inspector?

'Look, sir, although you speak perfect Italian, you're a
foreigner and I guess you must be unaware that a police
inspector has no say in—'

'Thank you for the compliment,' said Charles Zuck, 'but
I taught Italian for decades in the US. I fully realize that
you have no power to make the mayor receive me. But you
could try to persuade him.'

Why was he sitting there patiently listening to this man?
Because he aroused his curiosity?

'I suppose I could,' said the inspector, but wanting to
excuse the town's first citizen in the eyes of a foreigner, he
added: 'But the election is only three days away, and our
mayor is up for re-election. So it's actually his duty to
receive you.'

'All the more because I'm from Vigàta, or I used to be.'

'Ah, so you were born here,' Montalbano said, surprised,
but only a little. At a rough guess, the man must have been
born some time in the 1920s, when the port was doing well
and foreigners were ten a penny.

'Yes.'

Charles Zuck paused; his melancholy seemed to harden,
grow denser, and his pupils started bouncing off the walls.

'And I died here.'

✻

The inspector's first reaction was not surprise but anger – anger at himself for not having realized that the man was just a poor old fool, someone not quite right in the head. He decided to call one of his men to throw him out of the station. He stood up.

'Excuse me for a moment.'

'I'm not insane,' said the American.

The whole thing seemed according to script, madmen claiming their sanity like so many lifers protesting that they're as innocent as Christ.

'There's no need to call anyone,' said Zuck, standing up in turn. 'And please forgive me for having wasted your time. Good day.'

He walked past the inspector and headed for the door. Montalbano felt sorry for the man, who suddenly showed all his eighty-plus years. He couldn't very well let him go just like that. At his age, and if not crazy then surely addled and estranged, he was likely to get into trouble outside.

'Please sit down again.'

Charles Zuck obeyed.

'Do you have some kind of identification?'

Without speaking, the man handed him a passport.

There was no mistake: his name was as he'd said, and he was born in Vigàta on 6 September 1920. The inspector gave him back his passport. They looked at each other.

'Why did you say you died?'

'I'm not just saying it. It was written.'

'Where?'

'On the monument to the fallen.'

The monument to the fallen, which stood in a square along the main street of Vigàta, consisted of a bronze statue of a soldier raising a dagger in defence of a woman with a baby in her arms. The inspector had stopped a few times to look at it because in his opinion it was a good sculpture. It stood on a rectangular pedestal and on its most visible side had a stone plaque with the names of the local soldiers killed in the First World War, to whom the monument had been originally dedicated. Then, in 1938, a second plaque appeared on the right-hand side with the names of those who'd given up the ghost in the Abyssinian War and the Spanish Civil War. Finally, in 1946, a third plaque was added on the left bearing the names of the soldiers fallen in the Second World War. The fourth and last side remained empty for the time being.

Montalbano searched his memory.

'I don't recall having seen your name there,' he said in conclusion.

'In fact, the name Charles Zuck isn't there. But Carlo Zuccotti is – and that's still me.'

*

The old man told his story in clear, succinct, and orderly fashion. It took him just a little over ten minutes to give a summary of his seventy-seven years on earth. His father, he said, was named Evaristo, came from a Milanese family, and at a very early age married a girl from Lecco, Annarita Vismara. Shortly after their wedding, Evaristo, who worked for the railways, was sent to Vigàta, which at the time had no less than three train stations, one of which was exclusively reserved for commercial traffic and stood at the entrance to the harbour area. And so Carlo was born in Vigàta, becoming the couple's first and last child. Carlo spent the first twelve years of his life there, attending Vigàta's municipal elementary school and then the middle school in Montelusa, where he went by bus. Then his father earned a promotion and was transferred to Orte in central Italy. After finishing his high-school years there, he enrolled at the University of Florence, where his father had been newly transferred in the interim. One year before his graduation, Carlo's mother, Mrs Annarita, died.

'What did you study?' Montalbano asked at this point.

What the man was telling him wasn't enough; he wanted to know more.

'Modern literature. I studied with Giuseppe De Robertis and my thesis was on Foscolo's *Le Grazie*.'

Hats off, thought Montalbano, a literary enthusiast.

In the meantime, war broke out. Called up to serve again, Carlo was sent to fight in North Africa. After six months on the front, a letter from the Florence railway office informed him that his father had died, cut down by machine-gun fire. Now he was utterly alone in the world. He didn't even know the names of any relatives his parents might have had. Taken prisoner by the Americans, he was sent to a concentration camp in Texas. He spoke good English, and this was a big help, to the point that he became a sort of interpreter. That was how he met Evelyn, the daughter of the administrative director of the camp. Upon his release from the camp at the end of the war, he and Evelyn got married. In 1947, at his request, the University of Florence sent a certification of his degree. It wasn't valid in the United States, so he resumed his studies until he received a teaching certificate. After acquiring American citizenship, he changed his name from Zuccotti to Zuck, as the Americans already called him.

'Why did you come back here?'

'That's the hardest question,' said the old man.

For a moment he seemed lost in a labyrinth of memories. The inspector remained silent, waiting.

'At a certain point, Inspector, life for an old man like me becomes little more than a list of the dead. Which after a while becomes so long that you feel like you've been left alone in the middle of a desert. And so you try desperately to get your bearings, but you don't always succeed.'

'So your wife, Evelyn, is no longer with you?'

'We had one child, James. Just one. Apparently mine is a family of only children. And he lost his life in Vietnam.

My wife never got over it. And she rejoined our son eight years ago.'

Once again, Montalbano said nothing.

*

At this point the old professor smiled. It was a smile that made it seem to Montalbano as if the sky had darkened and a fist had emerged and grabbed his heart.

'What an ugly story, Inspector. Ugly in the literal sense, a cross between Giacometti's melodrama of civil death and certain situations such as you find in Pirandello. Why did I come back here, you ask? On impulse. All things considered, this is where I spent the best years of my life – the best, yes, only because I wasn't yet acquainted with grief. Which is saying a lot, incidentally. From my loneliness in Chicago, Vigàta started to shine as bright as a star. But the moment I set foot back in town, the illusion vanished. It was a mirage. I've been unable to find a single one of my old schoolmates, and even the house I used to live in no longer exists. Now there's a ten-storey apartment building in its place. And the three train stations have been reduced to one, with hardly any traffic. Then I discovered I was listed among the war dead, so I went to the records office. It was apparently a mistake on the part of the military. They thought I was dead.'

'Excuse me for asking, but when you saw your name there, what did you feel?'

The old man thought about this for a moment.

'Regret,' he said softly.

'Regret for what?'

'That things didn't go the way it says on the monument to the dead. I had to live instead.'

'Listen, Professor, I'm sure I could get you a meeting with the mayor by tomorrow. Where are you staying?'

'At the Hotel Tre Pini. It's outside Vigàta. I have to take

a taxi to come and go. In fact, could you please call me one now?'

*

That afternoon he was unable to talk to the mayor, who was in a meeting and afterwards had to go out for some door-to-door canvassing. The inspector wasn't received until the following morning. He told he mayor the life story of Carlo Zuccotti, the living dead man. When he'd finished, the mayor laughed so hard that tears came to his eyes.

'You see, Inspector? Our quasi-townsman Pirandello didn't really need much imagination to invent such stories! All he had to do was transcribe what actually goes on around here!'

Unable to box the man's ears, Montalbano decided not to vote for him.

'And do you, Inspector, have any idea what he wants from me?'

'No. He probably just wants you to have the plaque changed.'

'Good God!' the mayor said in irritation. 'That'd be quite an expense.'

*

'Professor? Inspector Montalbano here. The mayor can see you at five o'clock this evening. Is that OK? That way you can still catch your plane back to Chicago tomorrow.'

Total silence at the other end.

'Did you hear me, Professor?'

'Yes. But last night . . .'

'Last night?'

'I lay awake all night thinking of that plaque. I thank you for your kindness, but I've made up my mind. I think it's the best thing.'

'And what's that?'

'Well, since I'm already here . . .'

Montalbano bolted out of his chair, nearly ran into Catarella in the hallway, pushed him violently out of the way, got in his car and sped off. The mile and a half to the hotel outside Vigàta seemed like fifty.

He burst into the lobby.

'Professor Zuccotti's room?'

'There's no Zuccotti here.'

'Charles Zuck, idiot.'

'Room 115, first floor,' said the bewildered receptionist.

The lift was occupied on the upper floors. The inspector dashed up the stairs, taking two at a time. Out of breath, he knocked at the door to room 115.

'Professor? Open up! This is Inspector Montalbano!'

'Just a moment,' the old man said softly from within.

Then a gunshot rang out, sharp and violent, inside the room.

And Salvo Montalbano knew that the Mayor of Vigàta would be spared the expense of remaking the plaque.

SEVEN MONDAYS

1

The two men standing inside the new bus shelter, waiting patiently for the night circular to arrive, exchanged a little smile, though they didn't know each other. The reason for their mirth was the persistent snoring, louder than a chainsaw, coming from inside a great big cardboard box turned upside down — no doubt a homeless person, some poor bastard who had found temporary shelter from the cold and rain and who, comforted by the bit of body heat the box managed to retain, had decided it best to close his eyes, ignore the whole rotten world, and bid goodnight to all. At last the bus arrived, the two men got on, and it left. But then a man ran up.

'Stop! Stop!' he cried.

The driver must have seen him, but kept going. The man cursed and looked at his watch. There wouldn't be another bus for an hour, at 4 a.m. The man stood there thinking for a moment, and after a barrage of curses decided to walk to his destination. He lit a cigarette and headed off. At once the snoring stopped, the giant box teetered, and slowly the head of a tramp emerged, half hidden by an old hat full of holes and pulled down to his eyes. Stretched out on the ground as he was, the vagrant looked around carefully, turning his head slowly from side to side. When he was certain there wasn't a living soul about, and that the windows of the houses in front of him were all shuttered, the man crawled out of his box like a snake sloughing off its skin.

Standing up, he didn't look so much like a vagrant after all. Small in stature, he was close-shaven and was wearing a threadbare but well-made suit. He slipped two fingers into the front breast pocket of his jacket and extracted a pair of spectacles. Putting them on, he came out from under the shelter, turned right, and, after barely ten paces, stopped in front of a gate firmly shut with a big padlock and chain. Over the gate was a large neon sign, now turned off, that said: *Ristorante La Sirenetta — Every Kind of Fish*. It started raining. Not too hard, but enough to drench one's clothes. The man fiddled a bit with the padlock — which was more appearance than substance and, in fact, put up little resistance to his picklock — and soon he had opened one side of the gate, just enough to slip inside. Shutting it behind him, he put the chain back and reclosed the padlock until it clicked. There was a short, well-tended path leading to the front door of the restaurant. The man followed it, but halfway down it turned right and headed towards the garden behind the building, where some thirty tables would be set up as soon as the weather permitted. Despite the pitch darkness the man moved with assurance, not bothering to turn on the torch he had in his hand. He was getting soaked by the rainfall but paid no attention. Actually he felt hotter than if it was summertime, and even felt like taking off his jacket, shirt, and trousers and standing there naked in the cooling rain. Perhaps he even felt a little fever coming on?

The fish tank, pride of the establishment, was at the back of the garden, to the left. Whoever so wished could go to the tank and personally select the fish he wanted to eat. Equipped with a landing-net, he had to fish it out himself. This wasn't always so easily done, and in those cases everyone had a good laugh and a great time, with all sorts of innuendos and double-entendres about fish, especially if there were a few women in the group. The fun, however, usually ended when the bill arrived, as it was well known that the prices in that establishment were more than a little steep.

Standing at the edge of the tank, the man began muttering to himself in a sort of whisper that sounded both angry and plaintive. The night was so dark that you couldn't see a thing, not even whether the tank was full or empty. He lowered his hand slowly into the tank, cringing absurdly in fear that some fish, if there were any left, might attack him and eat one of his fingers. Feeling the freezing-cold water, he withdrew his hand at once. Then he decided to turn on the torch for a split second: the brief flash was enough to catch a silver gleam from the fish just below the surface of the water. There were a great many of them; apparently the tank had been refilled that evening. This — thought the intruder — would make matters easier since, for all intents and purposes, he had to catch a fish with a landing net in the dark. The less he used the torch, the better. Beyond the garden and across the street loomed a tall building of some ten storeys, and there was the danger that some idiot suffering from insomnia had seen the beam of the torch and raised the alarm. The intruder felt as if he was sweating all over, and indeed he was. He removed his jacket, which more than anything else impeded his movements, set it down on a plastic chair, and turned the torch on for another split second.

He spotted at least three little nets lying on the edge of the tank. Sometimes a group of customers would stage contests between themselves, such as whoever loses, pays for everyone. He grabbed a net, knelt down very close to the edge, dipped the net into the water, holding it with both hands, traced a broad semicircle with it, and pulled it back out. He could tell by the weight that he hadn't caught a thing. But he wanted to make sure, so he felt the net. There were only a few residual drops of water in it. He tried again several times, always with the same result.

He crouched down into a squat, dead tired, panting so
hard that he became afraid that someone in the apartment
building might hear him. He didn't have all this time to
waste. He had to be back outside the restaurant a good ten
minutes before the circular bus passed again at four o'clock,
because it was usually mobbed – with people still half-
asleep, yes, but still able, if necessary, to recognize someone.

He had an idea, and it seemed like a good one. Taking
the net into his left hand, he dipped it into the water and
traced a quick half-circle, but, before finishing, he turned on
the torch in his other hand. He had guessed right: a mass of
fish had taken refuge in the part of the tank the net didn't
reach. And so he stood up, found another net, balanced
himself on the edge of the tank, and waited about five minutes for the fish to calm down and resume swimming about
freely. He even held his breath. Then he sprang into action.
As he was tracing the usual semicircle with the first net, he
lowered the second one to head off the fleeing fish.

It worked. He could feel that at least three fish had
swum into the net all by themselves. Tossing aside the
empty net, he hopped down from the edge, put the other
one with the fish down on the ground, and turned on the
torch. He immediately noticed a big mullet. Smiling, he sat
down on the edge of the tank and waited for the fish to
finish their vain struggle against death. When he was certain
they had stopped moving, he tossed the other two fish back
into the water, since they were too small and of no use to
him, laid the mullet down on the edge of the tank, extracted
a pistol out of his back pocket, put a silencer on it, stuck the
lighted torch in his mouth and, holding the fish's body still
with one hand, shot at it with the other, holding the gun
vertically so that the bullet didn't decapitate it but only
reduced its head to a bloody pulp. He turned off the torch
and stayed completely still. Despite the silencer, the shot had
sounded to him as if it must have woken up the whole town

of Vigàta. But nothing happened. No window opened, no voice called out asking what was going on.

And so the man dug into the pocket of his trousers, extracted the already-written note he had brought with him, and slipped it under the dead fish.

The four o'clock circular bus was very long in coming, arriving some ten minutes late.

As it pulled away, among its sleepy passengers sat the man who had just murdered a mullet.

*

'Hey, Chief, do you know that restaurant called La Siren-etta, the one near the monument to Luigi Pirandello?' Fazio asked later that Monday morning, the 22nd of September, as he walked into Inspector Montalbano's office.

The inspector was in a good mood. The previous day had been cold and rainy, but with the new morning, an August-like sun had returned, offset by a crisp wind. And Fazio, too, to judge from his face, seemed free of unpleasant thoughts.

'Of course I know it, but that's nothing to boast about. I went there once with Livia, just to check it out, and that was more than enough. It's all smoke and mirrors. Well-dressed waiters, excellent, impeccable service, fancy cutlery, heart-attack prices, but when you come right down to it, no substance. The dishes they serve taste like they were made by a cook in an irreversible coma.'

'I've never eaten there.'

'Good for you. Why did you mention it?'

'Because early this morning, Mr Haber, the owner, who's also a distant relative of my wife's, called me up here and told me a very strange story that made me curious. So I went there. Did you know the restaurant's got a big tank full of living fish that you—'

'Yeah, yeah, I know everything. Go on. So what happened?'

'Well, last night someone picked the padlock and broke
in, took a fish out of the tank, and shot it in the head.'

Montalbano looked astounded.

'They shot a fish?!'

'Yes indeed. And then, under the corpse . . . I mean the
body . . . whatever . . . under the dead fish they slipped a
little piece of paper with some writing on it.'

'And what did it say?'

'That's just it. What with the rain, the water from the
tank, and the fish's blood, the ink dissolved. And the piece
of paper got completely soaked, so that when I picked it up,
it sort of fell apart.'

'Why the hell would someone go to all that trouble,
even risking arrest, just to shoot a fish?'

'I really can't say, Chief, but you're the boss here. Why
don't you tell me?'

'Are you sure the fish was shot?'

'Absolutely certain. The empty case was on the ground.
I've got it right here.'

He dug into his jacket pocket, pulled it out, and handed
it to the inspector, who took it and looked at it.

'Don't bother sending this to Forensics,' Montalbano
said by way of comment. 'They'll think we're insane. He
used a 7.65.'

He tossed the case into a drawer of his desk.

'Right,' said Fazio. 'If you ask me, it was some kind of
warning. Which probably means our man Haber missed a
payment.'

Montalbano shot him an irritated glance.

'With all your experience, how can you possibly talk
such tripe? If they'd missed a payment, the racket would
have massacred all the fish and burnt down the restaurant
for good measure.'

'So what could it mean?'

'It could mean nothing or it could mean everything. It

might just have been some kind of stupid bet between two customers . . .'

'So what do we do now?' Fazio asked after a pause.

'What kind of fish was it?'

'A mullet half the size of my arm.'

'Grey mullet or red mullet?'

'Grey, Chief.'

'The grey mullet's a salt-water fish, isn't it?'

'You can find them in fresh water, too, but they don't taste as good as the ones from the sea.'

'I didn't know that.'

'Sure, Chief. You don't even like fresh-water fish. What should I do about Haber?'

'I'll tell you what you should do. Go back to the restaurant and ask them to give you the fish. Tell them you need it for the investigation.'

'What am I supposed to do with it?'

'Take it home and cook it. I advise that you grill it, but be careful: the coals shouldn't be too hot. Stuff the stomach with rosemary and a little garlic. Then serve it with a salmoriglio sauce. It should still be edible.'

*

In the days that followed, Vigàta police headquarters fell back into its usual routine, with the exception of three occurrences requiring a little more attention than the rest.

The first involved a certain ragioniere, Pancrazio Schepis, who upon returning home at an unexpected hour had discovered his wife, Signora Maria Matildina, lying on the bed completely naked while the famous 'Magus of Baghdad', otherwise known as Salvatore Minnulicchia from Trapani, also naked, 'was using his sex organ as an aspergillum', in the words of Galluzzo's diligent report. After recovering from his initial shock, the ragioniere had grabbed his revolver and fired five shots in the direction of the magus, luckily striking him only in the left thigh.

The second occurred when the home of ninety-year-old Mrs Lucia Balduino was totally cleaned out by burglars. A lightning-fast investigation by Fazio established unequivocally that there was only one burglar: Mrs Balduino's grandson, the sixteen-year-old Filippuzzo Dimora, who grandma had refused to give the money to buy a moped.

The third involved three warehouses belonging to the deputy mayor, Giangiacomo Bartolotta, which all burned down in the same night. The event was seen by all as a clear warning to the deputy mayor to desist in his visibly strenuous efforts to combat the local Mafia.

It took only twelve hours to establish that the petrol used to set fire to the warehouses had been bought by the deputy mayor himself.

And so, what with one thing and another, a week went by.

*

It was a dark night. Not a single star was visible; they were all covered by clouds heavy with rain. The track was almost impassable: huge, jagged rocks jutted out here and there from the low stone walls on either side, and holes as big as chasms yawned in front of the car. The vehicle was old and falling apart and moved forward in fits and starts, gasping all the while. The man at the wheel, moreover, used the headlights only sporadically, a few seconds at a time, then turned them off at once. At that hour of the night, along a track like that, there were unlikely to be any other cars passing by, but it was still better not to arouse anyone's curiosity. At a glance he seemed almost to have arrived where he wanted to go. He turned the lights on full beam on and saw, about twenty yards ahead, a handwritten sign nailed to a post. The man stopped the car, turned off the engine, opened the door, and got out. The cool, humid air made the smell of the countryside more pungent. The man took a deep breath, thrust his hands into his pockets, and started walking. Halfway there something occurred to him, and he stopped. How long had it taken him to get there? And what if he was too early? He knew he'd left town just after eleven-thirty, but there hadn't been any traffic, and he couldn't work out how long he'd been in the car. He made up his mind. Pulling a torch out of his pocket, he turned it on for a split second. Long enough to see what time it was on his wristwatch. Ten past midnight. The new day was ten minutes old. Everything was on schedule. He resumed walking.

This time the man didn't need a silencer. The shot was heard only by a dog in the distance, which began to bark without conviction, just to show that it was earning its keep.

*

Around twelve o'clock noon on Monday, the 29th of September, Fazio walked into the police station carrying a plastic bag of the sort you get in supermarkets.

'You been shopping?'

'No, Chief. I brought you a chicken. You should eat it. I had the mullet for dinner last week.'

'What are you talking about?'

'Chief, the chicken I've got in here was shot. In the head, just like the fish last week.'

'Where did it happen?'

'At Masino Aiello's poultry farm, about a half-hour drive from here. It's a pretty secluded place. Here's the empty case.'

Montalbano opened the drawer, picked up the other case, and compared the two.

They were identical.

'And he left a note this time, too,' Fazio continued, taking a piece of paper out of his pocket and handing it to the inspector.

The words were written in ballpoint pen on graph paper, in block letters.

I'M STILL CONTRACTING

'What could it mean?' Montalbano wondered aloud.

'Can I say something?'

'Sure.'

'Maybe he man made a spelling mistake,' said Fazio.

'Think so?'

'Yeah. Maybe he'd meant to write: "I'm still contacting." Maybe he feels isolated for some reason, I don't know — taxes, or his wife's cheating on him, his son's taking drugs, that kind of thing. So he's trying to make contact, to tell the world.'

'By shooting fish and chickens? No, Fazio, there's no mistake here. He clearly wrote "contracting". And from this note we can infer what was in the first one, which we couldn't read because it was wet. Here he writes that he is "still" contracting.'

'So?'

'So the first note must have said something like, "I'm contracting", or "I'm starting to contract", something along those lines.'

'And what could it mean?'

'No idea.'

'What should we do, Chief?' Fazio asked, a bit worried.

'Is this stuff starting to make you feel uneasy?'

'Yes.'

'Why?'

'Because I can't make head or tail of it. And things that make no sense give me the creeps.'

'Well, there's nothing we can do about it for now, Fazio. We'll just have to wait for this gentleman to stop contracting, and then we'll see. But are you sure you don't like chicken?'

2

He'd slept well. All night long the light, refreshing breeze
dancing in through the window had cleansed his lungs and
his dreams. He got out of bed and went into the kitchen to
make coffee. Waiting for it to bubble up, he went out onto
the veranda. The sky was clear, the sea smooth and looking
as if it had been given a fresh coat of paint. Someone waved
to him from a boat, and he replied, raising his arm. Going
back inside, he poured the coffee into a big mug, drank it
down, lit his first cigarette of the day without a thought,
smoked it, then went and got into the shower, carefully
lathering himself up. No sooner was he covered with soap
than two things happened: the water in the tanks ran out,
and the telephone rang. Cursing the saints, and in danger of
slipping with every step because of the soap dripping from
his body, he ran to answer it.

'Chief, izzatchoo poissonally in poisson?'

'No.'

'Ah, 'scuse me, in't this the home o' Chief Isspecter Montalbano I's a-speakin' wit'?'

'Yes.'

'So, whooziss in 'is place?'

'I'm Arturo, his twin brother.'

'Reelly?'

'Hold on a second while I call Salvo.'

He was better off talking nonsense with Catarella than
getting all worked up over the sudden water shortage.
Among other things, the soap, as it dried on his skin, was
starting to itch.

'Hello, Montalbano here.'

'Y'know sump'n, Chief? Ya gots azackly the same voice
as yer twin brother Arturo!'

'That's often the case with twins, Cat. What did you
want to tell me?'

'Fazio called sayin' as how Mr Toggo got shot. 'E'll be comin' here now.'

'Was he killed?'

'Yessir.'

'And who is he, this Mr Toggo?'

'I coun't say, Chief.'

'Where'd it happen?'

'Dunno, Chief.'

He kept a reserve supply of water in a jerry can in the bathroom. He poured half of it into the sink. It was better not to use it all up, since it was anybody's guess when they would deign to refill the tanks. With some effort, he managed to peel the vitrified soap off his skin. He left the bathroom in a sorry state. Filthy. Adelina, the housekeeper, was sure to send a few heartfelt curses and ill wishes his way.

He arrived at the station at the same time as Fazio.

'Where'd this killing take place?' he asked.

Fazio looked flummoxed.

'What killing?'

'This Toggo guy.'

'Is that what Catarella told you?'

'Yes.'

Fazio started laughing, first softly, then more and more loudly. Montalbano got worried, in part because he also felt a persistent itch in the part of his body he had sat on to drive. And it didn't seem decent to him to start furiously scratching that area of his body. Apparently he hadn't managed to rid himself of all the soap stuck to his skin.

'If you'd be so kind as to tell me what's so—' he continued.

'I'm sorry, Chief, but it's just too funny! Toggo! I told Catarella to tell you a *dog* was killed!'

'Same guy as before?'

'Yes indeed.'

'One pistol shot and good night?'

'Yes indeed.'

'Today's the eighth of October, isn't it? This person operates on a weekly basis, and always on the night between Sunday and Monday,' the inspector observed, going into his office.

Fazio sat down in one of the chairs in front of the desk.

'Did the dog have an owner?'

'Yes, a pensioner named Carlo Iaccari, a former clerk at the town hall. He's got a little house in the country with a vegetable patch and a few animals. About ten chickens and a few rabbits. He was asleep at the time, but the shot woke him up and he grabbed his gun and—'

'What kind of gun?'

'Hunting rifle. He has a licence. He immediately saw the dead dog and a second later heard a car driving off.'

'Did he know what time it was?'

'Yes, he looked at his watch. It was twelve thirty-five. He told me he spent the rest of the night crying. He was very close to his dog. Then, first thing in the morning, he came here. So I went back with him to have a look.'

'Does he have any ideas?'

'None whatsoever. He says he can't work out why anyone would want to kill his dog. He claims he has no enemies and has never done anything wrong to anybody.'

'Is this Iaccari guy's house anywhere near the poultry farm of last time?'

'No, it's in the opposite direction.'

'How about the restaurant?'

'No, it's really far from that, too.'

'Did you find the empty case?'

'Yes, sir, got it right here.'

It was identical to the other two.

'But it took me a little longer this time to find the note. Last night's breeze blew it pretty far away.'

He handed it to the inspector. Same graph paper, same ballpoint pen.

I'M STILL CONTRACTING

'What a pain in the arse!' Montalbano burst out. 'How long is the idiot going to take to contract?'

At that moment Mimì Augello walked in, fresh, clean-shaven, and well dressed. He'd just spent a month in Hamburg as the guest of a girl he'd met on the beach the previous summer.

'Any news?' he asked, sitting down.

'Yes,' Montalbano replied drily. 'Three murders.'

Whenever the inspector saw Mimì looking so rested and cheerful, it got on his nerves and he found him obnoxious.

'Shit!' Augello reacted, literally jumping out of his chair.

But then, looking the other two in the eye, he realized something weird was up.

'You guys joking or something?'

Fazio started staring at the ceiling.

'Yes and no,' said the inspector.

And he told him the whole story.

'That's no joke,' Mimì said when it was over, falling silent and looking pensive.

'I'm only sorry that this time he killed an animal that neither Fazio nor I can eat,' said Montalbano.

Augello glared at him.

'Ah, so that's how you see it?'

'Why, how am I supposed to see it?'

'Salvo, he's going to get bigger.'

'I don't know what you mean, Mimì.'

'I was referring to the size of the . . .' He paused, tongue-tied. It didn't seem right to call them *victims* ' . . . of the animals. A fish, a chicken, and now a dog. You'll see, next time it'll be a sheep.'

✻

On Friday, 10 October, the inspector was sitting on the veranda, having just finished eating a first-class caponata, when the telephone rang. It was 10 p.m., and Livia, as usual, was dead on time.

'*Ciao, amore*, here I am, punctual as ever. What time does your flight arrive tomorrow?'

He had promised Livia a month ago that he would come to Boccadasse for a weekend so they could be together. In fact, when they'd spoken the previous evening he'd told her that now that Mimì was back, he could even spend Monday with her. Why, then, did he reply the way he did?

'You'll have to forgive me, Livia, but I'm really afraid I won't be able to get away. What's happened is—'

'Quiet!'

The silence seemed to have been cut with a scythe.

'It's got nothing to do with work, believe me,' he resumed, bravely, after a pause.

'So what happened to you?' asked Livia, her voice coming from somewhere in northern Greenland.

'You remember that bad toothache I had a while ago? Well, it suddenly came back, and it hurts so badly that—'

'I think *I'm* your bad tooth,' said Livia.

And she hung up.

Montalbano flew into a rage. OK, he'd told her a lie, but what if, in fact, he'd really had a toothache? Was that any way for a woman in love to react? To someone writhing in pain? How about a word of compassion, for Christ's sake? He went back onto the veranda and sat down, wondering why he had told Livia he wouldn't be coming to see her. Just one second before she called, he was set on leaving. But then those words came out of his mouth, just like that, beyond his control and without his realizing. Was it a sudden attack of laziness, an irresistible need to do absolutely nothing and loll about the house in his underpants?

No, he really did wish he had Livia beside him, so he could feel her living, hear her breathing in her sleep beside him in bed, bustling about the house, or laughing, so he could hear her voice calling him from the beach or from the other room.

So why, then? A sudden bout of sadism, as often happens between lovers? No, it was something to do with his own character. How could he have done something so senseless and irrational?

In the distance, at the outer reaches of audibility, a dog barked.

And, suddenly, *fiat lux!* That was the explanation! It was absurd, of course, but that was it, without a doubt. A moment before picking up the phone and talking to Livia, he'd heard the same dog barking. And, deep inside, at an almost unconscious level, he'd realized that it was time to take the matter of the murdered fish, chicken, and dog seriously. The phrases written on those little scraps of graph paper most definitely contained some sort of veiled threat, indecipherable but real. What would happen when the man had finished 'contracting', as he put it? And how was one supposed to interpret that verb, *contract*?

He went and looked up the number for the Sirenetta in the phone book and dialled it.

'Inspector Montalbano here. Is Mr Haber there?'

'I'll go and get him.'

The restaurant must have been full. He could hear animated conversations, men's and women's laughter, the tinkle of silverware and glasses, the notes of a piano, and a woman singing.

I'd like to see your faces when the bill arrives! thought Montalbano.

'At your service, Inspector!'

Haber sounded cheerful. Business must be good.

'Sorry to disturb you, but I'm calling about that fish from a couple of weeks ago . . .'

'Did you have it here? Was it not fresh enough?'

Eat at the Sirenetta? Not even under torture!

'No, I was referring to the mullet that was shot in your—'

'You're still thinking about that, Inspector?'

'Why, shouldn't I?'

'But it was obviously a prank! I got a little worried at first, I suppose, but after I thought about it a bit with a cooler head, I became convinced it was all just a silly joke . . .'

'A rather dangerous joke, don't you think? What if the nightwatchmen had come by on patrol and seen an armed stranger in the restaurant?'

'You're right, Inspector. But sometimes you have to take some risks to pull off a good practical joke.'

'I suppose so.'

'Listen, Inspector, I've got a full house here tonight and—'

'One more question and I'll let you get back to your customers. In your opinion, Mr Haber, was the kind of fish that was killed chosen randomly or on purpose?'

Haber seemed puzzled.

'I don't understand, Inspector.'

'Let me phrase the question a little differently. Can you explain to me how the man managed to take a mullet out the fish tank?'

'He didn't take just the mullet out of the tank, Inspector Montalbano. He caught three fish with the landing net. He probably picked the mullet because it was the biggest.'

'And how do you know he caught three fish?'

'Because that same morning I found a dead tench and a dead trout in the tank.'

'Also shot?!'

'No, asphyxiated, from being out of the water too long. In my opinion, he emptied the net onto the grass and waited for the fish to die. It would have been too hard for him to hold them in his hands while they were still alive. Then he took the mullet and threw the other two back into the tank.'

'In other words, he made a choice. In your opinion, he chose the mullet because it was the biggest, but he could have had other reasons, don't you think?'

'Inspector, how could I possibly know what's going through the head of a—'

'One last thing. What time was it when you closed the restaurant the night before the incident?'

'I always close at 12.30 a.m. – for customers, that is.'

'And how much longer do the staff stay?'

'Usually about an hour.'

The inspector thanked him and hung up. Then, equipped with pen and paper, he went back out onto the veranda and sat down. He wrote:

Monday, September 22 = fish
Monday, September 29 = chicken

He started laughing. It looked like a menu.

Monday, October 6 = dog

Why was it always in the wee hours of Monday morning? For now, at least, better gloss over this. He wrote down the first letters of each animal.

FCD

It made no sense. Then a puerile sense of humour got hold of him, and the only thing those three consonants suggested to him was:

FUCK COCK DICK

He crumpled the sheet of paper into a ball, threw it on the floor, and went to bed more confused than ever.

*

As Montalbano thrashed about in bed, trying to fall asleep after wolfing down a nearly industrial amount of sardines *a beccafico*, the man sat reading in a large room with crowded bookshelves covering the walls, the only light coming from a dim table-lamp. Looking up from the ancient, exquisitely bound tome he was reading, he closed the book, took off his glasses, and leaned back in his wooden armchair. He stayed that way for a few minutes, every so often rubbing his burning eyes with his fingers. Then, after heaving a deep sigh, he opened the right-hand drawer of his desk. Inside, amidst the paper, rubbers, keys, old stamps, and photographs, lay his pistol. He grabbed it and pulled out the empty magazine. He felt around further inside the same drawer, found the box of cartridges, and opened it. There were eight bullets left. He smiled. That was more than enough to do what he had in mind. He put only one bullet into the clip, just one, as he always did, then put the box back in its place and closed the drawer. He slipped the pistol into the right-hand pocket of his shapeless jacket, then felt the left-hand pocket: the torch was in its place. Glancing at his watch, he saw that it was already midnight. It was going to take him a good hour to get to the appointed place, which meant that he would be able to act at exactly the right time. Putting his glasses back on, he tore a small rectangle of graph paper from a notebook, wrote something on it with a ballpoint pen, then put the piece of paper in the small front pocket of his jacket. Then he stood up, went to get the telephone directory, and thumbed through it until he found the page he wanted. He had to be one hundred per cent certain that he had the right address. Next, he unfolded a map he kept within reach on his desk and double-checked the route he would take from his home. Actually, it looked like it would take a little more than an hour. So much the better. He went to the window and opened it. A cold wind hit him straight in the face, making him step backwards. He had better put something over his suit before going out. When he got into his car, he was wearing a heavy raincoat and a black hat.

He started the car, but after a few sputters the engine stalled. He tried again. Same result. He tried yet again, but the engine still refused to cooperate. He started sweating. If the car really was broken down, he would be unable to do any of the things he had in mind. So, what then? Should he skip this Monday's warning? No, that would mean failing to keep his promise, and he always kept his promises. He had no choice but to put the whole thing off and start again. But what if he missed the deadlines? Would he still be able to accomplish the extraordinary task he had set for himself? He felt lost. He tried again, feeling desperate, and this time the engine, after coughing a few times, decided to start.

3

Mimì Augello got it both right and wrong. He'd got it right as to the, well, *size* of the new victim, but he was wrong as to the species, since it wasn't a sheep.

On the morning of 12 October, Fazio came into the station with the news — which really wasn't news at all — that a goat had been killed. The usual shot to the head, the usual empty case, the usual piece of paper.

I'M STILL CONTRACTING

Nobody present breathed a word, nobody dared make a joke.

A dense, uncertain silence hovered in the inspector's office.

'He's certainly succeeding, I'll say!' said Montalbano, deciding he would be the first to speak.

It was his duty, after all. He was the boss.

'Succeeding at what?' asked Augello.

'At making us take him seriously.'

'I took him seriously from the start,' said Mimì.

'Congratulations, Deputy Inspector Augello. I'll recommend you for a solemn citation from his honour the commissioner. Happy?'

Mimì didn't answer. Whenever the inspector was in this foul a mood, it was best to sit tight and keep one's mouth shut.

'He's trying to tell us something else, in addition to keeping us abreast of his contraction,' Montalbano resumed after a pause.

He spoke in a low voice, mostly because he was trying to work things out for himself.

'What makes you think that?'

'Use your brains, Mimì, if it's not too hard. If he only wanted us to know that he was contracting – whatever he may mean by that – he didn't need to go running from one end of Vigàta to another, killing a different animal each time. Why change animal?'

'Maybe the first letter of each—' Mimì ventured.

'I've already thought of that. Does FCDG mean anything to you?'

'Could be the initials of some subversive group or movement,' Fazio timidly suggested.

'Oh, yeah? Give me an example.'

'I dunno, Chief, how about the Front for Communist Disruption and Grandstanding?'

'You think there are still revolutionary communists around? Give me a break!' Montalbano shot him down gruffly.

Another silence fell. Augello lit a cigarette, Fazio stared at the tips of his shoes.

'Put that cigarette out,' the inspector ordered Mimì.

'Why . . . ?' Augello asked, dumbfounded.

'Because, while you were screwing around in Frankfurt—'

'I was in Hamburg.'

'Wherever you were, while you were out of this beautiful country of ours, some minister woke up one morning and started worrying about our health. If you want to keep smoking, you're going to have to go for a little walk down the street.'

Cursing between clenched teeth, Mimì got up and left the room.

'Can I go too?' Fazio asked.

'What's keeping you?'

Alone at last, the inspector heaved a long sigh of satisfaction. He'd managed to give vent to some of the foul mood this idiot who went around killing animals had put him in.

*

Barely an hour went by before Montalbano's voice thundered through the police station.

'Augello! Fazio!'

They both came running. At the mere sight of Montalbano's face, Augello and Fazio became convinced that some gear inside the inspector's brain had started turning in the right direction. He had, in fact, a hint of a smile on his face.

'Fazio, do you know the name of the person who owned the murdered goat? Wait — don't say anything; just nod if you know.'

Bewildered, Fazio nodded his head repeatedly.

'Want to bet I know the first letter of the owner's surname? It begins with the letter *L*, right?'

'Right!' Fazio exclaimed in admiration.

Mimì Augello clapped his hands briefly, and ironically, and then asked:

'Have you finished your magic tricks?'

Montalbano didn't answer.

'Now, tell me the surnames of the other animals' owners,' he said instead, addressing Fazio.

'Haber, Aiello, Iaccari, Lomonaco — the owner of the goat, the one we were just talking about, is Stefano Lomonaco.'

'Hail!' Mimì shouted.

'Hail what?' Fazio asked, bewildered.

'That's what he wrote: "Hail",' Augello explained.

'You're right, Mimì,' said Montalbano. 'He is writing us another message using the first letters of those last names, not the names of the animals he's been killing.'

'Now I get it!' said Fazio.

'Then tell us, Fazio. We want to know too.'

'At the house of the old man whose dog he killed, there were also two goats. And this morning I was wondering why he hadn't gone back to Iaccari's place instead of dragging himself over ten miles outside town to kill another goat. Now I know why. Because he needed another surname, one beginning with *L*.'

'So what are we going to do?' Augello asked.

His tone was between agitation and anxiety. Fazio, too, looked at the inspector with the eyes of a dog wanting a bone.

Montalbano threw his hands up.

'We can't just wait for him to shoot a man before we intervene,' Mimì insisted. 'Because I'm more than convinced that, next time, he's going to kill somebody.'

Montalbano threw his hands up again.

'I don't understand how you can just sit there so calmly,' Mimì said provocatively.

'Because I'm not as foolish as you are,' said the inspector, cool as a cucumber.

'Would you please explain?'

'First of all, what makes you think I'm calm? And second, why don't *you* tell me what the hell you think we should do? Build an ark like Noah, put every kind of animal in existence in it, and wait for the man to come and kill one? And third: we have no way of knowing that next time he's going to kill a man. He probably won't kill anyone till the end of his message. For now, he's only written the first word: "Hail". He clearly hasn't finished his sentence yet. We have no idea how long it will be and how many words it will have. My advice to you both is that you sit tight and be patient.'

*

On the morning of Monday 20 October, Montalbano, Augello, and Fazio were all at police headquarters at the crack of dawn, without having made any prior arrangement. Seeing them all show up at such an early hour, Catarella nearly had a heart attack.

'Whass' goin' on? Ahh, wha'ss happened? Eh, wha'ss goin' on?'

He was given three different answers, three different lies. Montalbano said he hadn't slept a wink because of severe heartburn; Mimì Augello said he'd had to take a friend who'd been staying with him to catch an early train; and Fazio claimed he'd had to go out early to buy aspirin for his wife, who had a slight fever. But by common agreement they sent Catarella out to get three extra-strong coffees at the corner bar, which was already open.

After drinking his coffee in silence, Montalbano lit a cigarette. Augello waited for him to take his first drag and then launched into his private vendetta.

'No, no, no!' he said, shaking a reproachful finger. 'And what are you going to say to his honour the minister if he suddenly shows up and sees you?'

Cursing, Montalbano left the room and went down to smoke in the front entrance of the station. Taking his third drag, he heard the telephone ring. He dashed back inside like a sprinter.

All three of them, Montalbano, Fazio, and Augello, converged at once in the tiny doorway to Catarella's switchboard cabinet, which itself was scarcely bigger than a broom cupboard, and they began to struggle by way of shoulderthrusts. Seeing them all burst in like that, a terrified Catarella thought they were all coming at him for some reason. Dropping the receiver he had in his hand, he shot to his feet, eyes bulging, back against the wall, hands in the air, and yelled:

'I surrender!'

Using his authority, Montalbano grabbed the microphone.

'This is Chief Insp—'

'Hello! Hello! Whooziss talking?' a very shrill, hysterical female voice interrupted him.

'This is Chief Insp—'

'Hurry, hurry! Get over here right away! Quick!'

'Tell me, signora, has one of your animals been killed?'

'Animals? What animals? What, are you drunk first thing in the morning?'

'I'm sorry, please give me your personal particulars.'

'Whass' 'iss guy talkin' about?'

'Your name and address, signora.'

By the end of the strained phone conversation, they'd managed to gather that Mrs Agata Gaggiano, who lived in the hamlet of Cannatello, 'right azackly nex' to the water fountain', was scared out of her wits because her husband, Ciccio, had left the house with his rifle to go and kill a certain Armando Losurdo.

'An' you c'n b'lieve me, if 'e says 'e's gonna do it, 'e's gonna do it.'

'So why does he want to kill him?'

''Ow should I know? When's my husban' ever tol' me why 'e does anything?'

'Go and take a look,' Montalbano ordered Fazio.

Fazio left the room, muttering, and in turn ordered Galluzzo, who'd just come into the station, to come with him.

*

Mrs Agata Gaggiano, who was about fifty, was so skinny she looked like the personification of famine. The moment the two policemen appeared in front of her, she decided to break down in tears, resting her head against Galluzzo's chest. She told the two exhausted representatives of the law (the hamlet of Cannatello was located at the edge of a precipice and they'd had to climb for forty-five minutes on foot to get there, as the road was impassable by car) that her husband had gone out at five-thirty that morning to attend to their animals but had returned only ten minutes later, looking out of his mind, just like Orlando at the puppet theatre, hair standing straight up on his head, cursing worse than a wild Turk and bashing his head against the wall. She'd gone up to him to ask him what was wrong, but he acted as if he'd gone deaf and didn't answer. At a certain point he started yelling that this time he wasn't going to 'let it slide with Armando', he was going to 'shoot 'im as sure as the Lord was God'. And in fact he had taken the rifle he kept at the head of his bed and gone back out.

'This time they'll give 'im life! He'll never come out again! He's used 'isself up for ever!'

'Signora, before you start talking about life imprisonment,' Fazio cut in, thinking only of getting back to the station as quickly as possible, 'tell us who this Armando is and where he lives.'

It turned out that Armando Losurdo was a man with a few hectares of land bordering on the Gaggianos' property, and not a day went by without the two men squabbling with each other. One day, one of them would cut off the branch of the other's tree, saying it was jutting out into his field, the next day, the other would lay claim to a chicken that had strayed onto his land and make a soup of it.

'And do you know what happened this time, signora?'

'I don' know! He din't tell me!'

Fazio got her to explain to him where Armando Losurdo lived, and then he left on foot, followed by Galluzzo, who Mrs Agata had clung to all the while, soaking his jacket with tears and the mucus running from her nose.

When they got there, they found themselves in a scene

straight out of an American cowboy movie. Someone was shooting out of the only window of a rustic cottage at a fiftyish-looking peasant, obviously Ciccio Gaggiano, who, taking cover behind a low wall, answered with his rifle the other's pistol-fire.

Gaggiano was too absorbed in the gun-battle to notice Fazio coming up behind him. In a flash Fazio jumped on him and even managed, when the man turned around, to deal him a punch in the stomach. As Gaggiano was gasping for breath, Fazio handcuffed him.

Galluzzo, meanwhile, was yelling:

'Police! Armando Losurdo, don't shoot!'

'I don't believe you! Get outta here or I'll shoot you too!'

'We're with the police, idiot!'

'Swear it on your mother's head!'

'Just swear to it,' Fazio ordered him. 'Otherwise we'll be here all day.'

'But this is insane!'

'Just swear to it and stop messing about!'

'I swear on my mother's head that I'm a policeman!'

As Losurdo came out of the house with his hands up, Fazio asked Galluzzo:

'But didn't your mother die three years ago?'

'Yes.'

'So why did you drag your feet?'

'It didn't seem right to me.'

As soon as Gaggiano saw Losurdo outside, he thrust his shoulder and broke free from Fazio, handcuffs and all, charging at his enemy with head down like a ram. Galluzzo stuck a foot out and tripped him, laying him out on the ground.

Meanwhile, Losurdo was yelling:

'I dunno wha'ss got into him! He's crazy! He just set hisself down behind that wall and started shooting! I din't do nuthin' to 'im. I swear on my mother's head.'

'The man is fixated on mothers' heads,' Galluzzo commented.

Gaggiano, meanwhile, had risen to his knees but was so enraged he couldn't speak. The words got jumbled in his mouth and turned to froth as his face turned purple.

'The donkey! The donkey!' he finally managed to blurt out with a sorrowful voice on the verge of tears.

'What donkey?' Losurdo shouted.

'Mine, you bastard!'

Then, turning to Fazio and Galluzzo, he explained:

'This morning I found my donkey . . . dead! One shot to the head! An' it was this here bastard that killed him!'

At the sound of the words 'one shot to the head', Fazio froze and pricked up his ears.

'Let me get this straight,' he said slowly to Gaggiano. 'Are you telling me you found your donkey dead this morning, killed by one shot to the head?'

'Yessir.'

Fazio then literally disappeared before the eyes of Galluzzo, Gaggiano, and Losurdo, who all turned to stone as if an angel had passed, said, 'Amen,' and frozen everyone in the act of whatever they were doing.

'Why'd he run away?' Gaggiano and Losurdo asked in unison.

*

Fazio arrived at the Gaggiano house sweaty and out of breath. The donkey was still tied to a tree nearby, but lay dead on the ground. A trickle of blood oozed out of one ear. He found the empty case at once, practically between the animal's legs, and at a glance it looked exactly like the others. But there was no trace of a message anywhere. As he started looking around for it, thinking an early morning gust of wind might have blown it away, a window of the cottage opened and Mrs Gaggiano appeared.

'Did 'e kill 'im?' she asked in a powerful voice.

'Yes,' Fazio replied.

The floodgates opened, the shit hit the fan, and all hell broke loose.

'Aaaaaahhhhh!' Mrs Gaggiano wailed, vanishing from the window. Despite the distance at which he stood, Fazio heard her body hit the floor. He broke into a run again, went into the house, climbed up the wooden staircase, and entered the only upstairs room, the bedroom. Mrs Gaggiano lay under the window, unconscious. What to do? Fazio knelt down beside her and gently slapped her twice.

'Signora! Signora!'

No reaction. He went back downstairs, took a glass, filled it with water from a jug, went back up, wet his handkerchief with the water, then wiped the woman's face several times, continuously calling out to her:

'Signora! Signora!'

At last, with God's help, the woman opened her eyes and looked at him.

'Djou arrest 'im?'

'Arrest who?'

'My husband.'

'What for?'

'What? Din't he kill Armando?'

'No, signora.'

'So why'd you say 'e did?'

'I thought you were asking me about the donkey!'

'What donkey?'

As he was trying to come up with a contorted logical explanation for the misunderstanding, Fazio, from the window, saw Galluzzo approaching with Gaggiano and Losurdo. To keep them from attacking each other, Galluzzo had them both handcuffed and walking at a distance of about five paces from each other. Fazio forgot about the woman, who at any rate seemed to have recovered just fine, and went out to meet the trio.

With the help of Galluzzo and the two peasants, he

managed to move the donkey's carcass. Beneath it they found a piece of graph paper.

I'M STILL CONTRACTING

4

Fazio scrambled back to the station to tell everyone about the animal-killer's latest exploit, but the others didn't have time to absorb the information and ponder its meaning.

'Ahh, Chief, Chief!' Catarella shouted, bursting into the room. 'Whaa'? Dja fergit?'

'Forget what?'

'Yer meetin' witta c'mishner! He called jess now an' said they's aspecting you!'

'Shit!' said Montalbano, dashing out of the room.

A second later he stuck his head inside the door:

'In the meantime, you lot keep talking about this.'

'Thanks for giving us permission,' said Mimì.

Fazio sat down.

'Well, if we're gonna talk about it . . .' he said listlessly. It was a known fact that he wasn't terribly fond of Augello.

'All right, then,' Mimì began, 'our anonymous animal-hater—'

He wasn't even able to finish his sentence before Catarella burst into the room again.

'There's summon onna phone wants a speak to the Chief, but seein' as how the Chief ain't here, you wan' me to put the call tru to yiz poissonally?'

'In poisson,' said Mimì.

'Is this Inspector Montalbano?' asked an unknown and clearly annoyed voice.

'No, I'm Inspector Augello, his second-in-command. What can I do for you?'

'I'm a neighbour of ragioniere Portera.'

'So?'

'At this very moment, ragioniere Portera is shooting at his wife yet again. So my question is: when the hell are you guys going to put an end to this nonsense?'

'I'm on my way.'

Mrs Romilda Fasulo Portera was sixty years old, extremely short, with legs so bowed they looked like corkscrews, one eye looking east, the other looking west, and yet her husband was convinced she was a great beauty and had suitors galore to whom, every so often, she granted favours.

And so, on average about twice a month, after one of their ritual quarrels that could be heard as far as the neighbouring streets, the ragioniere would pull out the revolver he always kept in his jacket pocket and fire three or four shots at his spouse, always rigorously missing her. Mrs Romilda didn't even have to move; she would simply keep on doing whatever she'd been doing as the shots rang out, saying only:

'One of these days you're really going to kill me, Giugiù.'

Montalbano had tried once to make the man see reason, but there was no way.

'Inspector, my wife is the pure reincarnation of the slut Messalina!'

'Stop and think for a minute, Mr Portera. Even if your wife really was the reincarnation of Empress Messalina, can you tell me when she would have the time or opportunity to cheat on you? I'm told she never leaves the house alone, you never let her take a step without you, you accompany her everywhere, to church, to go shopping . . . And you yourself never go out for more than five minutes, to buy the newspaper. So you tell me when and how she meets these lovers of hers.'

'Ah, Inspector, when a woman sets her mind to doing something, she always finds a way, believe me . . .'

This time, however, Mimì Augello, who was on edge over the killing of the donkey, took off the kid gloves. He disarmed Portera (who at any rate hadn't the slightest intention of resisting), confiscated the weapon, and decided to handcuff the trigger-happy ragioniere to the bedpost.

'I'll come by this evening to free you,' he said.

'And what if I need to go? I took a diuretic!'

'Ask your wife to give you a hand, and I'd advise her to do just that. But if she won't, I guess you'll just have to piss yourself.'

*

Commissioner Bonetti-Alderighi was in a bad mood and made no effort to hide it.

'Let me begin by saying, Montalbano, that yesterday I held a meeting on this same subject with your counterparts from the other commissariats under my jurisdiction. With you, however, I thought it was better we meet alone, so I could devote the whole morning to you.'

'Why alone?'

'Because you – and please don't take offence – seem sometimes to have serious difficulty grasping the gist of the problems I present to you. And I don't think you do it in bad faith.'

For some time Montalbano had found that if he pretended to be utterly incapable of understanding the slightest thing, the commissioner would leave him in peace, summoning him to his office only when he had no choice. On this occasion the matter involved the measures to be taken in the face of recent landings of illegal immigrants on Sicilian shores. Their talk lasted more than three hours, because every so often Montalbano felt obliged to interrupt.

'I didn't quite get that,' he would say. 'If you'd be so kind as to repeat it more slowly . . .'

And his superior was always so kind as to start again at the beginning.

After the discouraged commissioner sent him on his way, the inspector ran into Dr Lattes, the chief of the commissioner's cabinet, known as 'Lattes e Mieles' for his unctuous falsity, in the hallway. Lattes grabbed Montalbano by the arm and took him aside. Then he got up on tiptoe and whispered in his ear:

'Have you heard the news?'

'No,' said Montalbano in a similarly conspiratorial tone.

'I've been told from a highly placed source that our commissioner, who so well deserves it, is going to be transferred. Would you be interested in contributing to a goodbye present, a nice little token of affection that I think could be—'

'Whatever you like,' said the inspector, leaving him in the lurch and walking away.

He went out of Montelusa Central Police singing *La donna è mobile*, so happy was he to learn that Bonetti-Alderighi would soon be out of his hair.

He celebrated at the Trattoria San Calogero with a giant platter of grilled fish.

*

They were finally able to meet again at five o'clock in the afternoon.

'So far,' Montalbano said at once, 'the guy has written "Hail g . . .". In my opinion, the statement will turn out to be "Hail God".'

'*Oh Madunnuzza santa!*' Fazio exclaimed.

'What are you so worried about?'

'Chief, whenever they start bringing religion into the picture, I get scared.'

'What makes you think that's what he means to say?' asked Augello.

'Before calling you both in here I did a little telephone investigation and got some specific information from the town hall. There are five people in the area who own donkeys, and their names are Di Rosa, D'Antonio, Gaggiano, Gerlando, and Musso. Di Rosa keeps his practically in town, and Gerlando's right on the outskirts, whereas our man went all the way out to that godforsaken mountain to

kill a donkey. Why? Because the animal's owner's last name
has two Gs in it on top of the first letter — whereas, for
example, Gerlando's only got the initial. Therefore we can
surmise that by choosing a surname that not only starts
with G but has two other Gs in it, he intended for the G in
his message to be capitalized.'

'That makes sense,' Augello admitted.

'And if my argument makes sense,' said the inspector,
'then this whole business is starting to look pretty nasty and
dangerous. With religious fanatics it's always better to steer
clear of them, as Fazio says, because they're capable of anything.'

'Well, if that's the way it is,' Mimì continued, 'then I
understand even less what he means when he says he's contracting. I've always read and heard that God makes Himself
manifest in all His greatness, power, and magnificence, not
in His smallness. Until proven otherwise, to contract means
to shrink.'

'That's what it means for us,' said the inspector. 'But
who knows what it means for him?'

'You could also interpret it another way,' Mimì resumed
after a reflective pause.

'And what would that be?'

'It's possible that he wants to say "Hail", comma, "God",
after which he's going to take the gun, shoot himself, and a
goodnight to all.'

'But how's he going to make a comma?' Fazio objected
timidly.

'That's his problem,' Augello cut him off.

'Mimì, among all the nonsense you've been spouting,
there was one thing you said that was right. Which was that
the things he was killing were growing in size. And that
worries me. A fish, a chicken, a dog, a goat, a donkey. What
animal's turn is it this time?'

'Well,' said Mimì, 'at some point he's going to have to

stop, since there aren't any elephants in this part of the world.'

He was the only one who laughed at his joke.

'Maybe it'd be better if we informed the commissioner,' said Fazio.

'Maybe it'd be better if we informed the Animal Protection Society,' said Mimì, who when he got going with the bad jokes could not control himself.

✳

The morning of Monday 27 October started out in nasty fashion, with high winds, lightning, and thunder.

Having slept poorly due to an excess of calamari and baby octopus, half of them fried and the other half dressed in olive oil and lemon juice, Montalbano decided to lie in bed a little longer than usual. His mood was so dark that if he were to run into anyone who wanted to talk, he was liable to attack him. Anyway, if there were any new developments at the station, everyone would certainly come running to let him know.

He dozed off without realizing it and woke up again around nine. How was that possible? Want to bet the phone was off the hook? He went and checked: all in order. Maybe the station had called him and he hadn't heard the phone ring?

'Hello, Catarella, Montalbano here.'

'I rec'nize yiz straightaways from yer voice, Chief.'

'Have there been any phone calls?'

'F'yiz poissonally in poisson, nah.'

'For anyone else?'

''Oo's "anyone else", Chief, if ya don' mine me askin'?'

'Augello, Fazio, Galluzzo, Gallo . . .'

'Nah, Chief, no calls f'them.'

'Then for whom?'

''Ere's one f'me, Chief, bu' I needed t'know foist if I's anyone else or not.'

As soon as he went into his office, Augello and Fazio came in. They were perplexed. There had been no news of any killing of humans or animals.

'I wonder why he skipped a Monday?'

'Maybe he was prevented from going out,' said Mimì. 'The weather's been bad and maybe he wasn't feeling well, maybe he got the flu. There could be any number of reasons.'

'Or else he did exactly what he had to do, but we haven't found out about it yet and nobody's reported it,' said Montalbano.

Montalbano, Augello, and Fazio spent the rest of that Monday morning practically running to the switchboard every time they heard the phone ring, each time making Catarella break out in a cold sweat, since he didn't know the reason for all this avid interest. The three men's agitation grew by the hour, to the point that to avoid the possibility of some violent scuffle, the inspector decided to go home for lunch — home, and not out, because on Saturday his housekeeper Adelina had left a note:

> *Isspecter, on Munnday I mekka yu pasta ncasciatta.*

Pasta 'ncasciata! A dish that made one moan with pleasure at every bite, but which Adelina rarely made for him because it took so long to prepare.

Since the wind had dropped, he ate out on the veranda amidst the lightning and thunder. But with that gift of God in front of him, which he relished not only with his palate but with his whole body, he no longer gave a damn about the bad weather. And since the good minister still allowed the so-called free citizen of the republic to smoke in his own home, he turned on the television, tuned into the Free Channel, which at that hour was broadcasting the news, dropped into an armchair, and lit a cigarette.

As his eyelids started drooping, he thought that a half-hour nap might be a good idea. Bending forward to turn the TV off, he reached out and then froze in mid-air.

On the screen was an image of a dead elephant. The TV camera did a slow pan of the animal's head, then zoomed in on an enormous eye mangled by a bullet. He turned up the volume.

'. . . utterly inexplicable,' said the voice of Nicolò Zito, his newsman friend, off-camera. 'The Wonderland Circus arrived in Fiacca on Saturday morning and gave its first performances that same evening. On Sunday, on top of the children's matinee, the circus gave afternoon and evening performances as well. Everything went fine, but at about three o'clock this morning, Mr Ademaro Ramirez, the circus's director, was woken up by some unusual trumpeting coming from the elephants' cage, which is close to his caravan. When he got up and went to the cage, he immediately noticed that one of the three elephants was lying on its side in an abnormal position, while the other two elephants seemed very agitated. At that moment the trainer, likewise awakened by the trumpeting, also arrived, and tried with great effort to calm the animals, which were dangerously upset. When she was able to enter the cage, the trainer realized that the elephant lying on the ground, whose name was Alachek, had been killed by a single pistol shot fired with great precision and cold calculation into its left eye.'

The image of the trainer appeared, a good-looking blonde who was crying inconsolably. Still off-camera, the newsman's voice continued the report as the camera showed other animals featured in the circus.

'One disturbing detail is that Marshal Adragna of the carabinieri, who is conducting the investigation, found a piece of graph paper inside the cage, on which was written the enigmatic statement: "*I've almost finished contracting.*" Investigation of this mysterious occurrence is . . .'

He turned off the TV. The first thing he did was call Mimì Augello.

'Did you know that there *are* in fact elephants in this part of the world?'

'What do you—?'

'I'll explain later. In an hour, max, at the station.'

Then he called Fazio.

'An elephant was killed.'

'Are you joking?'

'I'm in no mood for jokes. The elephant was part of a circus, in Fiacca. They found a piece of paper with a message. I think you're friends with Marshal Adragna, aren't you?'

'Yeah, he's an old friend.'

'OK then, I want you to go up to Fiacca, and see if your friend has recovered the empty case. If so, have him lend it to you for a day. Oh and, while you're at it, see if he'll let you have the message too.'

*

As he was driving to the station, he realized there was something in all this that didn't add up. If his theory was correct – and he sensed that it was – then the animal killer needed a name that began with the letter O. So how did the Wonderland Circus fit in? Even the elephant's name began with an A. And so?

He had his answer almost immediately. On the side of one of the first buildings in Vigàta was a large, colourful poster. He thought he saw, out of the corner of his eye, an image of a clown. He stopped the car, got out, and went to look. It was an ad for the Wonderland Circus and must have already been there for a few days because it looked a bit worn from the bad weather. It announced that the circus would be coming to Vigàta on the 20th of October. Too late for the killer.

Below this announcement was a calendar of the performance dates around the province, which must have been how the man who took himself for God, or at least thought he was part of the divine plan, had learned the date of the circus's performance in Fiacca. Standing out on the poster was the list of attractions. Second on this list, in gold lettering, was the name of Irina Orlovska, elephant trainer and star of the Moscow Circus.

So there was the letter O to put after the G. By now there was no doubt that the whole word would indeed be 'God'.

The man who thought he was God, or part of the divine plan, had clearly read the poster and acted accordingly, in a jiffy. What better opportunity could he have had?

But acting on the opportunity must not have been an easy task. The risks involved were enormous, so great that they might compromise the plan he had in mind. A night-watchman passing by, or a reaction of fear from one of the animals at the sight of a stranger approaching, would have been enough to ruin everything. And yet he'd gone just the same to the circus at night, or very early in the morning, and had succeeded in killing an elephant. Was he a madman who acted rashly, carelessly, taking things as they came, or was he one of those equally insane people who belonged to the category of obsessed, methodical madmen? Everything pointed to the likelihood that the man left nothing to chance.

Then there was the increasing size of the victims to consider. Surely this must mean something, and there was a hidden message that needed deciphering. After the goat was killed, the inspector had thought, with considerable concern, that a human being would be next. Whereas instead of a human, the madman had killed a donkey. Followed by an elephant. Now, between a goat and an elephant, there was plenty of room for a human body. But he hadn't done it. Why not? Because he thought little of humans? No, since for the humans he'd left the little messages communicating his stage of contraction — whatever that meant. And one could therefore conclude that he thought a lot about humans. He was alerting them to an imminent event. Maybe he would shoot a man on the coming Monday, which would mean that he put the man at the top of the pyramid of the animal kingdom. Yes, that must be it: next time around, it would be a human's turn. Man is, in fact, different from the other animals, being endowed with reason. And this makes him superior. Or at least that's what people still think, despite all the proof to the contrary that humans have never ceased to exhibit over the course of their age-old history.

5

The meeting started later than planned because Fazio, on his way back from Fiacca, had run into some heavy traffic. As soon as he came in, he handed the inspector two empty cases.

'Put these back in the drawer with the others.'

Montalbano looked bewildered.

'*Two* cases? Did he fire twice?'

'No, Chief, just once.'

'So why'd Adragna give you two?'

'Chief, these are from the ones we have here. See, it occurred to me that if I asked my friend to lend me the case and message, he would prick up his ears and start rightly wondering why we're so interested in the murder of an elephant. So I told him I was in Fiacca to see an old friend and had dropped in just to say hello. I casually got him to start talking about the circus incident, and he showed me the case and the piece of paper. At one point he had to leave the room for a few minutes, and so I compared his shell with ours, which I'd brought with me. They're identical. And this time, the message says: "I've almost finished contracting."'

'Yeah, I know, I heard that on TV.'

'I'm wondering what's going to happen when he stops contracting,' Mimì said pensively.

'Did Adragna tell you whether anyone saw or heard anything strange during the night?' Montalbano asked.

'Nothing. The animals' cages are set up rather far from where the stagehands and performers sleep. The trainer said she heard some . . . what do you call the noise elephants make?'

'Trumpeting?'

'Right, but since they often make noise when they're startled by something unusual, like someone passing close by, she didn't pay much attention.'

'And nobody heard the shot?'

'Nobody. He must have used a silencer. And he must have also brought along a powerful torch, because Adragna told me it's very dark around those cages at night.'

'So how the hell did he pull it off?'

'We have to assume he's a really good shot. Since he couldn't very well go and fire a big hunting rifle, since the bang would have been loud enough to wake up everyone in town, he climbed up the bars of the cage, getting practically as high as the elephants' heads, and then fired at the animal from about a foot and a half away.'

'How do they know that?'

'Adragna noticed the mud tracked by the soles of his shoes. So, anyway, he turned on the torch, pointed it at the eye of the nearest elephant, and fired.'

'He might be a good shot, but he's really bloody lucky, too,' Mimì commented, continuing: 'Now all he's missing is the *d* in God.'

Montalbano looked at them with concern.

'You know what?' he said. 'I think we have until Sunday night to prevent a murder.'

*

For the past three hours the man had been reading, never once taking his eyes off the book, turning the pages delicately, hands trembling.

He is one with His Power as the flame is one with its colours; his strength issues from his Oneness as the light of the gaze issues from the darkness of the pupil.

The one emanates from the other as scent emanates from a scent and light from a light.

In the emanation is all the Power of the Emanator, but the Emanator undergoes no diminution therefrom.

At this point the man could read no further. His eyes were full of tears. Of happiness. Nay, of joy. Superhuman joy. He looked at his watch: three o'clock in the morning. He let himself go, weeping convulsively, overwhelmed by emotion. He trembled as though feverish. He rose, had trouble standing, went over to the window, and opened it. An ice-cold wind was blowing. The man filled his lungs with air and screamed. The scream was so long it sounded like a howl. Then at once he felt his legs give out from under him. Unable to remain standing, he fell to his knees, the front of his shirt wet with tears.

Only seven more days until the Manifestation.

*

Montalbano looked at the clock: 3 a.m. What point was there in lying in bed if there was no way he could fall asleep? He got up, went into the kitchen, and put a pot of coffee on the hob.

Three questions kept drilling into this brain:

Why did the man always act on Mondays, in the early hours of the morning, at the start of the new day?

Why was he so keen that one and all should know that a contraction was taking place inside him? What the hell was contracting?

And what, exactly, did the madman mean by 'contracting'? Did it mean to shrink or grow smaller, as Mimì had said, or did it mean something only explicable by what was going through the unknown man's sick mind?

Montalbano felt that it was essential to interpret that verb correctly if they were ever to understand what the madman's ultimate intention was and where he wanted to go with it.

Was there an answer? No, there wasn't.

*

Early the following morning, which was a Tuesday, he turned up at the office with eyes bloodshot from lack of sleep and already in a foul mood that was then aggravated exponentially by the cold, windy weather.

'Listen to me,' he said to Augello and Fazio. 'I've given this business a lot of thought. I was up all night. This fanatic — since that's what he is, there's no point pretending otherwise — is without a doubt someone who was born and raised in Vigàta.'

'Why do you say that?' asked Augello.

'Mimì, think for a second. He knows exactly who owns what kinds of animals and what their last names are. Those are the kinds of things you either get from the town hall's records or you know directly by knowing the people.'

'*You* think for a second,' Mimì retorted sharply. 'What does it take to know that there's a fish tank at a seafood restaurant? Or that there are going to be chickens at a poultry farm?'

'Oh, yeah? So you yourself knew that Mr Lomonaco had a goat and Gaggiano had a donkey?'

Augello said nothing.

'Can I go on?' said Montalbano. 'I repeat: he's someone from Vigàta, and he's not too young, either.'

'Why do you say that?' asked Mimì.

'Because he knows pensioners, old people . . .'

'Bah,' said Mimì.

Montalbano didn't feel like having it out with him, so he just continued.

'He's an educated man. He has the handwriting of someone who's in the habit of writing.'

'Just a minute,' Fazio cut in. 'He can't be too old, either. It's unlikely a man of advanced age can so easily pick locks, roam the countryside at night, climb up elephant cages, and—'

'At any rate he's a fanatic, there's no doubt about that.'

'Yes, Salvo,' Augello cut in, 'but Fazio's question was—'

'I understood perfectly what Fazio's question was. And I am, in fact, answering it. Fanaticism leads people to do unthinkable things, it gives you strength you didn't know you had and courage you'd never have dreamed of. Anyway, there's no indication he's working alone. He might be sending other people out with the pistol and messages. An adept.'

'A what?' asked Fazio.

'An adept. It means "follower". It's not a dirty word, Fazio. So, here's what we're going to do. You, Mimì, are going to go to the town hall's records office and get a list of everyone in town with a last name beginning with D. Don't worry, there won't be hundreds of thousands.'

'Hundreds of thousands, no, but a lot just the same. I, for example, know a Mario Danieli and a Stefano Doni,' Mimì retorted.

'And I know three,' said Fazio. 'D'Arrigo, Delvecchio, and Dalla.'

'Not to mention,' Mimì continued, 'that Stefano Doni has ten children, five boys and five girls. And that three of the five boys are married and have children of their own.'

'I don't care about grandparents, children, grandchildren, nieces, or nephews, got that?' Montalbano fired back. 'I want the full list, newborns included, by tomorrow morning.'

'And what do you plan to do with it?'

'If by Sunday morning we still haven't worked this thing out, we'll bring them together in one place and post a guard.'

'Maybe we should put them all in the football stadium the way General Pinochet did,' Augello said ironically.

'You know, Mimì, I truly admire you. I knew you were an idiot, of course, but I had no idea you could reach such heights of idiocy. My most heartfelt compliments. *Ad majora.* Now get the hell out of here.'

Augello got up and left.

'So what am I supposed to do?' asked Fazio.

'Start hanging around town. See if you can find out whether the story of all these animals being killed has leaked out – and if it has, what people think about it.

✳

When he got home it was almost 10 p.m., but he really didn't feel like eating. His stomach was in knots. He was worried, but mostly unhappy with himself. Yes, he'd succeeded in connecting the dots between the different events, and he'd been able (perhaps) to predict the fanatic's next move, but none of this was of any help unless he discovered what maniacal idea, what sinister intention had lodged itself inside the mystery man's depraved mind and prompted him to act.

Not that he believed there necessarily had to be a specific, rational motive behind every crime. He'd once read a book by Max Aub on this question, called *Exemplary Crimes*, which, after the fun was over, had been more useful as a psychological study. On the other hand, it was equally true that the more you know about the person you're looking for, the more likely you are to find him.

The telephone rang.

'So, are you going to be able to make it here on Saturday?'

With a string of excuses that were many and various, and worthy of the first Nobel Prize for Lying, he'd managed to postpone the promised visit to Boccadasse from week to week, but felt that Livia was less and less convinced by his reasons. Perhaps it was best just to tell her the whole truth. He took a deep breath and plunged into the sea of things to say.

'In all honesty, Livia, I really don't think I can make it.'

'Could you at least tell me what's going on with you?'

'Livia, don't you know what I do for a living? Have you forgotten? I don't have the same working hours and rhythms as an office clerk. I have a very, very complex case on my hands at the moment. There's been a whole series of strange killings . . .'

'A serial killer?' Livia asked in astonishment.

Montalbano hesitated.

'Well, I suppose you could call him that, in a sense.'

'Who's he killed?'

'Well, he started with a fish — a mullet, to be exact.'

'What?!'

'That's right, a grey mullet, but of the fresh-water variety. Then he knocked off a chicken, then a—'

'Moron!'

'Livia, listen . . . Hello? Hello?'

She'd hung up. How was it that she never believed him, whether he told the truth or not? Maybe he should have put his words in a different order or used different ones . . .

Words, for Christ's sake! Words!

He'd used the right words when talking about the animal-killer — he'd called him a madman, a religious fanatic, someone who thought he was God, or at least that he had direct access to Him, but he had failed to draw the right conclusions from his own words! What an imbecile he'd been! That was the road he should follow, without wasting another minute. Frantic, he picked up the phone and started dialling. In his agitation he made a mistake. On the third try he got it right.

'Nicolò? Montalbano here.'

'What do you want? I'm about to go on the air.'

'I only need a few seconds.'

'I haven't got any. If you make me a dish of pasta, I'll come to your place after midnight, after the late edition.'

✳

Nicolò Zito the newsman sat down to a dish of spaghetti dressed in *oglio del carrettiere* and pecorino cheese and, as a second course, large black passuluna olives, a slice of caciocavallo cheese, and that's all, folks.

'You shouldn't have gone to all the trouble!' was his comment.

'I'm not hungry, Nicolò.'

'And because you're not hungry, you think I'm not either? What's with you? You're getting me worried if you, of all people, tell me you don't feel like eating. Now spit it out, what is it?'

Montalbano told him the whole story. As he was speaking, Zito became more and more attentive.

'This whole business,' he said when the inspector had finished talking, 'can only end in one of two ways: in tragedy or farce. As things stand right now, however, I think the former is more likely.'

'Me too,' said Montalbano, frowning darkly.

'So why'd you call me?'

'You can help me.'

'I can?'

'Yes. I need to get in touch immediately with Alcide Maraventano.'

The person the inspector wanted to see was a man of incredible erudition who a few years earlier had lent him a hand in solving the case that came to be called the Terracotta Dog. He lived in Gallotta, a little town near Montelusa. He may have once been a priest, maybe not, but he was certainly someone whose brain functioned in alternating currents. He was always wearing a sort of cassock that had once been black but had long ago turned a sort of mouldy green. Being frighteningly thin, he looked like a skeleton

who'd just climbed out of its grave, and yet he was mysteri-
ously alive. His house was an enormous, ramshackle hovel
without telephone or electricity. To make up for this it was
stuffed so full of books that there was no place to sit down.
When he spoke, he was in the habit of sucking milk from
a baby's bottle.

Upon hearing the man's name, Zito grimaced.

'What is it?'

'Well, just yesterday a friend of mine told me he'd gone
to see him, but Maraventano had refused to let him in and
would only talk to him through the door.'

'Why was that?'

'He told him he was near the end and had no time to
waste. He said he needs the little breath he has left for
breathing the days remaining to him.'

'Is he ill?'

Dying people frightened Montalbano.

'Who knows. He's certainly very old. He must be over
ninety by now.'

'Well, try anyway, as a favour to me.'

*

Around noon the following day, having still not heard from
Zito, he decided to ring him.

'Montalbano here, Nicolò. Have you forgotten the
request I made you last night?'

Nicolò Zito reacted as if he'd been stung by a wasp.

'Forgotten?! I've wasted all morning on it! Don't you
know Maraventano doesn't have a phone and you have to
send someone to his house when you want to talk to him?'

'So?'

'What do you mean, "so"? It's taken me until fifteen
minutes ago to find a volunteer in Gallotta. I'm waiting for
his answer.'

The answer arrived half an hour later. Alcide Maraventano had agreed to receive Montalbano. But it must be a

short visit. And the inspector, moreover, must come alone.
Otherwise he wouldn't be let in.

*

Alcide Maraventano's house was the way Montalbano
remembered it. Shutters unhinged, chips of plaster falling
off the facade and littering the ground, broken windowpanes replaced by sheets of cardboard and planks of wood,
the cast-iron gate half falling down.

The only difference was that the formless mass that
had once been the garden of the ex-priest (or maybe not) had
now become a sort of equatorial forest. Montalbano regretted not bringing a machete. He tore his jacket trying to
extricate himself from a tangle of branches and brambles,
cursing the saints as he reached the front door, which was
closed. He knocked. No answer. He knocked again, this
time with two powerful kicks.

'Who is it?' asked a voice that seemed to call from
beyond the grave.

'Montalbano.'

He heard a strange sound, as of iron against iron.

'Push, come inside, then close the door behind you.'

The bolt was operated by a metal wire that, when pulled
from somewhere inside the house, would raise it.

He entered the same large room as the previous time, a
vast space everywhere cluttered with books: in piles up to
the ceiling, on the floor, on the furniture, on the chairs. The
ex-priest (or maybe not) was sitting in his usual place behind
a wobbly table and had a gigantic thermometer in his
mouth.

'I'm taking my temperature,' said Alcide Maraventano.

'What kind of thermometer is that?' the bewildered
inspector couldn't refrain from asking.

'A fermentation thermometer. Afterwards I do the
maths,' said the priest (or maybe not), taking it out of his
mouth for a moment and then putting it back at once.

6

'Are you unwell?' the inspector asked.

'You mean the thermometer? No, I'm fine — I just like to run a little check every now and then.'

He'd answered again with the thermometer in his mouth, and his words came out sounding like a drunkard's.

'I'm glad to hear it, since I'd been told that—'

'That I was nearing the end? I'd said that to some idiot who took it the wrong way. All the same, I'm ninety-four years old and then some, my friend. So it's not entirely wrong to say that I'm nearing the end. Except that nowadays we say "nearing the end" to mean that we're in some sort of death throes, and it's time to call the priest for the final confession.'

What could he say to that? The reasoning was flawless. At last Maraventano took the thermometer out of his mouth, looked at it, set it down on the table, shook his head, picked up one of the three baby-bottles in front of him, and started sucking.

'I doubt that you came here to enquire about my health. What can I do for you?'

Montalbano told him everything, from the fish to the elephant, in a single breath. He even confessed his fears concerning the next move of this man who thought he was God or at least that he was in close communication with him.

Alcide Maraventano sat there listening, never once interrupting him. When Montalbano had finished, he asked him:

'Do you have any of the messages with you?'

The inspector naturally had brought them with him and handed them to the old man. Maraventano cleared away some space on his table, set them down in a row, and then looked at Montalbano and started chuckling.

'What do you find so amusing?' the inspector asked, perplexed.

And since the old man didn't reply, he tweaked him a little.

'Hard to make head or tail of it, eh?'

'Hard?' said Maraventano, taking the now empty baby bottle out of his mouth. 'Why, it's elementary, my friend! – as Sherlock Holmes might say to Dr Watson. Have you ever happened to read any of the *Sifre ha-'iyyun?*'

'I haven't yet had the chance,' said Montalbano, unruffled. 'What is it?'

'They're the so-called *Books of Contemplation*, probably written around the mid-thirteenth century.'

Montalbano threw up his hands, as if in regret. Not only had he never read them, he'd never even heard of them.

'But surely you've read a few pages of Mosè Cordovero,' conceded Maraventano.

And who on earth was he? For whatever reason, the name sounded Venetian to Montalbano.

'Was he a doge?' he guessed blindly.

'Don't be silly,' Maraventano replied severely.

Montalbano started to feel awkward and began to sweat. He was suddenly back in school, again the mediocre student he'd always been from elementary school through university. He didn't say another word, but only hung his head and started drawing circles with his forefinger in the dust on the table.

I'm done for, he thought. He's going to fail me.

'Come now,' Alcide Maraventano said to reassure him, 'you can't tell me you've never heard the name of Isaac Luria!'

Never, professor, never. And he was about to offer the classic excuse and say, 'It wasn't in my textbook,' but said instead:

'I can,' he said in a voice that came out sounding like

that of a young cockerel crowing meekly for the first time, 'but I really don't see what . . .'

Alcide Maraventano looked at him, sighed, shook his head, and started getting up from his chair. It seemed to take him for ever to stand up, so tall was the man. Finally, after uncoiling like a snake, that beanpole body that culminated in a tottering skull began to walk away.

'I'm going to get a book. I'll be right back,' he said.

The inspector heard him climb the stairs, emitting a painful 'ah' with each step. He felt almost ashamed to be making the poor old man go to all that effort, but Alcide Maraventano was the only person who might be able to tell him something about a problem that seemed to have no solution. He felt like lighting a cigarette, but was too afraid to do so: with all that paper around him, most of it dry, yellowed, and hundreds of years old, it wouldn't take much to set the whole place on fire.

A good twenty minutes went by. Try as he might to prick up his ears, he didn't hear the slightest sound upstairs. Maybe the old man had gone into a room that wasn't directly above where Montalbano was sitting.

Then all at once he heard a frightful boom, a terrible explosion that shook the whole house. A few pieces of plaster fell from the ceiling. Was it an earthquake? A bottle of gas that had burst? Having leapt so far out of his chair that he nearly hit his head on the ceiling, he noticed a sort of white curtain fall from the doorway that led to the stairs. It must have been dust, a cloud of dust formed by the plaster fragments falling from the floor above. The staircase was probably rickety and dangerous, but the inspector felt duty-bound to climb it, cautiously, to go and help the priest (or maybe not). The dense dust cloud entered his lungs, and he started coughing. His eyes began to water. Then he noticed some movement on the landing at the top of the stairs.

'Anyone there?' he asked, half-choking.

'Who else would it be? I'm here,' came the calm, unflustered voice of Alcide Maraventano.

Through the fog the priest (or maybe not) appeared, a large tome under his arm, his tunic having turned from mould-green to chalk-white from the dust cloud. Alcide Maraventano looked like the skeleton of a dead pope as he came down the stairs.

'But what happened?'

'Nothing. A bookcase fell, making another three or four stacks of books fall in turn.'

'And what's all this dust?'

'Don't you know that books gather dust?'

He sat back down in his chair, took a few sucks from a baby bottle, as his mouth had gone dry, cleared his throat, opened the large tome, and started turning the pages.

'This,' he said, 'is Vital's commentary on the thought of his teacher, Luria.'

'Thanks for clearing that up,' said Montalbano. 'But I'd like to know what we're talking about.'

Maraventano looked at him in shock.

'You still haven't caught on? We're talking about the Kabbalah and its interpretations.'

The Kabbalah! He'd heard mention of it, of course, but always as something mysterious and secret, something esoteric.

'Ah yes, here we are,' said Maraventano, finding the page he was looking for. 'Listen to this. "When the Ein Sof thought to create the worlds and produce the emanation, to bring the perfection of his actions into the light, he concentrated himself at the middle point situated at the exact centre of his light. The light became concentrated and retracted entirely around that central point . . ." Is that clear to you now?'

'No,' said Montalbano, flummoxed.

He understood the meaning of the words, of course, but couldn't grasp the connections between them.

'Then let me cite Cordovero,' said Maraventano, 'who claims that for human beings to be able to grasp his greatness, the Ein Sof, the supreme being, is forced to contract.'

'I'm starting to understand,' the inspector finally said.

'And when he's finished contracting, he shall appear to mankind in all his power and light.'

'*Madunnuzza santa!*'

He'd suddenly grasped what the madman who thought he was God was getting at.

'That imbecile hasn't understood a thing about the Kabbalah,' Maraventano concluded.

'That imbecile,' Montalbano added, 'isn't planning to kill just one man, he's preparing a massacre.'

Maraventano looked at him.

'Yes,' he said, 'I think that's a highly plausible hypothesis.'

Montalbano felt his throat go dry and was tempted to grab a baby bottle and start sucking.

'Why do you say he hasn't understood a thing about the Kabbalah?'

Maraventano smiled.

'I'll give you just one example. The point of greatest concentration of the light, the central point, is the locus of creation, not destruction, again according to Luria and Vital. That man, however, thinks it's the other way around. You must stop him. By any means necessary.'

'Can you explain to me why he always springs into action very early every Monday morning?'

'I can venture a guess. Because Monday is the dawn of the light, the day in which the Creator is believed to have started his work.'

'Listen,' Montalbano pressed him, realizing that every iota of additional information was a huge plus, 'do you know anyone in Vigàta or nearby who has had any dealings in these things? Think hard. There can't be many people around who've devoted themselves to such difficult and complex studies.'

Alcide Maraventano plunged deep into the bottomless well of his memory and in the end came up with something.

'There was one man, but a great many years ago. Sometimes he would come and discuss things with me. His name was Saverio Donzello, and he was a few years older than me. He died quite a while ago. Lived in Vigàta. I remember going to his funeral; he was buried there.'

'In the Vigàta cemetery?' Montalbano asked in surprise.

'And why not?' retorted Alcide Maraventano. 'He dealt in the Kabbalah not for religious reasons, but because he was a scholar.'

'Did he have any children?'

'He never told me anything about himself.'

After saying this, the old man sat back in his large chair, leaned his head back, and remained in that position. Montalbano waited a few minutes and then, pricking his ears up, heard an ever so faint snoring. Maraventano had fallen asleep. Or was he just pretending? Whatever the case, it could mean only one thing: that the visit was over.

The inspector got up and went out of the room on tip-toe.

✻

With an air of disdain, Mimì Augello slapped some ten pages filled with dense writing down on the desk.

'That's the list of everyone with last names beginning in D. For your information, there are four hundred and two of them in all, between men, women, lads, lasses, old bags, children, and newborns.'

'And they're all here?'

'Yes, they're all on that list.'

'Mimì, don't start acting like Catarella.'

'What's that supposed to mean?'

'I mean, are they all here in Vigàta? Physically present? Or are some of them away?'

'How should I know?'

'You have to know. When we decide to bring them all together, I want to be absolutely certain that they're all there. I want to know who's out of town on business, who's away studying or ill, that sort of thing. I also need to know who intends to go away before next Monday, and who, on the other hand, is going to be coming back before Monday. Is that clear?'

'Very clear. But how am I going to do that?'

'Work it out with Fazio, employ as many men as you need. Go from house to house and conduct a sort of census.'

'And what if people start asking questions?'

'Just give them some nonsense for an answer. You're pretty good at that, aren't you, Mimì?'

He picked up the list as soon as Mimì left. What did Maraventano say the Kabbalah scholar's name was? Ah yes, Saverio Donzello. There were three Donzellos on the list: Francesco, Tiziano, and, indeed, Saverio. He had to be a grandson. Who probably had nothing whatsoever to do with the whole affair. Since his last name began with a *D*, he was a potential victim, which meant he probably wasn't the insane fanatic. But everything had to be checked out.

✶

He slept badly that night, tossing and turning for hours in bed. Too many questions, doubts, uncertainties boring into his brain.

Should he inform the commissioner of what was happening? It was certainly his duty to do so. And if his boss didn't believe him, could he continue to act on his own? That the madman was planning a massacre he was certain. It was as if the man had told him poissonally in poisson, as Catarella would say.

And every so often the words of Alcide Maraventano

would force their way into his consciousness: *Because Monday is the dawn of the light, the day in which the Creator is believed to have started his work.* These words disturbed him, but he didn't know why.

There had to be a Bible somewhere in the house that he'd borrowed from someone but never given back. It took him a while to find it, but in the end he did. He went back to bed and started reading. 'And on the seventh day God ended his work which he had made; and he rested on the seventh day from all his work which he had made . . .' In other words, 'on the seventh day he rested'. And so? What importance could this sentence possibly have for the investigation he was conducting? He didn't know why or how, but he felt, in his bones, that it meant something, that seventh day, something important.

✻

The man walked slowly, head down as if watching where he was stepping, given the faint light cast by the streetlamps, a few of which were broken. There wasn't so much as a dog about. Everyone had gone to bed – or at least so they thought, whereas in fact they'd gone to a rehearsal of the eternal rest into which they would be cast a few days hence, thanks to his efforts. Everyone: old people who already felt death's breath on their necks, children and babies just born, men and women in their prime. The thought of the approaching day, the Day, triggered a shudder in the area of the man's groin that rose like an electric shock along his spine and went up into his brain, causing a sudden feeling of drunkenness so extreme that the shadows of the buildings started swirling around him. He closed his eyes, breathing heavily and moaning in pleasure. He had to stand still for a moment, until the drunken feeling passed and he could once again go on his way. He started singing voicelessly, in his head: '*Dies irae, dies illa* . . .'

✻

Late the following morning, Mimì Augello came in, saying thirty-five people had been taken off the list.

'If you want I can give you the details. Four have emigrated to Belgium, six to Germany, three are studying in Palermo—'

'Are you sure none of them will be back before Monday?'

'Absolutely certain.'

Then, after a pause:

'They besieged me with questions.'

'And what did you say?'

'I said that there was a brand-new law passed by the European Union requiring that a survey be made of people's displacements inside and outside the country in a random sample of cities.'

'And did they believe that?'

'Some did, some didn't.'

'And what did the ones who didn't say?'

'Nothing. They were probably just cursing under their breath.'

'Then why did they answer?'

'Because we represent the law, Salvo.'

'Which means that, in the name of the law, we have the power to make up whatever rubbish we like?'

'Has it taken you this long to work that out?'

Montalbano decided it was best not to probe the question any further.

'So now you know where they live. OK, listen to me, Mimì. I want you to do something for me, some very fine, subtle, but tedious work. I want you to take a road map of Vigàta and mark with an X every house inhabited by one of these people whose last name begins with D. Then trace the shortest possible route between them so that if need be, we can warn them all in the least amount of time.'

'OK.'

'If we're unable to stop the madman first, we'll have to talk to all these people, possibly even on Sunday evening right after dinner, and then transport them all to the Cinema Mezzano. I've already spoken to the owner; there's room for five hundred people there.'

Mimì turned pensive.

'What's wrong?' asked the inspector. 'I can see how it might get a little complicated trying to persuade people to leave their homes . . . There might also be a few old fogeys who'll be hard to move . . .'

'No, that's not the problem . . .' said Mimì.

Montalbano immediately saw red. He hated that expression. He kept hearing it uttered more and more in almost every meeting, and whoever said it intended, more or less secretly, to lead the ongoing discussion astray. He restrained himself and made no fuss because the case he had on his hands was too important.

'And what would be the problem?'

'Once we've managed to get all these people into the cinema, what then? Do you realize what we'll be dealing with? Little children screaming and crying and raising hell, old people needing to rest, men getting into scuffles . . .'

'That's not a problem. We'll just show them a nice movie. One of those that everyone can watch. And you, who have a pretty good voice, maybe you can sing them a few songs.'

He picked up the list of the people who were out of town and looked at it. The three Donzellos – Francesco, Tiziano, and Saverio – weren't on it. He handed it to Augello.

Mimì snatched it up and left the room without saying a word.

7

The following morning the inspector got to the office early, very early.

'Ah, Chief, Chief, 'ere's still nobody 'ere, asseptin' Fazio,' said Catarella as soon as he saw him.

'Tell him to come to my office.'

'Chief, the beforemintioned is sleepin' in Isspector Augello's office,' Catarella informed him.

Fazio was indeed in a deep sleep, his head resting on his folded arms on the desk.

'Fazio!'

'Huh?' said Fazio, raising his head but keeping his eyes closed.

'While you're at it, why don't you have your bed brought here from home?'

Fazio sat up, embarrassed.

'Sorry, Chief, but last night I had to take turns with Gallo, and so—'

'Why you? Couldn't you have had Galluzzo do it? Speaking of which, I haven't seen Mr Gallo for two days!'

Fazio looked at him in surprise.

'You mean nobody told you anything, Chief?'

'No. What were they supposed to have told me?'

'Gallo's mother died the day before yesterday.'

'What the hell! One of you could have had the decency to tell me! When is the funeral?'

Fazio looked at his watch.

'In three hours.'

'Quick, go to the florist's at once. I want a wreath. Tell him I'll pay whatever he wants, but I want a wreath.'

*

Three hours later, he attended the Requiem Mass and walked with the procession to the cemetery. He was about to leave after embracing Gallo when something occurred to him. He approached the sexton.

'Can you tell me where Saverio Donzello is buried?'

'In his grave, that's where,' said the sexton who, in keeping with literary tradition, was also a witty philosopher.

The inspector didn't feel like joking and gave him a dirty look, whereupon all the sexton's philosophy disappeared.

'Go down this path till you reach the end. Then immediately turn right and you'll find yourself in front of the church that's in the middle of the cemetery. Behind the church, almost attached to it, is the grave you're looking for.'

The grave wasn't a grave but a proper family chapel, and a rather imposing structure at that. Near the top of the facade was a broad frieze, a sort of scroll bearing the words *Famiglia Donzello*. It was well maintained. The inspector stuck his head between the wrought-iron bars of the gate that served as the door, but the thick grey glass between the bars prevented him from seeing inside. He addressed a short prayer in his mind to Saverio Donzello, the Kabbalist, asking him to lend him a hand, then left the cemetery.

*

He went to the Trattoria San Calogero but to the owner's great consternation wasn't able to eat a thing. His stomach was tied up in a knot, and even the smell of the fish on the plate before him bothered him.

He took a long walk along the jetty, but he was exhausted, at the end of his tether, tired and humiliated by his powerlessness, his inability to stop the plan of the man who thought he was God. He lucidly understood that he was forced to follow one step behind the mystery man's folly. He was unable to come up with any idea that might enable him, if not to get a step ahead of his adversary, at least to keep pace with him. He could only play defensively. And this was a novelty that had caught him completely unprepared.

The worst of it was that he was unable to change his feeling of frustration into anger. Anger, for him, was a powerful motivating force.

*

He'd barely sat down at his desk when the door slammed violently against the wall. Naturally, it was Catarella.

'Beg yer pardin, Chief, I los' my grip.'

'What is it?'

''Ere's summon wants a speack t'yiz poissonally in poisson. 'E says as how 'e's gotta 'ave assolute priority! 'E's says iss som'in rilly, rilly oigint!'

'Did he tell you his name?'

'Yessir. Algida.'

'Like the ice cream?'

''Ass right, Chief, jess like the ice cream.'

'Did he tell you his last name?'

'Yessir, Chief. Parapettàno.'

Alcide Maraventano! If he was calling, it must mean he had something really big and truly urgent to tell him.

'Ya wan' me to put 'im on, Chief?'

'No, I'll come to your post.'

He was afraid that Catarella, with his complicated manoeuvres at the switchboard, might lose the connection. He grabbed the receiver with hands already sweaty from the tension.

'Montalbano here. Where are you calling from, Mr Maraventano?'

'From my house.'

'You have a telephone?!'

'I wouldn't dream of it. There's a friend here who has one of those . . . whatever you call it . . .'

'Mobile phones?'

'Yes, and so I took advantage of the opportunity. I wanted to tell you that I've thought long and hard about everything you told me and I've reached a conclusion.'

Montalbano heard a strange noise at the other end, but it didn't take long for him to work out what it was. Maraventano was having a suck at his bottle. This irritated him. The old man was taking his time.

'Would you please be so kind as to tell me what your conclusion was?'

'My conclusion is this, my friend: what happens next, whatever it is, absolutely cannot occur, like the other things, during the first hours of Monday morning, because—'

'Because the cycle must necessarily end on Saturday,' Montalbano concluded.

He had managed, in a flash, to understand what had eluded his grasp when he was reading the Bible. Monday, the day that marked the beginning of Creation, couldn't also mark the end!

'Bravo!' exclaimed Alcide Maraventano. 'I can see you understand perfectly. Remember: whatever happens will happen before midnight on Saturday, because on Sunday our imbecile will have to rest. Along with many others, I fear. And bear in mind that the final contraction, in this individual's confused mind, will necessarily coincide with its becoming a blinding light that nobody can look at. Have I made myself clear?'

Perfectly clear. Feeling a sort of fever rising inside him, Montalbano didn't thank the man, didn't even say goodbye – he merely hung up and started yelling without realizing it.

'Hey, what day is it? What day is it?'

He had a gigantic calendar given to him by the Foderaro & Vadalà bakery right under his nose but couldn't see it.

'Iss the foist o' the munt'!' Catarella blurted out, infected by the panic he could hear in the inspector's voice.

And therefore the following day was 2 November, All Souls' Day: the Day of the Dead. There was no mistaking this. Montalbano and Maraventano were right. He was immediately, utterly certain of it. How did the prayer that he'd just heard at the funeral go? It was the Credo, and it ended with:

From thence he shall come to judge the living and the dead . . .

And on 2 November, the madman would have them all there at hand, the living and the dead, at the cemetery! And the last thing the living would see would be the manifestation of the ultimate light.

Like the people of Hiroshima, he thought.

All at once his wild agitation ceased, leaving a rational tension in its wake. He'd finally glimpsed a way to take the initiative, to throw his adversary off-balance. He was no longer one step behind. It was up to him to make the right move.

'Send me Augello and Fazio at once,' he said to Catarella, going back into his office.

*

'What's going on?' asked Mimì, rushing in with Fazio behind him. 'Catarella started yelling that you . . .'

He took one look at Montalbano, who was pale as a corpse, got scared, and fell silent.

'Now listen to me, you two. New orders. Whatever is going to happen will happen tomorrow, Saturday, not Monday.'

'How do you know that?' asked Augello.

'Nobody told me, I just worked it out. I'd been thinking of this possibility and somebody just confirmed it for me. Fazio, remember that as soon as we've finished here, I want you to send Gallo to inform Mezzano that his cinema must remain entirely at our disposal from nine o'clock this evening until midnight.'

The two looked at each other in confusion.

'This evening?!' asked Augello. 'But you said yourself that the whole business should be over by Saturday!'

'Mimì, this is the only chance we have of heading him off. If, for once, my hunch is correct, we'll beat him to the punch. But it would be too complicated for me to explain my reasoning to you now. The less time we waste, the better, believe me. We have very little time left. So you and the others, get a move on and inform all the families. Tell them to be there at nine on the dot. They have five hours to get ready. If anyone's unwell, they should let us know, and we'll have an ambulance come and pick them up. Mimì, I want you to stand outside the door to the cinema with the list and to check off people's names as they come in. If someone doesn't show up, tell Fazio, and he'll look into locating them. OK?'

'OK,' the other two said in unison.

'I repeat: I want to be absolutely certain that by nine-thirty this evening, every person of concern will be inside that cinema.'

'What are we going to tell them this time?' asked Fazio.

'The truth.'

'Meaning?'

'That if they don't do what we tell them, they'll be in mortal danger. They'll come running, you'll see.'

'Can I make an observation?' asked Mimì.

'Of course.'

'This business of moving things up to Saturday is because of something you worked out, is that right?'

'Yes.'

'Now let's assume for a minute that your reasoning is mistaken,' Augello continued. 'The result will be that the maniac will do what he plans to do this Monday, just like all the previous Mondays. And if that's the case, how are we going to persuade all those people to go back to the cinema on Monday?'

'We'll tell them there's a new movie for them to see,' said Montalbano. 'And there's a variety show before the film.'

✶

Carabinieri Lieutenant Romitelli listened in perfect silence to Montalbano's story and then proceeded to engage in a

systematic but no less useless re-ordering of everything on
his desk. When he'd finished, he looked up at the inspector.

'You put me in an awkward position,' he said, moving a
folder from his left to his right.

'Why do you say that?' asked Montalbano.

'Inspector, I believe the story you just told me. I really
do. And I'm ready to work together with you. But I have to
inform my superiors, and you don't want that, just as you
don't want to inform your own superiors. Am I right?'

'Yes.'

'We, however, are military officers.'

'I understand,' said Montalbano.

They sat there for a moment in silence.

'But everything would be different,' Romitelli resumed,
'if one of my patrols drove past the Cinema Mezzano and
noticed, by chance, a huge crowd outside. In that case, it
would be their duty to intervene and even, perhaps, to
request reinforcements. Understand what I'm saying?'

'Perfectly,' said Montalbano, standing up and shaking
the lieutenant's hand.

Exiting the carabinieri compound, he felt relieved. He
had also succeeded in getting the mayor to send some ten or
so municipal policemen. Alone with only his men he would
never have been able to control the hundreds of busybodies
who were sure to turn up as soon as the news began to
spread.

*

The summoned families entered the cinema between two
noisy mobs that a contingent of carabinieri and municipal
policemen had trouble holding back. For no apparent
reason, the whole affair had taken on a tone of festivity and
mutual mockery between the people going in and those
watching them.

But there were also protests and whisperings among
those summoned, especially the oldest of the lot. A young

man with long hair, earring, and beard came to a halt in front of the inspector and gave him the Fascist salute. Fazio dealt him a swift kick in the arse and he disappeared back into the crowd.

As people were going in, the cinema slowly turned into something between a nursery school and an old people's home.

At last the inspector was able to take the stage with Mimì following behind him. Aware of his woeful inability to speak in public, he was red in the face and his mouth was all puckered and dry, as if he'd just eaten a lemon.

'I am Inspector Montalbano. I apologize for the inconvenience, but I've done this all in your . . . in your . . .'

'Best interests,' Augello suggested.

'. . . best interests. There's a man who . . . a situation which . . . in short, I'm going to let my deputy explain.'

He stepped down from the stage, drenched in sweat. Mimì was quick and to the point, explaining what needed to be explained and reassuring those present that they were safe inside the cinema, as there were armed guards inside and out. He announced that a roll call would be taken, for greater security. Fazio then took the stage, list in hand, and stood beside Augello.

Giggles and a variety of twitterings and commentaries could be heard in the audience. The tension had dropped considerably. The roll call wasn't even half over when it hit a snag.

'Francesco Donzello.'

'Present.'

'Saverio Donzello.'

No reply.

'Saverio Donzello?' Fazio repeated.

Still no reply.

'I'm Tiziano Donzello,' said a man of about seventy, standing up. 'Francesco, who just answered, and Saverio are my sons.'

Meanwhile Francesco Donzello had also stood up and started looking around for his brother.

'I don't see him.'

'He was with me,' the father resumed. 'The three of us came together and were just inside the cinema when he turned to me and said he was going back outside for a second to buy cigarettes.'

A violent shudder worse than if he'd had tertian fever shook the inspector from head to toe. No, Saverio Donzello's absence was no accident. He was certain that he'd succeeded in making his adversary make his first false move.

He shot like an arrow towards the old man.

'Does your son Saverio live alone or with you?'

'He lives alone in the house that—'

'Do you by any chance have the keys?'

'Yes.'

'Give them to me, and the address as well,' he ordered him.

And while the man obeyed him without a murmur, Montalbano turned to Mimì and Fazio, who were still on the stage, and said:

'You two come with me. Gallo can finish the roll call.'

They dashed out of the cinema. There were no more gawpers or idlers about. A stone's throw away was the sign of a salt-and-tobacco shop. It had its shutter rolled halfway down. They all bent down and went inside.

'We're closed now!' yelled the owner, seeing the three men appear before him all at once.

'Police! Do you know a man named Saverio Donzello?'

'Yes. He buys cigarettes here sometimes.'

'Did you see him about an hour ago, an hour and a half?'

'No, I haven't seen him since yesterday.'

'Are there other tobacco shops nearby?'

'Yes, there's another one on the next street.'

In his haste, Mimì Augello miscalculated the height of

the shutter and crashed his head against it. He launched into a litany of curses. When they got to the other tobacco shop, the owner was locking up a display-window full of pipes beside the entrance.

'Do you know Saverio Donzello?' Fazio shouted from behind him.

The tobacconist literally leapt into the air and turned around in fear.

'What kind of fucking manners are these?'

Fazio had no time to discuss etiquette. He grabbed the man by his lapels and pushed him up against the display window.

'Police. Do you know Saverio Donzello or don't you?'

'No,' the tobacconist said, terrified.

'How many customers came in here over the last hour and a half?'

'F . . . four.'

'Do you remember what they bought?'

'Wait. A woman bought a box of matches, Ragionier Anfuso bought two sheets of stamped paper, a girl bought an envelope and a stamp, and my cousin Filippu punched out a lottery card.'

So, until proven otherwise, Saverio Donzello did not leave the cinema to go and buy cigarettes, as he'd told his father.

'We have to catch him immediately,' said Montalbano.

They started running back to the cinema, where the inspector had left his car. Fazio felt his heart racing: never had he seen his boss so worried.

8

Although the Donzellos' house was on the far outskirts of town, practically in the open countryside, they got there in the twinkling of an eye. The inspector had never before

tried to drive so fast. You could say a lot of things about
Inspector Montalbano, but not that he was someone who
knew what to do at the wheel. He missed hitting a stray dog
by a hair, while the driver of a Fiat 500 coming in the opposite direction looked death straight in the eye.

Montalbano pulled up right outside the front door of
the house. Everyone got out and had a good look at the
place from the outside. No light filtered through the shutters. The house was in total darkness. Saverio Donzello
might be hiding inside by a window, waiting for them with
a gun in hand — or then again he might not. The only way
to find out was to try. The inspector handed the keys to
Fazio, who opened the door. Montalbano went in first and
turned on the lights.

They found themselves in a large living room, nicely
furnished with nineteenth-century pieces, though a little
lugubrious in taste.

'Saverio!' Montalbano called.

No reply. Just to be sure, Augello and Fazio both drew
their guns, almost simultaneously. They had a thorough
look around the ground floor, which consisted of the very
large living room, a kitchen, a small bedroom-study, and
a lavatory. They found nothing. Not only was there not a
soul around, but the rooms, however perfectly clean, gave
the impression that they hadn't been lived in for a while.

They went carefully upstairs. Three bedrooms, three
bathrooms. They opened the wardrobes, looked under the
beds. Nobody.

Only one of the three bedrooms looked regularly inhabited, given the big mess it was in. The same for one of the
three bathrooms. That left the top floor, which consisted
of one very large room, a study with a work-table in the
middle. Thousands of books everywhere, on shelves, on
the floor, in stacks and piles. It immediately looked to the
inspector like a replica of Alcide Maraventano's study. And
it took him only one glance to realize that he was looking

at a specialized library full of esoteric books on magic, philosophy, the history of religions, and so on. The curious thing was that they didn't look like books that had been recently bought. The newest one must have been a good forty years old.

At any rate, there could no longer be any doubt: the animal-killer, the man who thought he was God, finally had a first and last name. Montalbano felt half satisfied, but the other half of him felt, if that was possible, even more scared. Yes, he had succeeded in making the madman make a bad move, but the game wasn't over yet. In fact, it hadn't even begun.

'This is our man,' said Montalbano. 'And it's a good thing he didn't stay at the cinema. He had all the Ds he could have wanted there.'

At that moment Fazio, who was rifling through the drawers of the desk, made a discovery.

'He left his pistol here. It's a 7.65.'

Montalbano's initial reply was to slap himself in the forehead.

'You stupid idiot!' he exclaimed.

Mimì and Fazio both turned and looked at him saucer-eyed.

'You talking to me?' they asked in unison.

The inspector didn't clarify that he'd actually meant himself.

'Lock this house up and come with me, quickly!'

They obeyed, not daring to ask why. Without any prior arrangement having been made, this time it was Augello who sat down behind the wheel. They'd seen too much on the ride out there, and the inspector didn't protest.

'Where are we going?'

'To the cemetery.'

As he was taking a curve practically on two wheels, Augello, upon hearing Montalbano's reply, went into a brief skid.

'Mimì, perhaps you don't realize that we're supposed to get there alive.'

'Would you please tell me what we're going there for?' asked Fazio, trying to make the question sound as respectful as possible.

'You both should know that the day I went to the funeral for Galluzzo's mother . . .'

He trailed off.

'Well?' said Mimì.

But Montalbano was following a thought in his head.

'Fazio, do you know this Saverio Donzello?'

Suffering from what Montalbano called a 'records office complex', Fazio knew the life story of many of the inhabitants of Vigàta.

'He's forty-two years old. He taught at the high school in Montelusa and lived an orderly life until three years ago, when his whole world changed.'

'Why, what happened?'

'He lost his wife and daughter in a car crash. The little girl was in the first year. He wasn't there – his wife was driving. Since then he's been living alone in the house his grandfather left him. The one we just visited, I think. He left his job and doesn't feel like doing much of anything any more. He hardly ever goes outside.'

The entrance gate of the cemetery was locked. They knocked at the door of the sexton's house, which was right beside it.

'Open up! Police!'

The sexton appeared, cursing. He was the same one Montalbano had already met.

'Unlock the gate.'

'Welcome,' said the man, opening the gate and standing aside.

'You come with us,' said Montalbano, who didn't want any guff. 'Listen,' he continued, 'has Saverio Donzello been around here lately?'

'He certainly has. Ever since his wife and daughter died, he comes practically every day. He's the first to come in and the last to leave. Poor bastard. He's no longer all there in the head.'

'And what does he do when he comes?'

'He holes himself up in the family vault and prays. At least that's what he's told me and my assistants. He's always carrying a small sort of suitcase. He says he's got prayer books inside.'

'But you don't really know what he's doing when he's inside the vault.'

'No, Inspector, it's got tinted windows. But what do you think the poor man's going to be doing in there? He's praying, I tell you. One time he talked to me about it. He said that he'd found a way to bring his wife and daughter back to life. He's nuts. We can't do nothing about it. That's some bad stuff that happened to him.'

They reached the Donzello family vault.

'Have you got the key?'

'No, sir, but it don't take much to open the door. If you'll allow me and step aside for just a second . . .'

Despite the darkness in the cemetery, Montalbano and Fazio looked at each other in amazement. The sexton was showing himself to be a very able lock-picker. But at that moment they had other things on their mind.

With the light turned on, the inside of the vault proved to be clean as a whistle and in perfect order. There were fresh flowers in front of the niches of Saverio Donzello's wife and daughter. Maybe the poor man really did come only to pray. But then the inspector noticed a sort of dark rectangle on the floor beside the altar. He went up to it. It was an open trapdoor; the thick slab that served to shut it was leaning against the wall. He bent down to look inside, but it was too dark.

'Where does this lead?'

'To the mortuary chamber,' replied the sexton, 'where

you put old coffins or fresh corpses waiting for a place to be buried. But I'm a little surprised to see that.'

'Why?'

'I didn't expect it from him. You need authorization to open the chamber. And Mr Donzello never asked us for it. And you're not supposed to leave it open.'

'Is there a light down there?'

Without answering, the sexton flipped a light switch near the entrance.

'Mr Donzello had it put in a couple of years ago.'

They went down in single file, the inspector leading the way. The chamber was as large as the vault above. The walls were unplastered. Three old coffins were arranged in the middle of the space. They'd been moved to free up the walls. And all four walls, up to a height of about six feet, were literally covered with sticks of dynamite. The sticks' fuses were bound together and linked up with a fatter, longer fuse that needed only to be lit to blow the whole place up.

'Shit!' said Augello, almost under his breath.

'So that's what he was carrying in his suitcase! Prayer book, right!' said the sexton, wiping his brow with his hand.

'We got here just in time. He was going to light the fuse tomorrow, on All Souls' Day, when the cemetery was packed. Let's go.'

They climbed back up in silence, each lost in thought. Once outside the vault, Montalbano said to Fazio:

'Get me Gallo on the mobile phone.

'Hello? Montalbano here. How are things over there?'

'All relatively calm, Chief.'

'Listen, I want you to send someone here to the cemetery – Imbrò or whoever you want. The sexton will show him which tomb he needs to guard, and I don't want him to move even one step from his post.'

'I'll send him right away, Chief. But I wanted to tell you something: that guy, Saverio Donzello, came back and is sitting in the stalls. He excused himself, saying that he had to take care of something really urgent before being shut up inside the cinema.'

Montalbano felt his blood run cold.

*

As soon as Gallo saw them getting out of the car, which had pulled in as fast as a bullet, he went up to them.

'Where is he? Where is he?' asked Montalbano, panting heavily as if he, and not the car, had been racing.

Gallo looked at him confusedly, being in the dark about everything.

'He sat down in the last row. He's alone. All the other seats in that row are empty. But what's going on?'

'Just listen to me and think before answering. Did he seem, I don't know, agitated or strange?'

'Well, yeah, a little. But they're all a bit agitated in there.'

'Was he carrying anything?'

'Yeah, one of those big carrier bags like women use when they go shopping.'

'Good God!' Mimì blurted out.

'But what's going on?' Gallo asked again, getting more and more worried seeing how worried everyone else was.

'You stay here in the lobby,' said the inspector. 'I'm going inside to have a look.'

He was ready for anything, except for Mr Mezzano to have had the brilliant idea of projecting cartoons, which now had the audience laughing and commenting. A few old people were sleeping.

Montalbano saw Saverio Donzello at once: he was alone with his head down, engrossed in the insane thoughts swirling around in his brain. The inspector approached him slowly. Donzello didn't even notice, and didn't move. Montalbano's eyes searched carefully on the floor beside him, but didn't find what he was looking for. And so he bent down as if to tie his shoe. This time he was sure: the large bag wasn't there.

He left the auditorium.

'He hid the bag somewhere before sitting down. We have to find it.'

They searched all over the lobby, between the curtains, behind the flower vases, inside the box office. Nothing. The inspector looked at his watch: one minute past midnight.

It was already the Day of the Dead. He had no more time to waste. He had to take immediate action. Saverio Donzello might have a remote-control device in his pocket that could at any moment set off the explosives in the handbag, wherever he happened to have hidden it.

'We have to arrest him,' he said. 'But we need to go about this carefully. You, Fazio, go into the auditorium to the aisle behind him and make sure he isn't holding anything in his hand. If he is, hit him on the head and put him out of commission. If he doesn't have anything in his hand, grab him and make sure he's unable to put his hands in his pockets. Got that?'

'Got it,' said Fazio.

'Mimì will go in after you and give you a hand. Then I'll come in right behind him. It's important that we arrest him with as little commotion as possible. If anyone notices and starts yelling, it could create a panic – the worst thing that could possibly happen. Now, let's go!'

Fazio went in, and five seconds later, Augello came in behind him. When the inspector finally entered the auditorium, he stopped dead in his tracks. Saverio Donzello was gone, and Fazio and Augello were just standing there looking at him, speechless.

Obeying a gesture from Montalbano, Fazio started going quickly up and down the central aisle, looking to his right and left.

'He's not there,' he said, coming back to the inspector's side.

Montalbano had a plan and knew that he had at most a few minutes left.

'You,' he said breathlessly to Mimì, 'get them to stop the projection, thank everyone for having cooperated, and send everyone home as quickly as you can. Tell them the danger has passed. And ask them to be orderly and not make any trouble. I want the cinema emptied in five minutes.'

Mimì dashed off.

'You come with me,' the inspector said to Fazio.

He headed decisively towards a door covered by a thick curtain over which, in neon lettering, was the word TOILETS. They went into the first one, the ladies'. The doors to the four stalls were open. There was nobody there. In the gents', the door to one stall was locked from the inside.

Montalbano and Fazio exchanged a glance and understood each other: Saverio Donzello had to be behind that door. In the silence they could distinctly hear his laboured breathing, which sounded like a rattle.

The inspector tasted blood in his mouth. He must have bitten his tongue. His teeth were clenched so tightly that his jaws hurt.

Montalbano explained his plan through gestures. He would count to three on his fingers, whereupon Fazio was to thrust his shoulder into the door and break it open. Fazio nodded to show that he'd understood, and handed the inspector his pistol. Montalbano refused it and started counting.

Fazio slammed his shoulder into the door so hard that it flew off its hinges. Montalbano was quick to pull it outside the stall. The sight that greeted them was worse than a nightmare.

In his hand Saverio Donzello was holding a blowtorch. At his feet lay some thirty sticks of dynamite. The bag was in the corner, empty. Donzello didn't move. His wild eyes probably didn't even see the two men standing in front of him.

Then Fazio, to his utter confusion, saw his superior bow deeply, his hand over his heart.

'Your greatness, I beg you to forgive my boldness and listen to me. Please deign to cast your gaze upon me!'

Montalbano took two slow steps forward, head bowed, and bent down on one knee.

'Your greatness, let your humble servant carry out your task! Grant me the grace of lighting the flame!'

Fazio likewise fell to his knees, arms spread in a gesture of devout entreaty.

Donzello gazed at them. Then, moving as though in slow motion, as a happy smile broke out on his face, he extended his arm and handed Montalbano the blowtorch.

Fazio sprang forward and grabbed the man by the arm. Saverio Donzello's face twisted up into a frown.

'You tricked me! You tricked me!'

He didn't try to struggle free. Big tears started streaming down his face.

'I could have brought them back, don't you see? I could have had them back again with me! With me! In my light! For all eternity!'

Montalbano understood. The meaning of those desperate words shook him to the core. He threw the blowtorch into a basin, left the bathroom, and went back into the auditorium, which was now empty.

He sat down and just stayed there, staring at the blank screen. He felt as if he was suffocating under a dense, heavy blanket of disconsolate melancholy.

✻

A short while later, Fazio came and sat down in the seat next to his.

'Inspector Augello's taking him to a clinic in Montelusa. I've already spoken to the father and the brother.'

'What did they say?'

'They can hardly believe what's happened. They didn't know Saverio went out at night. All they knew was that he would spend all day reading his grandfather's books. What kind of books were they, do you know?'

'They were the books of a Kabbalist.'

'You mean someone who divines the Lotto numbers?' Fazio asked in amazement.

'No, it's something else. He just kept reading that stuff and finally lost his mind, especially since his mind had already taken a hard hit with the death of his wife and child. And one day he ended up believing that if he could become God, he could bring his loved ones back.'

'OK, but what was that stuff about contracting?'

'Well, you see, God is so great that, in order to imagine Him, we have to make him smaller, and so—'

'No, wait, Chief, stop right there. I'm getting a headache. Do you have any orders for me?'

'Yes. The Donzello family tomb has to be cleaned out, tonight. I don't feel safe leaving all that dynamite there with all the people who are going to be at the cemetery tomorrow. In the morning you can buy two bouquets of flowers and put them—'

'Got it. It'll be done.'

✳

Back home in Marinella, the inspector didn't feel like washing then changing clothes. He'd made his decision. There was a flight leaving at 7 a.m. that always had vacancies. He needed Livia and would be at her place in Boccadasse by ten o'clock at the latest.

At the moment, however, he wasn't hungry and didn't feel sleepy. He went outside and sat down on the veranda. It was a warm night, and there wasn't a cloud in the sky. He started staring at a point in the sky that he knew well.

At that very point, a few hours later, the light of day would dawn and make its way through the darkness.

JUDICIAL REVIEW

The first time Montalbano saw the man walking along the beach was early one morning, but it really wasn't a day to be walking along the beach. On the contrary, the best thing you could do was go back to bed, pull the covers up over your head, close your eyes, and best wishes to one and all. Indeed a nasty, ice-cold north wind was blowing, and the sand got in your eyes and mouth; the breakers started high at the horizon line, lay flat and hid behind those in front of them, reappeared high above the shoreline, and then hurled themselves as though famished against the beach, eating it up. Little by little, the sea had managed to come almost all the way up to the inspector's wooden veranda. The man was dressed all in black. With one hand he held his hat firmly planted on his head to prevent the wind from carrying it away, while the heavy overcoat clinging to his body worked its way between his legs. He wasn't going anywhere in particular – you could tell by the way he walked, which, despite all the pandemonium, remained steady and regular. After going some fifty yards past the inspector's house, the man turned and headed back towards Vigàta.

He saw him other times as well, early in the morning, sometimes hatless, after the season had changed, but always dressed in black, and always alone. One time when the weather had improved enough to allow Montalbano a nice long swim in the cold water not yet warmed by the sun, as he turned round to swim back to shore he'd seen the man standing still at the water's edge, watching him. Continuing to swim in that direction, Montalbano was inevitably going to come out of the water right in front of him. And this made him uncomfortable, so he directed his strokes so that they would take him out of the water some ten yards down the shore from the man, who was still staring fixedly at him. When the man realized that the face-to-face encounter wasn't going to happen, he turned his back and resumed his customary stroll. And for a few months things went on in this fashion. One morning the man didn't come by, and Montalbano got worried. Then he had an idea. He stepped down from the veranda and onto the beach and saw, distinctly, the man's footprints in the wet sand. Apparently he'd taken his walk a little earlier than usual, when the inspector was still in bed or in the shower.

One night there was a lot of wind, but towards daybreak the wind dropped as if tired from being up all night. A clear day was in the offing, warm and sunny, if not yet summery. The wind in the night had cleaned up the beach, evened out the little holes, and the sand was all perfectly smooth and shiny. The man's footprints stood out as though sketched, but their path perplexed the inspector. After walking along the water's edge, the man had headed straight for Montalbano's house, then turned back towards the water. What had he had in mind to do? The inspector stood there a long time studying that sort of *V* traced by the footprints, as if through careful observation he might be able to enter the man's head and the thoughts that had driven him to make that sudden detour.

When he got to the office, he called Fazio.

'Do you know of a man who dresses in black and comes and walks along the beach every morning in front of my house?'

'Why, does he bother you?'

'No, Fazio, he hasn't bothered me at all. And even if he

had, don't you think I could handle it myself? I only asked if you knew of him.'

'No, Chief. I didn't even know there was a man dressed in black coming and walking along the beach. Do you want me to look into it?'

'No, never mind.'

The matter, however, kept popping back into his head every so often. By the time he went home that evening, he'd come to the conclusion that the *V* he'd seen in the sand was in reality a question mark. A question that the man dressed in black had determined to ask him but at the last minute lacked the courage to ask. For this reason, the inspector set his alarm clock for five the next morning. He wanted to avoid the risk of not seeing the man if for whatever reason he decided to come earlier than usual.

When the alarm rang, he bolted out of bed, made coffee, and sat down on the veranda. He waited till nine, time enough to read a detective novel by Lucarelli and drink six cups of coffee.

Of the man, however, not a trace.

'Fazio!'

'At your service, Chief.'

'Do you remember yesterday I mentioned a man dressed all in black who every morning—'

'Of course I remember.'

'He didn't pass by this morning.'

Fazio gave him a bewildered look.

'Is that a serious problem?'

'Serious, no. But I want to know who he is.'

'I'll try,' said Fazio, sighing.

Sometimes the inspector was downright bizarre. Why was he obsessed with this nab who liked to walk along the beach in peace? Why did this bother the good inspector?

*

That afternoon, Fazio knocked on the inspector's door, asked permission to come in, sat down, extracted from his pocket a couple of pieces of paper covered with dense writing, and cleared his throat with a gentle coughing sound.

'Are you going to give a lecture?' asked Montalbano.

'No, Chief. I'm going to give you the information you asked for concerning the person who walks past your house every morning.'

'Before you start reading I'd like to warn you that if you give vent to your records office complex and recite me all this man's personal details, which I couldn't care less about, I'm going to get up out of this chair and get myself a cup of coffee.'

'Tell you what,' said Fazio, folding up the pieces of paper and putting them back in his jacket pocket. 'I'll come with you for this coffee.'

They both left the room in silence, irritated. They went to the bar at the corner, and each paid for his own coffee. They returned to the office, still without speaking, and assumed the same places as before, except that this time Fazio didn't take the pieces of paper out. Montalbano realized that it was up to him to start talking. Otherwise Fazio was liable to remain silent and resentful for the rest of the day.

'What's the man's name?'

'Leonardo Attard.'

Therefore – like those named Cassar, Hamel, Camilleri, and Buhagiar – he was of distant Maltese origin.

'What does he do in life?'

'He used to be a judge. He's retired now. He was an important judge, a chief of the assizes.'

'And what's he doing here?'

'Dunno. Actually he was born in Vigàta and stayed here till he was eight. Then his father, who was chief harbour master, got transferred. So he grew up in the north, where he also studied and made his career. When he came here eight months ago, he didn't know anyone.'

'Did he own a house in Vigàta? Maybe an old family property?'

'No, sir. But he bought one. A nice big house with five large bedrooms, though he lives there alone. He's got a housekeeper to help him out.'

'He never married?'

'He did. And he has a son. But his wife died three years ago.'

'Has he made any friends in town?'

'You must be kidding! He doesn't know anyone. He only goes out early in the morning, takes his walk, and then vanishes from circulation. His housekeeper gets him everything he needs, from food to the daily paper. Her name is Prudenza . . . I can't remember her last name. Can I look at my notes?'

'No.'

'All right. Anyway, I talked to this housekeeper, and I can tell you straight away that the judge has left town.'

'Do you know where he went?'

'Of course. To Bolzano. That's where his son lives. Married and the father of two boys. The judge spends summers with his son.'

'And when will he be back?'

'In early September.'

'Know anything else?'

'Yeah. After he'd been living for three days in this house in Vigàta—'

'Where is it?'

'The house? Right where Vigàta ends and Marinella begins. About five hundred yards from where you live.'

'OK, go on.'

'So, as I was saying, after he'd been there for three days, an HGV turned up.'

'With the furniture.'

'No chance! You know how many pieces of furniture he has? Bed, bedside table and wardrobe in the bedroom; a refrigerator in the kitchen, where he also eats. He has no TV. And that's all.'

'So what was the HGV for?'

'To bring him his papers.'

'What papers?'

'From what the housekeeper told me, they are copies of all the documentation of every trial the judge presided over.'

'Good God! Don't you know that for every trial there are at least ten thousand pages of documents?'

'Exactly. The housekeeper told me there's not an inch of space in that house that isn't stacked up to the ceiling with files, papers, and binders. She says her primary responsibility is to dust all these papers, since they get dusty really fast.'

'And what does he do with the documents?'

'He studies them. I forgot to tell you that the furniture also includes a big table and an armchair.'

'He studies them?'

'Yes, Chief. Day and night.'

'Why does he do that?'

'You're asking me? You should ask *him*, when he comes back in September!'

✻

Judge Leonardo Attard reappeared one morning in early September, a morning that was shaping up to be languid — or perhaps, more than languid, downright exhausted.

The inspector saw him walk by, still dressed in black and looking like a crow. And he sort of had the same elegance and dignity that crows have. For a moment Montalbano felt like running up to him and welcoming him back in some way. Then he restrained himself, but felt happy to see him walking again along the wet sand, self-assured and harmonious.

Then, one morning in late September, as the inspector

was reading the newspaper out on the veranda, a sudden gust of wind blew in from the sea, with two immediate effects: rumpling the pages of Montalbano's newspaper and simultaneously blowing the judge's hat off in the direction of the veranda. As Mr Attard started running after his hat, the inspector hopped down, grabbed it, and handed it to the judge. In the end nature herself had intervened to bring the two together. Because it was natural, and inevitable, that sooner or later the two should meet.

'Thank you. Attard's the name,' said the judge, introducing himself.

'I'm Montalbano,' said the inspector.

They didn't smile, didn't shake hands. They just stood there for a moment, eyeing one another in silence. Then, each in turn, they exchanged a funny little bow, like the Japanese. The inspector returned to his veranda, and the judge resumed walking.

✻

Montalbano was once asked what, in his opinion, was the most essential talent for a policeman to have? Was it intuition? Perseverance in the search? The ability to find the connection between apparently unrelated facts? Knowing that if two plus two always equals four in the normal order of things, in the abnormality of crime two plus two can also equal five?

'A clinical eye,' was Montalbano's answer.

And everyone present had a good laugh over this. But the inspector hadn't meant to make a witty quip. The problem was that he hadn't explained his answer; he'd preferred to gloss over it, since there were two doctors amongst the company present. What he'd meant by 'clinical eye' was precisely that ability that doctors used to have to realize, at a glance, in fact, whether or not a patient was ill. Without needing – as so many doctors do nowadays – to subject the patient to a hundred different tests before realizing that he or she is fit as a fiddle.

Well, in the brief exchange of glances that Montalbano had with the judge, he became immediately convinced that the man was ill. Not physically ill, however. He had something eating at him inside, which made his pupils too still, too fixed, as though he was lost in some recurrent thought. Thinking this over carefully, however, he had to admit it was only an impression. But he'd had another impression as well, this one much more precise, which was that the judge had in his way been rather pleased to meet the inspector. He must certainly have already known, ever since he'd first stopped in front of his house months before, unable to make up his mind whether to knock or resume his walk, what line of work Montalbano was in.

✻

A week after their meeting, as Montalbano was drinking his morning coffee on the veranda, Leonardo Attard, when he came within earshot, looked up from the sand he'd been staring at as he walked, glanced at the inspector, and raised his hat in greeting.

Montalbano quickly stood up, cupped his hands around his mouth and shouted:

'Would you like a cup of coffee?'

The judge deviated from his customary route without altering his calm, measured step and came towards the veranda. Montalbano went into the house, and came back out with a clean demitasse. They shook hands, and the inspector poured the coffee. They sat down on the bench beside one another. Montalbano said nothing.

'It's very beautiful here,' the judge said suddenly.

They were the only words he pronounced. Having finished his coffee, he tipped his hat, muttered a few words that the inspector took to be 'Good day' and 'thank you', stepped down onto the beach, and resumed his morning walk.

Montalbano gathered that he'd won a point in his favour.

✲

The invitation to drink a cup of coffee, with the accompanying ritual of silence, was repeated twice more. On the third visit, however, the judge looked at the inspector and began slowly to speak.

'I would like to ask you a question, Inspector.'

He was laying his cards out on the table. Attard had never once asked him directly what he did for a living.

'Ask me anything you like, your honour.'

Montalbano too was laying his cards on the table.

'But I wouldn't want you to take this the wrong way.'

'That's unlikely.'

'Tell me, in your work, have you always been certain, mathematically certain, that the people you've arrested were truly guilty?'

The inspector was ready for anything except a question like that. He opened his mouth and immediately closed it again. It wasn't the sort of question you could answer off the cuff, without prior reflection. Especially with the firm gaze of the judge's eyes fixed on you. And he seemed very much the judge at that moment. Attard sensed Montalbano's uneasiness.

'You needn't answer me right now, on the spot. Think it over a little. Have a good day, and thank you.'

He stood up, raised his hat, stepped back down onto the beach, and resumed his walk.

Thank you, my arse, thought Montalbano, standing stiff as a pole. The judge had just bowled him a googly.

✲

That same afternoon, the judge phoned the inspector.

'Forgive me for bothering you at work. But the question I asked you this morning was, at the very least, inappropriate, and I apologize for that. Listen, if you've got nothing else planned for this evening, could you come by my place after work? It's on your way home, after all. Let me explain to you where I live.'

The first thing the inspector noticed upon setting foot in the judge's house was the smell. Not unpleasant, but penetrating – a smell similar to that of hay that has lain a long time in the sun. Then he realized it was paper he was smelling, old, yellowed paper. Hundreds upon hundreds of files stacked from floor to ceiling on solid wooden bookshelves in every room: bedrooms, kitchen, entrance hall. That wasn't a house, but an archive where a little space, just enough, had been made for a man to live in.

Montalbano was shown into a room with a large table in the middle covered with paper, as well as an armchair and a chair.

'My answer would have to be yes,' Montalbano began.

'Yes to what?'

'To the question you asked me this morning. I can say that I am mathematically certain – within the limits of my knowledge – that the people I have arrested were indeed guilty. Even though on a few occasions the courts didn't agree and acquitted them.'

'That's happened to you?'

'On a few occasions, yes.'

'Did it upset you?'

'Not at all.'

'Why not?'

'Because I'm too experienced to get upset. By now I know well that the truth of the courts runs on a track parallel to the real truth. But the two tracks don't always lead to the same station. Sometimes they do, sometimes they don't.'

Half of the judge's face smiled. The lower half. The upper half remained serious, and his eyes grew more immobile, colder.

'Your argument misses the point,' said Judge Attard. 'My question was another.'

With a broad gesture, opening his arms wide until he looked crucified, he indicated all the papers lying around.

'My question concerns a review.'

'What kind of review?'

'A review of the trials over which I presided during my life.'

Montalbano felt a little sweat start to form on his skin.

'I had the court documents of all my cases photocopied and sent here to Vigàta, because here I've found the ideal conditions for my work. I spent a fortune on it, believe me.'

'But who asked you to conduct this review?'

'My conscience.'

Montalbano finally reacted.

'No, you can't say that. If you are certain that you have always acted according to the dictates of your conscience . . .'

The judge raised a hand, interrupting him.

'That's the real question. The crux.'

'Are you afraid you made some judgements for the sake of convenience or due to outside pressure, things like that?'

'Never.'

'Then what is it?'

'You see, there are some lines of Montaigne that lay out the question somewhat crudely: "From the same sheet of paper on which he wrote out his sentence condemning an adulterer," writes Montaigne, "the same judge tears off a little piece to write a love-note to the wife of a colleague of his." It's a crude example, I repeat, but it contains a great deal of truth. Let me put it another way. What sort of state was I in — as a man, that is — at the moment in which I pronounced a harsh sentence?'

'I don't understand, your honour.'

'It's not so hard to understand, Inspector. Have I always been able to keep my private life separate from my application of the law? Have I always been able to prevent my bad moods, my idiosyncrasies, my personal concerns, sorrows, and lack of happiness from staining the white page on which I was about to formulate a sentence? Was I successful in this or not?'

The sweat had Montalbano's shirt sticking to his skin.

'I beg your pardon, your honour, but you aren't reviewing the trials you conducted – it's your whole life you're reviewing.'

He realized at once that he'd made a mistake. He shouldn't have said what he said. But for a moment he'd felt like the doctor who's just discovered that his patient is gravely ill: should I tell him or shouldn't I? Montalbano had instinctively chosen the first option.

The judge stood up brusquely.

'Thank you so much for coming. Good night.'

*

The judge did not pass by the following morning. Nor was he anywhere to be seen in the days and weeks that followed. But Montalbano did not forget about the judge. More than a month after that evening encounter, he summoned Fazio.

'Remember that retired judge, Leonardo Attard?'

'Of course.'

'I'd like some news of him. You met his housekeeper, didn't you? What was her name, do you remember?'

'Her name was Prudenza. How could I forget a name like that?'

That afternoon Fazio came in to report.

'The judge is doing fine; he just doesn't go out any more. Prudenza told me that since the floor above his became available, he bought it. So now he owns the whole house.'

'Did he take all his papers up there?'

'Not a chance! Prudenza told me he wants to leave the upstairs vacant, doesn't even intend to rent it out. She says he wants to be left alone in that house and doesn't want any bother. And actually Prudenza told me another thing that she thought was strange. The judge didn't exactly say he didn't want to be bothered; he said he didn't want any regrets. What do you think he meant?'

✶

Montalbano took all night to realize that the judge had not misspoken when he said 'regrets' instead of 'bother'. And when he came to this realization, he broke into a cold sweat. As soon as he got to the office, he attacked Fazio.

'I want the phone number of Judge Attard's son at once, the one who lives in Bolzano!'

Half an hour later he was able to talk to Dr Giulio Attard, a paediatrician.

'This is Inspector Montalbano, police. Listen, Doctor, I'm sorry to have to tell you, but your father's mental state has—'

'Has worsened? I was afraid of that.'

'You must come at once to Vigàta. Come and see me at the station, so we can work out a way . . .'

'Listen, Inspector, I thank you for your kindness, but at the moment I really can't come.'

'Your father is getting ready to kill himself, you know.'

'Let's not get melodramatic.'

Montalbano hung up.

That same evening, as he was driving past the judge's house, he stopped, got out of the car, and went and rang the doorbell.

'Who is it?'

'It's Montalbano, your honour. I just came by to say hello.'

'I wish I could invite you in, but it's too messy. Please come back tomorrow, if you can.'

The inspector was walking away when he heard his name called.

'Montalbano! Inspector! Are you still there?'

He ran back.

'Yes, what is it?'

'I think I found it.'

And that was all. The inspector rang again, repeatedly, but there was no answer.

✳

He was woken up by the persistent sirens of fire engines heading in the direction of Vigàta. He glanced at the clock: 4 a.m. He had a premonition. He went out on the veranda just as he was, in his underpants, and walked down to the water's edge, where he had the broadest point of view. The water was so cold it made his feet ache. But he barely felt it. He was looking, in the distance, at Judge Leonardo Attard's house blazing like a torch. Little surprise, with all the paper there was inside! It would take the firemen a very long time to find the judge's charred body. Of this he was certain.

✳

Two days later, a very large parcel with a long piece of string wrapped around it numerous times, and a large envelope, were placed on Montalbano's desk by Fazio.

'Prudenza brought them here this morning. The judge gave them to her the day before the house burned down, asking her to give them to you.'

The inspector opened the large envelope. Inside was a sheet of paper with writing on it and another, smaller envelope, which was sealed.

It took me a while, but in the end I found what I had always assumed and feared. I'm sending you all the documents relating to a trial of fifteen years ago, owing to which the court over which I presided sentenced to thirty years a man who to the very end proclaimed his innocence. I didn't believe his claims of innocence. Now, after careful review, I realize that I didn't want to believe his claims of innocence. Why not? If, in reading

these documents, you arrive at the same conclusion I did —
which was that I was acting more or less consciously in bad
faith — then, and only then, open the envelope included herewith.
Inside you'll find the story of a very troubled moment of my
private life. This story will explain, perhaps, my actions of
fifteen years ago. Explain, not justify them. I should add that
the man convicted died after twelve years in prison. Thank you.

The moon was out. With a spade he borrowed from Fazio, he dug a hole in the sand ten paces away from the veranda. And in it he put the parcel and the two letters. Then he went and took a jerry can of petrol from the boot of his car, went back to the beach, poured about a quarter of the liquid onto the paper, and set it on fire. When the flames went out, he stirred the paper with a stick, poured another quarter can onto it, and lit it again. He repeated this procedure two more times, until he was certain that the whole thing had been reduced to ashes. Then he started filling the hole. By the time he finished, dawn was peering over the horizon.

PESSOA MAINTAINS

Montalbano got up at six that morning, a fact that in itself would have made no difference to him had it not been such a dismal day. A sparse rain was falling, pretending it wasn't there, the very kind of rain farmers used to call 'peasant-drenching'. Once upon a time, when people still worked the land, a peasant wouldn't stop in the face of this sort of rain; he would keep toiling with his hoe, since the rain was so light it seemed hardly to be there at all, and when he returned home in the evening his clothes would be completely sodden. And this only worsened the inspector's already bad mood, since he had to be in Palermo, a two-hour drive away, by nine thirty that morning, for a meeting whose subject was the impossible – that is, finding ways and methods to distinguish, out of the thousands of illegal immigrants that landed on the island every year, those who were poor innocents down on their luck and those who were pure criminals who had finagled their way into the hordes of the desperate. Some genius of a minister claimed to have found a nearly infallible way to do this, and the honourable minister had decided that all law-enforcement personnel in Sicily should be duly apprised of it. Montalbano thought this ministerial genius should get the Nobel Prize, since, after all, he'd succeeded in creating nothing less than a method for distinguishing Good from Evil.

When he got in his car to go back to Vigàta, it was already five in the afternoon. He felt upset. The ministerial genius's revelation had been received with poorly concealed smirks and was practically unfeasible. A day wasted. As expected.

What he hadn't expected was the total absence of his men at the station upon his return. Even Catarella wasn't there. Where had they all gone? He heard some footsteps in the corridor. It was Catarella returning, out of breath.

'Ascuze me, Chief. I went to the phammacy t'get s'm assprin. I'm comin' down witta frou.'

'But where's everybody else?'

'Isspecter Augello's got the frou, Galluzzo's got the frou, an' Fazio an' Gallo's got—'

'The frou.'

'No, Chief. They're fine.'

'So where are they?'

'They wen' to the moider scene where summon was moidered.'

There you go: you can't go away for even half a day without people taking advantage and killing someone.

'Do you know where?'

'Yessir. Inna Ulivuzza district.'

And how did one get there? If he asked Catarella, he was liable to send him beyond the Arctic Circle. Then he remembered that Fazio had a mobile phone.

'But why bother to come, Chief?' said Fazio. 'The assistant prosecutor has already ordered the body removed, Dr Pasquano's already had a look at it, and Forensics are just finishing.'

'Well, I'm coming anyway. You and Gallo wait for me. Now tell me how to get there.'

He could just as easily have taken Fazio's advice and stayed put at the office. But he felt the need to make up in some way for a day wasted driving more than four hours and listening to a deluge of meaningless words.

✻

Ulivuzza district was near the administrative boundary with Montelusa. Another hundred yards and the matter would not have fallen under the jurisdiction of the Vigàta police. The house where they'd found the murder victim was completely isolated. Made of drystone, it consisted of three rooms in a row on the ground floor. There was a door that served as an entrance, with an opening in the wall beside it that gave onto a stall in which a solitary, melancholy donkey lived. When the inspector arrived, there was only one car there, Gallo's, parked outside the open area in front of the house. Apparently the bedlam of doctors, nurses, forensics experts, the assistant prosecutor and his retinue was over. So much the better.

Montalbano got out of his car and stepped straight into a foot and a half of mud. The peasant-drenching rain was no longer falling, but its effects still lingered. The threshold to the house was in fact buried under a good two or three inches of mud, and there was mud all over the room he entered. Fazio and Gallo were standing drinking a glass of wine in front of the fireplace. There was also an oven, closed by a piece of tin bent into a semicircular covering. The body had been taken away. On the table in the middle of the room lay a plate with the remains of two boiled potatoes transformed into purplish beetroots by the blood that had filled the plate and spilled over onto the wooden table.

On the table, which had no tablecloth, there was also a whole round of tomazzo cheese, half a loaf of bread, and half a glass of red wine. The flask was gone, taken by Fazio and Gallo to fill their own glasses. On the floor beside the wicker chair lay a fork.

Fazio had followed the inspector's gaze.

'It happened while he was eating,' he said. 'They executed him with a single shot to the base of the skull.'

It made Montalbano angry whenever television reporters used the word 'execute' to mean 'murder'. And he also got upset with his men when they did the same. But this time he let it slide. If Fazio had let it slip out, it was because he'd been shaken by that single shot to the base of the skull, coldly fired point-blank.

'What's over there?' the inspector asked, indicating the other room with an inclination of his head.

'Nothing. A double bed with no sheets, just the two mattresses, two bedside tables, a wardrobe, and two chairs like this one here.'

'I knew him,' said Gallo, wiping his mouth with his hand.

'The murder victim?'

'No, his father. His name was Antonio Firetto. The son's name was Giacomo, but I never met him.'

'What ever became of the father?'

'That's just it,' said Fazio. 'We can't find him. We looked all around the house and the general area for him, but he's nowhere to be found. If you ask me, he was grabbed and taken away by the people who killed his son.'

'What do you know about the man who was killed?'

'Chief, Giacomo Firetto is the man who was killed!'

'So?'

'Chief, the guy'd been on the run for five years. He was a Mafia foot soldier: small-time butchery jobs, mostly, or so they say. You're the only one who's never heard of him.'

'Did he belong to the Cuffaros or the Sinagras?'

The Cuffaros and Sinagras were the two Mafia families that had been fighting for years over control of the province of Montelusa.

'Giacomo Firetto was forty-five years old, Chief. When he still lived around here, he belonged to the Sinagras. He was just a kid at the time, but with a great future. To the point that the Riolo family from Palermo borrowed him for a while. For a long while, in fact, since he stayed with them till he was killed.'

'And so whenever he was in the area, his dad would put him up.'

Fazio and Gallo exchanged a lightning-quick glance.

'Chief, his father was a good and honest man,' Gallo said decisively.

'Why do you say he *was* . . . ?'

'Because in our opinion, by now they've already killed him too.'

'Well then, give me some sense of what you two think happened here.'

'With your permission,' said Gallo, 'there's something else I'd like to say. Antonio Firetto was around seventy, but he had the spirit of a child. He made poetry.'

'What?'

'Yes, sir, poetry. He didn't know how to read or write, but he made poetry anyway. Beautiful poetry. I heard him recite a few poems.'

'And what did he talk about in these poems?'

'I dunno, the Blessed Virgin, the moon, the grass. That kind of thing. And he never wanted to believe what people said about his son. He claimed that his son was incapable of doing such things, that he had a good heart. He just never wanted to believe it. Once he got into a violent tussle in town with a guy who'd called his son a Mafioso.'

'I get the picture. So you're telling me it was quite natural for him to put his son up, since he thought he was innocent as Christ.'

'Exactly,' said Gallo, almost defiantly.

'Let's get back to the subject. So what do you two think happened here?'

Gallo looked at Fazio as if to say it was up to him to talk.

'Here's how I think it went,' said Fazio. 'Giacomo probably came here in the early afternoon. He must have been dead tired, because he threw himself down on the bed with his muddy shoes still on. His father lets him rest, then makes him something to eat. When Giacomo sits down at the table, it's already dark outside. His father apparently isn't hungry, or is used to eating later, so he goes out to give a hand to the donkey in the stall. But there are two men outside, waiting for the right moment. They immobilize him, then tiptoe into the house and kill Giacomo. Then they bring the old man with them, and escape in the car that Giacomo drove to get here.'

'And why in your opinion didn't they kill the old man right here, when they killed his son?'

'Don't know. Maybe Giacomo had told his father something, and they wanted to know what they'd said to each other.'

'They could have done it in the stall next door.'

'Maybe they thought it would take a while. Somebody might come by. Which in fact happened.'

'What do you mean?'

'The murder was discovered by a friend of Antonio's who lives a few hundred yards from here. Apparently they would get together every evening after supper for a glass of wine and some conversation. His name is Romildo Alessi. Anyway, this Alessi, who has a moped, dashed to a nearby house where he knew there was a telephone. When we got here, the corpse was still warm.'

'Your reconstruction doesn't make sense,' Montalbano said brutally.

Gallo and Fazio looked at each other in bewilderment.

'And why not?'

'If you can't figure it out by yourselves, I'm not going to tell you. What was the dead man wearing?'

'Trousers, shirt, jacket. All light stuff, seeing how hot it is, in spite of the rain.'

'So he was armed.'

'Why do you say that?'

'Because anyone who wears a jacket in the summertime is armed and hiding a weapon under the jacket. So, was he armed or not?'

'We didn't find any weapon.'

Montalbano sneered.

'So you guys think a dangerous fugitive is going to go around without so much as a miserable handgun in his pocket?'

'Maybe his weapon was taken away by the people who killed him.'

'Maybe. Did you have a look around?'

'Yes, sir. And so did Forensics. We didn't even find the empty case. Either the killers took it, or they shot him with a revolver.'

A drawer in the table was half open. Inside was some raffia string, a packet of candles, a box of kitchen matches, a hammer, some nails, and some screws.

'Did you open this drawer yourselves?'

'No, Chief. That's how it was when we got here. And that's how we left it.'

On a shelf in front of the oven there was a roll of light brown packing tape about an inch and a half wide. It must have been taken from the half-open drawer and never put back.

Montalbano went over to the oven and removed the tin clip, which was simply resting against the edge of the opening.

'Could you give me a torch?'

'We've already looked in there,' said Fazio, handing him a torch. 'There's nothing.'

But in fact there was something: a rag once white but now completely black with cinders. On top of this, over an inch of very fine soot had fallen just inside the opening, as if it had been dislodged and fallen from the front part of the oven's vault.

The inspector put the makeshift latch back in place.

'I'm going to hang onto this,' he said, putting the torch in his pocket.

Then he started doing something that seemed strange to Fazio and Gallo. He closed his eyes and began walking, at a normal pace, from the wall on the side with the kitchen and oven to the table and then back again, then from the table to the front door and back again. In short, he was pacing back and forth with his eyes closed all the while, looking like he'd lost his mind.

Fazio and Gallo didn't dare say anything. Then the inspector stopped.

'I'm going to stay here tonight,' he said. 'You two turn off the lights, lock the doors and windows, and put the seals back up. We have to make it look like there's nobody in here.'

'Why would any of them want to come back?' asked Fazio.

'I don't know, but just do as I say. You, Fazio, drive my car back to Vigàta. Oh, and another thing: after you've put the seals back on the door, go into the stall and take care of the donkey. The poor animal must be hungry and thirsty.'

'Whatever you say,' said Fazio. 'Do you want me to come and get you tomorrow morning in my car?'

'No, thanks. I can walk back to Vigàta.'

'But it's a long way!'

Montalbano looked him in the eye and Fazio didn't insist.

'Inspector, could you tell me something before we leave? I'm curious why you think our reconstruction of Giacomo Firetto's murder doesn't work.'

'Because Firetto was watching the door as he was eating at the table. If anyone came in, he would have seen him and reacted accordingly. Whereas everything is in order in this room; there's no sign of any struggle.'

'So what? Maybe one guy came in first with a gun trained on Giacomo, told him not to move, while a second guy circled around the table and shot him in the back of the head.'

'And you think that someone like Giacomo Firetto — based on what you just told me about him — is the kind of guy who's going to let himself be killed just like that, scared stiff, without making a move? He's as good as dead, so he's going to try something desperate. There's your answer. Good night.'

*

He heard them close the door, heard them fumbling to put the seals back up (which consisted of a sheet of paper with something scribbled on it and a stamp, stuck to one half of the door with two pieces of adhesive tape), heard them tramping in the stall next door, cursing, as they saw to the donkey's needs (apparently the animal wanted nothing to do with the two strangers), heard them start up the car and drive off. He remained motionless in the total darkness, near the table. A few seconds later, the sound of rain reached his ears as it started falling again outside.

He took off his jacket and his tie, which he was still wearing, having had to put it on for the meeting in Palermo, and finally his shirt, remaining bare chested. With torch in hand, he walked resolutely towards the oven, removed the tin cover, set this down on the floor, trying to make no sound, stuck one arm inside the oven, and pressed the 'on' button on the torch. He was able to fit his entire torso into the oven, standing on tiptoe. Twisting himself around, he found himself resting with his back on the floor of the oven, half his body inside, and his buttocks, legs, and feet outside. A bit of soot fell into his eyes but didn't prevent him from seeing the revolver stuck to the ceiling of the oven, near the opening, with two strips of packing tape that glistened in the beam of the torch. Turning this off, he came out of the oven, put the cover back on, cleaned himself up as best he could with a handkerchief, put his shirt and jacket back on, and stuffed the tie into his pocket.

Then he sat down in a chair that was almost in front of the two burners. And to pass the time, but not only, the inspector started thinking of a book he'd read a few days

earlier. In it, the author, Fernando Pessoa, maintains —
through the words he puts into the mouth of his character,
Detective Quaresma — that if someone walking down a
street sees a man fallen on the pavement, he will instinctively
ask himself: why has this man fallen here? But this, Pessoa
maintains, is already an error of reasoning and therefore
possibly an error of fact. The man walking down the street
didn't see the man fall down; he saw him already on the
ground. It is not a known *fact* that the man fell down in that
spot. The only *fact* is that he's already there, lying on the
ground. He may have fallen somewhere else and been taken
there and laid down on the pavement. It could be any
number of things, Pessoa maintains.

So how to explain to Fazio and Gallo that the only *fact*
of the matter, aside from the dead body, was that Antonio
Firetto was not at the scene of the crime at the moment they
arrived? And that it was not a *fact* that his son's killers took
him away, but an error of reasoning?

He remembered another example, which supported the
first. Pessoa maintains, still through Detective Quaresma,
that if a man is inside, in a living room, while it's raining
outside, and he sees a wet man enter the room, he inevitably
will think that the visitor's clothes are drenched because
he's been out in the rain. But such a thought cannot be considered a *fact*, since the man inside did not see the visitor
outside in the rain. He may have spilled a bucket full of
water on himself inside.

So how to explain to Fazio and Gallo that a Mafioso
'executed' by a bullet fired precisely into the base of his skull
wasn't necessarily eliminated by the Mafia for having slipped
up or given signs of wanting to turn himself in?

Pessoa also maintains . . .

He never did find out what else Pessoa maintained at
that moment. The day's weariness came crashing down on
him all at once like a hood adding darkness to the darkness
already in the room. His head dropped onto his chest and

he drifted off. Before sinking into a deep sleep, he managed to give himself an order: sleep the way cats do — where they seem to be sleeping deeply, but the smallest thing is enough to make them spring to their feet and into a position of self-defence. He didn't know how long he slept, assisted by the constant sound of rain in the background, but then he was awakened suddenly, just like a cat, by a soft noise around the front door. It could merely have been some animal. Then he heard a key turn in the lock and the door open cautiously. He stiffened in his chair. The door closed again. He hadn't seen it either open or close, and had seen no change in the wall of total darkness either outside or inside. The man had entered but remained very near to the door without moving. The inspector, too, didn't dare move. In fact he was worried his very breath might betray him. Why didn't the person come forward? Perhaps he smelled a foreign presence in his home, like an animal returning to its den. At last the man took two steps towards the table and stopped again. The inspector felt reassured: he could now, if he so wished, leap up from his chair and grab the man. But there was no need.

'Who are you?' an old man's voice asked softly but firmly, without fear.

So he had indeed sniffed him out, a foreign shadow in the mass of shadows in the room, within which the man could by long-established habit distinguish what was in its proper place and what was not. Montalbano was at a disadvantage. However much he may have committed to memory the placement of every object in the room, he realized that the other man could close his eyes and move freely about, whereas he himself felt the absurd need to keep his eyes wide open in that total darkness.

He also realized that to say one wrong word at that moment would have been an irremediable mistake.

'I'm a police inspector; Montalbano's the name.'

The man didn't move, didn't speak.

'Are you Antonio Firetto?'

He'd addressed him using the polite form of *voi*, and in a tone that implied consideration and respect.

'Yes.'

'How long was it that you hadn't seen Giacomo?'

'Five years. Do you believe me?'

'I believe you.'

Therefore the whole time his son was a fugitive he'd never come here. Perhaps he didn't dare.

'Why did he come yesterday?'

'I don' know why. 'E was tired, very tired. 'E din't come in a car, 'e walked here. 'E came inside, gave me a hug, and trew hisself down on the bed wit' 'is shoes on. When 'e woke up a while later, 'e tol' me 'e was hungry. That was when I noticed he had a weapon – a revolver, on the bedside table. When I ast 'im why 'e was goin' roun' wit' a gun, 'e said it was 'cause there's a lotta bad people about. An' 'e started laughin'. It made my blood run cold.'

'Why?'

'It was the way 'e laughed, Inspector. We din't say no more, 'e stayed in bed, an' I came in here to make somethin' to eat. Just for him. I coun't eat. I felt somethin' like an iron hand close up my stomach.'

He interrupted himself, sighing. Montalbano respected his silence.

'That laugh kept echoin' inside my head,' the old man resumed. 'It said a lot. It said the whole truth about my son, the truth I never wanted to believe. When the potatoes was done, I called him. He got up and came in here, put his gun on the table, and started eatin'. An' so I ast 'im: "How many people you killed?" An' he said – cool an' calm like 'e was talkin' bout ants – he said: "Eight." An' then 'e said somethin' 'e never oughta tol' me: 'E said: "I even killed a nine-year-old boy." An' 'e kep' on eatin'. Great God almighty, 'e kep' on eatin'! An' so I grabbed the gun an' shot 'im in the back of the head. Just once, like they do when they's executin' a man.'

Executed, Fazio had said. He'd been right. The pause was very long this time. Then the inspector spoke.

'Why did you come back?'

''Cause I wanted to kill myself.'

'With the revolver you hid in the oven?'

'Yessir. It was my son's. It's missing a bullet.'

'You had all the time in the world to kill yourself. Why didn't you do so right away?'

'My hand was shakin' too much.'

'You could've hanged yourself from a tree.'

'I ain't Judas, Mr Inspector.'

Right. He wasn't Judas. And he couldn't throw himself into a well like a desperate wretch. He was a poet who until the end hadn't wanted to see the truth.

'So what are you gonna do now, arrest me?'

The same deep, steady voice, without fear.

'I should.'

The old man made a sudden, violent move, taking Montalbano by surprise. In the darkness the inspector heard the tin used to close the oven fall to the floor. Surely the old man now had the gun in his hand and was aiming it at him. But Montalbano wasn't the least bit afraid; he knew he only had a part to play. He stood up slowly, but once on his feet felt dizzy and as tired as if buried under slabs of cement.

'I got this gun trained on you, sir,' said the old man. 'An' I'm orderin' you to get outta this house immediately. I wanna die here, killed by my own son's gun. Sittin' in the same chair where I shot 'im. If you're a man, you'll understand.'

Wearily, Montalbano headed for the door, opened it, and went out. It had stopped raining. And he was certain he wouldn't find a lift into Vigàta.

THE CAT AND THE GOLDFINCH

Mrs Erminia Todaro, eighty-five years old and the wife of a retired railwayman, left the house as she did every morning to go first to Holy Mass and then to buy groceries at the market. It wasn't so much faith that made Mrs Erminia a churchgoer, but the fact that she couldn't sleep, as happens to almost all elderly people. The morning Mass helped her to pass a bit of time, as her days, who knew why, became longer and emptier. During those same morning hours, her husband, the former railwayman, whose name was Agustinu, would sit at the window giving onto the street and not move until his wife came home and told him that lunch was ready.

And so Signora Erminia stepped out onto the street, adjusted her overcoat – since it was a bit cool outside – and started walking. From her right arm hung an old black handbag with her ID card, a photo of her daughter Catarina who lived in Forlì, married to a man named Genuardi, a photo of their three children, three photos of the children of the Genuardis' children, a holy picture of Santa Lucia, twenty-six thousand lire in notes, and seven hundred and fifty in coins. Former railwayman Agustinu later said he saw a small motorbike being driven by someone with a helmet come up very slowly behind his wife. At a certain point the driver, as though fed up with going along at Signora Erminia's walking pace, which you certainly could not say was very fast, accelerated and passed her. Then he did a strange thing: after making a U-turn, he came back and headed straight for Signora Erminia. At that moment there wasn't another living soul on the street. When he was three paces away, the motorcyclist stopped, set one foot down on the ground, pulled a revolver out of his pocket, and pointed it at the lady. Who, being unable to make out even a dog from six inches away despite her thick glasses, kept walking, blissfully unaware, towards the man who was threatening her. When Signora Erminia found herself almost nose-to-nose with the man, she noticed the gun and was quite astonished that anyone should have any reason for shooting her.

'What are you doing, young man? Are you going to kill me?' she asked, more in surprise than fear.

'Yes,' said the man, 'if you don't give me your bag.'

Signora Erminia slid her bag off her arm and handed it to the man. By this point Agustinu had managed to open the window. He thrust his body out, at the risk of crashing to the ground below, and started yelling: 'Help! Help!'

The man fired. Just one shot – at Signora Erminia, not at her husband who was making all the racket. The lady fell to the ground, and the man turned his motorbike around, accelerated, and vanished. At the sound of the ex-railway-man's shouts, a number of windows opened, and men and women poured out into the street to help Signora Erminia, who lay in the middle of the street. To their great relief, they immediately realized that the lady had only fainted from fright.

*

Miss Esterina Mandracchia, seventy-five years old and a retired schoolteacher who had never married, lived alone in an apartment inherited from her parents. The distinguishing feature of Miss Mandracchia's three rooms with bath and kitchen was that the walls were completely papered with holy images by the thousands. In addition, there were many little statues: a Madonna under a bell jar, a baby Jesus, a St Anthony of Padua, a crucifix, a San Gerlando, a San

Calogero, and others not so easily identified. Miss Mandracchia always attended early morning Mass, and then went
back for evening vespers. That morning, two days after the
phantom shooting of Signora Erminia, Miss Mandracchia
stepped out of her house. As she later told Inspector Montalbano, she'd just set out for the church when a small
motorbike with a helmeted driver passed her on the street.
After going a few more yards, the motorbike made a U-turn,
came back, and stopped a few steps in front of her, whereupon the driver pulled out a revolver. The former teacher,
despite her age, had excellent vision. She put her hands up,
as she'd seen done so many times on television.

'I surrender,' she said, trembling.

'Give me your handbag,' said the man.

Signorina Esterina slid her handbag off her arm and
handed it to him. The man took it and fired the gun, missing her. Esterina Mandracchia did not scream, did not
faint. She simply went straight to the inspector and reported
the crime. In her purse, she declared, she had at least a hundred holy images and exactly eighteen thousand three
hundred lire.

'I eat less than a sparrow,' she explained to Montalbano.
'A panino will last me two days. Why would I need to go
around with a lot of money in my purse?'

*

Pippo Ragonese, the political commentator of TeleVigàta
News, had two outstanding features: a purse-lipped face
that looked like a chicken's arse, and a contorted imagination that saw conspiracies everywhere. An avowed enemy of
Montalbano, Ragonese didn't miss this opportunity to
attack him yet again. In fact he claimed that the unusual
bag-snatching served the precise political purposes of an as
yet not well identified group of leftist extremists, who with
these sorts of terrorist actions, aimed at dissuading believers
from going to church, in hopes of ushering in a new age of

atheism. The reason the Vigàta police hadn't yet arrested the pseudo-bag-snatcher must be looked for in the subliminal hindrance exerted by the chief inspector's political ideas, which certainly didn't tend toward the centre or the right. 'Subliminal hindrance,' the commentator said – and he said it twice, in case anyone had heard wrong the first time.

But Montalbano didn't get upset. Actually he had a good laugh over it. He didn't laugh the following day, however, when he was called in by Police Commissioner Bonetti-Alderighi – who, in the bewildered inspector's presence, didn't quite buy the news commentator's thesis, but nevertheless took out a trial subscription, inviting the inspector to 'accompany' him down the same path.

'But think about it for a second, Mr Commissioner. How many pseudo-bag-snatchers are there running around trying to dissuade all the little old ladies of Montelusa and its province from going to early morning Mass?'

'You yourself used the expression "pseudo-bag-snatchers" just now, Montalbano. You will admit, I hope, that we're not looking at a typical bag-snatcher's MO here. The man just pulls out a gun and fires! For no reason! All he has to do is reach out and take the bag at his leisure. What reason could there be to try to kill those poor women?'

'Mr Commissioner,' said Montalbano, who suddenly felt like playing with his boss's head, 'pulling out a weapon, a gun, in no way spells certain death for the person threatened; very often the valency of the threat is not tragic but cognitive. At least that's what Roland Barthes argues.'

'And who's that?' the commissioner asked, mouth agape.

'An eminent French criminologist,' the inspector lied.

'Montalbano, I don't give a damn about any French criminologist! This guy doesn't just pull out a gun, he shoots it!'

'Yes, but he never actually hits his victims. I think the cognitive valency is the predominant one.'

'Just get busy,' said Bonetti-Alderighi, cutting things short.

*

'In my opinion,' said Mimì Augello, 'it's classic drug-addict mischief.'

'But can't you see, Mimì? All the guy's managed to steal is forty-five thousand and fifty lire! He could get more just by selling the bullets in his gun! Speaking of which, have you found them?'

'We looked but couldn't find anything. Who knows where they ended up.'

'But why does this idiot shoot at the old ladies after they've already given him their handbags? And why does he miss?'

'What does it mean?'

'It means he misses, Mimì. Full stop. Look, the first time we might have thought he reacted instinctively when Mrs Todaro's husband started yelling out of the window. What's not clear is why, instead of shooting at the man who was yelling, he shot at the woman, who was barely a foot and a half away from him. You don't miss from a foot and a half away, Mimì. The second time, with Miss Mandracchia, he shot her as he was grabbing her bag with his other hand. They were probably about three feet away from each other. But he missed again. And you know what, Mimì? I don't think he missed either time.'

'Oh, yeah? So how do you explain that neither of the women was even injured?'

'It's because both shots were blank, Mimì. Here's something you can do: have the dress Mrs Erminia was wearing that morning analysed.'

*

He was right on the money. The following day, the Forensics lab in Montelusa informed them that even a superficial analysis of Mrs Todaro's dress at chest-level showed a large spot of gunshot residue.

'So he's a madman,' said Mimì Augello.

The inspector said nothing.

'You don't agree?'

'No. And if he is a madman . . . there's a lot of method in his madness.'

Augello, who hadn't read *Hamlet* – or if he had, he'd forgotten it – didn't catch the allusion.

'And what method is that?'

'Mimì, that's for us to find out, don't you think?'

✳

Very quietly, when people in town had almost forgotten about the two muggings and were no longer talking about them, the bag-snatcher (how could you call him anything else?) was heard from again. At seven o'clock one Sunday morning, he demanded the handbag of one Mrs Gesualda Bommarito, was given it, and then shot her. In the right shoulder, but the bullet only grazed her. Upon closer examination, the wound proved to be nothing. But it did send the inspector's theory of a gun filled with blanks up in smoke. Maybe the gunshot residue found on Mrs Todaro's dress was due to a sudden twist of the gunman's wrist, caused by an unexpected remorse for what he was about to do. This time the bullet was recovered and the Forensics lab informed Montalbano that the weapon was probably of antediluvian date. The purse of Signora Gesualda, who'd suffered more fright than harm, had eleven thousand lire in it. But how was it possible that this bag-snatcher (or whatever he was) went around robbing only old ladies on their way to early morning Mass? A serious, professional bag-snatcher, first of all, doesn't carry a weapon and, second, waits around for old ladies coming out of the post office after cashing their pension cheque, or else preys on smart-looking women on their way to the hairdresser's. No, there was something about the whole business that didn't add up. And after the wounding of Signora Gesualda, Montalbano started to get worried. If the idiot kept on shooting real bullets, sooner or later he would end up killing some poor old lady.

✳

And indeed, one morning Mrs Antonia Joppolo, fifty years old and married to Giuseppe Joppolo, a lawyer, was awakened from her sleep by the ringing of the telephone. It was seven o'clock. She picked up the receiver and instantly recognized her husband's voice.

'Ninetta, darling,' said the lawyer.

'What's wrong?' asked Signora Antonia, immediately alarmed.

'I had a little car crash just outside of Palermo. I'm in a hospital. I wanted to tell you personally myself, before anyone else did. But don't be alarmed, it's nothing.'

His wife, however, got alarmed.

'I'm getting in the car and coming,' she said.

This brief exchange was recounted to Montalbano by Giuseppe Joppolo when the inspector paid him a visit at the Sanatrix clinic.

It was therefore logical to assume that the signora got dressed in a hurry, went out, and rushed to the garage, which was about a hundred yards away. After taking a few steps, she was passed by a small motorbike. Annibale Panebianco, who at that moment was stepping out of the front door of the building he lived in, had managed to see the woman handing her bag to the man on the motorbike, hear a shot, and witness, petrified, the woman falling to the ground and the motorbike driving off. When he could move again, he ran up to Mrs Joppolo, who he knew quite well — but there was nothing more to do. She'd been shot square in the chest.

In his hospital bed, her husband Giuseppe was like Mary at the foot of the cross in his despair.

'It's all my fault! And to think I told her not to come,

to stay at home, because it was nothing serious! Poor Ninetta! She loved me so much!'

'Had you already been in Palermo a long time?'

'Not at all! She was still asleep when I left Vigàta and headed for Palermo in my car. Two and a half hours later I had the accident, so I called her and she insisted on coming to Palermo. And what happened happened.'

He was unable to go on, as he was sobbing so hard he could hardly breathe. The inspector had to wait five minutes before the man was in a condition to answer his final question.

'I'm sorry, sir, but did your wife normally carry large sums of money in her bag?'

'Large sums? What do you mean by large sums? We have a safe at home in which we always keep about ten million lire in cash. But she would only take what she needed. Anyway, nowadays, what with cash machines, credit cards, and chequebooks, who needs to carry a lot of money around? Of course, maybe this time, having to come to Palermo and thinking she'd probably have some unexpected expenses, she probably did take a couple of million with her. And she probably took some jewellery as well. It was a habit of hers, poor Ninetta; she would put some items of jewellery in her purse when she had to leave town, even for just a day or two.'

'And how did your accident happen?'

'Well, I must have nodded off, and I drove straight into a pole. I wasn't wearing my seat belt, and I broke two ribs, but nothing else.'

His chin started trembling again.

'And for something so stupid, Ninetta lost her life!'

*

'It's true,' noted TeleVigàta's political commentator, still harping on the same point, 'that the victim was not on her way to church, since she was headed for the garage.' But who could say with any assurance that before leaving for Palermo to comfort her husband, she would not have stepped into a church, even if for just a few minutes, to say a prayer for her dear husband, who lay in pain in a hospital bed? In which case it would all make sense, and this crime could also be ascribed to that same sect that wanted to terrorize the faithful into deserting the churches. Worse than in the days of Stalin. What we were witnessing, therefore, was a frightening escalation of atheist violence.

Commissioner Bonetti-Alderighi, in a fit of rage, used the same term.

'It's an escalation, Montalbano! First he fires blanks, then he grazes someone, then finally kills someone! So much for the cognitive valencies of your French criminologist – what was his name – ah, yes, Marthes! Do you know who the victim was?'

'To be honest, sir, I haven't had the time yet to—'

'Well, let me save you some time, then. Mrs Joppolo, aside from being one of the richest women in the province, was the cousin of Undersecretary Biondolillo, who has already phoned me. And she had some important friends – *extremely* important friends – in Sicilian political and financial circles. Do you know what that means? Look, Montalbano, here's what we're going to do – but don't take it the wrong way: the investigation's going to be led – with, of course, the agreement of the assistant prosecutor – by the chief of the Flying Squad. And you'll be working alongside him. Is that all right with you?'

For once, this was quite all right with the inspector. At the very idea of having to answer the inevitable questions of Undersecretary Biondolillo and all the political and financial circles in Sicily, he'd started sweating – not in fear, of course, but from the unbearable nausea he felt towards the world of Mrs Joppolo and her ilk.

※

The investigation conducted by the Flying Squad, which Montalbano took great care not to work alongside of (since, among other things, nobody from the squad had asked him to work alongside them), led to the arrest of two drug-addicted young criminals who owned small motorbikes. But the investigating magistrate refused to uphold the arrest, and the two youths were released. This brought the investigation to a halt, despite Commissioner Bonetti-Alderighi's anxious reassurances to Undersecretary Biondolillo and Sicilian political and financial circles that the killer would soon be found and arrested.

Naturally, Inspector Montalbano conducted his own parallel investigation, entirely submerged but just under the surface of the water. And he came to the conclusion that very soon there would be another mugging. He took care not to mention this to the commissioner, but did say something to Mimì Augello.

'What the hell!' Mimì exploded. 'You're sitting there all calm and collected and you tell me the guy's going to kill another woman? If you're so sure of what you're saying, we need to do something!'

'Calm down, Mimì. I said the guy would mug and shoot another woman, I didn't say he would kill her. There's a difference.'

'How can you be so sure?'

'Because he'll fire blanks this time, the way he did the first two times. Because it's no use telling me the killer didn't fire blanks but changed his mind at the last second and pointed the gun away . . . That's rubbish. There was an escalation, as the commissioner put it. Carefully and intelligently thought out. He'll fire blanks this time, I'd bet my house on it.'

'Let me get this straight, Salvo. Since we'll be lucky to catch the gunman, you're saying that there will be two more women shot with blanks, another grazed by a bullet, and a fourth one killed, in that order?'

'No, Mimì. If I'm right, there will only be one more old lady shot with blanks who'll have a terrible fright. Let's hope her heart holds up. But that'll be the end of it; there won't be any more muggings.'

*

About two months after the solemn funeral of Mrs Joppolo, one morning around seven o'clock, with Montalbano still asleep, having gone to bed at four, his telephone rang, waking him up. Cursing the saints, the inspector yelled:

'Who is it?'

'You were right,' said the voice of Mimì Augello.

'What are you talking about?'

'He shot another little old lady.'

'Did he kill her?'

'No. It was probably a blank.'

'I'll be right over.'

In the shower Montalbano sang, at the top of his lungs, '*O toreador ritorna vincitor.*'

*

A little old lady, Mimì had said over the telephone. Mrs Rosa Lo Curto was sitting in front of Montalbano, her back straight as a board. Fat, ruddy, and expansive, she looked ten years younger than the sixty she'd admitted to.

'Were you on your way to church, Signora?'

'Me?! I haven't set foot in a church since I was eight years old.'

'Are you married?'

'My husband died five years ago. We got married in Switzerland, a civil ceremony. I can't stand priests.'

'Why did you go out so early this morning?'

'I got a call from a friend, Michela Bajo. She's ill and had a bad night. So I said I'd come and see her. I even brought along a bottle of good wine, the kind she likes. But I couldn't find a plastic bag to put it in, so I carried it in my hand, since Michela lives only about a five minute walk away.'

'And what happened, exactly?'

'The usual thing. A small motorbike drove past me, made a U-turn, and came back. He stopped about two steps in front of me, pulled out a gun and pointed it at me. "Give me your handbag," he said.'

'And what did you do?'

'I said, "No problem." And I held my handbag out for him. And as he was taking it, he fired his gun. But I didn't feel anything. I knew immediately he hadn't shot me. So, with all my might, I smashed the bottle over his hand holding the handbag, which he had on the hand-grip with the throttle so he could drive off in a hurry. Your men picked up the pieces of broken glass afterwards. They're all covered with blood. I must have broken the bastard's hand. He still made off with my handbag, but I had barely ten thousand lire in it.'

Montalbano stood up and held out his hand.

'You have my sincere admiration, Signora.'

*

Since, upon being interviewed by Pippo Ragonese, Mrs Lo Curto declared that the thought of going to church on the morning of the assault was the furthest thing from her mind, the TeleVigàta political commentator let slide his personal theory concerning a forced desertion of the churches.

The person who didn't let anything slide was Bonetti-Alderighi.

'No, no, no! Are we back to square one or something? Look, public opinion will revolt if we sit still any longer! Actually, not "we", Montalbano: you!'

The inspector couldn't refrain from grinning, which enraged the commissioner even more.

'And what are you smiling about, for God's sake?!'

'Give me two days, and I'll have the two here in front of you.'

'What two?'

'The instigator and the material executor of the assaults and the murder.'

'Are you joking?'

'Not at all. I'd predicted this last assault, you know. I just did the maths, so to speak.'

Bonetti-Alderighi felt bewildered, his throat dry. He called the usher.

'Bring me a glass of water, please. Would you like one too?'

'No,' said Montalbano.

*

'Inspector! What a lovely surprise! What are you doing in Palermo?'

'I'm here on an investigation. I'll be staying just a few hours before I head back to Vigàta. I hear you've already sold all your late wife's properties in Vigàta as well as Montelusa.'

'Well, you know, Inspector, I just couldn't live any longer amidst all those sad reminders. So I bought this villa in Palermo, and I'll carry on from here. I brought the few things that didn't bring back painful memories with me, and I, well, alienated the rest, as we say in the legal profession.'

'Did you alienate the cat, too?' asked Montalbano.

'What cat?'

'Dudù. The cat your poor wife was so fond of. She also had a goldfinch. Did you bring them here with you?'

'Actually, no. I would have liked to, but unfortunately, in all the confusion of moving out of the old house . . . the cat ran away, and the bird flew away. Unfortunately . . .'

'Your wife was so fond of them, both the cat and the goldfinch.'

'I know, I know. The poor thing had these kinds of childish—'

'Excuse me, sir,' Montalbano interrupted him, 'but I didn't realize that there was a ten-year age difference between you and your wife. I mean, that you were ten years younger than her.'

Giuseppe Joppolo, the lawyer, bolted up out of his chair and made an indignant face.

'What's that got to do with anything?'

'Nothing, you're right. When there's love . . .'

The lawyer glared at the inspector with eyes half-closed and said nothing. Montalbano continued:

'When you got married, you were practically destitute, weren't you?'

'Leave this house at once.'

'I will, in just a minute. Now, however, with your inheritance, you've become very rich. At a glance I'd say you inherited about ten billion lire. It's not always a misfortune when a loved one dies.'

'What are you insinuating?' the lawyer asked, pale as a corpse.

'Only this: that you had your wife murdered. And I even know by whom. You conceived a brilliant plan. My compliments. The first two assaults were aimed at establishing a false purpose; the real purpose was the third — the fatal assault on your wife. It was never a question of snatching handbags, but of using phony muggings to conceal the true purpose: to murder your wife.'

'I'm sorry, but after my poor Ninetta was killed, I believe they tried to pull off another assault.'

'I've already complimented you once on your plan. That was the final flourish, the artist's touch intended to divert all possible suspicion away from you for ever. But you forgot about your wife's love of her cat Dudù and her goldfinch. And that was a mistake.'

'Would you please explain this idiotic reasoning to me?'

'It's not really so idiotic, sir. You see, I conducted an investigation. A careful one. When I came to see you in the hospital after your accident and your wife's murder, you told me that, when you spoke to your wife over the phone, you'd insisted that she stay in Vigàta and not come to see you in the hospital. Is that true?'

'Of course it's true!'

'You see, right after the accident, you were hospitalized and put in a room with two beds. The other patient was separated from you by a screen. You, shaken up by your fake accident, which nevertheless injured you, then called your wife. You were later moved into a single room. But the other patient had heard your phone call. And he's ready to testify. You begged your wife to come to Palermo to see you; you said you felt very bad. Whereas you told me, and just now repeated, that you'd insisted that your wife stay at home, in Vigàta.'

'How can you expect me to remember, after an accident that—'

'Let me finish. There's more. Your wife, extremely upset by what you told her over the phone, decided to leave at once for Palermo. But there was the problem of the cat and the goldfinch; she didn't know how long she'd be away from home. And so she woke the woman next door, who's a friend of hers, and told her what you told her, that you were practically on death's doorstep. So she had to leave at once. She left her cat and bird in her neighbour's care and went out into the street, where the killer was waiting for her, ready to bring your ingenious plan to a climax.'

Giuseppe Joppolo, the handsome lawyer, lost his cool.

'You don't have a shred of evidence, you fucking moron.'

'Perhaps you're unaware that your accomplice had his hand broken by the final victim, who smashed a bottle of wine over it. And he went to have it taken care of at Montelusa hospital, no less. We've arrested him, and my men are putting the screws to him. It's just a matter of hours now before he confesses.'

'Oh my God!' said Joppolo the lawyer, collapsing into the nearest chair. There wasn't an iota of truth in the story of the arrested accomplice; it was all a big lie, a bluff, a booby trap. But the lawyer had been unable to avoid stepping right into it, falling inside with all his clothes on.

MONTALBANO SAYS NO

The late April night was exactly as it had once seemed to Giacomo Leopardi as the poet sat and enjoyed it: *sweet and clear, without a breath of wind*. Inspector Montalbano was driving his car very slowly, relishing the cool as he headed back to his home in Marinella. He squirmed in fatigue the way you squirm in a dirty, sweaty suit, knowing that in a short while, after you shower, you'll be able to change into a clean, fragrant one. He had been at the office since before eight o'clock that morning, and now his watch said twelve midnight on the dot.

He'd spent the whole day trying to extract a confession from a nasty old lout who had molested a nine-year-old girl and then attempted to kill her with a stone to the head. The child was now in a coma at Montelusa hospital and thus in no condition to identify her attacker. After a few hours of interrogation, the inspector had little doubt that the culprit was the man he had arrested. But the dirty old codger had shielded himself in an iron-clad denial that revealed no chinks. Montalbano had tried to fool him with ruses, deceptions, and trick questions, but he would have none of it and merely repeated the same refrain:

'It wasn't me, and you have no proof.'

Of course he would have plenty of proof after the DNA tests of the sperm came back. But it takes too much time and too much straw for the sorb to ripen, as the peasants say.

Around five o'clock in the afternoon, after exhausting

the entire repertoire of police tactics, Montalbano began to feel like a walking corpse. Getting Fazio to replace him, he went into the bathroom, took off all his clothes, washed himself from head to toe, and got dressed again. When he returned to the interrogation room to resume questioning, he heard the old man say:

'It wathn't me, ant you haff no proof.'

Had the guy suddenly turned German? He looked at the suspect: a string of blood was trickling out of his mouth and one of his eyes was swollen shut.

'What happened?'

'Nothing, Chief,' Fazio replied with an angelic face that was missing only the halo. 'He sort of fainted and hit his head against the corner of the table. He may have broken a tooth, nothing serious.'

The old man said nothing, and the inspector resumed hammering away with the same questions. At ten o'clock that evening, not having managed to eat so much as a sandwich, Montalbano saw Mimì Augello come in, fresh as a rose. He immediately had his deputy replace him and dashed out straight to the Trattoria San Calogero. His hunger had gone so long unsated that with every step he felt he might collapse to the ground like a wasted horse. He ordered a seafood antipasto and could already taste it in his mind when Gallo burst into the restaurant.

'Chief, you gotta come, the old man wants to talk. He suddenly cracked and admits that he was the one who smashed the little girl's head with a stone after raping her.'

'How is that possible?'

'I dunno, Chief, it was Inspector Augello who persuaded him.'

Montalbano darkened, and it certainly wasn't because of the seafood antipasto that he wouldn't get the chance to eat. What? He'd spent all day sweating blood with the old pig, and now Mimì gets him to confess in the twinkling of an eye?

Back at the station, before going to see the nasty old man, he called his assistant aside.

'How did you do it?'

'Believe me, Salvo, it was only good luck. You know I shave with a straight razor, right? I really can't use those safety razors. Maybe it's something to do with my skin, what can I say?'

'Listen, spare me the details about your skin because I don't care. I want to know how you got the guy to confess.'

'Well, I'd just bought myself a new razor today, and I had it in my jacket pocket. As I was starting to interrogate the old man he said he needed to take a piss, and so I accompanied him to the toilet.'

'Why?'

'I dunno, he couldn't really stand up too well. Anyway, to cut a long story short, as soon as he pulled out his thingy, I opened my razor and gave him a little snick.'

Montalbano looked at him in dismay.

'*Where* did you give him a little snick?'

'Where do you think? But it was nothing, believe me. Of course, it did bleed a little, but nothing se—'

'Mimì, have you gone insane?'

Augello smiled at him condescendingly.

'Salvo, there's something you don't understand. Either he talked, or our men weren't going to let him out of here alive. So I solved the problem. The old man really thought I might cut it off, and so he cracked.'

The inspector resolved to talk to Mimì and all the men at the station the following morning. He couldn't stomach the way they'd behaved with the old man. He left the child-rapist and murderer to Augello, who in any case no longer needed to use his razor, and went back to the trattoria. His antipasto was waiting for him and washed away half of the worries on his mind. The mullet in tomato sauce banished the other half.

Outside the restaurant, the street was completely dark.

Either someone had broken the streetlamps or they had burnt out. After a few paces his eyes adjusted. Beside the entrance to a building was a man urinating, not against the wall, but onto a large cardboard box. When he came within close range of the man, he noticed that he was relieving himself onto an unfortunate wretch inside the box who was unable to react or speak because he was completely drunk.

'What is this?' said Montalbano, stopping.

'What the fuck do *you* want?' said the other man, closing his zip.

'You think that's right, pissing on a human being?'

'Human being? That's a piece of shit. And if you don't bugger off, I'm going to piss on you too.'

'Sorry to bother you, good night,' said the inspector.

He turned his back, took half a step, then spun around and dealt the man a powerful kick in the balls. The other collapsed on top of the wretch inside the box, winded. A fitting conclusion to a hard day.

Montalbano was almost home when he veered left, turned the car onto the little road that led to his house, arrived in the parking area, pulled up, got out, opened the front door, closed it behind him, and searched for the light switch. But his hand froze in midair.

What was it that paralysed him? A kind of flash, the sudden image of a scene glimpsed in passing just moments before, too quickly for his brain to process the information absorbed. He didn't turn on the light. The darkness helped him to concentrate, to reconstruct what had registered subliminally in his mind.

OK, it was when he had swerved before turning onto the little road: his lights on full beam had momentarily lit up a stage. In front of him, parked in the same direction as he was going, was a Nissan 4x4. On the opposite side of the street, three moving silhouettes. They looked as if they were performing a dance, first coming together as a single body, then breaking apart.

He closed his eyes and squeezed them tightly. The mere glow of the light left on outside on the veranda bothered him, as it tainted the darkness in which he was trying to immerse himself.

There were two men and a woman — now he was sure of it — dancing and, from time to time, embracing. No. That was what he *thought* he had seen. But there was something in the three people's body language that might lead one to imagine an entirely different situation.

Bring it better into focus, Salvo. A policeman's eye is always a policeman's eye.

All at once he had no more doubt. In his mind he zoomed in on a hand clutching the woman's hair fiercely, violently. The scene assumed its true meaning. A kidnapping! Two men were trying to force the girl into the Nissan.

He didn't need to think about it twice. He opened the door, went out, got in his car, and left. How much time had passed? A little over ten minutes, he thought. He drove around for two hours, obstinate, lips pressed tightly together, eyes peering forward and back, combing streets, alleys, lanes, and dirt tracks.

After he had given up hope, he spotted the Nissan parked in front of a house on a hill, a house that had always looked empty and uninhabited the few times he had happened to pass by. No light was visible in the windows in front. He waited a few minutes without moving. Then he got out of his car, leaving the door open and, hunching over, carefully circled round the house. In back, the glow of two lighted rooms, one on the ground floor, the other upstairs, filtered through closed shutters.

He went back to the front of the house, lightly pushed open the door, which had been left ajar, careful not to let it squeak. He was sweating. He found himself in a dark vestibule and went further inside. There was a living room and, beside it, a kitchen. In the kitchen were two young men in jeans with stubbly faces and earrings. Both were bare-chested. They were cooking something on two camping stoves and checking the level of doneness. One was attending to a small frying pan, the other stirring a big pot with a wooden spoon. There was a smell of fried food and sauce in the air.

But where was the girl? Could she have managed to escape her assailants, or had they simply set her free? Or had he been wrong about the whole thing? Maybe his mental reconstruction of the scene could be interpreted in an entirely different manner?

Something, however, deep in the core of his instincts, told him not to trust what he saw: two young men making dinner. It was the very normality of the scene that disturbed him.

Cautious as a cat, Montalbano started climbing the masonry steps that led upstairs. Halfway up the stairs, which were made of unjointed little bricks, he nearly slipped. A dark, dense liquid covered the staircase. He bent down, touched it with his index finger and smelled it. He was too experienced not to recognize it as blood. Clearly he had arrived too late to find the girl still alive.

He climbed the last two steps as if with great effort, weighed down already by what he imagined he would see, and which he in fact saw.

In the single lighted room upstairs, the girl, or what remained of her, was lying on the floor, completely naked. Still cautious, but partly reassured by the sounds of the voices of the two men downstairs, he approached the body. They had skilfully cut her up with a knife after raping her, using even a broom handle, which lay covered in blood beside her, for the latter purpose. They had gouged out her eyes, cleanly cut away the entire calf of the left leg, and amputated her right hand. They had even started opening up her stomach, but then had abandoned the idea.

After crouching down to look more closely, the inspector

was having trouble standing back up. Not because he'd gone weak in the knees, but for the opposite reason. That is, he felt that if he started to rise to his feet, the bundle of nerves he'd become might make him shoot straight up to the ceiling like a jack-in-the-box. So he stayed down long enough to calm himself and repress the blind fury that had invaded his body. He must not make any mistakes; at two against one, they would quickly get the better of him.

He descended the stairs with a light step and clearly heard the two men's voices again.

'The eyes are fried just right. You want one?'

'Sure, if you'll taste a piece of calf.'

The inspector went out of the house but didn't make back it to his car before he had to stop and vomit. He tried hard not to make any noise, which created sharp pangs in his stomach as he suppressed the retching reflex. When he got to his car, he opened the boot, took out a jerry can of petrol, which he always carried with him, went back to the house, and emptied it just inside the entrance. He was certain the two men would not smell the odour, as it would surely be covered up by the much stronger smells of two fried eyes and a calf boiled or simmered in sauce or whatever it was.

His plan was simple: set fire to the fuel and force the killers to jump out of the kitchen window at the back. He would be waiting for them there.

He returned to his car, opened the glove compartment, grabbed his pistol and loaded it. And then he stopped.

He put the pistol back into the glove compartment, stuck his hand inside his jacket pocket, and pulled out his wallet. Yes, there was a phone card. When driving through the neighbourhood earlier, he had noticed a phone booth a hundred or so yards before the house. Leaving the car where it was parked, he walked to the booth after lighting a cigarette. Miraculously, the phone worked. He stuck in the card and dialled a number.

*

A seventyish man striking the keys of a typewriter in the Roman night rose at once to his feet and went over to the phone looking worried. Who could it be at that hour?

'Hello! Who is this?'

'Montalbano here. What are you doing?'

'You don't know what I'm doing? I'm writing a story with you as the protagonist. I'm at the point where you're inside your car and have just loaded your gun. Where are you calling from?'

'A phone booth.'

'How did you get there?'

'None of your business.'

'Why did you call me?'

'Because I don't like this story. I don't want to go back into it. It's not me. This business of the fried eyes and stewed calf is totally ridiculous. Absolute rubbish, if you don't mind my saying so.'

'Salvo, I agree with you.'

'So why are you writing it?'

'Try to understand, son. Some people write that I am just a feel-good writer who tells only sugary, cosy stories; other say that the success I've enjoyed thanks to you hasn't been good for me and that I've become repetitive and care only about royalties . . . They claim I'm a facile writer, even if they break their heads trying to understand the way I write. I'm just trying to bring myself up to date, Salvo. A little blood on the page never hurt anyone. What, do you want to start splitting hairs? And let me ask you, since you're a true gourmet: have you ever actually tasted a pair of fried human eyes, perhaps with a little sauté of onions on top?'

'Don't try to be funny. And listen. I'm going to tell you something once and I'm not going to repeat it. To me, a story like this just isn't right. You're absolutely free to write others like it, but then you'll have to find another protagonist. Is that clear?'

'Perfectly. But meanwhile, how am I going to end this one?'

'Like this,' said the inspector.

And he hung up.

A KIDNAPPING

He was a true peasant, but he looked like a baby in a cot, with his beret squashed down on his head even inside the police station, his shapeless fustian suit, his hobnail boots of a kind that hadn't been seen around since the end of the Second World War. Seventy years old and gaunt, slightly hunched from a lifetime of working the mattock, one of the last remaining specimens of a vanishing breed, he had a pair of blue eyes that pleased Montalbano.

'You wanted to talk to me?'

'Yessir.'

'Take a seat,' said the inspector, gesturing towards a chair in front of his desk.

'Nossir. Iss no' gonna take very long.'

That was a relief. He must have been a man of few words, which was only proper for a genuine peasant.

'Consolato Damiano's my name,' he said.

Which was the surname? Consolato or Damiano? After a moment's doubt, the inspector decided that, in keeping with the rules of behaviour in the presence of a representative of the law, the peasant must have given his last name first, as was the norm, and then his first name.

'It's a pleasure to meet you. I'm listening, Mr Consolato.'

'You wanna talk to me formal-like or casual?' the peasant asked.

'Formally. I'm not in the habit of—'

'Well, then y'oughter know that my last name's Damiano.'

Montalbano felt a little irked at having guessed wrong.

'What can I do for you?'

'Yisterday mornin' I come down from the country into
town, seein' it was market day.'

The open-air market convened every Sunday morning in
the elevated part of Vigàta, near the cemetery that bordered
on an open countryside that was once all olive groves,
almond orchards, and vineyards and was now almost entirely uncultivated, invaded by increasingly vast stretches of
concrete, with and without planning permission.

Montalbano patiently waited for the man to continue.

'An' the donkey broke my *bùmmulu.*'

A *bùmmolo* was a terracotta jar that held water and kept
it very cold, and in the past peasants used to take one with
them when they went out to the fields to work. This confirmed Montalbano's impression that Consolato Damiano
was truly an old-style peasant. And in spite of the fact that
the story of the donkey and *bùmmolo* didn't seem to him the
sort of thing that might interest the police, he didn't say a
word, having decided to go along with the very slow flow of
Consolato's account.

'An' so, at the market, I bought myself a new one.'

So far, nothing out of the ordinary.

'Yisterday evenin', I put some water in it to try it out.
To see if it was cooked right, 'cuz if iss still raw, then it don't
keep the water cool.'

Montalbano lit a cigarette.

'So 'fore goin' a bed, I emptied it. An' when the water
come out, so did a piece o' paper that was inside the *bùmmulu.*'

Montalbano suddenly froze.

'I c'n read a little. Got as far as the third year.'

'Was it a note?' the inspector finally ventured to ask.

'Yes and no.'

Montalbano decided it was better to keep quiet and listen.

'It was a strip of paper torn off a newspaper. An' it was all wet. I put it next to the fire and dried it off.'

At that moment Mimì Augello poked his head inside the door.

'Salvo, don't forget that the commissioner's waiting for us.'

'Get me Fazio.'

The peasant waited politely. Fazio came in.

'This gentleman's name is Damiano Consolato. I want you to listen to what he has to say. Unfortunately I have to go out now. See you later.'

By the time he got back to the station, he'd forgotten entirely about the peasant and his *bùmmolo*. He went back out to the Trattoria San Calogero for lunch, wolfing down a good pound of baby octopus boiled and seasoned with salt, black pepper, olive oil, lemon, and parsley. They were so tender they melted in your mouth.

Back at the office, when he saw Fazio, he remembered about Consolato Damiano.

'So what did he want? The one with the *bùmmolo*.'

Fazio gave a little smile.

'Frankly, the whole thing seemed silly to me, which is why I didn't report back to you. He left me the piece of paper. It's the upper part of a page of newspaper from last year. You can read the date: 3 August 1997.'

'What newspaper is it?'

'That I don't know; the name's not visible.'

'Anything else?'

'Yes. There's also a few words written by hand. They say: "Help! He's going to kill me!" But—'

'And that seems silly to you?' Montalbano interrupted angrily. 'Let me see it.'

Fazio went out, came back, and handed Montalbano a little strip of paper. Written in block capitals and almost childish handwriting, it actually said: 'Halp! He gon kill me!'

'It must have been some joke somebody was trying to play on the old peasant,' a stubborn Fazio commented.

*

To a graphologist, certainly, handwriting speaks. And to Montalbano, who was not a graphologist, that ungrammatical handwriting also spoke: it represented a reality, an authentic cry for help. No joke at all, as Fazio maintained! This, however, was only an impression of his, nothing more. And that's why he decided it was best if he handled the matter himself, without involving his men. If his impression turned out to be wrong, he would be spared the snide smirks of Augello and company.

He recalled that the area where the market was held had been marked off and subdivided into compartments indicated by lines painted on the ground. Each compartment, moreover, had a number, to avoid disputes and quarrels among the merchants.

Montalbano went to the town hall and got lucky. The man in charge of allotting spaces at the market, Mr De Magistris, explained to him that there were only two compartments reserved for sellers of terracotta handicrafts. The first, which was number 8, was allotted to man named Giuseppe Tarantino. It was in the lower section of the market. The stand of the other seller of *bùmmoli* and *quartare*, a certain Antonio Fiorello, was in the upper part, the one closer to the cemetery, and had number 36.

'Mind you, Inspector, there's no saying that things on the ground will be the way they appear on my chart,' said De Magistris.

'Why not?'

'Because often the vendors will agree among themselves to exchange spots.'

'You mean the vendors of *bùmmuli*?'

'Not only. On the chart you might find, I dunno, that there's a greengrocer at number twenty, and then you go there and find someone selling shoes. Here we don't care, as long as they are in agreement and get along.'

*

He went back to the office, asked Fazio to explain to him how to get to Consolato Damiano's house, got in his car, and drove off. Contrada Ficuzza, where the peasant lived, was a secluded place between Vigàta and Montereale. To get there he had to park the car after about a half-hour drive and then walk for another half-hour or so. It was already dark by the time he arrived at a small farm. He made his way through a flock of chickens, and when within earshot of the door, he called out:

'Hey! Anybody home?'

'Who is it?' asked a voice from inside.

'Inspector Montalbano.'

Consolato Damiano appeared in the doorway, beret on his head, looking not the least bit surprised.

'Come on in,' he said.

The Damiano family were just sitting down to supper. There was an elderly woman whom Consolato introduced as Pina, his wife, a fortyish man, Filippo, their son, and his wife Gerlanda, around thirty and attending to their two small children, a boy and a girl. The room was spacious, and the part equipped as a kitchen had a wood oven.

'Would you like to join us?' Mrs Pina asked, getting up to bring another chair to the table. 'Tonight we're having some pasta with broccoli.'

Montalbano accepted. After the pasta, Mrs Pina went and pulled out of the oven half a roast suckling goat with potatoes, where she had been keeping it warm.

'You'll have to excuse us, Inspector. It's left over from yesterday, which was my son's fortieth birthday.'

It was exquisite, sweet and tender as a suckling goat is by nature, whether dead or alive. When they'd finished, seeing that nobody was asking him the reason for his visit, Montalbano spoke.

'Mr Damiano, do you by any chance remember which stand at the market you bought your *bùmmolo* from?'

'Of course I remember. The one closest to the cemetery.'

The compartment assigned to Tarantino. But had he exchanged places with Fiorello?

'Do you remember the vendor's name?'

'Yessir. His name's Pepè. I don' know his surname.'

Giuseppe. It could only be Giuseppe Tarantino. The whole thing could have been very easily resolved with a quick phone call. But if Consolato Damiano had had a phone, Montalbano would have missed the pasta with broccoli and the roast suckling goat.

✻

At the office he found Mimì Augello apparently waiting for him.

'What is it, Mimì? Look, in five minutes I'm going home. It's late and I'm tired.'

'Fazio told me the business about the *bùmmolo*. I guessed you wanted to work on it behind the scenes and not tell anybody.'

'You guessed right. What's your take on it?'

'The whole thing could just as easily be a serious matter as a waste of time. It might involve, for example, a kidnapping.'

'I'm of the same opinion. But there are certain factors that would tend to rule that out. It's been more than five years since there was a kidnapping for ransom around here.'

'Even more than that.'

'And last year there were no kidnappings of any kind reported.'

'That doesn't mean anything, Salvo. Maybe the kidnappers and the victim's relatives have managed to keep the news of the kidnapping and negotiations a secret.'

'I doubt it. Journalists nowadays know how many hairs you've got on your arse.'

'Then why are you saying it might be a kidnapping?'

'Not a kidnapping for monetary gain, Mimì. Have you forgotten the case of that worm who kidnapped a little boy to intimidate his father, who was planning to turn state's witness? He ended up strangling the kid and then putting him in acid.'

'I remember, I remember.'

'It could be something like that.'

'It could, Salvo. But then again, it could be that Fazio's right.'

'And that's why I don't want you guys in my hair. That way, if I'm wrong and the whole thing's a hoax, I'll be the only one laughing.'

✻

The following morning, he went back to the town hall at the crack of dawn.

'I've found out that the vendor of *bùmmuli* I'm interested in is named Giuseppe Tarantino. Could you give me his address?'

'Of course. Just one minute while I look at the files,' said De Magistris.

Less than five minutes later, he returned with a piece of paper in his hand.

'He lives in Calascibetta, in Via Alcide De Gasperi, number thirty-two. Do you want the phone number as well?'

✻

'Catarella, I want you to do me a special, important favour.'

'Chief, when y'ax me poissonally in poisson to do yiz a

favour poissonally in poisson, yer doin' me a favour jess by axin''

The baroque courtesies of Catarella.

'So, I want you to call this number. Somebody named Giuseppe or Pepè Tarantino will answer. Without telling him you're from the police, you're to ask him if he'll be home this afternoon.'

Catarella looked confused, clutching the little piece of paper with the number between his forefinger and thumb and holding his arm a short distance away from his body, as if the piece of a paper were some kind of repulsive animal.

'Is there something you don't understand, Cat?'

'Well, iss not azackly clear.'

'What's not exactly clear?'

'How's I asposta act if the man 'at ansers the phone is Pepè isstead o' Giuseppe?'

'It's the same person, Cat.'

'An' wha' if it in't neeter Giuseppe or Pepè 'at ansers the phone, but summon else?'

'You tell them to put Giuseppe or Pepè on.'

'An' wha' if Giuseppe Pepè in't there?'

'You say "thank you" and hang up.'

The inspector was about to go out when a doubt over-came him.

'Cat, why don't you tell me what you're going to say over the phone?'

'Straightaways, Chief. "Hallo?" axes the guy. "Lissen," I says, "if you's called Giuseppe or Pepè, iss the same ting." "Who's this?" axes the guy. "You jess fughettabout whoozz-iss 'ass talkin' t'yiz in poisson. An' I'm not wit' the police. Gott 'at? So: by order o' Mister Isspecter Montalbano, you can't leave yer home dis aftanoon." Izzat awright, Chief?'

In his throat Montalbano felt a scream of rage rise up, enough to shatter glass, but, sweating from the effort, he managed to suppress it.

'So iss not awright, Chief?'

Catarella's voice was trembling, and his eyes looked like those of a lamb before slaughter. Montalbano felt sorry for him.

'No, Cat, it's fine. But I decided that maybe it's better if I call. Give me back the piece of paper with the number.'

A woman answered after the second ring. She sounded young.

'Mrs Tarantino?'

'Yes, who's this?'

'This is De Magistris at Vigàta Town Hall, in charge of—'

'My husband isn't here.'

'But is he in Calascibetta?'

'Yes.'

'Will he be home for lunch?'

'Yes. But if you could tell me—'

'Thanks. I'll call back this afternoon.'

*

What with one thing and another it got to be well past eleven before he could finally get in the car and head for Calascibetta. Via Alcide De Gasperi was a little out of the way; number 32 corresponded to a sort of large courtyard packed full with hundreds of *bùmmuli*, *bummuliddri*, pots, amphorae, and jugs. There was even a broken down little truck. Tarantino's house of unplastered tufa stone consisted of three rooms in a row on the ground floor at the far end of the courtyard. The front door was closed. Montalbano knocked with his fist, since there was no doorbell. A young man a bit over thirty came and opened the door.

'Good afternoon. Are you Giuseppe Tarantino?'

'Yes. And who are you?'

'I'm De Magistris. I phoned this morning.'

'Yeah, my wife told me. What do you want?'

Montalbano had forgotten to think of an excuse on the

way there. Tarantino took advantage of his momentary un-
certainty.

'I've paid my taxes, and my licence is still valid.'

'We know that already.'

'So what is it?'

The man was neither overly hostile nor overly suspicious. Somewhere in between. Maybe he wasn't thrilled to
have a stranger interrupt his meal. A strong scent of ragù
wafted out from the house.

'Have the gentleman come in,' said a woman's voice from
inside, the same one that had answered the phone.

The man seemed not to have heard her.

'So, what is it?'

'Where's your workshop?'

'What workshop?'

'Where you work the clay. You know, the kiln, the—'

'You're misinformed. I don't make my own jugs and
bùmmuli. I buy them wholesale, and I get a good price for
them. Then I go round to the different markets and sell
them and I make a little money.'

At that moment they heard the shrill cry of a newborn.

'The baby just woke up,' Tarantino said to Montalbano,
as if to hurry him.

'I'll be on my way. Just give me the address of the workshop.'

'It's called Marcuzzo and Sons, in the Vaccarella district
near Catello. It's about twenty-five miles from here. Have a
good day.'

He shut the door in his face. The inspector would never
get to taste Tarantino's wife's ragù.

*

He drove around Catello and environs for two hours, but
nobody could tell him how to get to Vaccarella. And
nobody had ever heard of a clay works called Marcuzzo
and Sons that made jugs and *bùmmuli*. How could they not

know? Or was it because they'd sniffed him out as a police-man and didn't want to help? He made the difficult decision to go to the local carabinieri compound. He told the whole story to a marshal there, named Pennisi. When Montalbano had finished talking, Pennisi asked:

'What do you want from the Marcuzzos?'

'I couldn't really tell you, Marshal. I'm sure you know more about them than I do.'

'I've only got good things to say about the Marcuzzos. Their clay works was built by the father of the current owner, Aurelio, at the start of this century. Aurelio has two sons, both married, and at least ten grandchildren. They all live together, in a big house next to the factory. Do you really think they could keep a kidnap victim in a place with a good ten children running around? No, they're very honest, serious people, respected by everyone.'

'All right, Marshal, forget I ever mentioned it. But let me ask you a different sort of question. Do you think that someone who was perhaps kidnapped or threatened could have slipped that piece of paper into a *bùmmolo* without the Marcuzzos finding out?'

'Let *me* ask *you* a question, Inspector. What would a kidnap victim or someone whose life has been threatened be doing around the Marcuzzos' factory? Any criminal who knew what the Marcuzzos are like would have known to stay away.'

'Do they have any employees, any workers?'

'Nobody. Everything's done within the family. Even the women work.'

Then something clearly occurred to the marshal.

'Was there a date on that piece of newspaper?' he asked.

'It's from August the third of last year.'

'The factory was most certainly closed at that time.'

'How do you know?'

'I've been living here for five years. And for five years the factory has closed on the first of August and re-opened on the twenty-fifth. I know this because every year Aurelio phones me and tells me they're leaving. They all go to Calabria, to the house of the eldest son's wife.'

'I'm sorry, but why do they tell you they're leaving?'

'Because if one of my men happens to be passing by, he can keep an eye on things. Just to be safe.'

'And where do they keep their finished products when they're away?'

'In a large warehouse behind the house. With an iron-clad door. They've never been robbed.'

The inspector sat there in silence. Then he spoke.

'Could you do me a favour, Marshal? Could you call one of the Marcuzzos and ask him on what day last year he made a delivery to a certain market vendor just before he closed for August? The vendor's name is Giuseppe Tarantino; he says he's a client of theirs.'

Pennisi had to stay on the line for about ten minutes after making the request. Apparently they had to leaf through old registers. At last the marshal thanked them and hung up.

'The last delivery to Tarantino was made on the afternoon of July the thirty-first. After their holiday, they made other deliveries to him, one on the—'

'Thank you, Marshal. That's all I need.'

Therefore the note was slipped into the *bùmmulo* after it was already in Tarantino's possession — and stored in a place unprotected and accessible to everyone. Montalbano grew discouraged.

*

Turning the whole affair over and over in his head on the drive back to Vigàta, he became convinced he would never get to the bottom of it. The realization put him in a bad mood. He took it out on Gallo, who hadn't done something he'd told him to do. The telephone rang. It was Catarella calling from the switchboard.

'Chief? Iss a Mr Dimastrissi wants a talk t'yiz poissonally in poisson.'

'Where is he?'

'Dunno, Chief. I'll axe 'im where 'e is.'

'No, Cat. I just want to know whether he's here at the
station or on the telephone.'

''E's onna tiliphone, Chief.'

'Put him through . . . Hello?'

'Inspector Montalbano? This is De Magistris, you
know, the clerk at the—'

'What can I do for you?'

'Well, sorry for asking, really, but . . . did you, by any
chance, go to see Tarantino, the pottery vendor, saying you
were me?'

'Er, yes. But, you see . . .'

'No problem, Inspector, that's all I wanted to know.
Thank you.'

'Wait a second, if you don't mind. How did you find
out?'

'I got a call, at the town hall, from a young woman who
said she was this Tarantino's wife. She wanted to know the
real reason why I went to their house at lunchtime. I was so
taken aback, she must have realized she'd made a mistake,
and she immediately hung up. I just wanted to let you know.'

*

Why had she been so worried about the surprise visit? Or
was it her husband who'd put her up to making that call, to
find out more? Whatever the case, her phone call cast the
whole thing into doubt again. The game was starting again.
The piece of paper with Tarantino's phone number was on
the desk. He didn't want to waste any more time. The wife
answered.

'Mrs Tarantino? This is De Magistris.'

'No, you're not De Magistris. You have a different voice.'

'All right, signora. I'm Inspector Montalbano of Vigàta police. Let me speak to your husband.'

'He's not here. He left for the market at Capofelice just after lunch. He'll be back in two days.'

'Signora, I need to talk to you. I'm going to get in the car now and come.'

'No! For heaven's sake! Don't let anyone in town see you in the daytime!'

'What time do you want me to come and see you?'

'Tonight. After midnight. When there's nobody around on the street any more. And, please, park your car a long way from my house. And don't let anyone see you when you come to my place. Please.'

'Don't worry, signora. I'll be invisible.'

Before hanging up, he heard her sob.

*

The door was ajar, the house in darkness. He slipped in quickly, like a lover, then closed the door behind him.

'Can I turn the light on?'

'Yes.'

He fumbled around for the switch. The light revealed a humble living room: a small sofa, a little coffee table, two armchairs, two chairs, and a set of shelves. She was sitting on the sofa, face buried in her hands, elbows on her knees. She was trembling.

'Don't be afraid,' said Montalbano, standing motionless by the door. 'If you prefer, I'll go back to where I came from.'

'No.'

Montalbano took two steps and sat down in an armchair. The girl then sat up and looked him straight in the eye.

'Sara's my name.'

She might not even have been twenty yet. She was tiny,

delicate, with a frightened look in her eyes, like a little girl waiting to be punished.

'What do you want from my husband?'

Odds or evens? Heads or tails? How should he approach this? Beat around the bush or get straight to the point? Naturally, he did neither – though not, of course, out of any clever stratagem on his part, but simply because he suddenly found himself saying:

'Why are you so scared, Sara? What are you afraid of? Why did you want me to take all those precautions before coming to see you? Nobody knows me in this town. They don't know who I am or what I do.'

'But you're a man. And Pepè, my husband, is jealous. He can get crazy with jealousy. An' if he ever finds out that a man came in here, he gon' kill me.'

That was exactly the way she said it: *he gon' kill me*. And Montalbano thought: *So you also wrote: Halp!* He sighed, stretched his legs, and leaned back in the armchair, getting comfortable. So that was it. No kidnapping, nobody threatened with murder. So much the better.

'Why did you write that note and put it in the *bùmmulo*?'

'He'd beat the shit outta me an' then tied me to the bed with rope from the well. An' kep' me like that for two days an' two nights.'

'What had you done?'

'Nuthin'. Some guy came by, sellin' stuff, knocked at the door, an' I opened an' was tellin' 'im I didn't want nuthin' when Pepè come back, seein' me talkin' to this man. It was like he went crazy.'

'And afterwards? After he untied you?'

'He kep' beatin' me. I couldn't walk. An' since he had to leave to go to market, he tol' me to load the *bùmmuli* onto the truck. An' so I grabbed a newspaper an' ripped off five li'l strips an' wrote five notes, which I put into five different *bùmmuli*. Before leavin', he tied me back to the bed. But that time I managed to get free. It took me two days, an' I was really weak. Then I stood up, went straight into the kitchen, grabbed a knife, and slashed my wrists.'

'Why didn't you run away?'

'Because I love him.'

Simple as that.

'When he come back he foun' me bleedin' to death and took me to the hospital. I tol' him I did it 'cuz my mother died the week before, an' it was true. Three days later they sent me home. Pepè was changed. An' that night I got pregnant with my son.'

She was blushing and keeping her eyes lowered.

'And since then he hasn't beaten you?'

'Nossir. Sometime he still gets jealous an' he smashes everything around him, but he don't touch me no more. But then I started gettin' scared o' somethin' else, so's I couldn't sleep at night.'

'And what was that?'

'I's scared someone was gonna find the notes I left, now that things was all better. Cuz if Pepè ever found out that I was askin' for help to get away from him, he might . . .'

'Start beating you again?'

'No, Inspector, sir. He might leave me.'

Montalbano took this in.

'I managed to get four of 'em back, cuz they was still inside the *bùmmuli*. But I never foun' the fifth. Then you came here, an' after I talked to the man at town hall an' realized you used a fake name, I knew the police ha' foun' the note an' they might call Pepè thinkin' God knows what . . .'

'I'm going to go, Sara,' said Montalbano, standing up.

In the other room, the baby started crying.

'Could I see him?' asked Montalbano.

MONTALBANO AFRAID

He realized at once, the moment they sat down at the restaurant table, that Matteo Castellini the engineer was bad news. Castellini's wife Stefania, Livia's bosom friend, a fortyish brunette who spoke at the right moments and said intelligent things, was at least tolerable, if not quite charming. But the engineer, from the very first moment, had raised Montalbano's hackles. He'd shown up to dinner dressed all in white, a bit like the ice-cream man except that his tie tended a little towards ivory. Holding out his hand, Montalbano could hardly refrain from asking him:

'Dr Livingstone, I presume?'

Upon finishing his first course, a seafood risotto that had looked good to Montalbano, the engineer dived in.

'Well, let's get down to the matter at hand,' he said.

So there was a matter at hand? Livia hadn't told him anything about this. He gave her a questioning glance, and she replied with a look so imploring that the inspector promised himself that, no matter what this 'matter' turned out to be, he would restrain himself and not let the encounter take a bad turn, even though Livia had practically had to drag him there in chains.

'You know,' said Castellini, 'I've been begging Stefania for a long time to arrange a meeting between us. We share a common interest, and I envy you a great deal.'

'Why?'

'Because you are in a privileged position, with the observatory you have.'

'I am? What observatory do you mean?'

'The Vigàta police station.'

Montalbano hesitated. The Vigàta police station, a privileged observatory? Four ratty rooms inhabited by characters like the raving Catarella and Mimì Augello, who was always chasing after every woman who walked by? He glanced over at Livia, but she was deeply engrossed in conversation with her friend Stefania. The inspector could have sworn she was faking it.

'Absolutely,' Castellini continued. 'I design and build bridges. All over the world, in all modesty. But you can't find the man in a slab of reinforced concrete.'

Was he speaking seriously or joking? Montalbano gave him some rope.

'Well, in our part of the country, we used to do just that, every now and then.'

This time it was the engineer who hesitated.

'Really?'

'Of course. It was one of the ways the Mafia got rid of—'

'No, perhaps I didn't make myself clear,' Castellini interrupted him. 'You see, Inspector, I never wanted to become an engineer. I would have preferred to work in analysis.'

'Chemical analysis?'

'No, psychoanalysis.'

Montalbano was finally beginning to understand.

'Well, I'm sorry to disappoint you, but the Vigàta police isn't really the best place for . . .'

Could you imagine Catarella sitting beside a couch, listening to someone who'd stolen a handful of spinach?

'I know, I know. But still, you're in an excellent position to probe!' said the engineer, eyes lighting up.

He'd spoken so loudly that even Livia and Stefania had interrupted their conversation to look at him.

'To probe what?'

'Why, the human soul, of course! Its depths, its complexity, its tortured nature!'

Ah, so that was it. The engineer belonged to that category of people who wallowed beatifically in matters beginning in *psy-*. Psychology, psychoanalysis, psychiatry . . . Montalbano decided to give him rope.

'You mean to descend into its abysses?'

'Yes.'

'To explore their intricate labyrinths?'

'Yes, exactly.'

'Travel their dark meanders? Unravel their tangled webs? Their inscrutable—'

'Yes, yes, yes!' Castellini gasped, a mere step away from orgasm.

A kick from Livia under the table made Montalbano shut up. Luckily, since his repertoire of clichés and commonplaces was somewhat limited. Livia took advantage of the pause.

'You know, Matteo . . .'

Her sweet tone of voice made Montalbano suspicious. Whenever she spoke that way, it meant she was about to spray black ink like a squid – which was in fact what the waiter was serving them at that moment.

'. . . what you say is true. Salvo could do that, but he doesn't go that far. He stops at the evidence.'

'What do you mean?' said Montalbano, miffed.

'Exactly what I said. You always stop at a certain level – the one necessary for solving your investigations. Maybe you're afraid to look beyond it.'

She was trying to hurt his feelings, clearly. She was getting back at him for scurrilously mocking the engineer. Even Stefania seemed taken aback by her friend's comment.

'It's not my job. I'm not a priest, nor a psychologist or analyst. Now, if you'll excuse me . . .'

And he dived into the aromas and flavours of the squid,

which were cooked just right. After a few moments of silence, the engineer started talking about *Crime and Punishment*, which he said he'd reread 'in the silent darkness of the Yemeni night'. In his opinion, Dostoevsky was quite wanting in matters of psychology . . .

When it was time to say goodbye, Stefania took a set of keys out of her purse and handed them to Livia.

'Are you leaving tomorrow?'

Leaving? Where to? He'd barely been a week on holiday in Boccadasse and had no desire to go anywhere else.

'What's this business about leaving?' he asked Livia as she started up the car.

'Stefania and Matteo were kind enough to lend us their house in the mountains for a few days.'

Jesus Christ! The mountains! Montalbano was a man of the sea. It was just the way he was, through no fault of his own. The moment he was over fifteen hundred feet above sea-level he started to turn surly, ready to have it out at the slightest excuse, and sometimes he succumbed to bouts of melancholy that made him even more taciturn and solitary than he normally was. Of course there was no question the mountains were beautiful, but so was the sea. And what's more, Livia had unfairly taken him by surprise, worse than Gano di Maganza at the puppet theatre.

'Why didn't you tell me when I got here that you were planning to drag me off to the mountains?'

'Drag you off! What a sob story you're making it into! It's very simple. I didn't tell you because we would have spent every day arguing about it.'

'But what need is there to leave Boccadasse one week before the end of the holiday?'

'Because you come to Boccadasse to spend your holiday, whereas I live here. Got that? This is your holiday, not mine. And I decided that we will spend *our* holiday where I say so.'

'Could you at least tell me where this house is?'

'Above Courmayeur.'

Above? Amidst the eternal glaciers and the inviolate peaks, as the engineer Castellini would certainly have put it? The inspector shivered.

The spat was a long one, though Montalbano knew from the start that he'd lost. Then, before going to bed, they made peace. Later still, lying with eyes open, staring at the dim light filtering through the open window and hearing the sleeping Livia's rhythmical breathing, which blended with that of the sea, Montalbano at last felt at peace, ready to face the polar bears surely thriving across the ice floes above Courmayeur.

✽

The whole way there, for all those hours, Livia refused to let Montalbano drive. She wouldn't listen to reason.

'Come on, let me drive. Why do you want to tire yourself out?'

'You said I wanted to drag you off to the mountains. Well, now let yourself be dragged and shut up.'

Since, what with one thing and the next, they'd left Boccadasse rather late in the day and had even encountered traffic, Montalbano, seeing the sun go down, weighed his options and decided that the best thing to do was to take a nap. He was awakened by Livia's voice.

'Let's go, Salvo, we're here.'

Getting out of the car, he noticed that, except for the area lit up by the headlights, it was pitch black all around and that, to judge by his ears and nose, there wasn't a trace of human life anywhere nearby. The car was parked in a clearing, at one end of which a small path led almost vertically upwards, to some godforsaken place.

'Come on, don't just stand there in a daze . . . Grab your backpack and put on a heavy sweater.'

Livia had lent him the backpack, of course, though the sweater was his own, something he'd left in Boccadasse the previous winter. When the headlights suddenly went off,

Montalbano had the unpleasant sensation of being swallowed up by the night. He felt distressed. Livia turned on a torch and aimed it in the direction of the path.

'Follow behind me, and be careful not to slip.'

'How far away is the house?'

'About a hundred yards.'

After the first fifty, the inspector realized that a hundred yards at the seaside is one thing, while a hundred yards up the mountain are another thing altogether. And it was a good thing he was struggling uphill, otherwise the cold would have given him a heart attack in spite of the sweater. First he slipped, then he stumbled.

'Try to get there alive,' said Livia, who for her part was spry as a goat.

At last the path ended at a clearing. From the outside, there wasn't much Montalbano could tell about the house. It looked like thousands of other two-storey Alpine chalets. Inside, however, everything changed. The double door opened onto a vast living room with dark-brown wooden country furniture, massive and reassuring, a television, a telephone, and a spacious fireplace in the far wall. Also on the ground floor were a bathroom and a small kitchen with a huge refrigerator so stuffed with food they could have opened a grocer's shop. Upstairs were two bedrooms whose French windows gave onto a common terrace, as well as another bathroom. The inspector immediately liked the place.

'Do you like it?' Livia asked.

'Mm-hmm,' was all he said, not wanting to give her the satisfaction. And he added: 'It's cold in here.'

'I'll go and turn on the heating. You'll see, in ten minutes you'll be just fine. Meanwhile, I'll go and get you one of Matteo's heavy jackets.'

One of Castellini's jackets? He would rather freeze to death.

'No, no, it's all right. I'll be fine in a minute.'

And indeed, a minute later he was fine. And an hour

after that, he even sated the wolflike appetite the fresh air and climb had stirred up, emptying practically half of the refrigerator. Then they settled into the comfortable couch and Livia turned on the TV. By mutual consent, they decided to watch an American movie about a rich landowner in the South with a twenty-year-old daughter who was in love with one of the farmhands, which the father didn't appreciate one bit. Montalbano immediately fell asleep on Livia's shoulder, and when, ninety minutes later, she got up to turn off the television, he collapsed sideways on the couch, waking up in confusion.

'I'm going to bed. Thanks for the lovely evening,' Livia said sarcastically, starting up the stairs towards the bedroom.

*

He slept for seven hours straight, waking up in the same position he'd lain down in. Beside him, Livia appeared to have every intention of travelling a good deal more through ever new and scattered lands in the country of sleep. He got up, went downstairs, made a pot of coffee, had a shower, got dressed, opened the front door, and went outside. Without warning, he found himself inside an almost pitilessly beautiful day, with violent colours, blinding snow, and Mont Blanc looming so vast over his head that he felt slightly afraid. Then, at once, the stabbing cold attacked him, its frigid blades cutting his face, neck, and hands. Pulling himself together, he went behind the house, stopping under the bedroom balcony. A few yards away was a path that went up the side of the mountain and quickly vanished amidst the trees. It was a sort of invitation, and Montalbano, for no apparent reason, decided to accept it. Going back inside, he tiptoed into Matteo and Stefania's bedroom, opened the wardrobe, found a parka and a heavier sweater, put them on, took a pair of hiking boots from a shoe-rack, put these on, went back downstairs into the kitchen, and wrote a note for Livia: *I've gone out for a walk*. Then he put a sort of giant sock of heavy wool over his head and went out, locking the door behind him. Before heading off, he made sure he had his cigarettes and lighter in the parka's pocket. In the other pocket was a pair of gloves, which he put on.

After walking for about half an hour, feeling his lungs expand with each step, he found himself before a fork in the path and decided to turn right. He knew he was climbing, but he didn't feel tired. On the contrary, he felt a sort of increasing weightlessness, a lightness of body and mind. There were no more trees, only rock. At one point he sat down on a boulder before heading round a bend in the trail. He wanted to enjoy the view. Sticking a hand in his pocket, he pulled out the pack of cigarettes, lit one, took two puffs, then put it out. He didn't feel like smoking. Glancing at his watch, he gave a start. He'd been walking for an hour and a half without realizing it. He thought it best to go back. Livia might get worried if he was late. But before beginning his descent, he decided to go just a little bit further, past the bend that hid part of the landscape from view. And suddenly everything changed. Here the mountain appeared as it really was: rough, hard, and so harsh as to inspire a sort of fearful respect. The path became more arduous, squeezed as it was between a wall of rock and a sheer drop of dizzying height. Montalbano didn't suffer from vertigo, but at once, at the mere sight of the void before him, he instinctively recoiled against the rock face. Leaning back against the stone, he looked out over the mountaintops, down at the houses in the valley, which looked like little dice, at the snaking river disappearing and re-emerging behind the rises in the landscape. It certainly was beautiful, as far as that went, no doubt about it. But he felt rather out of place, like an awkward alien bewildered by a world not his own. He turned about to go back round the bend and head home, but then suddenly stopped. He thought he'd heard a human voice. Though he hadn't understood what the voice was saying, he'd grasped a sort of desperate tone in it. He pricked up his ears, all tense.

'. . . elll . . . lp!'

He turned back around. And heard the voice again.

'. . . ellllp! . . . elllp!'

He took three steps forward, certain that the voice was coming from somewhere around the sheer drop. Carefully approaching the edge of the path, he stuck his head out to look. Some twenty yards ahead, just below the trail, the rock jutted out, forming a sort of tiny bank over the abyss. And there, lying stomach-down, was a person, head hidden by a parka, making it impossible to tell whether it was a man or woman, holding a woman by the wrists, to keep her from plummeting into the void. Luckily the woman had managed to wedge her left foot into a crack in the rock face, otherwise the person holding her would not have been able to keep it up for very long. The scene immediately appeared so tragic to Montalbano that it seemed unreal, to the point that he was about to look around to see where the floodlights and movie cameras were placed. And without him realizing it, in a flash his legs brought him to a spot directly above the two unfortunate souls, where he noticed some five or six stairs cut directly into the rock; then he dashed down these and found himself behind the prostrate person. It was a man, and he'd heard the inspector come up behind him.

'Help,' he said.

He hardly had any voice left and, on top of that, his mouth was buried in his sweater and pressed against the ground.

'Can you hear me?' Montalbano asked, lying down beside him and removing his gloves. He looked down at the woman, whose eyes were squeezed shut. Her face had turned white as the surrounding snow, and her lipstick was smeared, making her look like a clown.

'Hang on!' the inspector shouted to her.

The woman kept her eyes shut, and was as still as a

statue. Montalbano dug himself firmly into the ground and said to the man:

'Now listen to me. I'm going to grab her left wrist with both hands. You do the same with her right wrist. Together we should be able to lift her up. Did you hear me? Do you understand?'

'Yes.'

Montalbano grabbed her left wrist. The man let go and wrapped both hands around her right.

'Got a good grip?'

'Yes.'

'Now I'm going to start counting. At the count of three, we're going to lift her up at the same time. Ready? One, two, three!'

Not an easy task to begin with, it was made more difficult by something the inspector hadn't taken into account, which was that the woman, as soon as she felt herself being lifted up, stiffened instinctively, making herself heavier, terrified at finding herself dangling in the void and keeping her foot wedged in the crack in the rock. Montalbano and the man had to execute complicated manoeuvres and counter-manoeuvres while panting heavily and rapidly losing their breath. Among other things, the inspector was convinced that the man, exhausted from the strain, would suddenly let go. Would he manage all by himself to lift the woman, who luckily was rather petite?

By the grace of God, some fifteen minutes later they were all lying on their backs on the embankment. The woman was moaning weakly, having probably broken a few ribs, and still kept her eyes tightly shut. She was young, around thirty. The man, who looked about forty, was breathing with his mouth open and making a snoring sound. The clothes they had on were visibly high-end, designer stuff. Montalbano rolled over until he was at the girl's side. Her face was still very white, the blood still having trouble returning.

'Signora, don't be afraid. It's all over. Open your eyes and look at me.'

Very slowly, the woman shook her head. The man was staring at him, apparently still in no condition to move.

'Do you have a mobile phone?' Montalbano asked.

The man gestured towards the inside pocket of his parka. Montalbano unzipped it and took the phone. But whom could he call? The man understood, asked for the phone back, propped himself up on one elbow, dialled a number, and started talking.

'Salvo!'

It was Livia's voice. Montalbano felt overjoyed. Apparently it had all been a nightmare, and Livia was now waking him up. None of it was true, it was all a dream.

'Salvo!'

He looked up. Livia was on the footpath above, eyeing him, spellbound. Then she came down to the embankment in a single bound. She was wild-eyed and short of breath. The inspector quickly told her what had happened.

'Go back home. I'll stay here with them.'

There was no way to make her change her mind.

'We'll sort things out later,' she added, as Montalbano was walking away.

*

Back at the house, the inspector stripped naked and took a shower to wash away the sweat on his skin. Then, without even bothering to put on his underpants, he sat down on the sofa, opened a brand-new bottle of whisky, determined to drink at least half of it.

He was still there when Livia returned four hours later. He'd drunk three-quarters of the bottle.

'Stand up!'

'Yes, sir!' said Montalbano, standing at attention. The slap Livia dealt him sent him falling, stunned, back onto the couch.

'Why'd you do that?' he asked, thick-tongued.

'Because you nearly scared me to death this morning when you didn't come back. You're an idiot!'

'I'm a hero! I saved—'

'Heroes can be idiots, too. And you're one of them. Now go and get some sleep. I'll wake you up later.'

'Yes, sir.'

＊

'Their names are Silvio and Giulia Dalbono, they've been married five years, and have a house on the other side of the mountain. He owns a factory in Turin, but they come here whenever they can.'

Montalbano was savouring a sort of lard, at once subtle and strong, that melted the moment he put it between his tongue and palate.

'I talked to the husband while they were examining the woman, who has two broken ribs. They were out for a perfectly normal hike and she wanted to go out onto the ledge, where she inexplicably fell. It may have been a momentary malaise, or a dizzy spell, or maybe just a misstep. Fortunately she managed to grab the edge as she was falling, just enough so that her husband could grab her wrists. Then, of course, you came along. He asked me about you. Who you are, what you do. He was impressed by your calmness. I think he's going to come by tomorrow to thank you. Are you listening to me?'

'Absolutely,' said Montalbano, slipping another slice of that sort of lard into his mouth.

Indignant, Livia fell silent. Not till the end of the meal did the inspector deign to ask a question.

'Has she opened her eyes?'

'Who?'

'Giulia. That's her name, isn't it? Has she opened her eyes?'

Livia gave him a look of surprise.

'How did you know? No, she won't open her eyes. She refuses. The doctors say she's still in shock.'

'I see.'

They sat down on the sofa.

'Feel like watching TV?'

'No.'

'What do you want to do?'

'I'll show you in a second.'

When she understood Salvo's intentions, Livia protested, but only half-heartedly.

'Let's go upstairs at least . . .' she said.

'No, this is where you slapped me, and this is where you'll expiate your sin.'

'Yes, sir,' said Livia.

*

The following morning he woke up at seven, and at eight he opened the door to go outside.

'Salvo!'

It was Livia, still in bed, calling him from upstairs. How could that be? Just ten minutes ago she was sleeping like a sack of potatoes!

'What is it?'

'What are you doing?'

'I'm going out for a little walk.'

'No! Wait, I'm coming with you. Just give me fifteen minutes and I'll be ready.'

'All right, I'll wait for you outside.'

'Don't go far.'

He felt furious. She treated him like a silly child! He went out. The day looked like a duplicate of the day before, crisp and dazzling. In the parking area stood a man, apparently waiting for him. He recognized him at once. It was Silvio Dalbono. He was unshaven, with dark circles under his eyes.

'How is your wife doing?'

'Much better, thank you. I spent the night at the hospital and came directly here. I was waiting for—'

'For her finally to open her eyes?'

The man gave him a look of amazement, opened his mouth, closed it again, and swallowed. He tried to smile.

'I knew you were a good detective, but that's very impressive! How did you work it out?'

'I didn't work anything out,' Montalbano said bluntly. 'I only noticed two things that didn't seem to make sense. The first was that your wife was obstinately keeping her eyes shut. At first, when we were holding her suspended over the void, I thought it was a kind of refusal to acknowledge the terrible situation she was in. But then she kept her eyes closed even after she was safe, and even in the hospital. And so I became convinced she was refusing to acknowledge your presence. The second thing was that when you were lying next to one another on the embankment, safe and sound at last, not only did you not embrace, you didn't even touch one another.'

'Believe me, I certainly didn't try to—'

'I believe you.'

'We've always walked past that ledge on our hikes. And yesterday morning, Giulia ran ahead, went down those few steps and then, as I was still on the path, I heard her cry out. She was gone. I went down, and that's when I saw . . .'

He trailed off, dug a handkerchief out of his jacket pocket, wiped away the profuse sweat glistening on his face. Then he resumed speaking, no longer looking the inspector in the eye.

'I saw her hands clutching a rocky spur along the edge. She called me once, then again, then a third time . . . I just stood there, silent, immobile, paralysed. The solution was right in front of my eyes.'

'You wanted to take advantage of the situation to be rid of her?'

'Yes.'

'Do you have another woman?'

'For the past two years.'

'Did your wife suspect it?'

'No, absolutely not. But at that moment, there, she finally understood. She understood because I didn't answer her cry for help. Then she suddenly fell silent. It was . . . it was terrifying, that silence, unbearable. And that was when I ran and grabbed her wrists. We . . . looked at each other. Endlessly. And then, at one point, she closed her eyes. And so I . . .'

Suddenly, for no apparent reason, Montalbano found himself back on the ledge over the sheer drop, and he saw the woman's face again, desperate, looking up like somebody drowning . . . And for the first time in his life he felt a sense of vertigo.

'That's enough,' he said gruffly.

The man stared at him, bewildered by the inspector's tone.

'I just wanted to explain . . . to thank you . . .'

'There's nothing to explain, nothing to thank me for. Go back to your wife. Good day.'

'Good day,' said the man.

He turned around and started descending the path.

✳

It was true. Livia was right. He was afraid. Afraid to plunge into the 'abysses of the human soul', as that imbecile Matteo Castellini had put it. He was scared because he knew perfectly well that, once he'd reached the bottom of one of those sheer drops, he would inevitably find a mirror. Reflecting his own face.

BETTER THE DARKNESS

1

At the crack of dawn, between sleep and waking, he'd distinctly heard the sound of water entering the storage tanks located on the roof of his little house in Marinella. Since the municipality of Vigàta deigned to bestow water on its citizens once every three days, the sound meant that Montalbano would again be able to take a proper shower. And in fact, after making coffee and reverently drinking his first cup, he rocketed into the bathroom and turned the water on full blast. He lathered himself up, rinsed, sang the entire triumphal march from *Aida* off key, and as he was reaching for the towel the telephone rang. He ran out of the bathroom naked, dripping water all over the floor — which his housekeeper would make him pay for later, probably by not leaving any food for him in the fridge or the oven — and picked up the receiver. There was only a dialling tone. Then why was the telephone still ringing? He suddenly realized it wasn't the phone, but the doorbell. He looked at the clock on the shelf in the dining room: it wasn't even 8 a.m. yet. Who could be knocking at his front door at that hour if not one of his men from the station? For them to come and bother him this way, it must be something serious. He went and opened the door just as he was. And when the priest who was waiting outside saw him there naked, he leapt backwards, speechless.

'I . . . I'm sorry,' he said.

'I . . . I'm sorry,' the inspector echoed him, equally flummoxed, trying awkwardly to cover his pudenda with his left
hand, which wasn't enough.

The priest did not realize it, but despite the embarrass-
ing situation, he'd already scored a point in his own favour
in Montalbano's eyes. Because the inspector couldn't stand
priests who dressed in civilian clothes, whether jeans and
sweater or jacket and trousers. It was as if they were trying
to hide, to camouflage themselves. This one in the doorway,
a slender, distinguished-looking man of about forty, was
wearing a cassock and looked like someone who knew what
was what.

'Why don't you come in while I get dressed,' said Montalbano, disappearing into the bathroom.

When he came out, he found his visitor standing on the
veranda, gazing at the sea. The morning was shaping up to
be crisp and colourful.

'Can we talk out here?' the priest asked.

'Of course,' the inspector replied, marking another point
in the priest's favour.

'I'm Don Luigi Barbera.'

They shook hands. Montalbano asked him if he wanted
some coffee, but he declined. The inspector's own desire for
a second cup faded when he noticed that the priest looked
agitated, as though anxious to tell him what he'd come to
tell him and at the same time reluctant to broach the
subject.

'What can I do for you?' the inspector prodded him.

'I came looking for you at police headquarters, but you
hadn't come in yet. One of your men was kind enough to
explain to me where you live, and so I took the liberty of
coming here.'

Montalbano said nothing.

'It's a delicate matter.'

The inspector noticed that the priest's forehead was now shiny with sweat.

'A week ago . . . a person . . . who's dying, wanted to confess. And this person revealed a secret to me. A grave misdeed, for which an innocent is paying the price. Well, I persuaded this person to get rid of this burden – to talk about it not only with God but with fellow humans. It wasn't easy. I encountered fierce resistance, outright rebellion. Finally, last night, with God's help, my powers of persuasion prevailed. Since I know you by reputation, I thought you might be the right person to . . .'

'To what?' Montalbano asked rudely.

Was this priest kidding, first thing in the morning? To begin with, Montalbano didn't like serial novels and would never let himself be dragged into one. And this whole business seemed just like a serial novel from the simple mention of a secret, a grave misdeed, an innocent in prison . . . And he was more than certain the rest of the repertoire would follow: the mistreated little orphan girl, the wicked, handsome young man, the thieving protector . . . Secondly, people on death's doorstep so scared him, stirred up something so dark and deep inside him, that when he encountered one he felt ill for the rest of the day. No, he wanted absolutely no part in this story.

'Look, Father,' he said, standing up to let the priest know that it was time to leave, 'I thank you for your faith in me, but I have too much to do to . . . Come to the police station and ask for Inspector Augello. You can tell him I said he should look into this case.'

The priest looked at him with eyes like those of a calf on its way to the slaughter. And in a voice so soft it was almost inaudible, he said:

'Don't let me carry this cross alone, my son.'

What was it that so struck the inspector? Was it the choice of words? The tone in which the priest said them?

'All right,' he said. 'I'll come with you. But are we sure we're not going to a lot of trouble for nothing?'

'I guarantee you that this person will tell—'

'I wasn't referring to that. I meant: are we so sure the dying man will still be alive?'

'The dying woman, Inspector. Yes, she's still alive. I made a phone call before coming here. Maybe we'll make it in time.'

✶

Since they'd decided that the inspector would follow the priest in his own car, Montalbano was unable to ask Father Barbera any more questions. And this lack of information made him feel more and more upset. He didn't even know the name of the woman he was going to see, and the strangest thing about the situation was that he was about to meet a person who, after a few hours had passed, he would never be able to see again.

Father Barbera headed towards the outskirts of Vigàta. Once on the road to Montelusa, he turned left, in the direction of Raffadali, and a couple of miles later he turned left again, drove through a large iron gate and onto a well-tended drive lined with trees, and finally pulled up in front of a large villa.

'Where are we?' the inspector asked after getting out of his car.

'This is a home for the elderly, Inspector. It's called La Casa del Sacro Cuore, the House of the Sacred Heart, and is administered by nuns.'

'It must be pretty expensive,' Montalbano commented upon seeing a gardener at work and a nurse pushing an elderly man in a wheelchair around the gardens.

'Right,' the priest said drily.

'Listen, before we go inside, tell me something. First of all, what's the . . . the lady's name?'

'Maria Carmela Spagnolo.'

'What's she dying of?'

'Old age. She's dying out slowly, like a candle. She's over ninety.'

'Does she have a husband? Children?'

'Listen, Inspector, I really know very little about her. She became a widow rather young in life and has no children, just a nephew who lives in Milan and pays the bills here. I know she was living in Fela, and then some time after her husband died she moved abroad. She came back to Sicily five years ago and was admitted here.'

'Why here?'

'That I can explain. She came to this home because an old childhood friend of hers was already here, though the friend died about a year ago.'

'Was the nephew informed of this?'

'I think so.'

'I hope you don't mind if I have a cigarette.'

The priest threw up his hands. Montalbano was looking for every available reason to delay the moment when he would find himself face to face with the dying woman. For his part Father Barbera couldn't understand why the inspector wasn't taking more interest in the case.

'And don't you know anything else?' asked Montalbano.

The priest looked at him very seriously.

'Of course I know more. But what I know was told me in the confessional. Understand?'

And so the serial novel continued. This was the scene where the priest couldn't reveal the secret confided to him in the darkness of the confessional. Oh, the only solution was to get it over with quickly, listen to the ravings of an old lady no longer in her right mind, and then take himself out of the game.

'Let's go.'

The place looked like a ten-star hotel, if such things existed. Nuns with rustling gowns were fluttering everywhere. A lift as big as a bedroom took them to the third and top floor. The sparkling corridor gave onto some ten rooms. From one of them came a desperate, continuous lament, from another some music from a radio or television, and from another a feeble feminine voice singing 'C'è una chiesetta, amor / nascosta in mezzo ai fior . . .'. The priest stopped outside the last door in the hallway, which was half open. He poked his head inside, had a look, then turned to the inspector.

'Come,' he said.

In order to take a step forward, Montalbano had to imagine that there was a someone behind him pushing and forcing him to move. In the room there was a bed, a small table with two chairs, a stand with a television on it, and two comfortable armchairs. And a door giving onto a bathroom. All extremely clean, all in perfect order. In a chair beside the bed sat a nun reciting the rosary while barely moving her lips. Of the dying woman only the small bird-like head was visible, her hair nicely combed. Patre Barbera asked in a soft voice.

'How is she doing?'

'She's almost on the other side now,' the nun replied in a singsong voice, getting up and leaving the room.

Father Barbera leaned over the tiny head.

'Mrs Spagnolo! Maria Carmela! It's Don Luigi.'

The old woman's eyelids didn't open, but fluttered a little.

'Mrs Spagnolo, I have here with me that person I mentioned to you. I'm going out now so you can talk to him. I'll come back when you've finished.'

The old woman didn't open her eyes this time either, but merely nodded ever so faintly. While walking past the inspector, the priest whispered:

'Be careful.'

Of what? At first the inspector didn't understand. Then he grasped perfectly what the priest was trying to tell him. Be careful, because this life is dangling from a non-existent thread, an invisible, very fragile spider's thread that your tone of voice, or a sudden cough, might suffice to sever irreparably.

He approached the bed on tiptoe and sat down cautiously in the chair.

'I'm here, signora,' he said in a soft voice, more to himself than to the dying woman. And from the bed came a voice very feeble, though clear and effortless, and apparently without pain.

'Are you . . . are you . . . the right person?'

'Actually, I wouldn't know,' he felt like saying, but luckily managed to restrain himself. How can anyone say with any certainty, to anyone, in any situation: I'm the right person for you? But perhaps the dying woman meant simply to ask whether he was a man of the law, someone who would make proper use of what he would learn from her. The old woman must have taken his silence for an affirmative answer, since she finally seemed to make up her mind, and with some effort moved her tiny head that little bit necessary to communicate this, while her eyes remained closed. Montalbano leaned his upper body towards the pillow.

'It . . . wasn't . . .'

It wasn't . . .

'. . . poi . . . son . . .'

It wasn't poison . . .

'Cristi . . . na . . . wan . . . ted some . . .'

Cristina wanted some . . .

'And . . . so . . . I gave . . . her . . . some . . . but . . .'

And so I gave her some, but . . .

'. . . it wasn't . . . it wasn't . . .'

It wasn't what?

'. . . poison.'

It wasn't poison.

In the absolute silence of the room, unbroken even by noises or voices outside, Montalbano heard a sort of hissing at once far away and near. He realized that Mrs Spagnolo had just sighed deeply, feeling perhaps liberated from the weight she had borne for so many years. He waited for her to resume speaking, to say something else, because what she'd said was not enough, and he didn't know how to begin to go about understanding.

'Signora,' he said very softly.

Nothing. Surely she'd nodded off, exhausted. So he got up ever so gently and opened the door. Father Barbera was gone, but the nun was there, standing a few steps away and still moving her lips. When she saw the inspector, she approached.

'The lady has fallen asleep,' he said, stepping slightly back. The nun went into the room and up to the bed, pulled the old woman's left arm out from under the covers and felt for the pulse. Then she took out the other arm and wrapped the rosary she kept attached to her sash around the old woman's hands.

Only then did the inspector realize that those gestures meant that Mrs Maria Carmela Spagnolo was dead. And that with that hissing noise she'd freed herself not of the burden of her secret, but of the burden of life. And he hadn't been afraid. He hadn't noticed anything. Perhaps because there hadn't been any of the sacred solemnity of death or even its everyday, horrendous, televised desecration. There was only death, simple and natural.

✳

Father Barbera returned after the inspector had smoked two cigarettes one right after the other.

'See? We got here just in time.'

Right. In time to swallow the bait, feel the hook catch in his gullet, and know for certain that it would be a long and difficult process to dislodge it. He'd been tricked. He looked at the priest almost resentfully. Father Barbera seemed not to notice.

'Was she able to tell you anything?'

'Yes, she managed to say that what she gave a certain Cristina was not the poison she'd wanted.'

'That corresponds,' said the priest.

'With what?'

'I wish I could help you, I really do. But I can't.'

'Well, I helped you.'

'You're not a priest bound to secrecy.'

'OK, OK,' said Montalbano, getting into his car. 'Have a good day.'

'Wait,' said Father Barbera.

From a slit in the side of his cassock he extracted a sheet of paper folded in four and handed it to the inspector.

'I had the administrative secretary give me everything they had on Mrs Spagnolo. I also wrote my address and phone number at the bottom.'

'Do you know whether they've informed the nephew?'

'Yes, they told him she's passed away. They called him in Milan. He'll be in Vigàta tomorrow morning. If you want . . . I can let you know which hotel he's staying in.'

The priest was trying to make it up to him.

But the damage was done.

2

'Chief, beckin' yer partin', but are ya feelin' OK?'

'I'm fine, Cat. Why do you ask?'

'Ah, I dunno . . . Iss like yer there but yer not.'

Catarella was perfectly right. He was there in the office because he was talking, giving orders, and thinking, but in his mind he was still in that small, clean, painted room on the third floor of an old people's home, beside the bed of a dying ninety-year-old woman who'd told him . . .

✻

'Listen, Fazio, come in and close the door behind you. I have to tell you what happened to me this morning.'

When he'd finished, Fazio gave him a doubtful look.

'And according to this priest, what are you supposed to do?'

'Oh, I dunno, start investigating, looking . . .'

'But you don't even know when or how this poisoning business happened! It might be something from sixty or seventy years ago! And was it something known to the public or did it remain hidden inside some posh household with nobody ever hearing about it? Take it from me, Chief, forget about it. I wanted to talk to you about yesterday's armed robbery . . .'

*

'Let me get this straight, Salvo. Did you tell me this story because you want my advice? Are you asking me whether you should get involved or not?'

'That's right, Mimì.'

'Why are you playing games with me?'

'I don't know what you mean.'

'You don't want any advice! You've already made up your mind!'

'Oh yeah?'

'Yeah! Is there any doubt that you're going to dive head-long into a story like that, with no beginning or end? And an old story at that! You'll probably be dealing with people a hundred years old, or almost!'

'So what?'

'You love to wallow in these journeys back in time. You have a ball talking to old people who can remember the price of butter in 1912 but have forgotten their own names! That priest was a shrewd one. He took one look at you and sized you up to a T.'

*

'You know what, Livia? This morning when I was in the shower the doorbell rang. I went and answered the door without any clothes on, dripping—'

'Wait a second, I'm not sure I got that. You went and answered the door completely naked?'

'I thought it was Catarella.'

'So what? Isn't Catarella a human being?'

'Of course he is!'

'So why do you want to inflict the sight of your naked body on another human being?'

'Did you say *inflict*?'

'That's what I said and I'll say it again. Do you think you're the *Apollo Belvedere* or something?'

'Tell me something. When I'm naked in front of you, do you think I'm inflicting the sight of my body on you?'

'Sometimes yes and sometimes no.'

This was the start of another of their ritual telephone quarrels. He could keep pretending not to notice, or he could make the whole thing take a nasty turn. He chose the former path. He tried to say something funny, but it came out flat since he was still feeling offended, and so he ended up telling Livia the whole story.

'Do you intend to pursue it?'

'Oh, I dunno. I thought about it all day. And in the end I've been leaning towards not doing anything.'

Livia let out an irritating giggle.

'Why are you laughing?'

'I dunno, just laughing.'

'Oh no you don't! You're going to explain to me why the hell you came out with that little *sconcica* giggle!'

'Don't you talk to me like that, and don't speak in dialect!'

'OK, sorry.'

'What's *sconcica*?'

'It means mocking, derision.'

'I had no intention of mocking you whatsoever. It was a giggle of pure and simple observation.'

'And what were you observing?'

'That you've aged, Salvo. Once upon a time you would have jumped right into a case like that. That's all.'

'Ah, so now I'm old and flabby?'

'I didn't say you were flabby.'

'Then why do you maintain that the sight of my body is some kind of torture?'

This time there was no stopping a full-blown spat.

*

Lying on the bed, he read the sheet of paper the priest had given him earlier that day.

Maria Carmela Spagnolo, daughter of Giovanni and Matilde née Jacono, born in Fela on 6 September 1910. Had a brother, Giacomo, four years her junior. Her father was a successful lawyer and well-off. She was educated at a boarding school run by nuns. In 1930 she married Dr Alfredo Siracusa, a rich chemist in Fela who owned lands and houses. The couple had no children. Widowed in 1949, by the middle of the year Maria Carmela had sold everything and moved to Paris to live with her brother Giacomo, a career diplomat. She subsequently followed him around to his various new posts. Then the brother died, leaving behind a wife and a son. Maria Carmela continued living all over the world with her nephew, Michele, a bachelor who'd become an engineer for the Eni energy giant. When Michele Spagnolo retired and settled in Milan, Maria Carmela requested to be admitted at the Casa del Sacro Cuore. She left all her money (and there was a lot of it) to her nephew – on the condition that he see to his aunt's needs for as long as she remained alive.

And there you have it. Have what? All things considered, that paragraph of information told Montalbano nothing. Or maybe there *was* something there – something that could be translated into a question: why, just a few months after losing her husband, would a woman sell everything to go and live abroad, leaving behind all her customs, habits, rituals, relations, and friends?

*

That night – surely because of the nearly two pounds of *purpi affucati* Adelina had made for him, which he had religiously wolfed down though perfectly aware that digesting them was a dangerous affair – he had several nightmares. In one of them he was walking down the road completely naked and wrinkled, skin sagging, leaning on two walking sticks, with a large crowd of women gathered around him, all of them strangely resembling Livia, mocking him and setting vicious dogs on him. He tried to take refuge in some houses nearby, but all their doors were locked. At last he found one open, went inside, and found himself in a smoky den full of burners with alembics and distillers. A sepulchral female voice said:

'Come closer. What do you want from Lucretia Borgia?'

He went closer and discovered that Lucretia Borgia was none other than poor Mrs Maria Carmela Spagnolo, the widow Siracusa, just deceased.

He thrashed about in bed until five or so, then fell asleep for four solid hours. When he saw that it was nine o'clock, he cursed the saints and dashed into the bathroom to wash and shave, then got dressed, opened the front door, and found Father Barbera's finger, which was about to ring the doorbell, in his eye. Jesus, what a pain in the arse! He had learned how to get to Montalbano's house and now would never forget it!

'Is somebody else about to die?' the inspector asked, with calculated gruffness.

Father Barbera didn't take it in.

'Could you let me in for a minute? I won't be long.'

Montalbano let him in, but didn't tell him to sit down. They both remained standing.

'I didn't sleep a wink last night,' said the priest.

'Did you also eat *purpi affucati*?'

'No, I had some broth and a little cheese for supper.'

He didn't say anything else. Was it possible he'd raced all the way to Marinella just to tell him last night's menu?

'Listen, I'm really in a rush this morning.'

'I've come just to ask you to drop the whole thing. What right did I have to bring to your attention, as a man of the law, something that happened so many years ago—'

'Shall we say in 1950, to be more precise?'

Father Barbera gave a start, taken aback. Montalbano realized he'd been right on the mark.

'Was it the dear departed who told you?'

'No.'

'Then how did you know?'

'I'm a policeman. Go on.'

'OK, well, I don't think I have the right – I don't think *we* have the right – to bring back out into the open something that over time had come to a close and been forgotten. It would be reopening old wounds, maybe even stirring up old resentments . . .'

'Stop right there,' said Montalbano. 'You talk of wounds and resentments, which is easy for you because you know more than I do. I'm not in a position to make any such judgement. For me it's all dense fog.'

'Well, then, I take it upon myself to ask you to forget the whole story.'

'I could, but on one condition.'

'What?'

'I'll tell you presently. But first I have to think about it a little. So, let's see. Very early in 1950, a certain Cristina asks Mrs Maria Carmela – a chemist's wife, or recently widowed – for some poison. For reasons of her own – which it would be hard for us ever to find out – or because she suspected that Cristina wanted the poison to kill someone, she gives her a harmless powder, pretending that it's poison. She pulls a fast one on her. Cristina administers the poison to the person she wants to kill, but the person remains alive. At the worst, he or she gets a stomach ache.'

The priest was listening to the inspector with his whole body bent forward. He looked like a bow tensed to the maximum.

'If that's the way it went,' Montalbano continued, 'Mrs Maria Carmela did not in the end have such great cause for remorse. It wasn't poison, and so? But if Mrs Maria Carmela turned it into such a cross to bear, carrying it all the way to her deathbed, that means things did not go as Mrs Maria Carmela had hoped. Does that make sense?'

'It makes sense,' said the priest with his eyes fixed on the inspector's.

'So we come to the point. Which is that, despite the fact that Cristina was not given any poison, somebody died just the same.'

It wasn't sweat but a waterfall that was pouring down Father Barbera's forehead.

'And I should add that the victim – whether a man or a woman, I don't know – was not killed with a firearm or knife, but with poison.'

'How can you make such a claim?'

'The poor old woman told me as she was dying: she carried the anguish around with her for her whole life. What must have happened was that once the murder was committed, she began to wonder whether she'd made a mis-take – whether she'd maybe accidentally given Cristina real poison instead of the fake one she'd prepared.'

The priest didn't speak or move.

'I'll tell you how I intend to deal with this. If whoever committed the murder paid for it, then the matter is of no more interest to me. But if there's something still unresolved, still to be cleared up, then I'll carry on.'

'Fifty years after the fact?'

'You know something, Father Barbera? Sometimes I ask myself what proof God had to accuse Cain of murdering Abel. If I could, I swear I'd reopen the case.'

Father Barbera gawked, his lower jaw dropping to his chest. He threw up his hands in resignation.

'Well, if you put it that way . . .'

He headed for the door, but before leaving, he added:

'Michele Spagnolo has arrived. He's at the Hotel Pirandello.'

*

He was late to the meeting at Commissioner Bonetti-Alderighi's office. His boss limited himself to glaring at him scornfully, then waited in silence — as if to emphasize the rudeness — for the inspector to sit down as he apologized left and right to his colleagues.

The commissioner resumed speaking on the topic of the meeting, which was 'What can the police do to regain the citizens' trust?'. One person proposed a competition, replete with prizes; another said that the best thing would be to organize a dance with sumptuous prizes and a cotillion; a third added that they could invite the press to help.

'In what sense?' asked the commissioner.

'In the sense that they look the other way when we make a mistake or are unable to—'

'Yeah, yeah, I get it,' the commissioner cut him off impatiently. 'Any other suggestions?'

The index and middle fingers of Montalbano's right hand raised themselves of their own accord, without his brain having ordered them to do so. Indeed he looked at his two raised fingers with some surprise. The commissioner sighed.

'What is it, Montalbano?'

'And what if the police simply did their duty, always and no matter what, without provoking or prevaricating?'

The meeting ended in an Arctic chill.

To return to Vigàta, he had to pass by the Hotel Piran-dello. He didn't expect Michele Spagnolo to be in, but it was worth a try.

'Yes, Inspector, he's in his room. Shall I get him on the phone for you?'

'Hello? Inspector Montalbano here.'

'Inspector? Of what?'

'Police.'

'And what do you want from me?'

The engineer Spagnolo seemed truly confused.

'To talk to you.'

'About what?'

'Your aunt.'

The engineer's voice came out of his throat sounding exactly like that of a strangled chicken.

'My aunt?!'

'Listen, Mr Spagnolo, I'm here at your hotel. If you'd be so kind as to come downstairs to the lobby, we can speak a little more comfortably.'

'I'll be right down.'

The engineer was a bit over sixty, rather diminutive in stature, with a face like fired clay, sunburnt from combing the desert in search of oil. He was a bundle of nerves who moved in fits and starts. He sat down, stood up, sat back down after Montalbano sat down, crossed his legs, uncrossed them, adjusted the knot of his tie, brushed some invisible dust from his jacket with his hands.

'I don't understand why the police—'

'No need to be alarmed, sir.'

'I'm not the least bit alarmed.'

One could only imagine how he acted when he was nervous.

'OK, well, your aunt, as she was dying, wanted to tell me a secret that I wasn't fully able to understand, some story about poison that wasn't poison . . .'

'Poison? My aunt?!'

Up from the chair, down again, legs crossed, uncrossed, tie-knot, jacket-brushing. On top of that, this time he took off his glasses, breathed on the lenses, rubbed them with his handkerchief, and put them back on.

If he carries on like this, before ten minutes are up I'll go insane, thought the inspector. Better cut things short.

'What can you tell me about your aunt?'

'She was a good woman. Like a mother to me.'

'Why did she move to Vigàta five years ago?'

Up from the chair, down again, legs crossed, uncrossed, tie-knot, brushing, eyeglasses, breathe, rub, glasses back on. Plus: nose-blow.

'Because after I retired I got married. And my aunt didn't get along with my wife.'

'Do you know anything about what happened to your aunt during the first six months of 1950?'

'Not a thing. But what in God's name is this all about?'

Up from the chair, down again, crossing, uncrossing . . . But the inspector was already outside the hotel.

3

As he was driving back to Vigàta he remembered something he'd read by a Shakespeare scholar about Hamlet. The scholar claimed that the ghost of the father – the late king murdered by his brother with the connivance of Gertrude, the widow who became the lover of the murderer and brother-in-law – in commanding his son, Hamlet, to avenge him by killing his uncle while nevertheless sparing his mother, was assigning him a task more fit for a melodrama than a tragedy. As is well known to one and all, while patricide and matricide are matters for tragedy, uncle-cide or auntie-cide are at best the stuff of third-rate melodrama or comedies of manners verging on farce. And thus the young Prince of

Denmark, in carrying out the task assigned him, goes through such a song and dance, such machinations, that he succeeds in promoting himself to the status of tragic character. And what a tragedy it is! Taking into account the differences of proportion between himself and Hamlet, and considering that Mrs Maria Carmela Spagnolo hadn't mentioned any ghosts – though she wasn't far from becoming one – and that the poor woman hadn't explicitly assigned him any tasks, and considering, finally, that if there was anyone assigning him a task, it was Father Barbera, a character who could easily be cut out (since there are no priests in Shakespeare's tragedy), why would he want, by investigating, to turn a serial novel into a detective novel? Because that was all he could aspire to: a good mystery – and never, ever, one of those 'dense, profound' novels that everyone buys and nobody reads even though the reviewers all swear that they've never come across such a book in all their days.

And so, as he entered the station he made the firm decision not to get involved in the story of the poison that wasn't poison, not even if he was dragged into it by the bridle, as one does with recalcitrant donkeys.

*

'*Ciao*, Salvo. You know something?'

'No, Mimì, I don't, at least not until you tell me. But if you tell me, then when you ask me if I know it, you'll have the satisfaction of hearing me say: "Yes, I know something."'

'Well, aren't you surly today! I just wanted to say, about that lady who died – what was her name? Ah yes, Maria Carmela Spagnolo, the one you're involved with—'

'No.'

Mimì Augello got flustered.

'What's that supposed to mean: "no"?'

'It means exactly the opposite of "yes".'

'Speak more clearly. Do you not want to know what I wanted to tell you, or are you no longer involved in the case?'

'The second thing.'

'And why not?'

'Because I'm not Hamlet.'

Augello hesitated.

'The "to be or not to be" guy? What's he got to do with it?'

'A lot. How's your investigation of the armed robbery going?'

'Great. I'm definitely going to catch them.'

'Tell me about it.'

Mimì told him in detail how he'd come to identify two of the three robbers. If he was waiting for the inspector to express his approval, he was disappointed. Montalbano wasn't even looking at him – he was lost in thought, head hanging down on his chest. After five minutes of silence, Augello stood up.

'Well, I'm going.'

'Wait.' The inspector had trouble getting the words out of his mouth. 'What were you saying a . . . about the dead lady?'

'That I found something out. But I'm not going to tell you.'

'Why?'

'Because you said you were no longer interested in the case. And because you didn't deign to utter a single word of approval of how I've been carrying on the investigation of the robbery.'

This was a police department? It was a kindergarten that ran on little acts of spite and resentment! You can't have my seashell because you wouldn't give me a bite of your snack . . .

'You want me to say you've been great?'

'Yes.'

'Mimì, you've been pretty good.'

'Salvo, you really are a bastard! But since I'm a generous man, I'll tell you what I found out. This morning at the barber's I saw Colajanni, the lawyer, reading the death notices in the paper, the way old people do.'

Montalbano flew off the handle.

'What do you mean "the way old people do"? Am I old or something? When I open the newspaper, the first thing I do is read the death notices. And then the news.'

'OK, OK. Anyway, at one point the lawyer called out: "Well, what do you know! Maria Carmela Spagnolo! I didn't know she was still alive!" That's all.'

'And so?'

'Salvo, this means there are still people around who remember her. And that the business of the poison must have made some noise. You therefore have an open road ahead of you: go and see Colajanni the lawyer and ask him for information.'

'Did you read the notice yourself?'

'Yes, it was quite simple. It said that the grieving nephew Michele announced the passing of his beloved et cetera . . . So what are you going to do? Are you going to talk to the lawyer?'

'But do you know Colajanni? He's completely lost his mind in old age! You say the slightest wrong thing and he'll break a chair over your head. To talk to him you have to put on riot gear. Anyway, I've already made my decision: I don't want to get involved any further in this matter.'

*

'Hello, Inspector Montalbano? This is Clementina Vasile-Cozzo. What happened? Did we quarrel or something the last time we got together? We never see each other any more. How are you?'

Montalbano felt himself blush. It had been quite a while

since he last got in touch with the paralysed former schoolteacher, who he was very fond of.

'I'm fine, signora. What a pleasure to hear your voice!'

'There's a selfish reason for this call, Inspector. A cousin of mine from Fela phoned me to tell me she'll be in Vigàta tomorrow. Since she's been badgering me for a long time to introduce you to her, I was wondering if you'd be so kind as to come to my place for lunch tomorrow? That way I'll get her off my back.'

He accepted, but for no apparent reason, he felt slightly alarmed. The hunter's instinct had reawakened in him, and it warned him of danger nearby, a trap in the ground covered by leaves into which, if he wasn't careful, he might fall. Nonsense, he said to himself. What danger could there be in a lunch invitation from Mrs Clementina?

*

'Just for curiosity's sake, purely for curiosity's sake,' the inspector reminded himself as he pulled up in the parking area behind the Casa del Sacro Cuore at half-past eight the following morning. He'd guessed right. Outside the rear gate was a hearse gleaming with gilded angels. Not far away, a taxi whose driver was pacing back and forth outside the car. There were also three mopeds. Clinics, hospices, and hospitals always have a back door that is used for quick, guarded funerals, which usually take place in the morning. Apparently they do this so as not to frighten the patients – who all hope to leave the place on their own two feet through the main entrance – with the sight of coffins and weeping relatives. A nasty wind was blowing, tousling some yellowish clouds. Four men came out carrying a coffin, followed by the nephew of the late Signora Maria Carmela. And that was all. Montalbano put the car in gear and drove off, feeling melancholy and angry with himself for the brilliant idea he'd had. Why the hell had he gone to a funeral so dismal and depressing as to be almost offensive?

Curiosity? To find out what new and imaginative tics Michele Spagnolo would come up with?

*

The moment Mrs Clementina Vasile-Cozzo's housekeeper opened the door for him, he realized, from the look she gave him, that the woman still harboured a profound albeit inexplicable antipathy towards him. Montalbano partly forgave her for this, because she knew what to do in the kitchen.

'How time flies, eh?' the housekeeper said to him, snatching the tray of cannoli rudely out of his hand.

What was that supposed to mean? That in less than a year he'd turned into an old man? And to top it off, upon seeing his enquiring, concerned expression, the villainess smiled.

In the living room, spilling out from an armchair beside Mrs Clementina's wheelchair, was a very fat woman of about fifty who the moment she opened her mouth revealed herself to be *vucciriusa* – which meant that instead of speaking she projected a voice exactly like an opera singer's full-chested C note.

'This is my cousin, Ciccina Adorno,' said Mrs Clementina in a tone beseeching the inspector to understand.

'Oh my God! It's such a pleasure to meet you!' said the cousin.

More than anything else it was a cross between the wail of a foghorn and the howl of a wolf that hadn't had anything in its stomach for a month. In the fifteen minutes or so that it took before they could sit down at the table, Montalbano – whose ears were starting to hurt inside – learned that Mrs Adorno née Adorno was also the widow Adorno ('I married my cousin'), and she was not fifty but seventy years old. He was also treated to a lengthy, thorough explanation of why and how the lady had been obliged to travel from Fela to Vigàta because of a dispute with a man to whom she had let a small house she owned and who no longer wanted to pay the rent because there was a broken gutter on the roof that leaked straight into the living room when it rained. Whose responsibility was it – she asked the inspector, who was a man of the law – to pay for repairing the gutter? Luckily at that moment the housekeeper came in to say that lunch was ready.

Head numb from all the yelling, Montalbano was unable to enjoy the *pasta 'ncasciata*, which must have been just slightly below the very highest level, beyond which there is only God. To make up for it, Signora Ciccina had moved onto the subject of greatest interest to her, which was to know, in the most minute detail, all the particulars of all the cases Montalbano had solved in his career. She remembered minutiae that the inspector had long forgotten all about.

When the fish arrived, Clementina Vasile-Cozzo made a final effort to rescue the inspector from that cyclone of questions.

'Ciccina, do you think the Empress of Japan will give birth to a son or a daughter?'

And while Montalbano was reeling from the sudden shift to the Empire of the Rising Sun, or whatever it was, Mr Clementina explained to him that her cousin knew everything about all the ruling houses in creation. But Signora Ciccina didn't take the bait.

'You want me to talk about things like that when we have our inspector here with us in person?' And without so much as pausing to take a breath, she continued: 'And what do you think of the Notarbartolo case?'

'What Notarbartolo case?'

'Are you joking? Don't you remember Notarbartolo, the one from the Banco di Sicilia?'

This was something that had taken place in the early twentieth century (or was it the late nineteenth?), but Signora Ciccina started talking about it as though it had happened yesterday.

'Because I know everything about every violent crime that has occurred in Sicily from the Unification of Italy to the present day.'

When she'd finished expatiating on the Notarbartolo case, she launched into the Mangiaracina case (1912–14), which was such a tortuous and complicated affair that when the coffee arrived they still didn't know who the killer was. At this point Montalbano, fearing that his eardrums were seriously damaged, glanced at his watch, got up from the table, pretended he was suddenly in a hurry, thanked Mrs Clementina and said goodbye. He was accompanied to the door by Ciccina Adorno.

'Excuse me, signora,' said the inspector, unaware of what he was saying. 'Do you remember a certain Maria Carmela Spagnolo?'

'No,' was the firm reply of Mrs Adorno, she who knew everything about every violent crime in Sicily.

*

Sitting on the flat rock under the lighthouse, he engaged in a kind of self-analysis. No doubt about it, Ciccina Adorno's negative reply had disappointed him. Which led to the question: did he really want to continue this investigation? Yes or no? He should make up his mind once and for all! A little initiative was all it would take. Such as going and introducing himself to Colajanni the lawyer and asking him to tell him, even at the risk of coming to blows, what he knew about Maria Carmela Spagnolo. Because there was no doubt that the lawyer had known her, given the way he'd reacted to reading the death notice at the barber's. Or perhaps going to the public library, requesting the collection of every day's edition of the island's major newspaper for 1950, and then patiently trying to find what happened in Fela during the first six months of that year. Or else assign to Catarella the task of looking for news of that sort on the Internet.

So why wasn't he doing it? All it would take was a little

goodwill for him to find out what there was to find out, and that would be the end of it. Was it perhaps because he didn't feel like supplementing therapeutic tenacity (endlessly talked about by doctors, priests, moralists, and TV hosts) and judicial tenacity (endlessly talked about by judges and politicians) with an investigative tenacity that nobody whatsoever would talk about? Or was it because – and this seemed to him the right answer – he preferred to remain passive about the whole thing? Which meant being like a coastline on which the remains of past shipwrecks occasionally washed ashore – some of which were swallowed back up by the sea, while others remained on the sand to cook in the sunlight. If so, the best thing was to wait for the waves to toss some new wreckage ashore.

*

He was on his way to bed, shortly after 1 a.m., when the telephone rang. Surely it was Livia.

'Hello, darling,' he said into the receiver.

There was silence at the other end, then a sort of world-ending thunderclap that left his ears ringing. Holding the receiver away from his head, he realized it was laughter. And the laughter could not have belonged to anyone but Ciccina Adorno, who apparently was not only *vucciriusa* but also an insomniac.

'I'm sorry, Inspector, but I'm not your darling. You gave me the wrong information!'

'I did? About what, signora?'

'About Maria Carmela Spagnolo. You didn't tell me her married name, Siracusa. Her husband was a chemist, and I've been up all night trying to work it out.'

'Did you know her?'

'Of course I knew her! Even personally. But there hasn't been any news of her for many years.'

'She died here in Vigàta just the other day.'

'Really?'

'Listen, signora, can we meet tomorrow morning?'

'I leave for Fela at eight o'clock.'

'Could you—'

'If you're not too tired, why don't you come over right now?'

'But what about Signora Clementina?'

'She's OK with it. We'll wait for you.'

Before leaving home he stuck a wad of cotton in each ear.

*

After Signora Ciccina had been talking for an hour, the neighbours upstairs started banging over their heads. Soon thereafter the downstairs neighbours did the same at their feet. Then others started banging on the walls. At this point Signora Clementina opened a large cupboard and sat the inspector and her cousin down inside it.

Montalbano finally left the place after three hours of discussion, six cups of coffee, and a whole pack of cigarettes. Despite the protective cotton, his ears hurt. This time the waves had washed not some scattered flotsam ashore, but a whole intact galleon.

4

At exactly 9 p.m. on 1 January 1950, the lawyer Emanuele ('Nenè' to friends) Ferlito sat down at the lansquenet table at the Patriots' Club, which everyone in Fela knew was often an illegal gambling den. And if it was one on normal week-days, one could only imagine what it became on holidays, especially the holidays that went from Christmas to Epiph-any, when the tradition in the towns was to gamble every-thing down to one's underpants. Nenè Ferlito, who was rich and basically idle, since he rarely practised his profession and almost always only as a favour to friends, was about fifty and had been around the block a few times. Aside from being capable of sitting at the gambling table for forty-eight hours straight without getting up even to go to the loo, he had women in Fela and the nearby towns, and it was known that in Palermo (where he often went – or so, at least, he told his wife Cristina – to argue lawsuits) he kept two more, a ballerina and a seamstress. He could down half a bottle of French cognac and more in a single evening. His daily consumption of unfiltered cigarettes was about a hundred and ten to a hundred and twenty. At around 11 p.m. on that New Year's Day, he was overcome by a sudden, severe malaise, just like the year before. That is, he turned as stiff as a salted cod (no pun intended), started shaking violently and vomiting, and could breathe only with great effort.

'Here we go again!' cried Dr Jacopo Friscia, who happened to be at the Patriots' Club that evening.

Having taken Ferlito into his care after the first such attack, the doctor had forbidden the lawyer above all to smoke, but the injunction had gone into one of Ferlito's ears and come out of the other. A nicotine-triggered relapse was inevitable.

This time, the matter appeared far more serious than the last. Nenè Ferlito was dying of asphyxia, and to reopen his jaws the doctor and some other people at the club had to resort to using a shoehorn. Finally Ferlito recovered a little, and they were able to carry him home while Dr Friscia ran off in search of medication. Ferlito's wife, Cristina, had them lay him down in bed (they slept in separate bedrooms) and then got on the phone to inform their daughter Agata, eighteen years old, who was spending the holidays in Catania with relatives. The helpers left upon the return of Dr Friscia, who found the patient in an immobile state. After clearly warning the wife that the patient's life was in danger, he wrote down on a sheet of paper the medicines she should give him and the times at which they should be administered. Seeing Signora Cristina understandably overwhelmed and as though absent, the doctor repeated that her husband's life depended on her strictly following his prescriptions. She would have to stay up all night. Cristina said she could manage. Feeling doubtful, the doctor asked her if she wanted him to send a nurse there to take care of everything. Cristina said no, and the doctor left.

The following morning, shortly after eight o'clock, Dr Friscia knocked on the door of the Ferlitos' house. Maria, the housekeeper who'd just arrived, answered the door and told him that Signora Cristina was shut up in her husband's bedroom and wanted to be left alone. The doctor, however, managed to persuade her to let him in. There was a horrendous stench of vomit, piss, and shit in the room. Cristina was sitting on a chair beside the bed, body stiff, goggle-eyed. On the bed lay the lawyer, dead. The doctor roused the wife from her state of shock and realized that the medications he'd given her hadn't even been opened.

'But why didn't you make him take them?'

'There wasn't time. He died half an hour after you left.'

The doctor touched the patient's body. It was still warm. But this was perhaps because there was a lit wood-burning stove in the room that Ferlito himself had stoked the previous evening before going out, since he didn't want to be cold when he got home from the club. Signora Cristina would later say that she loaded more wood into the stove fifteen minutes before her dying husband was brought home.

The funeral had to be postponed for a few days to allow the deceased's brother, Stefano, who lived in Switzerland, to attend. The day after her father's death, Agata, his daughter, went to talk to Dr Friscia, asking him to tell her in detail what her mother told him concerning the medications she hadn't had time to give her husband. The upshot was that Agata left home, asking some friends to put her up. What was this? How could a girl abandon her mother at the very moment when she should be by her side, sharing her grief?

Thus, in town, rumours that had already been communicated through gestures, allusions, and meaningful hints began to circulate openly.

Cristina Ferlito, when she first married, was a beautiful girl of twenty, daughter of the notary Calogero Cuffaro – at the time the most powerful representative, in Fela and the nearby towns, of the party in power. The local bishop received him almost daily. No public function, government grant, licence, contract, or statement got off the ground without Cuffaro's approval. In a short time Cristina learned what kind of stuff her husband, ten years her senior, was made of. Then they had a child, a little girl. Cristina behaved like a devoted wife; people had only good things to say about her. At least until February 1948, when her husband brought home a distant nephew of twenty-five, Attilio, a fine-looking young man, for whom he'd found work in Fela.

Having always lived with his parents in Fiacca, Attilio moved into a room in his uncle's villa. According to gossips, the nephew was always ready to console his Aunt Cristina when she suffered over her husband's unending infidelities. And by dint of daily consolation, Signora Cristina one day found it more convenient to get her consolation in bed. But she ended up falling in love with Attilio and gave the young man no rest. She became extremely jealous and started to make scenes even in front of outsiders. Her husband began to receive anonymous letters that left him indifferent – actually he was pleased that his wife was now in his nephew's hair instead of his. In October of the following year, Attilio – partly because he couldn't take any more of his mistress's shenanigans, and partly because he no longer felt like doing wrong by his uncle, to whom he was indebted for even his job – moved into a boarding house. Cristina seemed to lose her mind: she stopped eating, stopped sleeping, sent extremely long letters to her ex-lover using Maria, the housekeeper, as messenger. In some of them she declared her

intention — which Attilio didn't take seriously — to kill
her husband so she could be free again and live with him.

At the funeral the whole town was able to see Cristina
being shunned by her daughter, her brother-in-law Stefano,
who'd come from Switzerland, and by her mother-in-law,
who accused her, in no uncertain terms, right in front of the
coffin, of having murdered her son. At this point Cristina's
father, Calogero Cuffaro the notary, ran to comfort the
poor woman, letting it be known to one and all that she
was out of her mind with grief. But that same evening, at
the Patriots' Club, Stefano from Switzerland announced to
everyone present that he intended to demand that the
authorities perform a post-mortem on his brother's body,
and then withdrew with Russomanno the lawyer, who was
of the same political party as Cuffaro the notary, though
head of the opposing faction. Their intense, animated discussion, in a small consultation room at the club, lasted
three hours. Just long enough for Stefano, on his way home,
to be assaulted by two unknown men who beat him
viciously, telling him repeatedly, 'Go back to Swisserland,
Swisser!'

Despite a black eye and a gimpy leg, Stefano Ferlito,
summoned by Cuffaro the notary, who said he was owed a
'proper explanation', went to the home of the deceased in
the company of Russomanno the lawyer. Of the widow
Cristina, not a trace. To make up for this, there was the
honourable Sestilio Nicolosi, the court's top attorney, at the
notary's side. At about ten o'clock, after a small crowd had
gathered around the villa to hear the loud shouts being
exchanged by the lawyers Russomanno and Nicolosi as they
quarrelled, a sudden silence descended. What happened?
What happened was that the door to the living room had
opened without warning and Cristina appeared. Pale but
firm and decisive, she said:

'Enough of this. I can't stand it any longer. I killed
Nenè. With poison.'

Her father tried one last line of defence, saying she was delirious and raving, but it was no use. Twenty minutes later, the small crowd outside saw the front door open, and out came first Cristina, then her father the notary and Nicolosi the lawyer, followed by Stefano Ferlito and Russomanno the lawyer. The crowd fell in behind them and followed them all the way to the carabinieri station, where Cristina turned herself in. Interrogated by a certain Lieutenant Frangipane, Cristina said that after Dr Friscia had left and she was alone with her husband, instead of giving him the medications the doctor had prescribed, she gave him a glass of water in which she'd dissolved some strychnine-based rat poison.

'Where did you buy it?'

'I didn't buy it. I asked my friend Maria Carmela Siracusa, the chemist's widow, for it. She got it from the chemist and gave it to me. I'd told her I needed some because we had rats in the house.'

'Why did you kill your husband?'

'Because I couldn't stand his infidelities any longer.'

The following day, summoned by Lieutenant Frangipane, a weeping Maria Carmela Spagnolo confirmed that she'd given her friend the poison in mid-November, but never in the world could she have imagined that Cristina might use it to kill her husband. They'd seen each other at Christmas and talked for a long time. Cristina had seemed the same as usual . . . Around town, Maria Carmela, who was the same age as Cristina, had a reputation for being a woman of solid character. Her late husband, the chemist, had also been a skirt-chaser, but she'd never taken a lover the way Cristina had done. The lieutenant therefore had no reason to think Maria Carmela had been aware of Cristina's murderous intentions. And so he took her deposition and sent her home. Some people in town, however, started whispering that the chemist's widow was perfectly aware of Cristina's intentions. Thus many began to see Maria

Carmela as an accomplice. Indignant, the woman sold her properties and moved abroad, to live with her brother the diplomat. She would return for a few days in 1953, to testify at the first trial, where she confirmed her initial testimony. Afterwards she left immediately for France, never to return to Fela.

Before the trial, however, many strange things happened. A few days after Cristina's arrest, the prosecutor's office ordered the post-mortem that had been the reason for Cristina's confession. A number of body parts were removed from the corpse and put in eight containers that were sent to the Investigative Magistrate of Palermo, who then passed them on to Professor Vincenzo Agnello, toxicologist at the University of Palermo, and to Professor Filiberto Trupìa, who taught pathological anatomy. The two were also sent the vomit-stained sheets of the dying man as well as the underwear he had on. At this point Cristina made two statements to the investigating judge. In the first she claimed she killed her husband to spare him further suffering. A kind of euthanasia. In the second she said she wasn't sure she was guilty of murder because the amount of poison she'd given her husband was too small. Almost nothing, in fact, an invisible pinch between her thumb and forefinger.

A few months later, after intense discussions with her lawyer Nicolosi, Cristina made a third declaration in which she retracted everything. She never gave her husband any poison. If she'd told the carabinieri and the judge she had, it was because she was terrified by the death threats her brother-in-law Stefano, the one from Switzerland, had made to her. She'd been hoping that in gaol she would be safe and out of his reach. And she was keen to emphasize that what she'd said to Dr Friscia was true: that she hadn't been able to administer the prescribed medications to her husband because he'd died before she could intervene. She concluded by saying that the analyses of the two illustrious Palermo professors had proved her right. And indeed, shortly afterwards, a veritable bomb exploded, making a great deal of noise. In their findings, Doctors Agnello and Trupìa stated that although they'd conducted and re-conducted test after test, they had found no trace of strychnine or other poison in the bodily remains and fabrics they'd examined. Ferlito had died from acute nicotine poisoning, which had provoked a fatal attack of angina pectoris. Cristina was innocent. Stefano Ferlito, however, would not admit defeat and went on the counter-attack. Don't you know, he said to everyone left and right, that the two distinguished professors owe their careers in part to Cuffaro the notary, with whom they were inextricably linked? What else could you expect? Nicolosi had Cristina make that last statement when he was already certain of the favourable results of the tests. And many people took Stefano's side. So the public prosecutor of Palermo had a brilliant idea. Take all the material that the two Palermo professors had used for the report and send it to Florence, where their toxicological experts were known the world over. When the carabinieri went to pick up the eight jars with the mortal remains of the dead lawyer, they found very little inside them. One part had gone bad, another part had been lost during the testing. But, at any rate, the sealed parcel officially left for Florence on 1 July. In early September, however, a letter from a Florentine judge arrived in Palermo asking why they'd never received any package. So where had it gone? After endless searches high and low, the package was at last found in the Palace of Justice in Florence, forgotten in the attic. In late October of the same year, no fewer than six big-cheese Florentine professors submitted their report. They'd recovered enough strychnine to cast doubt on the professional integrity, or sanity, of Doctors Agnello and Trupìa, the two Palermo experts who hadn't found any (or hadn't wanted to find any). There was no doubt: Emanuele Ferlito died as a result of poisoning; his wife Cristina was guilty.

'What did we tell you?' Stefano Ferlito and Russo-manno the lawyer shouted triumphantly to one and all.

'I don't buy it!' Nicolosi the lawyer declared triumph-antly. 'The parcel arrived so late in Florence, it must have been tampered with!'

'This is a dirty trick by my political enemies,' Cuffaro the notary clarified. 'They want to get at me through my daughter.'

To be on the safe side, Nicolosi requested an examin-ation of his client's mental condition, but she passed it with flying colours and was declared perfectly mentally sound.

To cut a long story short, the first trial, which took place almost two years later, ended in a conviction and twenty years for Cristina — who, at one point, had said she remem-bered having given something to her husband that famous night, but it was almost certainly a pinch of bicarbonate of soda.

The most notable development of the second trial, which took place almost two years after the first, was the detailed counter-report presented by Aurelio Consolo, who claimed that his Florentine counterparts had been so care-less and incompetent that they had used the wrong reagent in their testing, and this was why they had found traces of strychnine. At this point Nicolosi said they needed to have further expert testing done that would override all the others. The request was denied, but the judges amended Cristina's sentence, reducing it from twenty to sixteen years in prison.

In 1957 the Supreme Court rejected an appeal and upheld the conviction.

From prison Cristina kept issuing requests for a pardon. Finally, three years later the Minister of Pardons and Justice, forgetting the second title of his office, and succumbing to pressures put on him by a number of influential members of his party — which was the same one that the uncowed Cuf-faro the notary belonged to — took the necessary measures to grant the woman her longed-for pardon. And Cristina could return home. The game was over, once and for all.

5

It was past five o'clock in the morning. He'd just come out of the bathroom – where he'd let the water run over his head a long time trying to lessen the numbness he felt from having been shut up in a small room all that time with the bellowing Mrs Ciccina – and was on his way to bed, feeling more confused than anything else by all those names of lawyers, experts, relatives of the deceased, and relatives of the murderess, which Ciccina Adorna remembered with maniacal, deadly precision, when the telephone rang. It could only have been Livia, probably worried at not having found him at home earlier.

'Hello, darling . . .'

'Again? I'm sorry, Inspector, it's Ciccina Adorno.'

Montalbano felt the numbness in his head returning and held the receiver a safe distance away from his ear.

'What is it, signora?'

'I forgot to tell you something concerning the first scientific analysis, the one conducted in Palermo by Dr Agnello and Dr Trupìa.'

Montalbano pricked up his ears. This was a delicate point.

'Tell me, signora.'

'When the experts from Florence said that their colleagues in Palermo were either incompetent or insane because they hadn't found any strychnine, Nicolosi called Professor Aurelio Giummara to testify. And this professor said that Professor Agnello, under whom he'd worked as an assistant, had died before signing the report that found no poison. And so the court told him to sign it himself. Which Professor Giummara did, but only after doing the tests all over again, because he was a conscientious man. And you know what? He said he'd used the same reagent as his colleagues in Florence. There wasn't any strychnine.'

'Thank you, signora. Do you remember the name of the judge presiding over the second trial?'

'Of course. Manfredi Catalfamo was his name. Whereas the judge in the first trial was named Giuseppe Indelicato, and the appeals judge was—'

'Thank you, signora, that's quite enough. Have a good trip.'

Naturally, he didn't care about Catalfamo and Indelicato. He'd asked her just so he could marvel again at the power of Ciccina Adorno's memory, a sort of living supercomputer.

＊

Lying on the bed, with the sound of a moderately rough sea in his ears, he thought about what he'd just learned. If what Maria Carmela Spagnolo told him just before she died was true, the Palermo experts hadn't found any strychnine because there simply wasn't any. Cristina had thought she was poisoning her husband, but all she'd given him was an innocuous little powder. So why had the Florentine experts found strychnine? Perhaps Cuffaro was right: the long, mysterious disappearance of the parcel had allowed his political enemies to get their hands on it and inject the body parts with a ton of strychnine. But this was hardly cause for scandal. Italian criminal justice was studded with cases of evidence disappearing and reappearing in due time. It was on old, cherished custom, practically a ritual.

Cristina was therefore convicted not for actually having poisoned her husband, but essentially for having intended to poison him. How could she ever have imagined that her bosom friend Maria Carmela had deceived her? And why indeed had Maria Carmela deceived her? Probably because she was aware of her friend's passion for her husband's young nephew Attilio, and because she knew that Cristina had lately been talking about wanting to kill her husband. Of course, it's one thing to open your mouth and spout nonsense and another thing to speak seriously. At any rate, just to prevent Cristina from one day doing something extremely stupid, Maria Carmela gave her a little powder, telling her it was rat poison. So far, so good. Maria Carmela was acting in Cristina's best interests. Then why, when speaking to the lieutenant of the carabinieri, and later at court, didn't she reveal the truth? All she had to do to exonerate her friend was to say to the lieutenant something like, 'Look, Cristina can't have killed her husband with the powder I gave her, because it wasn't poison.'

That would have sufficed. But she didn't say it. Actually, she put on a scene, crying in despair and saying she'd always been in the dark about Cristina's intention to commit murder. And, just for good measure, she hammered a few extra nails in her friend's coffin at the trial. She would wait another fifty years to say those words, when facing death, to ease her conscience.

Why? By not saying those words, Maria Carmela knew she was allowing an innocent person – even if only relatively innocent – to be convicted. It was an attitude that implied deep hatred; there was no other way to put it. What he was looking at was almost certainly a cold, lucid vendetta.

*

By now it was broad daylight. Montalbano got up, went and lit the gas under the espresso pot, then stepped out onto the veranda. The wind had dropped, and the sea, in withdrawing, had left the sand wet and littered with plastic bottles, seaweed, empty cans, and dead fish. Flotsam and jetsam. He shivered and went back inside. He drank three cups of coffee in a row, put on a heavy jacket, and went back out on the veranda and sat down. The chilly morning air cooled his brain. For the first time in his life he reproached himself for never taking notes. Something Signora Ciccina had told him was swirling around in his head and he couldn't make it hold still long enough to grasp it. He knew it was something important, but he couldn't bring it into focus. He'd always had an iron-clad memory. Why was it starting to fail him? At this rate getting older would no doubt mean going around with a notebook and a pencil in his pocket, like British detectives did. The horror of this thought jogged his memory better than any medicine, and he suddenly remembered everything. In the deposition she gave at the carabinieri station, Mrs Maria Carmela stated that Cristina had asked her for the poison in mid-November. And therefore until that date Maria Carmela cared so much for her friend that she protected her from any sudden brilliant ideas she might have by giving her a harmless powder. But less than two months later her feelings towards Cristina had changed completely; now she cared little for her – in fact, she hated her. And so she didn't belie her former friend's confession. This meant that something, in that short period of time, had happened between the two women. But not just any normal sort of quarrel of the kind that can come between even the closest of friends. No, it was something serious enough to inflict a deep, irreparable wound. Wait a second. Ciccina Adorno had also said that the two women had met over Christmas – at least that was what Maria Carmela had told the lieutenant. And there was no doubt that the meeting actually did take place. And it hadn't been a formal encounter, a polite but formal exchange of best wishes – no, the two women had chatted quietly and calmly as was their custom . . . This could only mean one of two things: either Maria Carmela started hating Cristina after or during their Christmas encounter, or her hatred began a few days after she gave Cristina the fake poison. If the latter hypothesis was true, then during the Christmas encounter Maria Carmela must have pretended to be the same old friend she'd always been, concealing skilfully what she was feeling for Cristina, waiting patiently for her friend sooner or later to pull the trigger. Yes indeed, because that fake poison was exactly the same as a revolver loaded with blanks. No matter how things turned out, the shot would ruin Cristina's life for ever. And of the two hypotheses, the second was surely the one closer to the truth, if Maria Carmela had been able to carry that secret inside her for all the years she had left to live.

Treacherously, the image of the dying woman appeared before his eyes – the tiny, featherless sparrow-head sunken deep into the pillow, the clean white sheets, the bedside table . . . Then the image froze, and his memory sort of zoomed in on the scene. What was on the bedside table? A bottle of mineral water, a glass, a spoon and, half hidden by the green bottle, a crucifix about six or seven inches tall on a square wooden base. And suddenly the crucifix came into perfect focus: the Jesus nailed to the cross was not white. He was black. It had to have been a sacred object she'd bought in some far-off African country when she was following her nephew the engineer around the world.

And suddenly he found himself standing up, from the thought that had come to him. Was it possible that that statuette was all that the woman had brought with her from all her journeys? Where were her other possessions, the objects, photographs, and letters we keep so that our memory has something to hang on to, something to bear witness to our lives?

✣

The minute he got to the office, he rang the Hotel Pirandello. They informed him that Mr Spagnolo had just left for the airport to catch the first plane to Milan.

'Did he have a lot of baggage?'

'Spagnolo? No, just a small carry-on.'

'Did he by any chance ask you to send him any large parcels or big boxes, anything like that?'

'No, Inspector.'

So Maria Carmela's things, if they existed, were still in Vigàta.

'Fazio!'

'Here I am, Chief.'

'Do you have stuff to do this morning?'

'So-so.'

'Then drop everything. I want to give you an assignment you're going to relish. You must head immediately for Fela. It's now eight-thirty. You should get there by ten. I want you to go to the records office there.'

Fazio's eyes sparkled with contentment. He had what Montalbano called a 'records office complex': when investigating someone, he didn't limit himself to reporting the person's birthdate, birthplace, mother's and father's names; he dug up the father's and mother's fathers and mothers, grandparents, uncles, cousins, and so on. And if Montalbano didn't interrupt him, usually in some violent way or another, he was liable, depending on the person's history, to trace his lineage all the way back to the dawn of humanity.

'What do you want me to do?' Fazio asked.

Montalbano explained it to him after telling him the whole story, including the part about Cristina and the trial. Fazio twisted up his mouth.

'So it doesn't just involve going to the records office,' he said.

'No, but you're a master at this sort of thing.'

Not five minutes later, the inspector himself went out, got in his car, and headed to the Casa del Sacro Cuore. By now he'd caught the bug – the irresistible desire to know, which was the mainspring of all his investigations. He no longer had any doubts or inner hesitations. Whether it was a serial novel or mystery novel, tragedy or melodrama, he needed to know everything about this story, all the whys and wherefores.

He introduced himself to the chief administrator of the

Casa, Ragionier Inclima, a fat, cordial man of about fifty
– who, upon hearing the inspector's first question, sat down
in front of a computer.

'You know, Inspector, normally it's my assistant, Ragionier Cappadona, who handles these sorts of things, but he's
got flu and didn't come in today.'

He fiddled around at the keyboard, pressing a few but-
tons here and there, but it was clear that computers weren't
his thing. Then he spoke.

'Yes, according to this, all of Mrs Spagnolo's personal
effects are in our storage facility, in a trunk of hers. But
I don't know whether or not it's already been sent to her
nephew in Milan.'

'And how could we find out?'

'Please come with me.'

He opened a drawer and extracted a set of keys. They
went out of the main door. On the left-hand side of the park
there was a low structure, a warehouse with a large entrance
over which was the word 'Storage', in case anyone had any
doubts. Parcels, boxes, suitcases, crates, cabinets, and containers of every sort were lined up in orderly fashion along
the walls.

'We take good care of everything and make it all readily
available,' said Ragionier Inclima. 'As you can imagine,
Inspector, all our clients are, er, rather well off. And every
now and then they feel like seeing some old dress or cherished object again . . . OK, here we are: Mrs Spagnolo's
trunk is still here.'

Why, thought Montalbano, don't the not-so-well-off
also feel sometimes like seeing some cherished objects of
their own again? Apparently not, because those objects
probably aren't readily available any more, having all been
sold or pawned.

The trunk wasn't really a trunk. It was a sort of small
wardrobe that stood straight up like a wardrobe and was as
tall as the inspector. The only place Montalbano had ever

seen trunks of this sort before was in films set in the late nineteenth and early twentieth centuries. And this one was literally covered – without a single inch left free – with those pieces of square, round, and rectangular coloured paper that hotels used to stick on baggage as a sort of advertisement. A part of this collage of stickers was covered by a white sheet of paper, with the glue on it still fresh, giving the Milanese address of the signora's nephew.

'The shipper will no doubt be here to pick this up tomorrow,' said Inclima. 'What else did you want to know?'

'Do you have the keys to the trunk?'

'Let's go and see whether we still have them or they were already handed over to the nephew.'

They'd already been given to the nephew.

*

He ate listlessly, with no appetite.

'You haven't done right by me today,' Calogero, the owner of the trattoria, reproached him. 'When a customer like you eats that way, I don't feel like cooking any more.'

The inspector apologized and reassured him that it was because he had too many worries on his mind and hadn't been able to block them out enough to enjoy the wonderful lobster that had been laid before him. Truth be told, he had only one worry, but it tormented him as much as ten. And, for lack of a better solution, he had to settle for the only course of action possible in the short time remaining before the trunk headed off to Milan: Orazio Genco. It was four o'clock in the afternoon, and at that time Orazio, a seventy-something burglar who had never committed an act of violence and was an honest man except for that one little vice of burgling people's apartments, was surely at home sleeping, making up for the sleep he'd lost during the night. He and Orazio were fond of each other, and the burglar had once given the inspector the precious gift of a set of picklocks and skeleton keys.

Gnetta, Orazio's wife, came to the door.

'Inspector? What happened? Is something wrong?'

'No, it's nothing, Gnetta. I just came to see your husband.'

'Come in,' said the woman, reassured. 'Orazio's ill. He's in bed.'

'What's he got?'

'Rheumatic pains. Doctor says he oughtn't to go out at night when it's humid. But how's the good man gonna work otherwise?'

Orazio was half asleep, but upon seeing the inspector he sat up in bed.

'Inspector! What a nice surprise!'

'How's it going, Orà?'

'So-so, Inspector.'

'Would you like a little coffee?' asked Gnetta.

'I'd love some.'

Taking advantage of the fact that Gnetta had left the room, Orazio was anxious to set things straight.

'Look, Inspector, I haven't worked for over a month, so if there was anything—'

'That's not why I'm here. I had a little job for you, but I see you're unable to move for the moment.'

'No, Inspector, I'm sorry. You're gonna have to go it alone. Don't you know how it's done? Didn't I teach you?'

'You did, but this is a trunk that has to be opened and then closed so that nobody knows. You know what I mean?'

'Of course I do. But let's have a quiet cup of coffee now and we can talk about it afterwards.'

6

Fazio checked back in at around seven that evening, looking pleased. He sat down comfortably in the chair in front of the inspector's desk, pulled a sheet of paper folded in four out of his jacket pocket, and started reading.

'Siracusa, Alfredo, son of Giovanni Siracusa and Emilia née Scarcella, born in Fela on the—'

'You want to fight?' Montalbano interrupted him.

Fazio grinned.

'Just kidding, Chief.'

He folded up the page and put it back in his pocket.

'I got lucky, Chief.'

'How's that?'

'I was able to talk to the chemist Arturo De Gregorio.'

'And who's he?'

'The current owner of the shop that used to belong to Alfredo Siracusa. See, Chief, this De Gregorio, as soon as he graduated in 1947, went and did his training at the Siracusa chemist's. Siracusa was a man who spent his whole day either playing cards or chasing women. On the 30th of September 1949, as he was driving back from Palermo, Dr Siracusa got in an accident and died on the spot.'

'What kind of accident?'

'Well, it looks like he fell asleep at the wheel. He'd probably been up all night gambling or with a woman. Anyway, he was alone in the car. And to cut a long story short, less than a week later, Dr De Gregorio told his widow that, if she agreed to it, he would like to take over the shop. The lady stalled a little, and then, towards the end of November, she said OK and they agreed on a price.'

'So why the hell should I care about this story, Fazio?'

'Just be patient, Chief, I'm getting to the point. So, De Gregorio starts taking an inventory. Aside from the back room of the shop, which was used for storage, there was a small room off to the side with a desk that Dr Siracusa used for paperwork, accounts, correspondence, purchase orders. But one of the drawers was locked and the key was nowhere to be found. So De Gregorio asks the widow. She rounds up all her husband's keys, goes to the shop, tries one after the other, finally hits on the right one, and opens the drawer. De Gregorio sees that it's full of papers and photographs, but then he hears the automatic entrance bell ring and goes to attend to the customer, who is followed immediately by another customer. Finally the chemist is free to return to the little office. He finds Mrs Maria Carmela lying on the floor, unconscious. De Gregorio revives her, and she tells him she fainted. Some of the papers and photos are on the desk, others are on the floor. Dr De Gregorio bends down to pick them up, and the widow springs like a viper.

'"Don't touch anything! Leave them alone!"

'He'd never seen her act that way, De Gregorio told me. The lady was known for being polite and affable, but just then she'd seemed possessed by the devil.

'"Go away! Get out of here!"

'The chemist went back out to serve some more customers. Half an hour later the signora reappeared holding two large bags.

'"How are you, signora? Do you want me to take you home?"

'"Leave me alone!"

'And from that day on, Maria Carmela was never the same again, according to the chemist. She never set foot in the chemist's again. And with De Gregorio she continued to be rude and hostile. Then the whole affair of Ferlito's death broke out, and people in town started saying that she was an accomplice of Cristina, the lawyer's murdering wife. And so the widow Siracusa sold her properties and went to live abroad. Of all the things De Gregorio told me, the fact that she fainted in that office seemed the most interesting.'

'Why do you say that?'

'Come on, Chief, it's plain as day! And you know better

than I do! In that drawer, the just-widowed Mrs Maria Carmela found something she'd never dreamed she'd find.'

*

Around midnight, he'd run out of strategies for making the time pass. Unable to concentrate, he couldn't read: he would finish one page and then have to start all over again because he'd forgotten what he'd just read. The only solution was TV, but he'd already listened to a political debate moderated by two journalists who looked like Laurel and Hardy, one thin as a rail and the other fat as an elephant, over the resignation of an undersecretary with a reptilian head who was a lawyer by profession and had tried to have the judges presiding over the cases he'd lost arrested. Defending the undersecretary and sitting beside him was a minister who looked like a death's head and spoke in such a way that you couldn't understand a damn thing.

The inspector bravely turned the TV back on. The debate was still raging. Then he found a channel broadcasting a documentary on the lives of crocodiles and stopped there.

He must have fallen asleep, because it was suddenly two o'clock. He went and washed his face, left the house, and got in his car. Twenty minutes later he drove past the closed gate of the Casa del Sacro Cuore, took the first right turn and pulled up in the area behind the villa as he'd done before when he went to watch the funeral. He got out of the car and noticed that many windows were illuminated by dim lights. He realized why: the insomnia of old age, the kind that condemns you to spend every night awake, in bed or in an armchair, reviewing your life minute by minute, enduring every episode again, passing from one to the next like beads on a rosary. And so you end up wishing for death because it's an absolute void, a nothingness, free of the damnation and persecution of memory.

He clambered over the small gate without any problem,

as the moonlight sufficed to let him see where to put his feet. Once inside the park, however, he froze. There was a dog pointing straight at him, one of those terrible, murderous dogs that don't bark — that don't do anything, in fact, but the instant you move they tear your throat out. He felt his shirt suddenly wet with sweat and sticking to his skin. He remained perfectly still, and so did the dog.

Tomorrow morning they're going to find us still like this, he thought, *with me eyeing the dog and the dog eyeing me.*

With one difference between them, however: the dog was in his own territory, whereas he had entered it illegally.

The dog's in the right, he thought, repeating the famous line of Eduardo De Filippo.

He absolutely had to make up his mind and do something. But luck took care of things and lent him a hand. A pine cone, or dry fruit, fell from a tree and onto the animal's back, making to his great surprise a *Ping!* sound.

The dog was fake, put there just to frighten idiots like him. He opened the warehouse door in no time at all. Closing the door behind him, he turned on the large torch he'd brought with him and, following Orazio the burglar's instructions, he easily opened the trunk-wardrobe. Ten or so dresses hung from coat hangers; the shelf below them was crammed full of objects: a tiny Eiffel Tower, a papier-mâché lion, a wooden mask, and other mementos. The inside part of the trunk was actually a chest of drawers. There were panties, bras, handkerchiefs, scarves, woollen socks. Two large, other drawers were located under the shelf full of objects. The first contained shoes. The second, a cardboard box and a large envelope. Montalbano opened the envelope. Photos. On the back of each, Maria Carmela had diligently written the date, place, and names of those portrayed. There were Maria Carmela's father and mother, her brother, nephew, sister-in-law, a French girlfriend, a black housemaid, a number of different landscapes . . . No photos of her wedding, however. And there wasn't a picture of her husband to be found for love or money. As if the signora had wanted to forget what he looked like. And there weren't any of Cristina, either, her former bosom friend. He put the photos back into the envelope and opened the box. Letters. All sorted in orderly fashion and put into different envelopes according to who they were from. 'Letters from Mamma and Papa'; 'Letters from my brother'; 'Letters from my nephew'; 'Letters from Jeanne' . . . The last envelope had nothing written on it. Inside were three letters. He needed only to read the first to realize that he'd found what he was looking for. He slipped the three letters into his jacket pocket, closed the trunk and locked it, also locked the warehouse door, patted the fake dog on the head, clambered back over the gate, got in his car, and drove back to Marinella.

*

Three long letters, the first dated 4 February 1947, and the last, 30 July of the same year. Three letters ardently testifying to a torrid love affair that had blazed like burning straw and fizzled out just as fast. Letters to the chemist Alfredo Siracusa and signed by Cristina Ferlito, always starting the same way: 'My beloved Alfredo, blood of my life'; and ending with: 'Yours in every thing and every way, Cristina'. Letters which the woman had sent to her lover, the husband of her best friend, and which the husband carelessly kept in a locked drawer of his desk in the pharmacy – the one Maria Carmela opened at the request of Dr De Gregorio. Upon reading them that day, Maria Carmela must surely have felt mortally wounded and offended, even more by the words her friend wrote about her than by the twofold betrayal of her husband and best friend. For they were words of scorn and mockery: *Alfredo, how can you stand living with such a prissy goody-two-shoes? . . . When you wake up in the morning with her beside you, how do you keep from getting sick to your stomach? . . . You know what Maria Carmela told me in confidence the other day? That ever since your wedding night, making love to you has always been an ordeal for her. Then why is it for me so great a pleasure as to have no equal in life except, perhaps, for the release of death?*

Here Montalbano couldn't help but imagine another pleasure, one far more wicked and refined: that of the chemist enjoying the wife of his closest gambling and skirt-chasing companion, with him none the wiser. And who knew how much longer it might have lasted if her husband's good-looking nephew Attilio hadn't come into the picture?

So, upon finding the letters, Maria Carmela decides to take revenge. She'd already given Cristina the fake poison before discovering the betrayal, and she certainly must have regretted having grasped her friend's murderous intentions in time. Had she already known about the affair, she would have given her real poison, so her husband would die by her own hand. But now all she can do is wait for her former friend to make a false move. And when Cristina does, Maria Carmela is ready to grab the chance, doing her best to help send Cristina to gaol though she knows she couldn't have killed her husband with the powder she gave her. If she'd told the lieutenant of the carabinieri the truth, things would have turned out much better for her former friend. But that's exactly what she doesn't want. And only at the moment of death, when her palate had become insensitive to all tastes, even the sweetness of revenge, did she decide to reveal her misdeed. But why did she hang on to those letters? Why didn't she throw them away with the photos of her husband and their wedding? Because Maria Carmela was a smart woman. She knew that one day the anger that drove her to do what she did would start to lessen, the memory of the offence would fade, and she might end up telling someone what really happened. And Cristina might very well be set free . . . Whereas all she had to do was to pick up one of those letters, and the motives for her vendetta would be revived and as ferocious as on the first day.

✵

The following morning he went out early, after barely sleeping a wink. When he entered the church, Father Barbera had just finished saying Mass. He followed the priest into the sacristy. Father Barbera took off his vestments with the help of the sacristan.

'Please leave us now, and don't let anyone in.'

'Yes, sir,' said the sacristan, going out.

One look at Montalbano and the priest knew that the inspector now knew what Maria Carmela Spagnolo had told him in the confessional. But he wanted to be sure.

'Did you work everything out?'

'Yes, everything.'

'How did you do it?'

'I'm a policeman. It was kind of a bet with myself, more than anything else. But now it's over.'

'Are you sure?' asked the priest.

'Of course. Who do you think is going to care about a fifty-year-old case? Maria Carmela Spagnolo is dead, Cristina Ferlito too—'

'Who told you that?'

'Nobody, I just assumed . . .'

'You're wrong.'

Montalbano looked at him in astonishment.

'You mean she's still alive?'

'Yes.'

'Where?'

'In Catania. She lives with her daughter Agata, who forgave her when she got out of prison. Agata married a bank clerk, a good man named Giulio La Rosa. They have a small house at Via Gomez 32.'

'Why are you telling me that?' asked the inspector, but he already knew the answer.

'So that you will go and do what I, as a priest, cannot. You are in a position to bring peace of mind to a woman at the very moment when she no longer expects anything from life. To illuminate, with the light of truth, the last dark passage of that woman's existence. Go and do your duty, do not wait any longer. Too much has already been lost.'

And he practically pushed Montalbano toward the door, hands on his shoulders. In a daze, the inspector took a few steps, then stopped dead in his tracks. A sort of flash had lit up his brain. He turned around.

'You had a precise plan that morning when you first came to me! You machinated the whole thing! You used me and I fell for it like a total idiot! And you even put on that little act of trying to talk me out of it, knowing I would never let it drop. You knew from the very start that we would get to this point, and that we would say these words to each other. Isn't that true?'

'Yes, it is,' said Father Barbera.

✳

He drove in a nervous rage, ready to fight any motorist who happened to cross his path. He'd let himself be tricked like a babe in arms. But how? How could he have gone so long without realizing that Father Barbera had set him up? Never trust a priest! The Sicilian proverb said it all: *Monaci e parrini / sènticci la Missa / e stòccacci li rini.* Listen to the monks and priests when they say the Mass, but when they've fin-ished, give them a good hiding! Ah, folk wisdom, gone for ever!

✳

Driving through the traffic in Catania, he had no lack of opportunities to give the finger to motorists and yell obscenities left and right. Finally, after endlessly circling round and round, he pulled up in front of a little house in Via Gomez. A rather young woman was watching over two small children playing in the tiny garden.

'Are you Mrs Agata La Rosa?'

'No, she's not in. I'm just looking after the kids.'

'Are they Signora Agata's children?'

'Are you joking?! They're her grandchildren!'

'Listen, I'm a police inspector.'

The woman got scared.

'What?! Has something happened?'

'No, nothing's happened. I just need to give Mrs Cristina a message. Is she here?'

'Of course she's here.'

'I sort of need to talk to her. Would you take me to her?'

'And what am I supposed to do with the children? You can go by yourself. It's the second door on the left, after you enter. You can't miss it.'

The house was tastefully furnished and orderly despite the presence of the grandchildren. The second door on the left was ajar.

'May I come in?'

No answer. He went in. The old woman lay sprawled out in an armchair, asleep, warmed by the sun bursting through the windowpanes. Her head was thrown backwards and from her open mouth dripped a shiny string of spittle, as her laboured, raspy breathing broke up moment by moment, only to restart with increased effort. A fly passed undisturbed from one eyelid to the other, which had become so thin that the inspector feared they might cave in under the insect's weight. Then the fly slipped inside one of her transparent nostrils. The skin on her face was yellow and so taut and close to the bone that it looked like a layer of colour painted on a skull. The skin on her inert, gnarled hands was instead wizened and discoloured by large brown splotches. Under a tartan blanket her legs shook with a perpetual tremor. There was an unbearable stench of rot and urine in the room. Was there still anything to communicate with inside that body so obscenely deformed by time? Montalbano doubted it. Worse yet, if there was still something there, would it be able to stand the knowledge of the truth?

Truth is light, the priest had said, or something similar.

Right, but might not a light so strong risk burning the very thing it was supposed to illuminate? Better not to disturb the darkness of sleep and memory.

He withdrew, went out, and was back in the garden.

'Did you talk to the signora?'

'No. She was sleeping. I didn't want to disturb her.'

Notes

*page 10 — **Settimana Enigmistica*** An immensely popular Italian weekly magazine of puzzles and rebuses that was first published in 1932.

*page 11 — **polipetti alla strascinasale*** These are baby octopus simmered in water and salt.

*page 13 — **'Ibis redibis non morieris in bello'*** This was traditionally said to be the phrase uttered by the oracle to the soldier about to go off to war in Ancient Rome. The sentence's syntax is so conceived as to create a perfect ambiguity between opposite meanings. Depending on where one inserts commas — or pauses, since Latin had no commas — the statement changes meaning. If you read it *Ibis, redibis, non morieris in bello*, it means 'you'll go, you'll come back, you'll not die in war'; if you read it as *Ibis, redibis non, morieris in bello*, it means 'you'll go, you'll not come back, you'll die in war.'

*page 34 — **napoletana*** The traditional espresso pot of Naples, formerly made of aluminium. When the water boils, one must turn the pot upside down to let it filter through the coffee grounds in the middle.

*page 36 — **touching the lobe of his right ear with the tip of his index finger. [. . .] What did he mean? That we had to become gay to understand the malaise of our young people?*** One of the ways to say 'homosexual' in Italian is *orecchione* ('big ear'), sometimes communicated nonverbally by touching the lobe of one's ear repeatedly. As it has generally a negative connotation, it has recently fallen into relative disuse.

page 45 – **Valley of the Temples** Probably the finest group of Ancient Greek ruins in Sicily (and there are many), the Valley of the Temples is just outside Agrigento, the city on which the fictional Montelusa is based.

page 64 – '. . . **Rosa** [. . .] . . . **Because it's a colour'** *Rosa* means 'pink' in Italian.

page 92 – *cavatuna* Hollow tubes of pasta, rather like rigatoni or, when larger, cannelloni.

page 102 – *Andiamo a mietere il grano, il grano, il grano* . . . A 1966 song by Louiselle, the *nom d'artiste* of Maria Luisa Catricalà (Vibo Valentia, born 1946). The title means 'Let's go and harvest the wheat . . .'

page 102 – *Amore amor portami tante rose* A 1934 song covered in 1967 by I Camaleonti ('The Chameleons'), a pop-rock band.

page 107 – **'La donna è mobile, qual piuma al vento'** 'Woman is light, like a feather in the wind'. The famous canzone from act III of Verdi's *Rigoletto*, sung by the Duke of Mantua after he has ravished Gilda, Rigoletto's daughter.

page 110 – **a small octopus, ever so soft,** *a strascinasale*, **followed by a little fried** *nunnato* Nunnato are tiny baby fish, just born. The word is Sicilian for 'newborn' (*neonato* in Italian).

page 122 – **he concluded on a questioning note, bringing both hands, cupped like artichokes, to his forehead, and agitating them** This is the common Italian hand gesture intended as a question. In Sicilian it's called *cacocciola*, dialect for 'artichoke'. Bringing the cupped hands to one's forehead is for emphasis, as if to say that the thing in question is so incomprehensible that one can't get it through one's head.

page 130 – **Dottor Montalbano** In Italy anyone with a university degree is considered a 'doctor' or *dottore*, and anyone who rises to Montalbano's rank of Commissario di Pubblica Sicurezza must have a university degree.

page 140 – *lupara* The Sicilian term for sawn-off shotgun, a former favourite weapon of the Mafiosi and bandits of the island. It is so called because it was once used by shepherds to defend their flocks against wolves (*lupi*).

page 141 – **Bonpensiero . . . despite his name** *Bonpensiero* literally means 'good thought' or 'good idea'.

page 156 – **that dense atmosphere of palpable desolation and visible despair, which filled the compartment with a rotten yellow smell** As the reader of the novels in this series will know, Montalbano has a synaesthetic sense of smell: that is, he sees odours as having colours.

page 175 – *Tu che a Dio spiegasti l'ali* An aria from act III scene II of Donizetti's *Lucia di Lamermoor*. The phrase means 'You who spread your wings to God.'

page 189 – **fifty billion lire** At the time, this was worth about twenty-five million US dollars.

page 193 – *vo' cumprà* A reference to the ambulant foreign vendors, usually from the Maghreb or sub-Saharan Africa, whom one encounters on Italian streets and beaches. The phrase *vo' cumprà?* is a corrupted form of Italian meaning 'do you want to buy?' Since the vendors repeatedly utter this question, they are known as such in common parlance in Italy today.

page 197 – **with a logic worthy of Monsieur La Palisse** A reference to the legendary Jacques de la Palisse (1470–1525), a French nobleman and military officer active in Francis I's Italian campaign, during which he was killed in 1525. His epitaph reads: *Ci gît Monsieur de La Palice: S'il n'était pas mort, il ferait encore envie* ('Here lies Monsieur de la Palisse: were he not dead, he would still be envied'). This was originally misread — by mistake, presumably — as saying ' . . . *S'il n'était pas mort, il serait encore en vie*' ('Were he not dead, he would still be alive'), due perhaps to the potential confusion between *f* and *s* in serif script. The misreading gave rise to a whole tradition of burlesque song variants, with similar tautological plays on words (such as *Il n'eût pas eu son pareil / S'il avait été seul au monde* ('He would have had no equals / Had he been alone in the world.')) The many variants were brought together into *La chanson de La Palisse* by Bernard de la Monnoye in the early eighteenth century, though other versions exist as well.

page 212 – **Being unmarried, Mimì . . .** This story was written before Mimì Augello got married.

page 227 – **over two hundred million lire** At the time, over one hundred thousand dollars.

page 233 – **Via Giovanni Verga [. . .] Vicolo De Roberto [. . .] Made sense.** Giovanni Verga (1840–1922) and Federico De Roberto (1861–1927) are two Sicilian authors of national and international renown, particularly Verga.

page 249 – **'With cream? Or *corretto*?'** One way of taking espresso coffee in Italy is with a shot of strong alcohol added, in which case it is called a *caffè corretto*, or 'corrected coffee', presumably because the alcohol, being a sedative, is supposed to offset the stimulant effect of the coffee. A *caffè corretto* is usually cut with brandy, cognac, grappa, or one of the herbal *digestivi* popular in Italy.

page 265 – **pasta in Trapanese pesto sauce** *Pesto alla trapanese*, like its cousin, *pesto alla genovese*, is a sauce for pasta using ground or finely chopped basil as its foundation. The Trapanese version (from the Sicilian city of Trapani), however, uses finely chopped and toasted blanched almonds instead of pine nuts, as well as several finely chopped, uncooked tomatoes, which are ground into the blend with garlic, olive oil, and black

pepper. Finally, after serving it on the pasta one adds a sprink-
ling of toasted bread crumbs in the place of cheese.

page 274 – **Don't you know what Arquà rhymes with?** *Quaquaraquà.* In Sicilian, a *quaquaraquà* is a worthless person of no
account, treacherous and a snitch who talks too much.

page 285 – **Inside was only a little money in cash, not even two
hundred thousand lire** At the time, about a hundred dollars.

page 285 – **large sums from fifty million lire upwards** From
about twenty-five thousand dollars upwards.

page 286 – **smaller loans, from one hundred thousand lire up
to twenty or thirty million** From about fifty dollars to ten or
fifteen thousand.

page 286 – **amounting to figures in the billions of lire** In the
thousands of dollars, divided by two.

page 286 – **Over three hundred thousand lire** Over a hundred
and fifty dollars.

page 292 – **old issues of *Topolino* covered the floor** *Topolino* is
Mickey Mouse in Italian. Starting in 1932, the *Topolino* comics
became an Italian industry in their own right, with stories
featuring Disney characters but written by Italian comic-book
writers and illustrated by Italian comic artists. It started first
as a newspaper and then became a twice-monthly book-sided
'review' of sorts. It still exists today.

page 296 – **It was about a dirty old man of the upper classes
who plots to kidnap a beautiful young girl and make her
yield to his desires. After a number of vicissitudes, the kidnapping is pulled off successfully, and the dirty old squire
can finally contemplate Alba (that was the girl's name) naked
and imploring, in his very own bedroom.** This story line is
mischievously reminiscent of one of the principal plot threads
of the nineteenth-century classic Italian novel, *I promessi sposi*
(*The Betrothed*), by Alessandro Manzoni.

page 305 – **Inside the cardboard box was eight hundred million lire** About four hundred thousand dollars.

page 323 – **Being Here . . .** Title in English in the original.

page 326 – **the Abyssinian War and the Spanish Civil War** The so-called Abyssinian War was a war that Fascist Italy fought in Ethiopia in 1935–36 to secure colonial control of that country. In the Spanish Civil War (1936–39), Fascist Italy fought on the side of General Franco's far-right Phalange. Italian left-wing militants also fought in significant numbers on the side of the Spanish Republic, but it is not clear whether the monument here evoked would include their names among the fallen.

page 327 – **Giuseppe De Robertis** (1888–1963) was a distinguished Italian literary scholar who taught at the Conservatorio Cherubini in Florence.

page 328 – **a cross between Giacometti's melodrama of civil death and certain situations such as you find in Pirandello** Paolo Giacometti (1816–1882) was an Italian dramatist and the author of the play *La morte civile* (1861); novelist and dramatist Luigi Pirandello (1867–1936) wrote many works involving loss of identity, real or imagined, most notably the novel *The Late Mattia Pascal* (*Il fu Mattia Pascal*, 1904), which involves a story similar to the present one, in which the protagonist when travelling finds his obituary in the newspaper and decides to assume a new identity.

page 356 – **looking out of his mind, just like Orlando at the puppet theatre** The traditional Sicilian puppet theatre often interprets episodes from Italian chivalric romances rooted in the Carolingian tradition, most notably Ludovico Ariosto's Renaissance classic, *Orlando Furioso* (1532), in which the lovesick Orlando (Roland) loses his mind and becomes uncontrollably violent.

page 361 – **the slut Messalina** Valeria Messalina, Empress Consort of the Roman Empire from AD 41 to 48, was reputed to be promiscuous by her political enemies.

page 392 – **'Algida.' 'Like the ice cream?'** Algida is a famous brand of ice cream in Italy.

page 396 – **'We, however, are military officers.'** The carabinieri, like the gendarmerie in France and the guardia civil in Spain, is a branch of the military.

page 396 – **some ten or so municipal policemen** The *vigili urbani*, or municipal police in Italian cities, are a separate department from the *commissariati*, the criminal police departments of which Montalbano's unit is one.

page 398 – **the sign of a salt-and-tobacco shop** Since salt and tobacco are government monopolies in Italy, they are sold at licensed shops that have rectangular black signs with white lettering outside, featuring a large white T for tobacco.

page 425 – **Pessoa Maintains** The title of this story, 'Sostiene Pessoa', is a nod to the Italian novel by Antonio Tabucchi (1943–2012), *Sostiene Pereira* (translated by Patrick Creagh as *Pereira Maintains*, 1994). Tabucchi, a scholar of Portuguese as well as writer, wrote extensively on the great Portuguese modernist poet and author Fernando Pessoa (1888–1935).

page 438 – **twenty-six thousand lire in notes, and seven hundred and fifty in coins** Just over thirteen dollars at the time.

page 440 – **eighteen thousand three hundred lire** Just over nine dollars.

page 442 – **forty-five thousand and fifty lire** Around twenty-three dollars.

page 443 – **eleven thousand lire** About five and a half dollars.

page 445 – **ten million lire in cash** Around five thousand dollars at the time.

page 448 – *'O toreador ritorna vincitor'* Montalbano is conflating the 'Toreador' aria from Bizet's *Carmen* and the 'Ritorna vincitor' aria from Verdi's *Aida*.

page 449 – **barely ten thousand lire** Barely five dollars.

page 451 – **ten billion lire** About five million dollars.

page 482 – **worse than Gano di Maganza at the puppet theatre** Gano di Maganza is the Italianized name of Ganelon of Mainz, the archetypal traitor who betrays Charlemagne's armies to the Muslims in *La Chanson de Roland*. As the archetypal traitor he appears in many Italian romances in the Carolingian tradition from which much of the material for the Sicilian puppet theatre is derived.

page 506 – *purpi affucati* Or, literally, 'drowned octopuses'. This is octopus cooked in a Neapolitan-style tomato sauce.

Notes by Stephen Sartarelli